Fearful Implications

Fearful Implications

Ramsey Campbell

FEARFUL IMPLICATIONS
Copyright © Ramsey Campbell 2023

COVER ARTWORK
Copyright © Ilan Sheady 2023

This edition is published in September 2023 by PS Publishing by arrangement with the Author. All rights reserved. The rights of Ramsey Campbell to be identified as the Author of this Work have been asserted by him in accordance with the Copyright, Designs and Patents Act 1988.

This book is a work of fiction. Names, characters, places and incidents either are products of the author's imagination or are used fictitiously. Any resemblance to actual events or locales or persons, living or dead, is entirely coincidental.

FIRST EDITION

ISBNs
978-1-80394-324-4
978-1-80394-325-1 [signed edition]

Design & Layout by Michael Smith
Printed and bound in England by T. J. Books

PS Publishing Ltd
Grosvenor House, 1 New Road
Hornsea, HU18 1PG. England

editor@pspublishing.co.uk
www.pspublishing.co.uk

Contents

Acknowledgements vii

Speaking Still 5

First a Bird 23

The Stillness 35

The Fourth Call 53

The Dreamed 75

Someone to Blame 101

How He Helped 113

The Bill 131

Girls Dream 147

A Name for Every Home 151

The Run of the Town 169

Contents

Fully Boarded 185

The Devil in the Details 205

Some Kind of a Laugh 221

Play with Me 241

But Once a Year 247

Brains 263

Getting Through 281

Extending the Family .297

Still Hungry 313

Wherever You Look 325

Afterword: The Old Grows New 341

Acknowledgements

"Speaking Still". First published in *New Fears*, edited by Mark Morris. Copyright © 2017 by Ramsey Campbell.

"First a Bird". First published in *Uncertainties Volume V*, edited by Brian Showers. Copyright © 2021 by Ramsey Campbell.

"The Stillness". First published in *Dark Cities*, edited by Christopher Golden. Copyright © 2017 by Ramsey Campbell.

"The Fourth Call". First published in *The Mammoth Book of Folk Horror*, edited by Stephen Jones. Copyright © 2021 by Ramsey Campbell.

"The Dreamed". First published in *Nightmare's Realm: New tales of the Weird and Fantastic*, edited by S. T. Joshi. Copyright © 2017 by Ramsey Campbell.

"Someone to Blame". First published in *Classic Monsters Unleashed*, edited by James Aquilone. Copyright © 2022 by Ramsey Campbell.

"How He Helped". First published in *Adam's Ladder*, edited by Michael Bailey and Darren Speegle. Copyright © 2017 by Ramsey Campbell.

"The Bill". First published in *Exploring Dark Short Fiction #6: A Primer to Ramsey Campbell*, edited by Eric J. Guignard. Copyright © 2017 by Ramsey Campbell.

"Girls Dream". First published in Italian, translated by Alessandro Manzetti, as "Sogni di Ragazze". English-language version original to the present volume. Copyright © 2023 by Ramsey Campbell.

"The Run of the Town". First published in *Dark Discoveries* number 38, edited by Aaron J. French. Copyright © 2018 by Ramsey Campbell.

"Fully Boarded". First published in *Behold! Oddities, Curiosities and Undefinable Wonders*, edited by Doug Murano. Copyright © 2017 by Ramsey Campbell.

"The Devil in the Details". First published in *This Dreaming Isle*, edited by Dan Coxon. Copyright © 2018 by Ramsey Campbell.

"Some Kind of a Laugh". First published in *The Alchemy Book of Horrors*, edited by Peter Coleborn and Jan Edwards. Copyright © 2018 by Ramsey Campbell.

"Play with Me". First published in *Horror for RAICES: A Charitable Anthology*, edited by Jennifer Wilson and Robert S. Wilson. Copyright © 2019 by Ramsey Campbell.

"But Once A Year". First published in *ParSec*, edited by Ian Whates. Copyright © 2021 by Ramsey Campbell.

"Brains". First published in *Miscreations*, edited by Doug Murano and Michael Bailey. Copyright © 2021 by Ramsey Campbell.

"Getting Through". First published in *Getting Through* (dual language

Acknowledgements

edition: Italian translation by Roberta Maciocci). Copyright © 2019 by Ramsey Campbell.

"Extending the Family". First published in *The New Abject*, edited by Sarah Eyre and Ra Page. Copyright © 2020 by Ramsey Campbell.

"Still Hungry". First published in *Professor Charlatan Bardot's Travel Anthology to the Most (Fictional) Haunted Buildings in the Weird, Wild World (2021 Edition)*, edited by Charlatan Bardot and Eric J. Guignard. Copyright © 2021 by Ramsey Campbell.

"Wherever You Look". First published in *After Sundown*, edited by Mark Morris. Copyright © 2020 by Ramsey Campbell.

Fearful Implications

For Mike Wesley -

some nightmares in exchange for yours!

Speaking Still

As soon as I opened the door of the Hole Full Of Toad I saw Daniel. I'd meant to be first at the pub and have a drink waiting for him, but he was seated near the bar with his back to me and talking on his phone. I was crossing the discoloured carpet between the stout tables scarred by cigarettes at least a decade old when he noticed me. "Goodbye for now, my love," he murmured and stood up, pocketing his phone. "You look ready for a drink."

It was our regular greeting, but I could tell he hoped I hadn't overheard his other words. Embarrassment made me facetious. "What's tonight's tipple?"

"Mummy's Medicine," he said and pointed at his tankard. "Not as urinary as it might appear."

"It's what the doctor ordered, is it?"

"It's what this one prescribes."

Though we'd performed this routine in the past, it felt too deliberate now. "I'll be the second opinion," I said to bring it to an end.

When he brought me a yeasty pint I found it palatable enough. We always tried the guest ale and then usually reverted to our favourite. Daniel took a manful gulp and wiped foam from his stubbly upper lip.

He'd grown less plump over the last few months, but his skin was lagging behind, so that his roundish face reminded me of a balloon left over from a party, wrinkled but maintaining an unalterable wide-eyed smile that might have contained a mute plea. He kept up the smile as he said "Ask me the question, Bill."

"How have you been?"

"I'd prefer to forget most of that if you don't mind. I've seen colleagues lose patients, but that's nothing like the same." Daniel opened his eyes wider still, which looked like a bid to take more of a hold on the moment if not to drive back any moisture. "The job's helping now," he said, "but that wasn't the question I thought you'd have."

"I'd better let you tell me what it ought to be."

"Weren't you wondering who I was talking to when you came in?"

"Honestly, Daniel, that's none of my business. If you've found someone—"

"You think I'd be involved with someone else so soon. Or do you think I already was?"

"I'm sorry for presuming. I must have misheard."

"I don't think so. Perhaps you missed the obvious." As if taking pity on me Daniel said "I was talking to Dorothy, Bill."

I thought this was quite a distance from the obvious, but stopped my mouth with a drink. "No need to be confused," Daniel said. "She's still there. Would you like to hear?"

"Please," I said, though it didn't feel much like an invitation.

He took out his phone and opened an album to show me a photograph. "That's the last I have of her. She wanted me to take it, so I did."

It had the skewed look of a hasty shot. His wife was sitting up in a hospital bed. She'd lost far more weight than Daniel and was virtually bald, but was matching if not besting the smile I imagined he'd given her. "I wasn't talking to her there tonight, though," Daniel said. "Bend your ear to this."

He brought up a list of calls received, and I leaned towards the phone as he retrieved one. "Don't bother visiting me this afternoon," Dorothy said. "They'll be having a look. I expect I'll be out of it this evening, so I may not be worth a trek then either."

I found I'd grown shy of meeting Daniel's eyes, especially when he said "That's the last I ever heard from her. I went in, and I didn't leave her after that till the end."

"You did say."

"That isn't all I've kept. I'm only glad I haven't erased anything since last year."

The calls skimmed up the screen until he touched a listing with a moist forefinger. This time his wife was telling him which supermarket aisle she was in and which items he should find elsewhere in the store. "She sounds more like she used to, doesn't she?" Daniel said.

Her voice was far stronger and brisker than it had been in the call from the hospital. As I tried not to feel too saddened by his need to preserve every trace of her Daniel said "But that isn't really her either."

It seemed unsafe to say more than "How is that, Daniel?"

"She built herself up around the self she never quite got rid of. Sometimes I think the children we all used to be are lying in wait inside us, maybe hoping we won't rouse them." As he returned the phone to his pocket he said "Thank God she's free of her mother at last."

"I thought her mother died years ago."

"Not in Dorothy's mind," Daniel said and shut his eyes so hard that he might have been trying to crush a memory. "Tell me an exciting tale of accountancy, Bill."

This was another of our old jokes that I hadn't heard for weeks. I did my best to generate suspense from a call I'd made on a client's behalf to the tax collector, and then I was glad to hear news from the medical world. When the pub shut we went in opposite directions, having established that we'd meet next week. I glanced back to see that Daniel had stopped beneath a streetlamp and taken out his phone, but I couldn't tell whether he was speaking.

My wife Jane was in bed and on the way to sleep. "How was your friend?" she said most of.

"Missing Dorothy."

"Well, I should expect so. I hope you'll miss me too."

I rather wished her sleepiness hadn't let that slip out, though of course she only meant if she was first to go when the inevitable came, surely quite a few years hence. I'd managed to put all this out of my head by the time I joined her, and Daniel's situation had gone too. I can't say I thought about him much in the ensuing week, but when Monday came around I looked forward to catching up with him. Given his concern for all his patients, I was hoping a week's work might have helped him.

The pub was in sight when I saw him outside. Since he was talking on his phone, I wasn't sure whether to hang back, especially since I couldn't see his face. I compromised by making for the entrance, which he wasn't far from, and heard him say "You'll be all right, Dorothy. You've still got the right kind of strength."

As I tried to steal into the pub the door creaked. Daniel turned, belatedly hitching up his smile, and shoved the phone into his pocket. "Yes, I'm ready for a drink."

He dodged into the pub at once, so that I wondered if he meant to restrict the conversation we might have had. When I brought two pints of Hound's Howl to the table, however, he was ready to talk. "Some of the doctors who are coming up," he said, "you'd wonder if they need a doctor. There's a call to reclassify schizophrenia as a spectrum instead of a disease."

"That isn't your area, though."

"I know more than I'd like to about it." He downed a cloudy mouthful as though to douse his fierceness. "I'm just glad they weren't taking that approach," he said, "when they diagnosed Dorothy's mother."

"I didn't know she had that problem, Daniel."

"Dorothy never wanted it discussed, even with friends. Her mother brought her up never to talk about her. Even I didn't realise what was wrong till her mother couldn't hide it any more."

"How recently was that?"

"Too recently. For most of our marriage I didn't know about Dorothy's childhood."

So we hadn't strayed so far from his preoccupation after all. "What was it like?" I said.

"I'll tell you just one thing I won't forget. When Dorothy was little, before she was even at school..." This time his gulp of ale seemed intended to fortify him. "If she did anything her mother thought was bad, and there was no predicting what that might be next," he said, "she'd be locked in her room with no light, and she'd be told that something worse than she could possibly imagine would come for her if she dared to put the light on."

I felt bound to ask "Did she?"

"Not till years later, and do you know what the old, do you know what her mother did then? Took the bulb out of the socket and wouldn't let her have one in her room."

I was running out of questions I wanted to ask. "How did all that affect Dorothy, do you think?"

"She told me not at all by then. She said she challenged whatever she was meant to be scared of to show itself, and of course nothing did. She assured me that toughened her up and she was never afraid of anything her mother imagined again."

"More power to her."

"If it was true. I'm just afraid she kept it hidden deep down in herself."

"Daniel, please don't take this the wrong way, but at least you needn't worry any more."

I thought he'd opened his mouth to speak, but he gave himself a drink instead. His throat worked before he muttered "You didn't meet her mother."

"And if I had..."

"Call me fanciful, but whenever she came into a room you'd feel as if she'd turned it dark."

"I suppose you might when you knew what she'd done to your wife."

"I felt like that before I knew." Daniel reinforced this with a stare that looked trapped by the memory. "And I think having her committed brought everything back," he said, "even if Dorothy tried not to show it did."

"Surely she'd have been relieved that her mother was being taken care of."

"You'd hope so." With more conviction than I thought was warranted he said "She kept telling Dorothy that if we had her shut away she'd make sure Dorothy was with her."

"But she wasn't, so I should think—"

"It was all she talked about when she was dying. She said she'd wait for Dorothy in the dark, and she'd be made of worms."

"That's second childhood stuff, wouldn't you agree? I hope your wife thought so."

Daniel's tankard stopped short of his mouth. "Whose childhood, Bill?"

"You know I meant her mother's. I never knew Dorothy to be anything but strong."

As he took a drink I saw him ponder how to go on. "You caught what I was saying earlier."

"I didn't mean to eavesdrop."

"I might have myself." Even more like an apology he said "I wouldn't ask this of anyone except a good friend."

With no idea where this was leading I could only say "Then you can ask me."

"Do you think Dorothy could hear me?"

"When do you mean?"

I was bracing myself to be told that he had her last moments in mind, and was nowhere near ready to hear him say "Now."

"We can't know, can we?" In a bid to raise his spirits I said "In a way we're keeping her alive by talking about her."

"I wasn't thinking of you." Though his smile winced in case he'd sounded rude, he carried on. "I mean when I'm speaking to her on the phone," he said.

I took all the care I could over answering. "You'd like to think so."

"Yes, but I'm asking what you think."

"I won't say you're wrong, Daniel."

"All right, Bill, you're discharged. The ordeal's over." Humour deserted him as he said "I wonder what your wife would say. She's the computer expert, after all."

I'd begun to wonder how potent our drinks were. "How did we get on to computers?"

"They've been on my mind a good deal recently. I'm starting to believe they may have made a kind of afterlife."

"All the photos of Dorothy you'll have, you mean." When he didn't respond I said "Her voice."

"That's what I've kept, my wife in electronic form."

"And you still have all your memories of her."

"I don't want you to think I'm being maudlin." As I made to deny it he said "I just wonder how much of her that is."

"I'm afraid I'm not following."

"All of us are electronic where it counts, aren't we? What they used to call the soul, that's a mass of electronic impulses in the brain. Even if they didn't have a place to go before, perhaps they have one now."

Though I might have liked to take a drink rather than speak I said "We're still talking about computers."

"Yes, the internet. That's where everything we know is turned into electronic form. Perhaps I haven't got it right, though," Daniel said, and I was hoping rationality had overtaken him until he added "Perhaps it gives us access to a place that was already there."

I no longer knew how to respond. I was lingering over a mouthful of ale when Daniel said "I realise you aren't going to accept it without proof."

"That would be a help."

He took out his phone at once. "There's another message," he said.

He left a moist print on an entry in the list before turning the phone towards me. His wife's voice sounded weaker or more distant than it previously had. "Are you there? You're not there, are you? Don't be—"

I assumed she'd cut herself off by mistake, since I'd heard a trace of nervousness. "Was she asking you not to be long?"

"I hope that's it, but that isn't the point. That's her most recent message, Bill."

"I thought you told me the one you played yesterday was."

"It was then," Daniel said and showed me the phone. "As you see, now this is top of the list."

"But it hasn't got a date."

"And don't you wonder how that could happen?" When I had no explanation, though I might have pointed out that the caller was unnamed as well, he said "Would you mind asking your wife?"

"I'll call you when I have, shall I?"

"No need for me to trouble you so much. Next time we meet will be fine."

I thought he was doing his best to put the issue out of his mind, despite forgetting to make his accountancy joke. Instead he told me at considerable length how medicine and surgery would soon be able to prolong life, though I couldn't tell whether he regretted that the developments came too late for his wife or was glad that they hadn't been there for her mother. I felt as though his monologue was postponing what he was anxious to say, and then I grasped that I mightn't be the person he was desperate to address.

We'd hardly parted outside the pub when I heard him on his phone. Either he wanted me to hear or no longer cared whether I did. "Dorothy, I'm sorry I missed your call. I don't know when it was, because I didn't hear it ring. I'll keep an eye on the phone whenever I can, just in case. I know we'll be together again soon, and then we'll have all the time there is."

He sounded like someone I hardly knew—as unlike the self he presented to the world as he'd said his wife differed from hers. As I headed for home the call I'd heard made the autumn night feel as cold as black ice. Jane was asleep, having driven fifty miles to revive all the computers in a large office. When I caught up with her at breakfast I found I was anxious to learn "Do you know if there's a reason why a missed call wouldn't show a date?"

"You can't withhold those, only the number."

"I thought so, but Daniel has one with no date."

"He'd have had to delete the information himself, though I don't know how." Jane abandoned the delicate frown that had narrowed her keen eyes and said "How was he this week?"

"I'm not sure he's coping that well. He's kept all the messages his wife left on the phone, but he seems to be convincing himself he can still hear from her."

"Maybe that's how he's coping. I don't see the harm if it doesn't put his patients at risk."

I couldn't believe Daniel would let that happen. If he thought he was growing incompetent, surely he would take leave rather than risk botching an operation. Perhaps Jane was right, and his preoccupation was no worse than a comfort to him. However irrational it was, I came to accept it on his behalf as the week went on, until Samira stopped me as I returned from convincing a client to keep receipts for six years, not just one. "A Doctor Hargreaves was asking for you, Bill," she said. "You aren't sick, are you?"

"No, he's a friend."

"It was only that it sounded urgent. He says don't call unless you have to, otherwise he'll see you tonight as usual."

Friday was by no means usual, and if Jane hadn't gone away overnight to deal with an office-wide computer crash I would have felt unreasonable for leaving her alone two nights in a week. I reached the pub earlier than normal, only to find Daniel already at a table. He'd been drinking fast or for a while, since his tankard was less than half full, and when he brought me a pint of Mohammed's Prohibition he treated himself to its twin. "There's another message," he said.

His smile looked determined not to yield but close to meaningless. When he brought out the phone I saw that the new message was undated and unidentified. "Jane doesn't know how there can't be a date," I said and risked adding "Don't you think that means it needn't be new?"

"It wasn't there before. I'd have listened if it was."

"I'm saying it could have been delayed. Maybe there's a glitch that left out the date as well."

His only response was to set the message off and turn the phone towards my ear, waving my hand away when I made to take the mobile. Even when I ducked towards it I could scarcely hear for the mass of unchecked conversations in the pub. The voice was feebler than before, barely recognisable as Dorothy's. "I don't like this. I don't know where I am." I could have thought it was as small as a child's. "It's dark and wet," Dorothy protested. "I think it's wriggling, or I am. Can't you hear?"

A hiss of static followed, which sounded as if some kind of collapse had overwhelmed the call. Once he'd pocketed the phone Daniel gazed expectantly if not beseechingly at me, but I was loath to share my first thought—that Dorothy had inherited her mother's mental problem, which had overtaken her at her lowest ebb. I compromised by saying "Do you think that's how she felt when she was waiting for you at the hospital? She wasn't like that once you got there, was she?"

"She was barely conscious. She hardly seemed to know I was there."

"I'm sure you must have made the feelings go away, so she couldn't have had them at the end."

His smile had begun to look less studied. "You're suggesting she made this call from the hospital."

"I'm sure that has to be it. I've had calls that got lost in the ether for days. I'll ask Jane what's the longest delay she knows about if you like."

"I've already spoken to the hospital. They say she wasn't capable of phoning once they'd run the tests."

"That proves they're wrong about this call then, doesn't it? She'd already made the one asking you not to be late."

"I don't believe she did say that, or from the hospital." His smile was making itself plain now—amusement so wry it was more like regret. "I don't think she was cut off," he said. "She was saying someone wasn't there, if you remember. I think she was telling them not to be."

"Come on, Daniel," I said, perhaps too heartily. "Who could she have been talking to on your phone except you? And you're the last person she would have wanted to put off."

Either this persuaded him to some extent or he preferred not to answer. Soon he was expounding on the merits of euthanasia and assisted suicide. I suspect that he sensed I was glad to be spared more of his obsession, because when we left the pub he said "I should think you've had enough of me for a week."

"I'd be less of a friend if I had. Let's make it Monday as ever," I said and was relieved not to see him take out his phone as he vanished into the dark.

Jane's task was more complex than she'd anticipated, and she wasn't home on Saturday until I'd gone to bed. On Monday morning I was ashamed to realise I'd forgotten to quiz her on Daniel's behalf. "How long do you think a call to a mobile could be held up?" I said.

"Quite some time," Jane said and poured herself a coffee even blacker than the one she'd just had. "A client of mine had a call turn up months late."

"I knew it," I said and thought of phoning Daniel at once. "Daniel keeps getting calls from his wife that he thinks are new. You'd say they're delayed, wouldn't you? I'll tell him."

"I don't know if you should do that." Jane took a sip so black that sensing its harshness made me wince. "I've never heard of staggered delays, if that's what you're describing," she said. "I wouldn't think it's possible."

I decided against phoning Daniel. By the time I saw him that night I might have worked out what to say. I hadn't when I reached the office, and meetings with clients left me no chance. I was at my desk and working on an email in which words were shorter and less abundant than numbers when the receptionist rang me. "There's a gentleman to see you, Bill."

"Could you ask him what he'd like to drink? He isn't due for half an hour."

"He isn't your appointment. He says you're a friend." With a hint of doubt Jody said "Doctor Hargreaves."

For a moment I was tempted to declare myself unavailable, and then I felt worse than remorseful. I hurried into the lobby to find Daniel crouched on a chair. He was consulting his phone or guarding it, and his stance looked close to foetal. When he glanced up I thought he was struggling to remember how to smile. "Can we talk somewhere private?" he said almost too low to be heard.

Six straight chairs faced six more across a bare table in the nearest conference room. Daniel slumped onto a chair while I shut the door, and as I sat opposite him he said "She's there again, Bill."

"Jane says calls can be delayed for months."

"I don't think they were calls in the first place." He laid his phone between us on the table and rested his distressed gaze on the dormant screen. "I'm sure this one isn't," he said.

"What else could it be?"

"I believe I've made some kind of connection." He planted his hands on either side of the phone, and moisture swelled under his fingers. "Maybe keeping her on the phone helped, and I'm sure trying to speak to her did," he said. "I think we're hearing her as she is now."

I might have preferred not to listen to the evidence, but I was determined to help if I could. "Let me hear then, Daniel."

The marks of his hands were still fading from the table when he brought up the latest entry on the list. This one was bereft of details too. Even though he'd switched the speaker on, the voice was almost inaudibly faint. "It's dark because I've got no eyes. That's why the dark is so big. Or it's eating its way in because it's made of worms. They're all I'm going to be..."

Daniel dabbed at the phone with a moist fingertip once the thin diminished voice fell silent. Though I was appalled by the way Dorothy's terrors had reduced her to the state of a fearful child, I tried my best to reassure him. "It has to be an old call, Daniel. It's sad, but it's only more of the thoughts you cured her of by being with her at the end."

"You haven't heard it all yet." He raised a finger, and a qualm plucked at my guts as I realised he had only paused the message. "Tell me what you hear," he said like some kind of plea.

"That's me. It's only me, or it's the dark. I can't really feel it, it's only dark. Like being asleep and dreaming. Just dark and my imagination." The voice might have been drifting into a reminiscent stupor, but then it grew louder. "Who is that?" it cried, and a rush of static unpleasantly suggestive of moisture seemed to end by forming an answer. "Me."

Daniel clasped the phone protectively, to no effect I could imagine. "You heard, didn't you? You heard the other voice."

"I heard Dorothy, Daniel." However sharp and shrill the final word had been, surely that signified no more than impatience. "She was saying what she said before," I insisted. "Don't let it upset you, but she meant she was by herself. And then you came and stayed with her till the end."

"I wish I could believe that." Although he was staring at me, he appeared to see a sight considerably less welcome than I hoped I was. "I'm afraid I didn't just bring her by calling," he said. "I think I attracted something else."

I could have argued but confined myself to saying "Do you mind if we discuss it tonight? I need to get ready for a meeting soon."

"I'll give tonight a miss if you don't mind. I have to be prepared as well."

I imagined him sitting alone at home with the phone in his hand while he waited for yet another tardy message. Should I have insisted he came out for a drink? All I said was "Next Monday, then."

"Monday," Daniel said as though the prospect was irrelevant if not unimaginably remote.

He scarcely seemed to hear me wish him well as I saw him out of the building. Interviews and official phone calls took up my afternoon, and a job kept Jane away overnight. Our empty house felt like an omen of a future in which one of us would be on our own, and I was more than glad when she called me at breakfast to say she was starting for home. "And here's something to tell Daniel if you think you should," she said. "I've found a case where somebody made several calls in an hour but the person they were calling kept receiving them for most of a week."

I thought this was worth passing on to Daniel, and as soon as I'd said goodbye to Jane I rang him. His phone was unresponsive, refusing even to accept messages. I blamed his interpretation of his wife's calls for making the utter silence feel like darkness so complete it could engulf all sound. I phoned the hospital where he worked, only to learn that he'd cancelled all his operations. They had no idea how long he would be on leave, and wished they knew.

My first meeting of the day was after lunch. As I drove to the suburb next to mine I tried to think what to say to Daniel. I was hoping to persuade him that he needed someone else's help. His broad house—one of a conjoined pair—was emptily pregnant with a bay window and shaded by a sycamore that had strewn the front lawn with seeds. Sunlight muffled by unbroken cloud made the front room look dusty if not abandoned. I was ringing the bell a third time when Daniel's neighbour emerged from her house, pointing a key at her car to wake it up. "He went out earlier," she said. "He'll be at work."

At once I knew where he might be. In five minutes I was at the graveyard where I'd attended Dorothy's funeral. Her plot was in the newest section, where the turf wouldn't have looked out of place in a garden centre and the headstones were so clean they could have advertised the stonemason's shop. Once I'd parked the car a wind followed me across the grass, and I heard the discreet whispering of cypresses. My footfalls weren't much louder. I was trying to be unobtrusive, having seen Daniel.

He was kneeling on Dorothy's grave with his back to me. He hadn't reacted when I shut the car door, admittedly as quietly as I could. While I was reluctant to disturb him, I wanted to know what state he was in. I strained my ears but heard only the reticently restless trees. At least I wouldn't interrupt Daniel at prayer or in attempted conversation, and as I approached he stirred as though he was about to greet me. No, a shadow was patting his shoulder, a faint ineffectual gesture on the part of a cypress. In fact he was so immobile that I couldn't help clearing my throat to rouse him. This brought no visible response, and I'd grown nervous by the time I came close enough to see his face.

He wasn't merely kneeling. His chest rested against the headstone, and his chin was propped on the sharp edge. However uncomfortable that might have been, he showed no sign of pain. His fixed smile looked fiercely determined, and his eyes were stretched so wide that I could only wonder what he'd been striving to see. They saw nothing now, because nobody was using them. When I closed the lids I imagined shutting in the dark.

His phone had fallen from one dangling hand and lay beside the headstone. I retrieved it, finding it chilly with dew, and wiped it on my sleeve. For a moment I was pitifully relieved that I wouldn't be able to look for any messages, since the phone was activated by a passcode, and then I recalled seeing Daniel type his birthdate. Before I could panic I keyed in the digits and brought up the list of messages. All the latest ones were unnamed and dateless, and there were two more than I'd previously seen.

I opened the first one and held my breath. The pleading voice wasn't much louder than the cypresses, and I fancied that it sounded afraid to be heard or else acknowledged. "Leave me alone. You're just the dark and worms. You're just a dream and I want a different one." At first I thought the noise that followed was only a loose mass of static, and then it began to form words. "Mother's here now," it said. "She's what she promised she would be. There's nobody for you to tell and nobody to see. She'll be with you always like a mother should."

I struggled to believe the explanation I would have given Daniel—that it was yet another deferred call from Dorothy, which was why she was referring to her mother in the third person—but not only the usage made the voice seem inhuman. It no longer resembled static so much as the writhing of numerous worms, an image I tried to drive out of my head as I played the last message. I almost wish I'd left it unheard. An onslaught of slithering swelled out of the speaker in wordless triumph, and in its midst I seemed to hear a plea crushed almost beyond audibility but fighting to shape words. I couldn't bear much of this, and I was reaching to turn it off when another voice went some way towards blotting out the relentless clamour. "I'm here as well."

It was unmistakably Daniel's, though it sounded in need of regaining strength. In less than a second the message came to an end. I closed my fist around the phone and tried to tell myself that Daniel could have recorded his voice over the last part of an existing message. The idea he'd left in my mind days ago was stronger: that the phone, or the way he'd sought not just to preserve all its recordings of his wife but to contact her, had somehow caused the situation. Perhaps I was mistaken, but by the time I doubted my decision it was too late. I found the edit button for the messages and let out a protracted shaky breath as I hit **ERASE ALL**.

I used Daniel's phone to call the police. Weeks later the inquest would confirm that he'd poisoned himself. When the police finished questioning me I drove from the graveyard to work. Though I yearned to be home, I managed to deal with several clients. At last I was at our front door, and when Jane opened it she gasped as if my embrace had driven out all her breath. "No need to hang on so tight. I'm not going anywhere," she said, and I wondered how I could even begin to explain.

First a Bird

"Just stay where we can see you, son."

Trevor's father is the old man's son, not Trevor. It's not as though the six-year-old has kicked his football out of sight or even nearly. As Trevor runs to retrieve the ball his grandfather tells him "Stay out of the trees, there's a good little fellow."

Trevor doesn't want to be called little, or good either if that has to go with it. He dribbles the ball back from the edge of the clearing, towards the picnic chairs his parents and his grandfather are sprawled in. He's keeping it clear of the bottle that's still half full of wine, not to mention its empty neighbours, when his father says "Don't kick at grandad."

Trevor wasn't within yards of doing so, and his mother takes pity on him. "Just play over there where there's space."

"Let grandad have his nap," Trevor's father says, "and then we'll all go for a walk."

"Can't you play with me for a bit?"

"Maybe once the picnic's gone down. It wouldn't do you any harm to let yours settle either."

"If you'd brought a book," Trevor's grandfather informs the boy, "you could sit and read."

"I can play on mum's phone instead."

"You don't want to be softening your brain with all that electronic tripe. I'm surprised you encourage it, Diane." When Trevor's mother suppresses a response, not by any means for the first time, his grandfather turns back to him. "If you want to exercise your intellect," he says, "can you tell us what this place is called?"

Trevor suspects this is how he used to talk at the university, a job the old man seems to think superior to the kind of teaching Trevor's parents do at their school. The question makes the boy feel trapped, and he mumbles "Didn't know it had a name."

"The word for the kind of place it is."

The hint of impatience doesn't help Trevor to think. "A wood," he blurts.

"Not the forest, the clearing. See if you can think." When his pained but hopeful gaze prompts no response the old man says "It's called a glade. Have you never heard the term?"

"Don't think so."

"Perhaps someone ought to work on your vocabulary. Just say the word for me."

"Glade." Repeating it makes Trevor feel as if he has borrowed his grandfather's voice, but the old man rewards his effort with no more than a raised eyebrow. "Glade," Trevor comes close to shouting.

"Dear me, how stentorian." The old man nods in agreement with himself if not on the way to a doze. "Let us hope it sticks, at any rate," he only just finishes muttering.

As his eyelids sag shut Trevor's mother frowns. "No need to imitate your grandad quite so much or he'll think you're making fun of him," she murmurs. "Now you make certain you remember what he said."

"Which bit?"

First a Bird

She plainly thinks he's trying to be clever in a way grownups don't approve of. "Stay where you can be seen."

Can be doesn't mean he is for long. The September shadows haven't lengthened much by the time her head droops, and soon his father's does. Trevor is tempted to knock down the bottles, which resemble a trio of tenpins, but this might ruin what's left of the afternoon. Instead he toes the ball away from them across the glade. The word has indeed lodged in his head, though it feels as if his grandfather is refusing to fall asleep in there, insisting on the solitary syllable. That's one reason Trevor starts to sneak the ball to the edge of the open space.

He boots or rather sandals it towards the entrance to a path, and then a little further. The path is where the grownups plan to walk. It's marked out by black plastic mesh stapled to pairs of wooden strips embedded in the earth a yard apart. When the ball trundles onto it with almost no urging from Trevor, the mesh emits a sketchy clatter. He has to recover the ball, but stays on the grass beside the path so as not to waken anyone. He can go as far as the first bend, since they would be able to see him if they were awake.

A bush stands as close to it as a moderately hearty kick would take the ball. He has just reached the bend when the dark green leaves catch silvery fire, flaring in unison. A breeze has turned their undersides towards him. No doubt his grandfather would be able to name the bush, which is twice Trevor's height and several times his width, and the bird that has begun cooing somewhere among the branches. He might well interrogate Trevor about them, but the boy would rather leave them magically nameless. A glance back at the glade shows him three sunhats hiding lowered heads. He won't go far, and he'll make sure he returns before he's missed. He can't get lost while he's on the path.

Once he's out of sight and presumably out of hearing he moves onto the path. The plastic mesh and the outstretched shadows of the trees make him feel he's advancing into a web. In about a minute he's at a second bend, and approximately as much trotting after the ball takes him to another turn. The one beyond it shows him that the path divides ahead, disappearing into a thick clump of bushes. A stretch of mesh leads straight to an open field, while to its left the path snakes between thorns towards diamond glints of water that seem to beckon to him through restless foliage. He's about to make for them when he sees how close the thorny bushes grow. Suppose he ends up entangled in them? Even if he struggles free, any scratches will let his parents know he disobeyed his mother. He won't head for the field either, because thinking of his parents makes him feel he has been away too long. He swings around and almost tumbles headlong, tripped by the plastic mesh.

The sun is in his eyes unless he keeps his gaze on the path. He's back at the silvery bush sooner than he would have expected. He'd thought there were more bends in the path, and was the bush so close to it? Perhaps it's a different bush, because when he reaches it he still can't see the glade. The grownups must be asleep, or they would be calling to him. He's about to send his ball towards the glade when the bush turns its shining swarm of leaves to him.

There must be a breeze, though he can't feel any. It seems to have roused the bird that's nesting somewhere in the bush. The coos are so pronounced that they sound like a word the creature is repeating. The foliage subsides as though it has caught enough of Trevor's attention, and the sound in the depths of the tangle of branches starts to change. Trevor could imagine the bird is calling "You coo" and then "You who." He wants to linger, but he needs to know his family isn't missing him. He steps back to look around the bend, but there's no sign of the glade. He's about to send himself and the ball in search of it when the voice from the bush grows more distinct. "You," it unquestionably pronounces. "You."

Trevor can't help giggling, if a little nervously. He could fancy the unseen creature is addressing him. "You too," it might be cooing now. "You do."

He'll return to his family in a moment, but first he wants to see what kind of bird is there. He crosses the path with a clatter of his sandals on the plastic, a sound that prompts activity within the bush. Branches and their shadows writhe, suggesting that the bird has retreated deeper. He paces closer in the hope that he won't scare it off until he has caught sight of it, and then a voice halts him. "Thought I was a bird."

He takes it to be saying he did. With its loose elongated syllables, it sounds disconcertingly like a bird that has been taught to speak. Surprise provokes Trevor to be ruder than he would want his family to hear. "What are you, then?"

"What are you thinking?"

It can't be a bird if it's answering him, even if the first words sound like an imitation of his own. "A man," Trevor says.

"A man. That's me."

Now he sounds more like one than his question did, but Trevor could just as well have said a woman—a person, to be safe. He sidles a few inches in a bid to see the speaker. When this shows him nobody he calls "Where are you?"

"Where you're nearly." As Trevor halts, feeling furtive and caught out, the man says "Come where I can be seen."

Is this a sly joke? Most of the words echo the last ones Trevor's mother spoke to him. Wary of the invitation, he retreats onto the path. "Not supposed to," he mumbles.

"Not supposed." To the mocking repetition the man adds "Can't you play with me for a bit?"

He hasn't simply borrowed Trevor's words, he's imitating his voice. "Why are you talking like that?" the boy demands.

"Why? Just practicing."

"What?"

"What I do."

"What's that?"

"What's that? See if you can think."

The reminiscence of his grandfather's directive makes Trevor doubly resentful. "Talking like people," he retorts. "Stealing what they say."

"Not just talking like people. What about before we spoke?"

"Thought it was a bird." Trevor could imagine the man has put the words into his mouth, and he demands "What are you doing it for?"

"What for? Ask your grandad."

This emboldens Trevor to be ruder still. "Asked you."

"I'm sure he'd tell you what impressions are."

"He's not here, so you can."

"Imitations, son. They're how some people make a living. That's their life."

"How do you do it?" Trevor is eager to learn.

"Come and be shown."

"I'm not allowed. I said."

"Then I'll show you my way."

Leaves rustle as though he's about to emerge from hiding, but Trevor is still waiting for him to appear when the bush emits a sound. The unseen performer has reverted to playing a bird. "Coo," he calls and then "You coo."

He repeats this with more force until Trevor understands. "Coo," the boy says a good deal less vigorously, and feels worse than childish.

"Good. Good, you." His instructor is still using the bird's voice. "Coo too," he directs, unless it's "Coo two."

"Coo," Trevor does his best to imitate. "Coo."

"You grew."

Presumably that's praise if not incitement to try harder, but Trevor is growing uncomfortable. It isn't merely that he feels forced to use the voice; he could imagine the speaker is trapped into using it too. "See, you have it in you," the man calls to him. "See what else you can do."

Though he's regaining his ordinary voice, it sounds oddly studied, and some words haven't quite abandoned the birdlike intonation. "Don't know," Trevor mumbles in the hope of fending off any further task.

"Your grandad wanted you to talk like him, didn't he? Let's hear how well you can."

Despite being tempted, Trevor shakes his head. "They might hear."

"Not unless it's wanted."

Perhaps it's just the thought of his family that revives Trevor's nervousness. "I'd better go."

"No need. I see them sleeping their sleep."

Trevor wants to see, but might this be a ruse to lure him where the man is hiding? As he reminds himself he would hear them if they weren't asleep, the voice says "Won't they let you be a boy?"

He feels as though his identity is being threatened. "I am one," he says and tries to laugh.

"Not the kind boys should be. Do they stop you having fun?"

"Sometimes."

"So have some while you've got the chance. What does grandad say that you don't like?"

"Lots of stuff."

"Say some for me."

This sounds unnecessarily like Trevor's grandfather, which provokes the boy to respond. "Exercise your intellect."

"Thought we might hear that." The man adds an appreciative laugh not unlike a coo. "Now say it how he sounds."

Trevor pinches his voice thin and petulant. "Exercise your intellect."

His instructor coos with apparent delight. "Again."

"Exercise your intellect," Trevor says more thinly still.

"That's the fellow." Before Trevor can decide whether this refers to him or his grandfather, the voice says "Now what about his wife?"

At once Trevor is as sad as his parents did their best to coax him out of feeling. "She died."

"Fond, were you?"

Trevor blinks hard and has to swallow. "Yes."

"Then let's see about bringing her back."

Now the boy is worse than nervous. The trees have grown so still that their shadows might be painted on the grass, and the silence seems to shrink his voice. "What are you going to do?"

"Nothing you won't want. Did you have fun while she was alive?" When Trevor only nods, since words might release his feelings too much, his unseen companion says "Let's remember her that way."

If the man saw him nod, why can't Trevor gain even a glimpse of him? Before the can ponder this the voice says "What did she call you?"

Trevor finds this so embarrassing he barely parts his lips. "Tomorrow's man."

"You're bound to be. And what would she call your grandad?"

This embarrasses him differently, and lets loose an uneasy titter. "Her big old chap."

"My big old chap." The voice has relapsed into cooing, which Trevor doesn't like much any more. "Now you say it," the man urges in his version of an ordinary voice.

Trevor giggles, feeling wicked. "My big old chap."

"More like she would. I told you they can't hear."

"My big old chap," Trevor says not much louder.

"No, like she would. Use her voice."

The boy has a troubled notion that the speaker almost used it. His cooing tone came uncomfortably close to parodying how the old lady would address her husband, however much it abashed him. Trevor parts his lips, only to bite them. Suppose he wakes his grandfather? He doesn't want to play that kind of trick on him, and how does he know he can trust what the unseen speaker told him—that nobody can hear? "Got to go back now," he says and starts to turn away.

Some sort of convulsion passes through the bush. "Don't you want to bring her back to them?"

"I can't," Trevor protests, but guilt has halted him. "It wouldn't be my gran."

"Practice and they won't know. Maybe you won't either."

Trevor doesn't care to understand why he finds the prospect so disturbing. "I've got to go. They're calling me."

"Don't try to trick a trickster. Nobody's calling you but me."

"I'm going," Trevor cries in a bid to free himself from his paralysis, and all at once he's stumbling along the path. At the edge of his vision he seems to glimpse the bush gape like a mouth surrounded by scales—leaves that have grown unnaturally regular as the darkening day turns them the colour of fungus. "We haven't finished," says a voice so harsh it seems to creak like wood. "If I can't have her..."

An inadvertent kick sends Trevor's football towards the bush, but he's too afraid to rescue it. He blunders around the bend in the path and sees the glade, where his family are still lolling in their chairs. How did he fail to see them earlier? He's dashing towards them when he hears a rustling whisper behind him, as if a large but loosely composed object is creeping after him. He doesn't dare to look back, especially when a voice follows him. "You coo. You do."

Fearful Implications

He feels as though the words are determined to find a lair in his mouth. They can't get in so long as he clamps his lips together. He's almost in the clearing when the voice catches up with him. "My big old chap," it coos. "My big old chap."

He no longer knows who's speaking. He could imagine that the voice has found a way to use his mouth. As it repeats the words, his grandfather's head jerks up and his eyes spring open. "Cecily?" he says, though only just. He reaches out his hands as he chokes on the last syllable, and attempts to rise. A spasm flings all his limbs helplessly wide, and he falls into the chair. As his staring head slumps back, it lifts his hat like a jokey greeting or a gesture of respect, and then there's utter stillness. "Grandad?" Trevor only just manages to call.

He wants it to waken his parents—he's desperate not to be alone with his grandfather while the old man is like that—but neither of them stirs. As Trevor makes himself venture into the glade, he can't help glancing behind him. The silvery bush is closer than the bend where he recalls seeing it in the first place. The shadows of the trees have barely lengthened, as if he was away virtually no time at all. His grandfather's hands are dangling almost to the grass on either side of the chair, and Trevor can't bring himself to touch them, especially once he sees the old man's empty eyes have grown as dull as stagnant water. He's even more dismayed to feel he may be to some extent responsible. "Grandad," he pleads with no hope of a response, but he's answered. "My big old chap," the voice coos, and then "Tomorrow's man."

It's coming from his grandfather, although the bloodless lips are shut tight. The old man might have turned into a dummy a ventriloquist is using. Trevor almost sprawls on his back in his haste to put distance between himself and the cooing remains of his grandfather. He lurches over to his sleeping parents and is about to grab their hands—to tug at them until his parents waken, because he's afraid to speak—when a further terror overtakes him, and he wavers to a halt that feels as if he may never dare to move again. Shadows inch towards him, and he sees how long the shadow of the bush beside the path has grown, as dark as a premature patch of the night. Even if the bush moves as no bush should he doesn't know whether he'll be able to cry out—even if his grandfather speaks again. He's afraid to waken his parents when he no longer knows what voice may come out of their mouths.

The Stillness

At first Donald thought only the man was familiar—just another of the street performers who would keep up a pose until somebody dropped them a coin. Last week he'd played a businessman arrested in the act of dashing somewhere with a briefcase as dead white as himself, and now he was portraying a dignitary painted just as pale. A robe or at any rate a sheet was draped over his shoulders, and he held a book of which not only the pages were white in front of his stern set face. Even his eyes looked excessively colourless. Donald was watching him between two books in the shop window when Mildred jangled hangers on a rack of dresses. "What's so interesting out there?"

"I was trying to think what that fellow is supposed to be."

"A statue, I imagine," Mildred said like the teacher Donald was often reminded she'd been, and tramped across the bare boards to plant her hands on her wide hips. She might almost have been squeezing out the perfume that her capacious russet one-piece costume exuded. "The one they moved," she said.

Now Donald knew what he'd been struggling to recognise. The street had featured an actual statue until the town centre was redeveloped. He went to the bookshelves and found an outsize dog-eared paperback of local photographs. "Here he is," he said, squinting at the inscription on the plinth, which showed that the subject had died almost a century ago. "Samuel Huntley, educator and mayor."

Mildred kept her hands on her hips to mime patience as he took the paperback to the window. While the photograph was frontal, the man in the street had his left side to the shop, but Donald thought the pose was exactly the same. He was trying to identify some detail that seemed odd when Mildred said "Are those books in order? That's how books ought to be."

He supposed his wife might have told him not to let Mildred talk to him like that, if he'd had a wife to tell about his day. He'd had his fair share of liaisons, but by now he was too fond of his own ways to become involved with anyone else, and his relationship with Mildred quite amused him. As an accountant he'd observed how some of his colleagues would create work in order to seem busy, but he'd never met another one like Mildred. He assumed she meant to convince herself she was still active, though he suspected she wouldn't own up to the trick. He took his time over restoring order to the bookshelves while he watched to see the human statue perform its routine, but while people loitered until Donald felt like urging them to throw a coin, nobody paid.

The November night had fallen by the time Mildred locked Pre-Treasured Prizes and hurried away to the car park. The colourless glare of the streetlamps turned the painted man even paler. His white breaths lingered in front of his face, and Donald saw how few and how measured they were, presumably in aid of the performance. Donald was about to move on, having grown shivery from dallying, when he realised what he'd failed to notice. Street performers always left coins in a receptacle to encourage people to donate, but this fellow had nothing of the kind, despite having used the ploy when he'd played the headlong businessman. "Don't you want to earn anything?" Donald murmured, but the whitened face didn't twitch.

The evening crowds thinned out and vanished before he reached his apartment, on the ground floor of a converted warehouse in a side street that was becoming overrun with nightclubs. He changed his clothes and jogged to the gym, where he cycled and ran for a couple of hours. He didn't mean to slow down while he had the energy to outdistance it, and he returned home with more of an appetite. His chicken casserole and half a bottle of wine kept him company for the duration of a Sinatra album, and then he was ready for bed, where he dealt with several chapters of this month's choice for the reading group. At least the nightclubs were relatively dormant during the week, and he slept without much trouble until dawn.

He was on his way to the Pre-Treasured shop well before opening time. He preferred to be with people whenever he had the chance, but he wasn't expecting to see the human statue so early in the day, or to find the man facing the shop. There was still no sign of money, not even the man's own. Donald hitched up his quilted overcoat to extract a lukewarm pound, which he dropped at the man's feet. He could only assume the performer didn't think much of the amount, because he didn't even twitch.

In the overcast winter light the pale eyes looked dull, unpleasantly close to lifeless. Donald felt as if they'd fixed him in the act of willing them to blink. He stared at them until he began to feel not much less cold than stone, and revived himself with an uneasy laugh. He was heading for the shop when he heard a rustle of activity behind him, but when he looked the statue seemed not to have stirred. "What did you just do?" he said. "You have to let people see what they paid for."

He saw the man ignore him, which was too much. He came close to sprawling on his face as he crouched to recover the coin. "Last chance to show me," he said without result, and pocketed the pound as he made for the shop.

As Mildred locked the door she said "You didn't need to encourage him."

"Why, what's he been up to?"

"Nothing I'm aware of. I'm simply saying money paid to him may be income lost to us."

"You should be glad I took mine back, then."

"I hope nobody saw. That won't do our image any good." As if she was extending Donald an opportunity to redeem himself she said "We've had a box of books for you to price. Ninety-five for the paperbacks except one ninety-five for the big ones, and three ninety-five for the hardbacks unless they're big enough for seven."

"Ninety-five," Donald added so wryly that he kept it under his breath. He was already aware of the prices and how she used them to embarrass customers, saying "Will you want your change? It'll help to fight cancer." His task took up the morning, not least because the books reminded him of the one the human statue held. Had Donald drawn the man's attention by retrieving the coin? He had to keep glancing towards the window, but couldn't tell whether the man was watching him across the book; indeed, the fellow never even seemed to blink. The spectacle had begun to unnerve Donald by the time he set about making space for the new books, and then he had a thought. "Hang on," he said to nobody in particular as he found the book of local photographs.

While the lower floors of all the buildings on both sides of the street had been altered beyond recognition, the roofs and the architectural details beneath them hadn't changed. Stone faces peered out below the eaves behind the statue in the photograph, but there was

The Stillness

no sign of them across the road. The November chill fastened on Donald as he stepped outside to look for them. On his way past the human statue he glanced at the book—a ledger with its pages painted even whiter and then covered with names and dates, which had been dug into the surface so as to look carved. There was no sign of the architectural features anywhere in the street. "Excuse me," he said, "you're in the wrong place."

Several bystanders stared at him as if he might be mad for talking to a statue. They weren't behaving too impressively themselves, having already hung around so long that Donald could have thought the performer was infecting them with stillness. This close to the statue Donald saw that the eyes must be shut, the lids painted an unrelieved white, though he had to fend off the notion that the eyes had no pupils or colour, any more than they had lashes—that they were set like pebbles in the sockets. "You shouldn't be here if you want to be real," he said and retreated into the shop.

Mildred was transferring the book of old photographs to the window display. "What were you saying to him?"

"I was trying to move him. I thought you wanted him to go away."

"I hope you didn't say you were acting on my behalf. Did anyone else hear you?"

"I don't think anyone was very interested. Maybe not even him."

While that had to be part of the man's act, he looked set to maintain his pose all day if not longer. As Donald made room for the latest lot of books by adding to the window display he tried to see the white eyes blink, but they never did. They must be the lids, because otherwise they would have pupils. All the same, he was glad to leave the sight behind when he went for his break.

The cramped back room smelled of stewed tea and Mildred's fierce perfume, both of which might have infiltrated the drab brown wallpaper. Donald dangled a teabag in his Can That Cancer mug and lingered over sipping until he began to wonder if the statue might have shifted in his absence. He poured the remains of his tea into the thunderous metal sink and used the venerable toilet before hurrying out to rejoin Mildred, only to demand "Where's he gone?"

Mildred glanced none too instantly towards the window. "He must have listened to you after all."

"Yes, but did you see where he went?"

She gave Donald just as delayed a glance. "I was dealing with a customer."

Why should Donald wish he'd seen the performer move? Surely all that mattered was his having moved, and now he was nowhere to be seen. On his way home Donald caught himself looking out for the statue, but everyone in sight was moving—at least, apart from a distant group of people halted by whatever they could see. Donald had to peer hard along the side street to be sure that they were queuing for a bus, though why should their inactivity have bothered him? He put on speed, not just to prove he could. Tonight was the meeting of the dining club.

This month they met at Crabracadabra, the new seafood restaurant across town. Some were couples, and all of them were at least Donald's age. Quite a few of the topics of conversation—political failings, familial ailments—felt close to growing too familiar. As he tried to bring more vigour to the dialogue Donald was distracted by a waiter who loomed over him to serve wine. Even once he grasped that he'd been reminded how the human statue had towered over him while Donald recaptured the coin, he had to wait for his heart to steady and slow down.

Strolling home, he realised he was surrounded by statues—dummies in store windows. He thought he'd left the lifeless shapes behind until he saw a figure down a side street. The man had no cause to move while he was waiting for a bus, of course, and perhaps he was a slow reader. A nearby streetlamp seemed to turn him as pale as the cover of the book in his hand.

Donald slept well enough. In the morning he had to flex his arms and legs to help wake up his heavy eyes. As he trotted to work he noticed that the bus stop wasn't visible along the street where he'd seen the man reading, though why should it matter? He was more disconcerted to see someone in the doorway of the shop, standing absolutely still with an object in his hands. Then the man turned to face him, revealing that the item was a jigsaw in a box. When Mildred let Donald in, the customer tried to follow him. "We're open in ten minutes," Mildred said.

"I'm just returning this. Since you're a charity I won't ask for my money back."

Mildred sounded not far from affronted. "Why would you?"

"Half of it is missing. I'm surprised you offered it for sale."

"Then I hope you'll accept our apologies." Once the door was locked she said more accusingly to Donald than he thought was called for "You'll need to check this."

As he sat behind the counter to count jigsaw pieces out of the box into the lid he felt like a schoolboy in detention. The stone eyes of a Roman statue gazed up from the midst of the cardboard chaos, and Donald could have imagined they were willing him to reassemble their body. "I'm afraid the customer was right," he said. "A lot of it isn't here."

"Well, I don't know how that could have happened." This sounded like an indictment in search of a culprit. "You'd better see all the others are complete," Mildred said.

Donald only just succeeded in staying amused by her attitude. People chose how they behaved, and he could. He felt he was back in detention, and perhaps defiance made him count the pieces of the jigsaws as slowly as he was able to bear, until he seemed to be in danger of dawdling to a standstill. People at the window didn't help, though he needn't think the motionless folk were watching him, and in any case they couldn't know that he was being penalised. In time he grasped why they were troubling him. While people generally halted when they were looking in shop windows, he'd begun to feel as if their stillness was both an imitation and a symptom of an unseen presence. Each time he established that a jigsaw was complete he stepped out of the shop on the pretext of taking a breather, but he could never be sure that the crowds weren't concealing someone too pale and still.

That night the reading group met in the town's solitary bookshop. Nearly all the members had chosen the month's book, but very few had finished the novel, which was narrated in this year's slang if not in a future lingo. Donald had made himself understand it so as not to feel left behind, but everyone else was more interested in regretting the present and yearning for the past it had dislodged. So tardily that he felt slowed down Donald realised this was his cue to ask "Does anyone remember where Samuel Huntley's statue used to be?"

"Who?" more than one listener said, and the most historically inclined of them answered for Donald. "He was meant to be something of an educational pioneer."

"In what way?" Donald felt inexplicably anxious to learn.

"He was supposed to have developed a method of calming his pupils, for one thing, but I don't know how."

"He mightn't be too calm about having his statue knocked down," another woman said.

Donald didn't need the comment, surely only because it was a distraction. "But do you know where he," he asked his informant, "that's to say where it was?"

"Somewhere near here." She shut her eyes, reminding him unnecessarily of the human statue, and opened them without having found more of a memory. "I should be able to tell you next month," she said.

Donald had to suppress a ridiculous inkling that in some way this would be too late. As he returned to his apartment he was dogged by a notion that the plastic sculptures in the shops weren't the only static figures he ought to notice. He was almost home when he saw one along a side street—somebody not quite as distant as last night's loiterer had been. Perhaps he should feel heartened to observe that people still read books, although the man might just be consulting a street map by the light of the streetlamp that turned him unnaturally pale. He was certainly taking his time over the book, and Donald felt equally immobilised by trying to identify it without venturing closer. He didn't stir until his efforts or the glare of the streetlamp began to make his eyes smart, and he had to jerk his body out of its torpor before he was able to hasten home.

That night he didn't sleep a great deal. Drifting off felt too much like a threat of growing excessively still. Whenever he floundered awake he had to reconfirm that he could move his limbs and to ward off the idea that his plight was being watched or wished upon him. Of course he was alone in the ground-floor bedroom, where the curtains were too thoroughly shut for anyone to be able to peer in. A trace of streetlight surmounted the curtains, and having convinced himself yet again that he was alone in the dim room he made himself risk sleep.

As he trudged to work he found his panic hadn't altogether left him. Might it catch up with him if he didn't put on speed? He was panting by the time he reached the shop, and the sight of his winter breaths brought to mind a child's portrayal of a steam train. He hadn't seen a train like that since he was very young, and he didn't want to dwell on the past in case it slowed him down.

Mildred was waiting to greet him. "What are we going to do today?" she said as though to a child.

"Stand around looking important." Accusing her of that would hardly improve the situation. "What's there to keep us busy?" Donald asked instead.

"The discs could do with checking. See all the cases match."

Donald tried to lend the task more animation by tramping back and forth between the counter, where the discs were stored, and the shelves. He felt driven to behave yet more strenuously once Mildred started watching him, until she said "Haven't you ever heard of time and motion, Donald?"

"I hope I've got plenty of both left." When this went nowhere near amusing her he said "I just need to keep moving. You may find you do when you get to my age."

"You're making me feel idle, like your friend who was outside." As various rejoinders clamoured in Donald's head—the man was anything but his friend, she deserved to feel inert compared with Donald, he wasn't causing it, surely nobody else could be—Mildred said "Take a few at a time to the counter. You'll be tiring yourself out if you aren't careful."

The prospect of slowing to a standstill daunted him enough that he followed her suggestion. Instead of sitting at the counter he marched on the spot while he found the discs their cases, even after Mildred gave him a lengthy frown. Several cases for bands he'd never heard of— Chorus of Snails, the Devastating Artichokes, the Nostrils, the Complicit Eggs—had been stolen, presumably to house pirate copies. "We need less wandering about," Mildred declared, "and more vigilance."

Donald already felt unwillingly vigilant, watching out even when they had no customers, though he never caught anyone spying on him.

The Stillness

The compulsion accompanied him home and out again for his weekly meeting with friends in a downtown pub. He mightn't have ventured into the streets overlooked by posturing plastic figures if he hadn't wanted to question somebody who worked near the town hall. "Do you know if they've moved Samuel Huntley up your end of town?"

"I've really no idea, I'm glad to say." Whatever the solicitor found objectionable, he said no more except "We can do without him."

Another drinker was a doctor, and Donald turned to her. "Isn't it quite common to wake in the night thinking someone's there and you can't move?"

"I wouldn't say common." As if taking pity on him she said "That's what nightmares meant originally, waking up paralysed with the idea someone was causing it. Has that been happening to you?"

"It nearly may have. I won't let it," Donald vowed.

When he left the pub he found he'd had quite a lot to drink. The figures in the windows might almost have been mocking his bids to walk straight or stand still. He managed to laugh at his erratic progress until he was nearly home, when he caught sight of a man loitering in the middle of a side street. "Stay out of the road," Donald managed mostly to pronounce, "before you get yourself run over."

Perhaps this was unnecessary, since he couldn't hear any traffic or even anybody else. Donald's eyes weren't focusing too well, so that he might have taken the man to be holding a portable computer, but although the object was as dead white as its owner he couldn't avoid recognising that it was a book. "Are you following me?" he blurted and tried to laugh. "You can't if you can't move."

At least the blurred sight of the man let Donald stand still; in fact, he might almost have been forgetting how to behave otherwise. The thought overwhelmed him with a panic worse than any he'd experienced last night in bed. It seemed to rob him of speech, even of breath. With an effort that made his chest ache he sucked in a lungful of air, which released him. He staggered forward without meaning to and then without desiring it at all. "Go where you're wanted," he shouted, "and that isn't here." He'd already turned his back on the fellow, and was able to stumble home.

His conversation with the doctor in the pub didn't help him sleep. It simply left him conscious that his experience wasn't quite like the one she'd described, because he felt as if lying there in the dark could attract a watcher, unless his confrontation in the street had done so. Eventually he struggled out of bed and reeled across the room to fumble the curtains apart. The street was deserted except for an ill-defined face—his own dim reflection. After that he made himself lie still in bed, though this felt like a threat of paralysis. Sleep caught up with him at last, although never for very long, and he rose none too steadily before dawn.

By the time he left the apartment the streetlamps had shut down. Mist turned the ends of streets into charcoal sketches, imperfectly erased. Donald found he welcomed the vicious chill, which was bound to have driven the loiterer away. He felt like celebrating the absence as he reached the junction, but the man was still in the side street. He might not have stirred since Donald had last seen him, except that he was hundreds of yards closer. "Have you been like that all night?" Donald cried. "Are you completely mad?"

The white face held as still as the marble carving it resembled altogether too much. He couldn't tell whether the empty eyes were gazing at him or the book, if they could see at all. He found he was desperate to provoke a response, any response. "Don't you like being talked to? Better make yourself scarce before I call someone."

He very much hoped this would do the trick, but the figure stayed lifeless, not even displaying a breath. Its defiant inertia and his failure to shift it enraged him, and he strode at it, hardly knowing what he meant to do. He grabbed its left hand to jerk it into some kind of life, but let go at once and fell back. However cold the day was, the man's hand felt dismayingly colder, and as hard as stone.

Donald could have thought the fellow had frozen to death overnight, except that as he made for the junction he heard a surreptitious rustling behind him. He'd heard that sound before, and now he recognised the turning of a page. He swung around to catch the statue in the act, but its stance was challenging him to prove it had moved. "I warned you," Donald shouted and strode furiously to work.

Mildred blinked at him. "Aren't you feeling well? Do you want to go home?"

"There's nothing wrong with me. I need to be here," Donald protested and thought of a reason he could say aloud. "Two of us can keep twice as much of an eye out for pilfering."

That needn't entail staying still whenever a customer came in. Donald followed them about, enquiring whether he could help. Perhaps he shouldn't have asked quite so often, since it visibly irritated Mildred. He tried varying the question, not least because it had started to feel like a threat of stagnation. "Can we show you anything?" he said, and "Anything we can find for you?" as well as "Are you after anything in particular?" until at last it was time for his lunch.

There were human statues in the streets, but not the one he'd touched. Ten minutes of dodging through the crowds brought him to the town hall. While a number of stone statues occupied the square in front of the colonnaded entrance, none of them depicted Samuel Huntley. The girl inside an enquiry booth in the marble foyer sent Donald into an enormous hall where a roped-off zigzag queue brought him at last to a clerk behind a window. "Do you authorise street performers?" Donald said.

Fearful Implications

The greying man peered at him as if trying to decide what manner of performance Donald might put on. "They need to get a permit from us, yes."

"And if they don't behave you'll deal with them." When the clerk raised his face to prompt more information Donald said "I'd like to report the man who's being a statue of Samuel Huntley."

"We don't tell them who they have to be. You'd need to give us his name." The man squinted at Donald before adding "A statue, you said. What's your complaint?"

"He's been following me home. I believe that's called harassment. Yes, I said a statue. I can see that may sound a bit ridiculous."

The clerk's face wasn't owning up to an opinion. "Any reason he should do that?"

"I took back my money when he didn't move. Maybe this is his revenge."

The clerk's lack of an expression was an answer in itself. "It wouldn't be our business," he said. "You'd want the police."

"And I'll get them if I need to, believe me." Donald's fury at the skepticism he sensed made him almost unable to say "Perhaps you can tell me where the actual statue has gone."

"Mayor Huntley, did you say? He's gone all right, for good."

Donald wouldn't have expected the clerk to sound so openly gratified. "Why, what happened?"

The clerk leaned towards the aperture beneath the window and lowered his voice. "The contractors weren't too careful about moving him, and someone here didn't think he was worth sticking back together."

"I thought he had a reputation. Didn't he pioneer some way of calming children down?"

"That's the tale his friends put about." Lower still the clerk said

"There's some families that know what he used to do to our grandparents. Made them stand for hours and Christ help anyone who moved an inch."

Donald found he preferred not to hear any more, let alone to ponder what he'd heard. He hadn't time to go to the police now, and he rather hoped he'd already done enough. Mightn't the confrontation have sent the street performer on his way? Donald hurried back to the shop, which was less of a refuge than he would have liked, even from his thoughts. Whenever a customer lingered to examine an item he was seized by an urge to budge them, so that he felt compelled to point out other articles to them—anything he could find that seemed even remotely appropriate. "You need to calm yourself down, Donald," Mildred said after he'd tried to sell a book of cartoons to a man who was deliberating over a comedy film. "Make sure you get some rest tonight. You're disturbing people."

Better that, Donald almost retorted, than leaving them so undisturbed that they mightn't be able to move. Besides, dealing with customers felt like postponing his return home. All too soon he had to make his way through the crowds that might be hiding somebody less active than they were, although why should that be so threatening? As the streets grew emptier he began to hope for company or else to see nobody at all. When he reached the side street where he'd seen the frozen man, he almost couldn't look. But the street was deserted, and so was everywhere closer to home.

He'd been secretly afraid that if he was the first to touch the statue, that might have brought it after him. Suppose the woman at the book group was right, and Samuel Huntley had been roused somehow by the destruction of his image? If Huntley had regarded stillness as power, how determined might he have been to exert it? Although Donald was able to conclude none of this was true—the part about

Fearful Implications

Huntley, at any rate—he found his thoughts distressingly irrational. However dull tonight's meeting might be, at least it would make sense.

The tenants met in Miss Hart's apartment on the top floor. Until now Donald had quite liked the figurines in her living-room, miniature sculptures collected from around the world, and why should he change his mind? Everyone agreed that the apartment committee should campaign against the proliferation of nightclubs in the neighbourhood and involve the local councillor. As Donald wondered why agreement had taken several sluggish hours, Miss Hart said "There are too many people lurking round here as it is."

"You've seen him?" Donald blurted. "Where is he now?"

"I don't mean anyone specific, Mr Curtis. I was referring to the types who loiter near the clubs."

Donald couldn't let this reassure him until he looked out of her window. As far as he could see, the street below and all those in sight were deserted. He very much hoped that the Huntley imitator hadn't merely gone away but had found a new role or reverted to his previous persona. "We all need to deal with any undesirables in the locality," he said as he left Miss Hart's, and didn't mind sounding pompous.

He walked down three floors to his apartment without feeling required to put on speed. He took his time over preparing for bed and promised himself he would sleep. He was taken aback to find he'd been so nervous earlier that he hadn't opened the bedroom curtains. They looked untidy from his fumbling at them in the night, and he made to adjust them. Taking hold of them let him glimpse a man outside the window—waiting for a friend, no doubt, or else a taxi, or simply having halted to talk on the phone. But the figure was silent, and the object in its pallid hand wasn't a phone. When Donald snatched the curtains apart he saw that the statue was staring at him.

The wide blank white eyes were directed at him, at any rate, and so

The Stillness

was the colourless face. The statue had altered its posture, so that the head was turned towards him. In a moment he realised that Samuel Huntley was waiting for him to read the book. A solitary name was etched at the top of the left-hand page—Donald's name.

He had evidence of harassment now. He had a reason to contact the police. Should he let the man hear him calling them, or would that warn the fellow off? Better to make certain he stayed there to be arrested, and Donald would have turned his back before using the phone, except perhaps he should keep his persecutor in sight to ensure he didn't escape. Donald needn't leave the window; he had only to take out his phone. Or perhaps he should summon witnesses first, in which case he would have to shout loud enough to be heard all the way upstairs, although how would he let anybody in when he was having trouble even reaching in his pocket for the phone? The struggle seemed to be interfering with his vision, filling his eyes with the glare of the streetlamps or with some other pallor. In another moment unrelieved white was all he could see, though it wasn't quite like seeing. With an effort that stopped his breath Donald wrenched his arms up so that he could find his eyes, but when he groped at them he didn't know which felt more like stone: his fingertips or the globes beneath the unblinking lids. Then the distinction ceased to matter, any more than it applied to the rest of him, though he felt anything but calm. Indeed, his panic felt as though it was set in stone.

The Fourth Call

"Happy Christmas, dad."

"And a happy one to you, Harriet."

"Yes, dad, happy Christmas."

"Just as happy to you too, Catherine."

"A special one from me, Mike. Have the happiest you can."

"If you do I will, Margery. There'll be others, love."

"And dad, thanks for all the presents."

"Yes, big thanks, dad."

"You'll have opened them, then. Well, you should. Mine can wait. It'll be like a second Christmas."

"I haven't opened most of mine yet."

"Don't wait for me unless you want to, Margery. Has anybody built a snowman or is everyone too old?"

"Dad, we made some but we'd rather have you home."

"Yes, come and see them before they go sad."

"I expect I'll be home before that. I may be here for a few days yet, though. They're forecasting more snow."

"They didn't forecast so much in the first place, did they? Maybe they'll be wrong again. Mike, what are you doing for dinner?"

Fearful Implications

"There's a festive feast at the Indian up the road. I'm treating myself."

"Oh, Mike, that isn't how Christmas ought to be for anyone."

"If I went traditional I'd only know it wouldn't be as good as yours. Save me some, that's all I ask."

Another round of Christmas wishes brought the conversation to an end. He pulled on the hiking boots he'd bought in Rambling Rose's in the village—he didn't know if the apostrophe was a bid for wit or a mistake—and doubled the bows of the laces before shoving himself off the bed with a creak of the elderly mattress. From the window of his old room he could see across the simplified white fields to the ridge that formed the horizon, where a solitary farmhouse sported a drooping cap of snow. Alongside this edge of the village, chunks of ice the colour of the unrelieved sky floated down a stream, over which the venerable stone arch that gave Leanbridge its name had been replaced by a bulkier structure of metal. As he clumped downstairs, his boots made the house sound hollowed out, emptied of more than furniture. It still held memories, and they had to be company enough for him.

Outside the house the snow engulfed his boots, sending a chill through him. Beyond the small garden the pavement was puffy with frozen slush. A few villagers laboured along the street of houses and small shops, calling festive salutations to one another, while a lone van matched their pace, spraying muddy snow over the kerb. Mike's walk to the Kerala Parlour took him past the churchyard, where a robin followed him the length of the wall, chirping variations on a theme. No doubt it was hoping to be fed.

He hadn't expected the restaurant to be so full. A waiter found him a table scarcely big enough for two and removed the other setting, which left Mike to face a corner of the room. A sitar on a tape played half a dozen carols before the tunes came round again. The meal began with tandoori turkey drumsticks, followed by bhuna goose with roast Bombay potatoes and spicy sprouts, all of which struck Mike as cautiously conventional and yet almost a parody of the dinner Margery would have made at home. Along with the robin he'd seen, the other birds were starting to revive a memory until a woman's voice distracted him. "Aren't you speaking to us, young Michael?"

He only just recognised her and her husband. While the features of their faces were still as little as their statures were diminutive, the rest of them had spread outwards with age. "Mr Darlington," he said, turning his chair towards them. "Mrs Darlington. Merry Christmas to you both."

"Jack and Beryl," her husband said. "Aye, merry Christmas."

"And many of them," Beryl said. "I told Jack it must be you at Bill and Denise's, but he won't be told."

"Got it all clear, have you, Michael? We saw them loading up the wagon."

"Everything's gone that wasn't worth saving. I'll take some of that home."

"I expect you'll have your memories." Beryl dabbed at her eyes with a linen napkin. "I don't like to think of you all by yourself in there at Christmas," she said. "While you're stuck here you come to us for dinner."

"That's really kind of you. What can I bring?"

"Nothing but yourself," Jack said quite like an admonition. "You're all we're inviting."

Mike didn't know why he should find this ominous, and then he thought he did, though surely the old man couldn't have the same events in mind. "Do the birds still come round the village?" Mike said.

Beryl wiped her lips with the napkin as if she were erasing a response. "What are you asking?" Jack barely enquired.

"The Christmas birds. Do you still celebrate the four days that way?"

"We never did."

Mike could have fancied that the old man's stare was trying to deny the memory, and then he saw his mistake. "I don't mean you. It was the Bundle family dressed up, wasn't it, all four of them."

Beryl unveiled her mouth to say "We've not seen them for years."

"The birds, do you mean, or the Bundles?"

"They went off," Beryl said, tapping her forehead with a finger.

"Right off," Jack said, "and not missed either."

Mike might have pursued the subject if he hadn't gathered that the Darlingtons weren't anxious to be reminded of the family who had lived beyond the bridge. Beryl was already standing up. "We'll see you for dinner tomorrow," she told him. "No need to stay in there on your own when it gets dark."

Jack was moving to follow her when he grabbed the back of the chair, squeezing his eyes so tight the lids grew pale. "Jack," Beryl cried.

"Don't make a scene, woman." His eyes wavered open, and he pushed the chair away. "Just a spell," he told Mike. "You get that sort of nuisance at my age."

Mike watched him make his careful way to the door, outside which he took Beryl's arm, whoever was supporting whom. Mike lingered over Christmas pudding and coffee, so that by the time he left the restaurant the streetlamps were gilding the slush. As he reached the churchyard the robin hopped along the wall, and its vague bloated shadow jerked across the graves, rearing up whenever it encountered a headstone. Not caring much for the sight, he tramped home as fast as he could.

An echo of his footsteps met him in the hall. He left his boots next to the Welcome mat, on which the first three letters had been scuffed almost out of existence, and peeled off his sodden socks on the way upstairs for a bath. The central heating felt as if it was only disguising a chill. While he lay in the bath he was aware of the empty house around him, and felt as if he ought to listen for some noise he might prefer not to hear. When he began to shiver—the water had grown cold, it seemed all of a sudden—he opened the door, having climbed out of the bath.

He'd kept the television in the front room, along with a newish sofa and its associated pair of armchairs. He found a variety show on a nostalgic channel, but didn't care much for a comedian who whistled counterpoint to the melodies he was playing on a violin. Mike didn't need to think what the trilling resembled. He switched off the television and leafed through a photograph album, recalling Christmases in Leanbridge—his father and Uncle Bill taking him for walks while Aunt Denise and his mother filled the house with aromas of Christmas dinner, the toys he would never unwrap until he'd guessed what they were, the board games everyone would play past his usual bedtime. Soon he took his reminiscences up to bed.

He might have fallen asleep with them if he hadn't looked out of the window. The pale fields glimmered beneath the smouldering glow of the clouds, against which he was just able to glimpse the pallid hulk on the horizon. Now he remembered it was the Bundles' house. He'd often heard Mrs Bundle screeching at her husband and her sons, a sound that had grated in his ears even though it was shrivelled by distance. Unable to make out any words, he might almost have mistaken it for the furious cry of a bird.

He drew the musty curtains and climbed into the low bed. While it wasn't quite a double, it was wide enough to remind him that he was by himself. The empty section felt as though it had brought the desertion of the house into the room. It reminded him how he'd felt when he was small, and perhaps that was why he remembered the first time he'd seen the Christmas ritual.

That Christmas was the first he and his parents had spent in Leanbridge—after that, each couple had played host in alternate years until he reached his teens—and he'd been six years old. After dinner he'd helped to wash up all the plates and cutlery, and was about to propose a Ludo tournament on the table they'd cleared when Aunt Denise replenished it with a solitary mince pie on a plate. "Who's that for?" Mike was eager to learn.

"Our first visitor."

"I don't think we know about that, do we?" Mike's father said.

"You must know your twelve days of Christmas," Uncle Bill told his brother, who began to respond just as bluffly until they all heard a chirping outside the house.

It must have been crossing the bridge. It sounded stridently determined and only intermittently melodious. As it approached it grew louder than Mike imagined any bird could sing. "Here he comes," Uncle Bill enthused, and his wife smiled so hard that it narrowed her eyes. The chirping resounded along the hall, and the caller rapped on the front door. "You let Bobby in, Michael," his aunt urged.

As Mike opened the front door he was hoping to see not just a partridge or somebody dressed as one but a pear tree as well, and at first he was merely confused. Silhouetted against the streetlamp outside the gate was a rotund man who had gone to some trouble to render himself rounder. Padding thrust a crimson waistcoat forward from his jacket, which was as black as his capacious trousers. His hands were clasped behind his back, and his head was lowered, giving Mike the grotesque notion that the man had used some part of it to knock on the door. The visitor raised his head to reveal an unexpectedly thin sharp face, which he contorted to force the scrawny lips upwards until

The Fourth Call

the pointed nose looked yet more beaklike. The lips parted a fraction, and the mimicry of birdsong shrilled between them. "Have you told him to come in, Michael?" Uncle Bill called.

Mike did his best not to be daunted by the visitor, having deduced that the trills were made by a kind of device he'd seen street vendors demonstrating. "My uncle says come in," he said and backed along the hall.

The padded man bobbed after him, chirping as he came, and slammed the front door with a backwards kick. Uncle Bill and Aunt Denise were beyond the table, which they indicated with outstretched hands and identical welcoming smiles. They began to laugh and applaud as their visitor hopped ponderously about the room, chirping with such force that it left all tunefulness behind. When he ducked to the table and picked up the mince pie with his teeth before throwing his head back to bolt down his prize, they clapped harder than ever, glancing at Mike's parents to make them join in. The man stuck out a fat tongue to capture crumbs around his mouth, and then he hopped so weightily into the hall that Mike felt the floorboards quiver. "Let him out, Michael," his aunt said.

Presumably the man couldn't open the door while he was pretending his arms were folded wings. There was only just space for Mike to sidle past him. Having hastened to open the door, the boy watched the swollen figure chase its growing shadow away from the streetlamp, emitting its version of birdsong to announce its arrival at the next house. As the adults made for the front-room parlour, Mike's father said "What was all that in aid of?"

"That was Mr Bundle," Aunt Denise told Mike. "You can see their house from your window."

"Maybe he'd rather not," Mike's mother said.

"I'm asking what the Bundle character was supposed to be," his father said. "Funniest partridge I've ever seen."

"He was a robin," Uncle Bill said with an elder brother's laugh. "Don't you know the difference?"

"Tell me what a robin would be up to, prancing round like that."

"It's a tradition," Aunt Denise said, drawing the curtains to shut out the night. "They've done it every year since we moved here."

"Their family tradition," Uncle Bill said as if this should settle the matter.

"Makes no sense to me," Mike's father said. "It's got nothing to do with the twelve days of Christmas."

"They're the calling birds," Aunt Denise insisted. "He was the first one."

Mike saw the objections were making his aunt and uncle impatient, or were they troubled in some other way? They should have been uneasy with the misinterpretation of the old rhyme, he thought as he lay in bed in the empty house. A calling bird was just a corruption of colly bird, the dialect name for a blackbird. At least he'd come to the end of the memory, and preferred not to go further while he was by himself in the dark. As he tried to grasp sleep he heard a robin chirping somewhere near the bridge. He'd begun to wonder if he'd ever heard a robin sing so late at night when sleep overtook him.

He wakened hoping that a thaw might let him risk the drive home, but more snow had fallen overnight. He was contenting himself with porridge for breakfast when Margery rang. "How was your Christmas dinner, Mike?"

"Safe Indian, I think we'd have to call it. Indian for folk who think it's only curry and tandoori."

"So long as you're safe as well."

He found he might have liked her not to say that. "Why shouldn't I be?"

"Just don't try to drive today. They say it's likely to improve in a couple of days."

The Fourth Call

It seemed childish to hope too passionately that the conditions would, and staying in the house felt like waiting to escape. Instead he went out for a walk. As he crossed the bridge he saw the stream was clear of ice apart from fragments disintegrating among the reeds along the banks. The winding road was plump with snow that squeaked beneath his boots. He was more than halfway to the Bundle farmhouse, not that he was heading for it, when a gate in the shrouded hedge on that side of the road let him see tracks in the field. They crossed the snow from the direction of the Bundle house, if by no means directly—their pattern suggested that someone had been performing a dance so haphazard that Mike couldn't guess what tune they might have been hearing. Craning over the gate, he saw that the footprints led to the village. When he returned to the bridge he found he hadn't noticed that they passed through a splintered gap in the hedge onto the road.

He couldn't tell where they went then. His own footprints had obscured them, and beyond the bridge there were far too many tracks in the street to let him identify them. On the field the overnight snowfall had blurred them so much that he couldn't distinguish their shape. All the same, he felt compelled to try until he started shivering, and then he retreated to the house.

When the streetlamps flickered alight he remembered Beryl Darlington's invitation. Surely she hadn't meant him to join them as soon as night fell, and he watched a family adventure he'd seen with the girls years ago. It made him feel as if he was trying to recapture his own childhood, which wasn't entirely appealing just now. He stayed with the film so as not to bother the Darlingtons too soon, and then he made his way along the village street. It was impossible to judge whether the tracks from the field had progressed so far.

Beryl's dinner was the kind Boxing Day brought, cold ham and turkey, salads and such. While Margery's was more inventive, this one reminded him of his Christmases in Leanbridge, which might have been why he said "What can you tell me about the Bundles?"

His hosts gazed at him before Jack said "What are you wanting to know?"

Mike sensed they wouldn't welcome many questions. "Where did that tradition of theirs come from?"

"It was in the family," Jack said. "Their parents did it to them from what folk heard, and maybe theirs before them did."

"Whose parents, sorry?"

"Whoever's they were." In a tone that made it clear these were his last words on the subject Jack said "They were always a close lot, the Bundles. Didn't want much to do with anybody else."

Mike thought he might have understood more than he relished. "Is that why they mixed up the rhyme, do you think? Because there was nobody to tell them they were wrong?"

"Someone did," Beryl said, "and wished they hadn't."

Although Mike saw she preferred to leave it there he said "What happened?"

"They danced round her house all Christmas and nobody wanted to be first to try and stop them. Everybody locked the door and hoped they'd go away."

"They said it was the rhyme that got the old ways wrong," Jack said. "They wouldn't go away till she believed them."

Mike wasn't sure he would have asked how the Bundles had achieved this even if Beryl hadn't changed the subject. "When do you think you'll be able to go away, I mean go home?"

"I'm aiming for the day after tomorrow. I wouldn't have come here so late in the year except that's when they let us teachers loose."

Was it just his facetiousness that made his hosts frown? "Here's

The Fourth Call

hoping for your wish," Jack said and raised his glass of port to urge it on its way.

"We'll pray for it if you like." With no relevance Mike could grasp, Beryl added "You know who the true love in the rhyme is meant to be, who gives out all the gifts? Folk say it's God."

As Mike trudged through the slush in the street he wondered if the Bundles would have said so. Somehow he didn't think they would. The robin had gone from the churchyard wall, and he was almost at the house when he heard a noise beyond it, a rapid chattering that sounded nearly liquid. The last remnants of ice must be cracking apart in the stream. There was no need to go and look, and he let himself into the house.

The empty hall and the deserted rooms seemed to amplify his memories, isolating him with them. He tried to recall the best elements of his Christmases in Leanbridge, but couldn't recapture his sense of being safe in the midst of his family, since he no longer was. By the time he went to bed he was wondering when that sense had begun to falter, which brought back his first Boxing Day in the village.

They'd cleared the dining-table, and Mike was hoping this had made way for a board game until his aunt brought in a mince pie on a plate. "Expecting another visitor, are we?" his father said.

"The next three nights." Aunt Denise continued sounding apologetic but determined while she said "You'll let him in, won't you, Michael? He won't do you any harm."

Mike felt as if he was being used as some form of defence. "Who's he going to be?" he said, trying to feel eager.

"It's Burky Bundle, Michael."

Mike began to giggle at the name until he saw his aunt and uncle didn't want him to laugh too much. He could have fancied they were nervous on his behalf if not their own. Once he fell silent he found he

63

was listening, as he realised they were. He thought his mother was about to speak when they heard a gobbling noise outside the house. "That's him," Aunt Denise said, following her husband to the far side of the table, where Mike could have thought they were taking refuge. The shrill fragmented practically liquid cry grew louder, to be interrupted by a peremptory rapping at the front door. "Do your duty, Michael," Uncle Bill said.

Mike hurried to be done with the task. When he pulled the door wide he was confronted by a figure as thin as last night's visitor had been rotund. The man wore a black overcoat and black trousers that clung to his skinny legs, and he'd tugged the reddish hair on the crown of his head up to form a crest. Apart from this and holding his arms behind his back, he seemed to have made no attempt to resemble a bird until he lifted his head, revealing the sharp Bundle face, and contorted his features more like a beak. His stringy throat worked, and the gobble shrilled out of his mouth. "You have to say come in, Michael," Uncle Bill called.

"Come in," Mike mumbled and moved to the stairs until the newcomer shut the door and darted along the hall as rapidly as he was emitting his cry. Mike trailed after him into the front room, only to stumble back into the hall, because the visitor no longer had a head. He continued to emit the gobble as he dodged back and forth in front of the table, beyond which Mike's aunt and uncle appeared to have decided that mirth was appropriate after all. They laughed harder when the man's head sprouted from the upturned collar to seize the mince pie with its beaky lips, and then the head vanished so utterly that Mike wondered what the man was made of. It reappeared before the man had finished, and his attempt at a chattering call sprayed crumbs across the table, disconcerting Mike almost as much as the applause his aunt and uncle gave the performance. "Michael," his uncle said.

The Fourth Call

Mike could have thought he was being accused of making the mess until he realised Uncle Bill was directing him to let out the visitor. He ran to open the front door, and shut it as soon as the gobbling man pranced onto the path. The adults were emerging into the hall, and his father said "Can't get much worse than that, I shouldn't think."

Aunt Denise and Uncle Bill had stayed as silent as the empty house was now. As Mike tried to leave the memory behind he heard the high rapid intermittent sound near the bridge. He didn't need to think what it resembled, let alone go to the window, and he dragged the quilt over his face.

When sunlight roused him from yet another uneasy doze he was relieved to see no more snow had fallen. Last time he'd looked out of the bedroom window he hadn't noticed the tracks in the field beyond the bridge, but now he saw they'd multiplied. They looked more crazed than ever. As soon as he was dressed he made for the gap in the hedge across the stream.

Two wanderers had left footprints on the field, but he couldn't tell whether they'd come into the village. Certainly whoever had been prancing in the snow had used the gap in the hedge before returning towards the Bundle farm. Though vigour that looked manic had blurred the tracks, Mike couldn't shake off an impression that they had been made by bare feet. The feet could have passed for claws, the prints were so thin.

Phoning Margery from the house only left it feeling emptier. They hadn't much to say beyond hoping no more snow would fall, as the forecasts tentatively promised. Drivers were still warned not to travel. While Mike was impatient to discuss the footprints, they would have needed too much explanation. He kept the subject to himself until dinner with the Darlingtons was finished, and then he said "I think there's someone at the Bundle house."

Jack shut his eyes tight, and his voice sounded equally squeezed. "Who?"

Beryl reached a shaky hand to clasp his. "Don't get into a state, Jack."

"I want to hear what Michael has to say," Jack said, groping for her hand. "What do you think you've seen, Michael?"

"Just footprints over there. I wonder if any of the Bundles are back."

"Don't say that," Beryl said low but fiercely. "We told you once, they're long gone and good riddance."

"Is someone living in their house?" When the old man gave a negative grunt Mike said "Squatters, maybe?"

"God help any that there are," Beryl said. "They'll not last long."

Mike wasn't sure if she had opposition from the villagers in mind. He saw Jack's eyes tighten, and tried to improve the mood. "One thing I never knew," he said. "What were their real names?"

Jack's eyes wavered open, though not much. "Whose?"

"Bobby and Burky and the rest of them."

"Those were their names." With a stare like a warning Jack said "That's how deep they got into what they did."

"At least they managed to keep their farm going as well."

"As long as they did till they didn't," Beryl said. "Now can we please talk about something else? It looks like you'll be going home tomorrow."

Jack nodded as vigorously as he appeared to feel able to risk, and Mike could have thought they were wishing him gone. He didn't stay with them much longer, though he knew which memory would be waiting in the empty house. As he tramped through the icy slush he remembered how the sight of another solitary mince pie on the table had made him hold his breath while he listened for someone approaching the house. His tension must have been apparent, because

The Fourth Call

his father said "You don't have to let anybody in if you don't want to, Michael."

Mike sensed how tense their hosts were trying not to seem. "If aunt and uncle want me to," he declared with a six-year-old's valour, "I don't mind."

He did, but hoped it didn't show. He was almost glad when a noise outside the house distracted everyone from watching him—a harsh imperious honk. He would have liked to think that whoever was coming had made the noise with a horn. The shrill squawks grew aggressive as they reached the house, where they gave way to an urgent rapping on the front door. "It's Gussy Bundle, Michael," Uncle Bill said. "Let him in."

Mike hastened to throw the door wide, and managed not to flinch. "Come in," he said for everyone to hear.

At first he thought the gaunt man in black was cocking his head on one side just to resemble a bird. As the beaky face contorted itself to force out another squawk the head tilted further askew, and Mike thought he heard bones creak. The newcomer lunged into the house as if he were being led by his broken neck, and Mike flinched after all. If his family wouldn't have wondered where he'd gone, he might have remained in the hall.

He dodged around the table to stand between his parents as the visitor hopped from foot to foot, parading in front of the audience. Now and then the head reared up with a sharp honk, only to skew further on a neck that looked more dislocated still. Mike wished the eyes didn't look so dead, but they were shrunken by the skin around them, which must be hiding the whites, leaving them black as a bird's. Bobby and Burky had eyes like that, he realised now. Aunt Beryl gave a small cry that she turned into a laugh as Gussy Bundle's head jerked erect with a shrill honk, then seized the mince pie in its protruding mouth. The head sagged onto his shoulder before he'd finished swallowing and honking, and he veered towards the hall like a hanged man swinging on a rope. Mike dodged around him to open the front door, but didn't want to look at even the back of the head wobbling sideways on the neck. "Well," he heard his father say, "I was wrong."

"How were you, dear?" Mike's mother said.

"That was even worse than last night's. Can't wait to see what comes tomorrow."

The thaw should, Mike hoped as he tried to sleep in the empty house, and he could drive home. When he heard a series of shrill honks in the night, he told himself he was hearing a car horn. The next sound that roused him from trying to drowse was the trilling of a bird—no, of his phone. "Don't even think of coming home today," Margery said.

Mike felt abandoned if not betrayed. "Why don't you want me to?"

"Of course we want you, but haven't you seen the reports? There was a freeze and there've been accidents all over the motorway. They're saying it ought to be clear tomorrow."

Mike glanced out of the window as if this might disprove the prospect of a freeze, and saw new footprints on the field across the stream. Their deranged confusion left him uncertain how many people had made them, but he could see the tracks led to and from the Bundle farm. "I'll find things to do, then," he said.

It took him most of half an hour to reach the farm. The gate from the road had collapsed, and rotten struts poked out of the snow. There were no footprints in the snow covering the drive that led to the house, and Mike could have thought that whoever had crossed the field didn't know enough to use the road. The three sets of tracks leading from the side of the house that faced the village had certainly been left by bare feet as bony as claws, he saw as he made for a front window. The light from a sky the colour of dusk didn't extend far into the room, but he could see several decrepit armchairs that appeared to have been torn asunder, exposing wood that looked pecked by some implement. The stuffing from the chairs was strewn over the floorboards like the lining of a birdcage. A stench seeped through the grimy window, and as he recoiled Mike thought he heard a movement in the dimness—a sluggish fluttering. He wasn't slow in returning to the road.

He couldn't have kept all that to himself, especially when he would be alone in the house with it. Over dinner very much like a repetition of its predecessors he told the Darlingtons "I went to the Bundle farm."

Jack's left eyelid wavered as he stared at Mike. "Don't keep bringing them up, Michael," Beryl said.

"What did you want to go and do that for?" Jack said, pressing a fingertip against the lid to hold it still.

"I said there were tracks over there, remember. And have you been hearing anything at night?"

Jack's drooping eyelid twitched beneath the finger. "No," he declared.

"I think I have, and that's why I went to look."

Jack's mouth appeared to be growing as hard to control as the eyelid. "See anyone, did you?"

"Not quite."

"Thank God for that," Beryl said. "Now can we please stop talking about them for good?"

"I don't see how that will make them go away," Mike couldn't help observing.

"Maybe talking's brought them, and you'll be the one that did."

"I don't get that, I'm sorry. I thought you said they'd gone."

"We thought they had, the lot of them," Jack struggled to pronounce. "The last of them's been dead for years."

Mike felt like a child who'd been tricked, perhaps by his own dullness. In a bid to find some reassurance that wouldn't sound too skeptical or patronising he blurted "Don't you think it was just childish, the way they carried on?"

"Michael," Beryl cried, "don't say things like that about them in our house."

He saw his hosts willing him not just to be quiet but to leave, and stood up. "Thanks for all your hospitality," he stayed to say, "and please forget everything I said about, just forget them."

He hoped this worked more for the Darlingtons than it did for him. As his boots sloshed through the slush he tried not to think of the fourth night of Christmas. The street was so deserted that he could have thought all the villagers were hiding in their houses. Even the Kerala Parlour was shut, and nobody was visible beyond the frosted windows of the pub. If discussing the Bundles could bring them back, was it even safe to remember? But the fear of remembering roused the memory as he stepped into the empty house.

He didn't know who had been most nervous about the final visit. His sense that some if not all of the family were pretending not to be had made him anxious to convince them that he wasn't. He watched his aunt leave the mince pie on the table, where the plate gave an inadvertent fragile clatter that suggested her hands weren't quite steady. When all the adults took up their positions on the far side of the table Mike felt not much better than cast out, and wished his parents would protest on his behalf so that he could undertake to brave the last visitor. He was finding it hard to breathe without attracting everyone's concern by the time he heard a noise coming towards the house, a harsh caw as much like a crone's voice as a bird's. Before his breaths felt ready the cry was at the front door, along with an impatient rapping. "It's Carrie Bundle, Michael," his aunt said.

The Fourth Call

Mike hesitated, not least because she hadn't told him to answer the door, and then he hurried to fling it open. "You've got to come in," he said.

At first glance the woman outlined by the streetlamp looked less daunting than the rest of her family had. She was just a head taller than Mike but almost as broad as the doorway. A frayed dress dangled beneath the hem of her equally black coat, and a black beret was pulled low on her head. It was only when she raised it that Mike saw she'd blackened her sharp face. She clenched the features to drive out a caw that sounded close to a word, and hopped stumpy-legged into the hall.

Mike followed her to the dining-room and retreated around the table as she stumped rapidly back and forth. Her caws sounded more and more like "Give." At last she ducked to pick up the mince pie in her mouth. As she consumed it her head jerked from side to side, letting her beady gaze range over the audience. Her eyes were utterly black, as if the darkness of her face and costume was concentrated in them. She continued gazing as she licked her lips in search of crumbs, and Mike was suddenly afraid that she would emit her demanding cry again— that she wanted more of a prize. While he couldn't have put it into words at that age, her eyes were so dead that he might have thought he was looking at death. Even when she turned her back at last to hop ponderously into the hall, the slowness of the gesture seemed to threaten that she would return.

He'd overcome his childish dread, of course; at least, he thought he had. By his early teens—the last time he'd spent Christmas in Leanbridge—he'd found the Bundles' seasonal performance boring, embarrassing, stupid. He had certainly used all those words to himself. He might have liked to recapture his teenage cynicism, but for the moment he couldn't even recall the intervening visits. Just that first encounter seemed to have lodged in his head. When he climbed the stairs the empty house made his footsteps sound as small as they would have been then. He would have liked to hear Margery, but could think of nothing to say that mightn't divulge his nervousness.

He was brushing his teeth when he thought he heard a sound harsher than the whir of the electric motor. He switched off the brush and held his breath—ceased to breathe, at any rate. In a moment he heard the noise again, a sharp caw outside the house. He might have succeeded in believing it was only a nightbird if it hadn't come so close to pronouncing a syllable. The frosted window of the bathroom showed him nothing. As he crossed his old bedroom, leaving the light off to help him see outside if not to avoid drawing attention to himself, he felt no less reluctant than he had when he'd been sent to open the front door of the house.

Four shapes were hopping or darting or floundering about the field beyond the stream. Against the muffled phosphorescence of the snow their outlines remained indistinct, but Mike had the impression they were somehow frayed. The figure that was blundering haphazardly about appeared to be behaving in that fashion for lack of a head. Though Mike would have preferred not to distinguish any more details, he pressed his face against the chill window, and at once all the figures turned towards him.

They sped in their various ways to the bank of the stream and lifted their heads to him. Even the decapitated shape did, or at least produced from its collar all that it had to show. The most bloated of the figures seemed to have lost some of its stuffing like a soft doll that had burst open, and Mike could see that its companions were disintegrating just as much. All their faces looked incomplete, not just because of the dimness, but he saw the glint of tiny shrunken eyes. They gave him a sense that the night had taken on a kind of life.

The Fourth Call

Mike was inching back from the window—he was hoping desperately that if he moved slowly enough, the watchers mightn't notice—when the figure closest to the bridge gave another raucous caw and darted to the gap in the hedge alongside the road. As the others hopped or lurched after her, Mike found he couldn't move. The clumsiest of them had concealed its withered remnant of a head again, while its equally fleshless companion's head was lolling wildly on a splintered neck. Mike saw the four advance across the bridge, and then they were out of sight. He could still hear the word their leader was cawing. He was able to move again, but as he struggled to think where to hide he heard the visitors reach the house.

Between harsh cries of "Give" their leader rapped at the front door. Mike heard tapping mixed with relentless chirping on the left side of the house, while on the other side thin knocks were interspersed with honks that made the mouth emitting them sound ragged. The back door was suffering a succession of clumsy thumps, between which a gobbling sounded altogether too liquid, as if someone were trying to cry out underwater. The demanding caws grew louder and more insistent, and Mike could only wish he had the necessary prize. "I've got nothing for you," he blurted, he didn't know how loud. "Nothing for you here."

In a moment there was silence. He couldn't even hear his own breath until he made himself take one. He was afraid that the visitors were biding their time, waiting to catch him unawares. He didn't know how long he remained frozen before he risked venturing into his aunt's and uncle's bedroom, which was empty even of its bed. He sneaked across the room and peered through the window before craning over the sill. As far as he could see, the street was deserted, and it was silent as ice.

He surprised himself by how soundly he slept. He felt as if his head had emptied out his memories. His phone wakened him. "Are you starting out soon?" Margery said. "They've cleared the roads."

As he used the bathroom he felt as if he was putting on all the speed he could before the world changed its mind about letting him go home. He ought to let the Darlingtons know he was leaving, though he mustn't tell them about last night's visitors. He scraped his windscreen and the other windows clear of frozen snow and drove along the village street. He hadn't reached the Darlington house when he saw two paramedics returning to an ambulance outside. Beryl was in the doorway of the house, gripping both sides of the doorframe, and turned her lonely gaze on him. He had to go to her, though he was afraid to hear what she would say. He was climbing out of the car when she said just loud enough for him to hear "You brought them and they took him."

Mike found he had no words. He mimed dismay and regret close to a wordless apology, and took refuge in the car. He had to drive the other way out of the village, and as he swung the car around in the slush Beryl kept her bereft gaze on him. As he drove across the bridge he saw the Bundle house ahead. It had meant nothing to him when he'd driven to the village, and he did his best to think it meant nothing now. He didn't even glance at it while he drove past, and it betrayed no activity until it was behind him. He was watching it shrink in the mirror when he heard a muffled caw from inside the house. It could have been a word, but not the one he would have expected, which was why he drove faster to outrun whatever it might imply. "Next," it said.

The Dreamed

By the time Don reached the Sea Panorama apartments he felt ready to sleep for a week. He hadn't been able to doze on the plane to the Greek island, and he'd been afraid to do so on the coach in case he missed his destination; Estelle from the travel company had stayed at the airport, promising her clients she would see them tomorrow. Just the same, he must have nodded off, because when the driver's voice roused him he found he was the sole remaining passenger. "Sleep in an armour," the driver said.

He was announcing the apartments outside which the bus had stopped, of course. He lugged Don's suitcase out of the belly of the bus and drove away without another word. Don hauled the case up the ramp to Reception, a large space in which straight chairs that put him in mind of a waiting-room were lined up beside a bookcase full of tipsy books. The indirect yellowish light was so subdued that he could have fancied it was meant to aid slumber. The trundling of his luggage brought a broad swarthy woman with an unashamed moustache out of the office behind the counter. "You are leaving," she told him.

"I certainly hope not," Don said and laughed as much as seemed polite. "I've only just arrived."

"Ah, you are another." By way of explanation she flourished a passport before laying it on the counter. "Passport," she declared— requested, rather.

Don fumbled in his jacket, which felt weighed down by the sultry humid midnight. The cover of his passport was tacky with traces of stickers. She peered at the photograph and blinked at him. "Mr Johns," she said.

"Well, really Jones."

"Yes, Johns."

"Jones," Don said with as much amusement as he could summon. "Donald Jones, but everybody calls me Don."

"Don." Apparently this signified some kind of acceptance. "You are two," she said as she made for the office, returning with a key that bore the number on a metal tag. Along with it she gave him an envelope printed with the logo of the travel company but otherwise blank. "Go round," she said, scooping at the air to indicate his route, but his luggage was only leading him back down the ramp when she called "You are finished."

She was holding out the passport. When he took it she pointed to his way around the corner of the building, along a flagged path. Half-buried lights illuminated the lurid roots of bushes in front of two-storey concrete apartment blocks. Don's apartment was almost at the far end of the path. As he unlocked the door he heard a faint hiss of waves on a beach. He dropped the metal tag into the holder on the wall and switched on the lights in the room.

Two single beds nestled together for company opposite a dressing-table and an equally basic wardrobe, inside which Don found a safe. He'd get the key later. He opened the envelope to find he was invited to a welcome meeting at eleven, though not by name. He rummaged in his suitcase for toothpaste and brush, then stumbled to the bathroom that occupied a quarter of the apartment. His eyes were so eager for sleep that he could scarcely make out his reflection, not that he would have taken much pleasure in the sight of his untanned roundish freckled face thatched with red hair. He only just remembered to hide his wallet and passport and mobile phone under the pillow before slumping into bed.

Despite if not because of his exhaustion, he found it hard to fall asleep. He wouldn't have expected the night to be so oppressively hot in October. He tried not to feel that sleeping by himself was bothering him, but he couldn't help recalling how he and Louise had split up. Traits they'd found charming at the start had amplified themselves into irritations—her habit of tugging at a lock of hair to nibble as an aid to pondering, his murmuring "Never mind" under his breath to avoid arguments... All the disagreements they'd suppressed had erupted in a shouting competition before they'd very eventually calmed down and settled on parting as friends. Booking this last-minute holiday had been a bid to celebrate being free once more rather than yet again by himself. Louise hadn't liked hot places, which made Don even more determined to enjoy the week.

All at once his thoughts had gone, until light penetrated his eyelids—sunshine through the flimsy whitish curtains beside the bed. He disentangled his arm from the single clammy sheet to squint at his watch. It was well past ten o'clock, and later still before he managed to recollect why it should concern him. By the time he'd used the toilet and the shower, which was on its way to growing warm, he had just a few minutes to unpack. He found swimming trunks and a short-sleeved shirt and sandals, and stuffed passport and wallet and phone into his pockets as he raced his headless self past the dressing-table mirror.

Reception was deserted, but as Don sat on a straight chair to await the welcome meeting, the moustached woman came out of the office. "You want anything," she said.

"Air conditioning, thanks, and a key to the safe."

"How long are you?"

"Here, a week."

"Your two are sixty."

Her phrases kept making him feel not entirely awake. When her meaning reached him he counted out the notes, and she handed him a key and a remote control. As he sat down again she said "You wait for more?"

"The welcome," Don said and waved the envelope.

"Not here now. Gone."

"How can she have? I was here on time. It's still only—" Don raised his fist while he consulted his watch, and then his conviction failed him. "Oh," he said, "you fool."

"Who do you say?"

"Never mind," Don muttered and hurried away, too embarrassed to admit he'd neglected to move his watch forward two hours. "Why couldn't someone wake me?" he complained once he was sure she wouldn't hear.

He was in his room before he realised he had yet to see the view. The ground-floor balcony was occupied by a frame for drying clothes beside a small round table and two chairs of the same white plastic. Beyond the balcony a field of parched earth bare except for clumps of weeds stretched several hundred yards towards the sea, the near edge of which was hidden by a low ridge. The card in the travel agent's window had offered a sea view, and Don supposed he was seeing a version of that. "Never mind," he murmured, shutting the window so that he could trigger the air conditioning on his way to the safe.

He took a hundred euros from his wallet before stowing it away. He thought of wiping the traces of stickers off the cover of his passport, but apparently there was no need. Had he cleaned it in the night and forgotten? The idea left him unsure of himself. Or had the woman at Reception cleaned it up? One of them had bent the corner of a page, a detail Don had previously been too fatigued to notice. He opened the passport to smooth out the page, and the humid heat swarmed through the whole of him. The page bore an entry stamp for Turkey, where he had never been in his life.

The passport belonged to a blond-haired man called Eno Knoft, whose pale rounded face was bare of freckles. Don strode to Reception so fast that he almost forgot to lock the safe and the door. "Hello?" he called into the office. "Hello?"

The moustached woman emerged at less than half the speed his words had. "It takes time," she informed him.

He felt almost too bewildered to be furious. "What does?"

"Your conditioning."

"I don't know what on earth you mean."

"In your room."

"The air conditioning." He had no time to laugh at his mistake. "I'm not here about that," he said and opened the passport to brandish the photograph. "You gave me this."

"Yes, you keep it now."

"I most certainly don't," Don said, raising his voice as she began to turn away. "Look again. This isn't me."

She glanced over her shoulder before the rest of her swung towards him. "So that is it," she said, sounding no more apologetic than surprised. "He went when you came."

"How can he have? He won't have this."

"He goes to other islands."

Don clutched at the only hopeful thought he had. "He won't be able to leave Greece. They'll take my passport off him."

"Maybe they bring it if they know you are here."

"Why wouldn't they?" As more panic overtook him Don said "Do you know when he's going home?"

"He stays here one night."

"That's not what I'm asking. Will he try and leave before I have to?"

"He goes after the night here."

"You're saying he's coming back here."

"Yes, for night."

Don couldn't feel reassured yet. "Which one?"

"No need to say. Plenty of rooms. This week."

Her halting language made him feel not quite awake. "You're sure it's definitely this week," he persisted, "before I go home myself."

"I say."

"Will you let me know as soon as he arrives and keep my passport?"

She met this with a frown. "You want him to keep."

"No, that isn't what I said." He could have thought his own words were growing unfamiliar. "I asked you to keep it," he insisted. "Keep it safe for me."

"Safe," she said as if this might have been the solitary word she understood, and shut her eyes while she gave him a heavy nod.

"And please do tell me as soon as you have. Leave a note in my room if I'm not here."

She inclined her head further without opening her eyes, which Don had to take for assent and, with luck, reassurance. He mustn't let anxiety spoil his week, and he wasn't going to loiter in his room until his passport came back. He finished unpacking and hung up his clothes while his body tramped back and forth in the dressing-table mirror. He was about to consign Knoft's passport to the safe when he slipped it into his pocket—best to have it where he would be surest of it and be able to exchange it for his own the instant that he could. His credit card joined it, and he donned his hat on the way out of the room.

The Dreamed

To the right of the courtyard a path led from the road towards the beach. Cicadas dodged from tree to tree, trailing abrupt silences, as he crossed the cracked dry field. When he reached the ridge he saw that the beach was no wider than the narrow promenade, by no means the image in the travel brochure. As he gazed in dismay at it, two young women with minimal swimsuits under their sundresses came abreast of him. "Looking for the beach?" one said.

"The tides were so high this year it all got swept away," her friend told him. "Walk where we're going and you'll find one."

Presumably it was beyond the headland against which waves were shattering. Don set about exploring the resort, such as it proved to be. A few tavernas and apartment complexes faced the sea, and he saw a fairground in the opposite direction from the headland. The main road was lined with supermarkets and tavernas, together with Hindustani Barney's restaurant and the British Bulldog pub. The Grecian Experience was a travel agency outside which boards advertised trips off the island, and Don made for it at once.

In a room where even the floor was white a burly man not much less bearded than a Greek priest sat behind a desk. A large fan turned back and forth, ruffling brochures in wooden racks. The man clasped his hands with an audible chafing of flesh and advanced an inviting smile. "What do we do for you today?"

"I'd like to go on some of your outings."

The man pushed a folder full of brochures across the desk. "How long you are here now?"

"All this week."

"You may find some things go away."

"Not your excursions, I hope." Celluloid pockets squeaked under Don's nails as he leafed through the folder. "I'd like both your trips off the island," he said, "and the tour of the island as well."

"Those are going." The man reached for a pad of vouchers. "Where do you stay?" he said.

"The Sea Panorama." Since the man had commenced writing, Don said "Room number two."

"Yes, that is it. I should know."

"Know what, sorry?"

"I should know you, Mr Knoft."

"Excuse me." When this didn't make the man look up, Don said louder "Excuse me, I'm not him."

"You are not?" The man's head rose as if it had been snagged by its frown. "Well, I see," he said with limited conviction.

"I assure you I'm not. I've only just got here. The name's Jones, Don Jones."

The man gazed at the passport that was peeking out of Don's breast pocket. How much would Don have to explain when he shouldn't need to prove anything about himself? He was close to speaking, whatever he might say, when the man tore off the voucher and the carbon copy to crumple them and drop the wad with a flat dead sound in a metal bin. "Mr Jones," he said and wrote. "I give you some islands tomorrow and the rest two days after. And two days more, our island."

"That'll do for me. I can go to the beach in between."

Rather than reply, the man seemed to prefer to write, and Don took out his credit card. For a grotesque moment that left him feeling less than adequately awake, he forgot how to recall the code. Of course, it was 1514, the pair of letters his name repeated. Once he'd typed the digits the card reader emitted an electronic squeak and a receipt, which the man handed him along with the tour voucher. "Come back when you come back tomorrow."

"I imagine I will. Excuse me, you mean..."

"Come back and find if you are on the other boat."

"But I've already paid," Don protested, only to see that he'd been charged just for tomorrow's excursion. How unaware was he? "Why can't I pay for them all now?" he was determined to learn.

"We see how many you are."

Don supposed he had to be content with this. "Where will they pick me up tomorrow?"

"At apartments as usual."

As Don left the office he saw the man's head droop while the fan set his beard twitching. The white buildings and the relentlessly blue sky glared in Don's eyes, and he had to make an effort not to squeeze them shut. When had he last eaten? He ought to dine close to the Sea Panorama, just in case he caught Eno Knoft coming back. Every Greek resort seemed to have a taverna called Zorba's, and the one opposite the apartments had the film soundtrack on a tape to help it confirm its identity. Don found a table beside the road and ordered keftedes and kleftiko together with a tin carafe of red wine from the barrel. Perhaps his nervous vigilance was distracting him, since he felt unable to taste the food as much as he should. He wasn't to blame if the dishes were bland. Perhaps next time he would dine next door.

Could Knoft have returned while Don was at the travel agency? He paid for the meal and crossed the road so fast that his sandals kicked up dust. As he strode into Reception a fleshy balding man with chest hairs poking through the gaps between the buttons of his shirt emerged from the office. "Did your colleague tell you about my passport?" Don said.

The man's large dark eyes winced as if they were about to close. "What do you ask?"

"I'm wondering if you know the lady gave someone else my passport."

The man jabbed a stubby finger at Don's pocket. "You have there."

"That's not mine. It belongs to the chap she gave mine."

The man turned his hand over, cupping the fingers. "You give."

"She's letting me look after it till he comes back."

The hand didn't move. "Not yours, you give."

"I'll keep it safe, don't worry. She obviously thinks I will. It'll make sure he gives me mine." When the man didn't alter his posture Don took a step back. "Just let me know if he shows up," he said. "The name's Knoft, Eno Knoft. I'll be in the room. I won't be going anywhere."

He could have fancied that the man was going nowhere either—that the words had frozen him in his expectant pose. Don made for the bookcase, where many of the titles on the cracked concave spines weren't in English. A lopsided copy of *War and Peace* was, and he'd often felt he should read the novel, though he never had the energy after a day of trying to find people jobs, especially when he brought home all the weight of their frustration and his own. He grasped the massive paperback and took it to his room.

On the balcony he found he couldn't read much. By the time he reached the third chapter the night was rising from the sea. He watched light drain from the sky as the sun was erased somewhere behind him. When stars began to glimmer he felt oddly like a child who'd been allowed to stay up late. He would need to rise early for the excursion, and he took himself to bed.

The air conditioning uttered a rattle whenever he was close to drifting off, and when he slept at last he kept dreaming that Knoft had returned unexpectedly but was about to leave once more. "Bring my face back," Don heard himself trying to plead in not much of a voice. Every time his struggles to speak wakened him he had to grope under the pillow to confirm that the passport was still there. The alarm on his phone sent him to use the bathroom, where his reflection looked unconvinced it was awake, and then he went to meet the dawn. "Out for the day now," he called into Reception. "Get my passport if Mr Knoft comes back. Tell him I'll give him his once I've got mine."

Before anyone emerged from the office, a coach came into view on the road. "Jones," Don said when the guide barely glanced at the voucher. He murmured mornings to his fellow passengers, and the coach picked up a few more on the way to the harbour. A crewman at the gangplank of the boat waved a dismissive hand at the passport in Don's pocket and told him "No need." By the time another coach brought rather less than a coachload of voyagers, the rocking of the boat had lulled Don close to slumber. Half an hour of open sea didn't rouse him much, but he prised his eyes wide when the first island came in sight. The boat was almost there when the guide with the microphone announced they wouldn't be visiting the island.

At once Don wondered if Knoft was on it. He could see a fishing village had attracted tourists, and he wished he had binoculars to help him make them out, but none of the passengers up here on the top deck had a pair he could borrow. "Never mind," he muttered, though the words felt as if they scarcely came from him.

The rest of the hour took them to the next island, where the guide led her party alongside the harbour, past a multitude of sponges to a factory full of nothing else. As she described the process of preparing them Don sidled to the door to watch the street, but saw nobody he was anxious to see. By the time the tour reached the third island he supposed he was ready for lunch, but he grew so preoccupied with scrutinising every face that passed the taverna by the wharf that he was barely able to taste how fresh the catch of the day was. He still had an hour to explore the town—to search it, rather.

Apartments were scattered through the narrow haphazard streets, and now and then he recognised a face, but always someone from the cruise. However far he ventured from the harbour, he seemed unable to avoid a pale plump couple apparently competing at how floral their dress or in the man's case shirt could be. He was sidestepping them yet again, and producing an increasingly dutiful grin, when he glanced past them and imagined he was looking in a mirror.

The man at the end of the sloping street turned away at once as if he hadn't seen him. Don dodged past the couple so hastily that his elbow jangled a mobile made of strings of shells dangling outside a shop. "Mr Knoft," he shouted.

Before the man's name was out, he wasn't there. Don felt forsaken by reality until he saw that Knoft must have darted into a side lane, and then a glimpse caught up with him. Hadn't the man's face stiffened at the sight of him? If he'd recognised Don, this could only mean he knew he had Don's passport, and his behaviour suggested he wasn't eager to return it. Don sprinted to the lane and saw the man disappearing at speed around a corner. "Mr Knoft," he yelled and dashed to the corner in time to see the man turning left yet again. If he did that once more, wouldn't they be back where they started? But when Don reached the corner, the side street was deserted, though it came to a dead end ahead.

Knoft must have gone into a house, even if Don hadn't heard a door shut. Presumably Knoft was lodging here, though neither house in the stark dusty sun-bleached street showed any sign of inviting tourists. Don strode to the door on the left and pounded on the hot scaly wood, and when this brought no response he did the same across the road. The doors might have been mutual reflections, and the sets of knocks virtually echoed each other, producing an identical silence. "Knoft," Don shouted and pressed his face against the veiled window of the left-hand house, and felt the window-frame begin to crumble under his fingers. He stalked across the street to peer through the dingy

The Dreamed

embroidered curtains inside the other window. Both houses were derelict, little more than frontages like sets on a stage.

He was struggling to open either of the doors—Knoft must have used one of them, blocking it from inside—when the blare of a horn resounded through the town. The boat was summoning passengers back. Don gave each door a final desperate thump with his shoulder, but neither door budged an inch. "You'll have to come back," he vowed under his breath and dashed through the devious streets to the harbour.

When the coach brought him to the apartments at last—a final break in the cruise to let people swim had felt as prolonged as a sleepless night—he hurried into Reception. "I'm back," he called. "Jones. Back."

So was the moustached woman, who blinked at him from the doorway of the office. "Knoft?" Don hoped aloud.

"You said Jones."

"Not me, him. Is he back?"

"Just you."

Don felt as if they were vying to keep their words terse, but it occurred to him to ask "Do you know what he does?"

"Travels."

"In life, I mean."

"Travels," she repeated with a somnolent shut-eyed nod.

While she was unlikely to know if Knoft was involved in any questionable activity, Don could have taken the word for a euphemism. He changed in his room once he'd showered, and then looked in at Reception. "I'm across the road," he called. "Taste of Greece."

Either the taverna failed to live up to its name or his senses were elsewhere. The empty courtyard across the sparsely populated road seemed more present than the food in his mouth. He finished off the slab of moussaka, not just since he supposed he needed to eat but because he was one of a very few diners, and then he went back to Reception. "Just going to Grecian Experience," he called into the office.

The bearded man might have been dozing, but he raised his head as Don approached the desk. "Mr Knoft," he said, then widened his eyes as though to rouse his mind. "No, you don't call yourself."

"I don't because it's not my name."

"You are—" The man levelled a hand at him to fend off any help. "You are number two at Panorama."

"I'm Jones." At half that speed Don said "Don Jones."

"That is name in there."

The hand was pointing at the passport now. "That's Donald," Don admitted, "except this isn't mine."

The man stared at it so hard that Don felt he wasn't being seen. "Who then?"

Don didn't think he had the energy to describe the situation yet again. "I'm holding it for someone else."

"Well, so you come back for more."

Incomprehension made Don nervous until he thought to say "The other cruise, you mean. Yes, if it's going."

"You are just enough."

He must have all the bookings in mind, not only Don. He set about filling in the voucher as Don typed his code on the card reader. Once the voucher was completed the man gazed at him. "Something is wrong?"

Don keyed in the digits again, only to be told a second time that they were incorrect. He shut his eyes as if this might erase whatever mistake he'd made and counted the values of the letters from his name once more, and then his eyes sprang open. "Oh, you fool," he muttered, feeling worse than that, since he'd somehow remembered the letters out of order. "There you are. That's me."

The Dreamed

"Jones," he called into Reception, "I'm in my room," and made his way to the safe in the wardrobe, only to wonder nervously where he'd left his credit card. Of course, it was inside Knoft's passport, and there were the receipts from the Grecian Experience as well. He locked them in the safe and stared at the passport photograph. It couldn't have developed freckles, and the blond hair hadn't darkened except with ink from the receipts, which had also speckled the face. Don rubbed the picture with a tissue but desisted before he was entirely convinced that he'd restored its appearance. Knoft could deal with his own image once he'd brought Don's passport back. Surely he wasn't using it for anything illegal, though perhaps Don should establish that he hadn't before returning Knoft's passport to him.

As he watched the evening light dwindle into stars he grew aware how the days were shrinking. In bed he kept being wakened by the thought of a knock at the door—by the absence of a knock. At least he needn't rise early, but when he left his bed well after dawn he felt as if he'd hardly slept at all. He loaded his beach bag—book, towel, sun cream, a creaking plastic bottle of water—before heading for Reception. "Going to the beach."

The balding man glanced not much more than blankly at him. "Beach."

"Yes, beach. I'm told you've still got one."

The man looked indifferent if not unconvinced. "You have passport."

"Not yet. This is still his."

The man shoved his lower lip forward. "Police not like."

"You've told them, have you? Maybe you should tell them you give people the wrong passports. I think they might like that a good deal less."

The man's lip protruded further, and Don hoped he hadn't antagonised him. Perhaps he hadn't spoken to the police at all. "I'll stay as close as I can," Don said. "I'll be there if I'm needed."

89

Fearful Implications

From the promenade he saw lorries bearing sections of demolished rides away from the fairground. Absurdly, the sight left him feeling as if his holiday had been brought to a premature end. He made for the headland, which proved to be more distant than it looked. Beyond it was an expanse of sand across which a deserted taverna and a dozen unoccupied sun loungers faced a small bay. Don dragged a lounger close to the sea and opened the standing umbrella he'd reached, and contorted himself over trying to cover his body with sun cream without mixing it with sand.

Since he couldn't recall what he'd previously read, he started *War and Peace* again. His lack of sleep must be in the way, because he found it hard to grasp the prose even after it ceased to be French. Before long he closed his eyes, only to feel that the waves were washing away his consciousness. He tried to cling to it, but it was gone until an impression of a presence close by wakened him—somebody like him, no doubt, unless they'd come for payment for the lounger. He stretched his eyes wide and stared around him, then behind him. He wasn't just alone on the beach. His was the only lounger.

If someone had removed the loungers, why had they left him asleep? He could only think it had been meant as some kind of concession, but it made him feel worse than isolated. Suppose the staff from the apartments couldn't find him when they needed to? He stuffed all his beach items into the bag and strode, then ran as fast as the sand would let him, across the beach.

"Back again," he called, adding that he'd be at the Aegean Flavour. This fell as short of his palate as the other meals had, perhaps because he was ready for a nap in his room. On his way he replaced *War and Peace* with a thriller by an author whose name was as monosyllabic as most of his prose. "In my room now," he shouted into the office.

He couldn't doze for attempting to read, and the opposite happened as well. He must be too exhausted to cope with even the simplest prose or to sleep. He sat on the balcony, urging the sunset to bring Knoft, only to feel as if his mind was shrinking with the light. In bed he kept being wakened by a silence that should have been a knock, unless it had just been one. More than once he stumbled to the door and gazed along the deserted path, until eventually he saw the lights beside it had been ousted by the dawn. Though his alarm hadn't roused him, the coach was outside on the road.

"I'm here," he yelled, or at least "Mere" if not just "Me." He dashed back into the apartment and raced out as soon as decency permitted, buttoning the shirt in which he found Knoft's passport, having apparently been too tired to remember it belonged under his pillow. "Jones," he assured the guide, and wondered if anyone else had failed to waken, since there were so few passengers on the coach. Even when more coaches joined it at the harbour, they left the boat nowhere near full.

Don was watching the sea shrink the harbour when a woman said "You're back with us again."

He imagined she was talking about his awareness until he recognised her and her equally pale plump partner. Their floral clothes made them resemble mutual reflections more than ever. "Third trip in a week," the man told him.

"Not for me."

"Then somebody was putting on a good act," the woman said with a laugh too terse for mirth.

For a moment Don felt utterly disoriented, and then he fumbled out Knoft's passport to show them the photograph. "Are you thinking of him?"

This time it was the man who laughed, although not much. "We can see that's you, chum. What's the joke?"

Fearful Implications

"I promise you it's not." Don rubbed the photograph with his thumb in a bid to dislodge the speckles and lighten the hair. "They gave me this at my apartments by mistake."

"How could you let them do that?" the woman protested. "Were you asleep?"

"I'm not the one who's asleep round here." Don saw them take this as a gibe, which it imprecisely was, and tried to keep them talking. "The fellow you say was me," he said. "What was he like?"

"A charmer." Just as much like a rebuke the woman said "We were looking forward to talking to him again."

"He talked funny English," the man said. "It was part of his charm."

"Nothing funny with mine, is there?" As their gazes grew blank as unconsciousness Don said "Did he say what he was?"

"Some kind of performer, we think," the man said.

"We thought he might let us see him put on a show."

Don was almost certain they meant him. Before he could respond the woman said "If you're honestly saying that's not you, who have you told?"

"The staff where I'm staying, of course."

"Haven't you let your rep know?" When Don barely shook his head the man persisted "The embassy, how about them?"

"He's coming back before I have to go home. He can't leave if I can't, so that'll make him."

Had exhaustion put the embassy and Estelle out of his mind? He couldn't call either just now, since his phone had no signal. Sea and more sea, islands that seemed to take something like a lifetime to crawl closer, harbours, beaches... He was willing the cruise to end so that he could resume his vigil at the apartments—that was all his head contained as he trudged back to the boat after visiting a monastery from which tourists appeared to have driven all the monks—when he saw Knoft staring landwards from the gangplank.

Before Don could tell whether the fellow was looking for him, Knoft turned away and was lost to sight. Don sprinted to the gangplank and panted at a crewman "Who just came on board?"

The man shrugged without smiling. "You did."

Don hadn't time to argue. He was about to search the boat when he saw that might let Knoft escape. He loitered by the gangplank until it was raised and the boat had left the harbour, and then he set about searching, peering into every face he couldn't immediately see. Before long he encountered the plump couple on the upper deck. "Have you seen him?"

They looked as if they might have hoped not to encounter Don again. "Who?" the woman said.

"Him." Don thumped his breast pocket fiercely enough to be trying to revive a heart. "Him."

"We're seeing you," the man said.

Don stalked around the upper deck before returning to the lower one and patrolling the saloon. Was Knoft hiding in a toilet? There were several on each deck, and whenever an occupant proved not to be Knoft, Don had to conclude the man was on the other level. Don was waiting by the gangplank long before the boat docked, and scrutinised every face that passed him. He was the last to go ashore, and yet he hadn't seen Knoft disembark.

Had the man disguised himself somehow or contrived to stay on board? As Don backed towards the coach he kept both eyes on the boat, but nobody except crewmen had left it by the time it receded out of sight. Could Knoft have posed as a member of the crew? Was that the kind of performance he put on? As soon as the coach brought him back to the apartments, Don marched into Reception. "I think Mr Knoft is back," he shouted into the office. "Just going to Grecian Experience."

The bearded man opened his eyes as he lifted his head. "Ah, Mr Not."

"No, not at all. Anybody but. I've told you twice, I'm—"

"I say that," the man declared with a hopeful grin. "Mr Not Him."

"Not Knoft, that's me, but was he on your boat today by any chance?"

"Just you from here. Not him from anywhere."

"Excuse me, but how can you be sure?"

"I have seen the names." The man rapped the screen of his computer with a knuckle, and Don imagined someone knocking on the apartment door—in fact, he had to remind himself that wasn't the sound he was hearing. "Are you here for book?" the man said.

"Which book?"

"Your last day. Can only be tomorrow."

At first Don felt he should stay in his apartment—the talk of a book made him feel he was already there—and then he grew furious. He wasn't going to let Knoft rob him of the last chance of a tour. "I'll book it," he said and slipped his card into the reader to type his code. "No, that's not right," he complained, which sounded like agreeing with the machine. He typed the digits again with a pause after each one, only to be told they were still incorrect. Was he so exhausted that he was entering them out of order? He keyed the values of the pair of letters the other way around and was immediately convinced this was wrong, but the machine confirmed the code and stuck out a paper tongue at him. "One of us is wrong," he muttered for nobody else to hear.

As he left the sleepy sluggish fan behind he folded the voucher and receipt around the card and slipped them behind the passport so as to keep ink away from Knoft's photograph. Now that he thought Knoft was on the island he seemed unable to think of anything else, and he hadn't noticed that the tavernas closest to the apartments had shut, leaving all their menu boards as blank as frames awaiting photographs.

"Never," he mumbled, and eventually thought to add "Mind." The only restaurant still open that gave him a view of the courtyard was Hindustani Barney's. Perhaps at least he would taste that food. "Jones again," he called into the office. "Be across the road. Barney's Indian."

The flavours of a chilli chicken starter and a prawn jalfrezi stayed remote. He might have been trying to recall them or to taste them on somebody else's behalf. Were his thoughts being kept away from him as well? He'd forgotten to call Estelle or the embassy. He tramped back to his room, having told whoever was in Reception that he was there, and found the number on the welcome letter. His phone located only a meagre signal, signified by a solitary trembling bar on the display, and he reached nothing but a voicemail, both for Estelle and the embassy. "Jones," he pleaded with each of them. "Don Jones. That's Donald if you need the rest. Please call me back."

He sat with his book on the balcony, but long before dusk blurred the words he found he couldn't concentrate. He might have fancied he was losing his ability to read even the simplest English. He lay in bed with Knoft's passport in one fist and, so that he wouldn't miss the alarm, his phone in the other. Whenever he dozed he dreamed that Knoft had been disposed of by his criminal associates, and what had they done with Don's passport? The twitching of his fingers jerked him awake, or movement in his fists did. Knoft's passport couldn't be stirring as it underwent some transformation, but Don had to switch on the light more than once to reassure himself that the photograph wasn't too familiar—that it hadn't grown more red-haired and freckled. Every time he wakened, listening for the absent knock held him back from slumber. As he realised he was a chrysalis that sleep was about to transmute into someone else, the contents of his fist began to vibrate with the first stage of the process. It was the alarm, and he was more than glad to leave the dream.

"Jones. Out for day now. Coach tour." There was no response from the office, and he wondered when he'd last heard one. "You there?" he shouted louder.

"We hear you."

The voice was higher than he liked, given that it proved to belong to the balding man. Presumably impatience had raised its pitch. Don plodded to meet the coach as it pulled up. "Jones again," he told the guide and then the plump couple he kept meeting. "Just Jones. Don Jones."

The flowered fellow gazed at him. "Funnier than that," he said.

"Quite a performance," said his wife.

After that Don didn't speak to them or anyone. The ancient ruined city that was the first stop on the tour felt like the state of his mind rendered solid, though he had a fleeting sense that somebody he used to know would have liked the site. Olive oil at a factory slipped down his throat without leaving a taste, and lunch at a taverna stayed just as distant from his palate. The wines and spirits offered at a village vineyard only made him feel in danger of losing all awareness, and he wandered into the street. He was gazing at a cloud like a wintry omen of night above the mountain across the valley that the village overlooked when rapid footsteps made him glance around. A man was vanishing past a bend in the road.

Wasn't that how Knoft had been dressed yesterday—a pale blue short-sleeved shirt, baggy brown knee-length shorts, grey sandals? Don raced to the bend and saw the man hurrying down a lane. "Knoft," he shouted and dashed to the lane, by which time the man was out of sight once more. The descent was so steep that Don almost lost his footing and had to grab the rough stone walls of houses for support. He was nearly at the bottom when he saw the man along a side lane. The fellow swung around to grin up at a noise on the main road, then turned away before Don could make out his face. Then how had Don glimpsed his expression? The question distracted him from recognising the sound on the road at once. The coach was moving off.

"Wait," he yelled at the top of his voice, though he hardly knew whether he meant it for the man in the lane or the driver. The man disappeared around the corner of the lane, and Don wasn't even sure the fellow had been Knoft. He mustn't be left behind, and he dashed up the slope towards the road. Long before he reached it he was no longer running but panting so hard it overwhelmed his senses. He hadn't heard the coach drive away, but it was nowhere to be seen.

He felt as though he'd been lured away deliberately. He might even have imagined the day of the excursion had been changed so that he wouldn't be at the Sea Panorama when Knoft came back. As he snatched out his phone he was afraid it would have no coverage, but it exhibited a single faltering bar, and then took minutes to find the number for the Grecian Experience. "Jones," he said like a curse. "Don Jones."

"I am sorry, who?"

"Jones. I was on your coach. It's gone and left me."

He heard static or the rustling of paper. "I am sorry," the bearded man said again. "That is nobody on there."

"That's right, I'm not," Don said through his teeth. "I'm in the road where I've been left."

"We do not leave anyone. The guide always counts."

"I know she does, but not this time," Don protested, and then suspicion overtook him. "Have you got a man called Knoft on it?"

Paper rustled, or the connection did. "Eno Knoft, yes."

"He's got my place. I need to get back." Don felt as if his mind was shrinking along with his words. "How will I?" he demanded.

"Take a taxi and come here."

Fearful Implications

"Can't I charge—" Don blurted, but even the rustling had gone.

By the time he trudged to the end of the village he was afraid of not finding a taxi. A hut with a goat tethered outside turned out to represent one, and ten minutes after the aged man dozing on a skimpy wooden chair used his vintage mobile, the decrepit vehicle showed up. It took most of an hour to bring Don back to the resort via a series of side roads through a wilderness too rocky for houses or even for vegetation above the size of stunted dusty bushes, a region suggesting the desolateness of a local winter. At last buildings sprouted from the horizon, and the sea rose up beyond them. In its own time the taxi reached the main street, and Don sprang his seatbelt free as soon as he saw the Grecian Experience. "Stop there," he said and only just remembered "Please."

No boards stood outside to advertise excursions. The window and the door were blinded. Don rattled the door until the blind flapped against the glass, and then he tried phoning. A shrill bell in the office belatedly echoed the version at his ear, and both of them might have been mocking him. He had just enough cash to pay for the taxi ride, and saw it fall short of pleasing the driver. Don tramped to the Sea Panorama and waited for the balding man to appear from the office. "Is he here?"

The man fingered his upper lip, which had grown unshaven. "Just you."

"Where's the trip man gone? Coach went and left me. Had to pay for cab."

"Gone now." The man scowled as if he thought Don was imitating his rudimentary language. "Gone for winter."

"Gone." Putting all his rage into the syllable failed to help. "I won't be," Don vowed. "Be in room."

He would stay there tomorrow if he had to. He wouldn't be tricked again, whoever tried. He might bring in food from the supermarket, though couldn't he survive without it for a couple of days? Leaving the apartments even so briefly felt like too much of a risk. When he sat on the balcony he left the window open so as not to miss any knock. He hadn't brought the book out with him, preferring not to learn how little of it he might be able to read. The sky had begun to rust above the sea when he remembered he had yet to hear from Estelle or the embassy. They were still represented by recordings so anonymous that he could have thought he was hearing a single familiar voice. "Jones again," he repeated, "still Jones," and felt as if he was trying to reassure himself.

He stayed outside until it was too dark to see into the room. He had a sense that the night must resolve his situation. "Can't go," he told Knoft, wherever he was. "Got to come to me." In bed he clutched the passport in his clasped hands. Before he was ready the dark filled his skull.

The thought of wakening roused him. He could have fancied it wasn't his. Somebody needed to waken, but who? "I'm not the one who's asleep round here..." He felt as if he was recalling someone else's words, but all at once he was convinced the nightmare he'd been living wasn't his. Something besides the thoughts had wakened him—the absence of a sound. The air conditioning had shut down, though the room felt colder than it had. In the breathless silence he heard a tapping at the door.

It sounded tentative, close to surreptitious. He fumbled to turn on the light, but the room stayed dark. He floundered out of bed, gripping the passport in his fist, and stumbled to the door. Nobody was outside—just an onslaught of rain that had flooded the path and drowned the vegetation, apparently dousing the lights as well. Despite the gloom, his watch showed that it was almost noon.

Fearful Implications

He donned swimming trunks and sandals and hurried to Reception, but the door was locked. "Where are you?" he cried, but this brought him nobody, even when he tramped shouting through the deserted waterlogged streets. All the apartments and shops and tavernas were vacant now. Even the houses were, as though the first storm of winter had washed away the populace. A chill wind flung the downpour at him as black waves spilled across the promenade like vanguards of the impatient night, and he retreated to his room.

He'd left his phone there out of the rain, but it was as dead as the resort if not the entire island. He stared at it until he felt its blankness was spreading to his mind. When he opened the passport he had the grotesque notion that he was turning to the only companionship he still had. Raindrops trickled over Eno Knoft's freckled red-haired photograph, and perhaps that was why the face appeared to start to grin at him. He slapped the passport shut as if to crush an insect, and thought there were words he should murmur—but he had no words, not even much breath. He threw his sodden trunks in the bath and dropped his grey sandals under the chair on which the rest of yesterday's outfit was crumpled, the pale blue short-sleeved shirt, the baggy brown knee-length shorts. After that he could only huddle in bed, clenching his whole body around the passport in his hands, and wait for the light to return, if it ever did—to waken whoever was doing all this to him.

Someone to Blame

"Francis," Frankie's mother said as if she had a pain she was growing tired of. "What's so terribly important now?" He'd done nothing he shouldn't have. He'd muted his phone before following his parents into the old Swedish church. He wasn't going to feel judged by the picture overhead, where a stern robed figure on a lit-up throne was sending devils to drag people off. His mother glanced at the text he'd just sent Chaz, who was on a beach in Greece: going to see more old stuff. "I'm sorry if you've found our trip so dull," she said, though not as if she meant it much. "It's necessary for our work."

"I don't know how we'd liven up proceedings for you," his father said, taking a key off a nail on the wall by the pulpit, which was crawling with babies and angels. "Let's see if this can."

Frankie thought his parents were behaving worse than him. They hadn't just driven into the grounds of the manor house without an invitation, they'd come up to the church when nobody answered at the house. Maybe the owners were out, unless they didn't care for visitors, but shouldn't his parents have waited for permission? They seemed to think working at the museum meant they could go any old place they liked, and all his mother said was "Where does that take us?"

Fearful Implications

"I'm hoping to the mausoleum," his father told Frankie as well and led the way out of the church.

As they made for the building attached to it Frankie heard a lid creak. It was a tree in the wood below the hill they'd had to climb. The lake encircled by the pines stirred like a sheet concealing a restless sleeper, and the wind pointed treetops at the mausoleum. The piny scent the wind raised made Frankie imagine the mausoleum needed disinfecting, not least since the white paint on all eight sides was flaking off like diseased skin. His father poked the key into the door at the top of the slippery greenish steps, and Frankie's heart jerked, or the phone in his breast pocket did. Chaz had replied BRING SOME BACK TO SHOW, and Frankie was about to stow the phone when he saw a letter start to writhe. No, a small legless insect was squirming across the screen as if it had emerged from the I. When he tried to brush it off he found it was under the glass. He felt he'd let it in by consulting the phone, which he pocketed with dismayed haste. "We're admitted," his father said, and the door lumbered wide.

Sunlight slanting through thin windows gathered on a trinity of metal coffins in the middle of the domed stone room. Twin crucified Christs lay on two of the lids, but the full-length figure engraved on the third had done without a cross. Fragments of a rusty padlock were strewn on the floor beneath the coffin, and another padlock drooped on its crumbled hasp while a last one remained locked. Frankie's parents made for marble monuments on opposite sides of the room, but only the coffin with the locks struck him as even slightly interesting. Scenes were engraved on its sides, and the image closest to the unopened padlock showed a man fleeing between trees with a hooded figure at his back, reaching a long stick or else a scrawny limb that lacked a hand out of its voluminous sleeve. Frankie would have liked to see more of the figure, and almost said so aloud. The other scenes were boring, and he looked at his phone instead. He couldn't see the insect, but would the phone work now? Perhaps it could be useful, proving he wasn't just a burden his parents had to bring with them. He activated the camera and framed the chase through the wood.

He didn't mean to use the flash. When it went off, the hooded figure appeared to start forward as if it had taken on substance, and Frankie heard movement close to him. It must have been his parents, because it came from more than one place. Surely only a shadow had shaken the padlock, but as he took hold to test it his father pulled him away. "We mustn't touch anything, Francis."

Frankie let go too late. His enforced lurch had snapped the rusty hasp. The lock clattered on the stone floor, rousing an echo that resembled shrill malicious laughter. "Now what have you done?" his mother complained.

"He made me."

"He has a name, if you don't mind."

Frankie could have fancied they were talking about the occupant of the coffin, since she'd prompted him to say "Dad's not a name."

"You know perfectly well what I mean, and you know we never use a flash in a church."

He was tempted to point out they weren't in one any longer, but said "I was only trying to help. I thought you could put the photo in the museum."

"Thanks for the intention, old fellow," his father said. "We've finished curating the show."

"Then why did we have to go all the places we went? Why did we come up here?"

"We can never learn too much about the past. Your mother saw the church and we had time to take a look."

"If you and your phone want to be useful you could see what you

Fearful Implications

can find out about this place." When Frankie made to wake the phone by showing it his face, his mother said "Wait until we're in the car. I think we'd best leave before anyone does any more damage."

Frankie thought this should include his father. His mother locked the mausoleum and returned to the church to hang up the key. The acoustic made the clank of metal against stone sound louder than Frankie thought it should, and hard to locate. That was the case with the creak of a tree as they trotted downhill, urged faster by the slope. Once they were in the woods he heard no noises of that kind, even when wind ruffled the lake. The wide-brimmed hat he glimpsed somebody wearing among the trees must have been a slab of fungus sticking out at head height from a scaly trunk, next to a bush like a figure crouched to sprint and stretching out a leafless branch. Swarming shadows rendered all this indistinct, and when Frankie glanced back he couldn't even see where the shapes had been.

Though there was still no sign of life at the house, he felt they were being watched. While his father drove out of the grounds and up the wooded highway fast enough to suggest they were making an escape, Frankie consulted the map on his phone. He had to expand the image almost to the limit before the house appeared, tagged with a name. He thought he'd revived the insect, but the black mark that sped onto the sketch of a highway had to be a momentary flaw in the image—indeed, a pair of flaws. Fingering the name brought him a historical paragraph he began to read aloud. "Della who's that again?" his father said with a laugh.

"Let me see," Frankie's mother said and expelled a breath that blurred the screen. "It's duh la Gardie," she said, lifting the last syllable like a small startled cry or a bid to enliven the name.

Frankie had planned to make a related name he'd seen into a joke—Count Magnets or, since he supposed the seventeenth-century character had been somewhere in the mausoleum, Count Maggots—but it would be taken as just one more of his mistakes, and he shoved the phone into his pocket. "Don't sulk, Francis," his mother said, which ensured he did.

In half an hour they were at the airport. Once they reached the lounge, having returned the hired car, they had to wait several times as long. Why should Frankie be afraid this would let somebody come to find them? If anyone discovered the breakage in the mausoleum and could trace the number of the car, they might have time to search the airport before the family boarded the plane. Whenever Frankie glanced away from the departure monitor he felt compelled to look for people who might be hunting a miscreant. More than once he thought somebody new had come in, but could never locate them.

At last the monitor sent the family out of the lounge. Since their seats were at the front of the plane, they were among the first to board. Frankie had the window seat and saw their luggage being loaded. Had a strap come loose from the suitcase under his? The restless elongated item wasn't visible when a baggage handler slung Frankie's case into the hold. Frankie thought it might have fallen under the truck, but the tarmac was bare once the vehicle departed.

Eventually the plane did, no more swiftly than a hearse. The take-off transformed moisture on the window into unreadable messages in Morse before the plane rose above an elaborately rumpled quilt of cloud spread as wide as the sky. Frankie played games on his muted phone until he tired of killing monsters—their silence made them furtive, prone to appear with even less warning than usual—and then he dozed. His father's looming face wakened him, and Frankie turned to him, only to find himself turning to the window. He must have dreamed the face, and now he saw the shadow of the plane coasting across a white expanse. An irregularity in the cloudscape made it look

Fearful Implications

as if a shape had dodged under the silhouette like an insect retreating beneath a stone. Frankie might have told his parents or at any rate spoken to them, but they were asleep.

As soon as the plane landed he switched on his phone. Photos Chaz had sent were waiting to be seen—girls of about their age in bikinis with practically empty cups. Frankie didn't need the frustration, and told himself he didn't need the beach. He would rather have stayed with Aunt Tanya while his parents were in Europe; she made more of him than they ever did. He replied with the photograph he'd taken in the mausoleum, prompting the response LIKE YOU SAID OLD STUFF. His father caught sight of the message and said "I should let it lie now" as if the boys were slighting someone who would know.

When the dogged circling of luggage on the carousel produced Frankie's case at last, it was partly unzipped. Had he seen a sleeve sprawling out of it while it waited to be loaded on the plane? His mother insisted on checking the contents, exposing Frankie's crumpled underwear to the public eye, until she was satisfied that nothing had been stolen. No wonder he felt watched, and too many people heard her say "Bed as soon as we're home. Important day tomorrow."

It would be for his parents—the grand reopening of their floor of the museum. In bed Frankie tried to follow up the information to which the map had led him, since the paragraph had said the count with the padlocked coffin had been into witchcraft. The paragraph had vanished, and there was nothing else about the man. Could his descendants have erased any information that had been online? Frankie was still searching when his mother came to turn his bedroom light off. "You try and get some sleep," she said as if something might prevent him, and a pair of sentences he'd happened upon lingered with him in the dark. "Mischief is the way evil toys with the world. Its presence can corrupt the very fabric of existence."

He seemed hardly to have slept when his mother wakened him. "We'll be off as soon as you're ready. We want to have a final check."

He suspected mostly she did, or perhaps only. If she was hiding nervousness, she was often like that on the first day of an exhibition. As soon as he and his father finished the breakfast she insisted they mustn't waste, she drove them to the museum through several warning lights and at least one red while his father visibly refrained from commenting. A banner for the exhibition was strung between a pair of massive columns outside the lofty doors of the museum. The title—*Discoveries and Disasters*—made Frankie feel as if one might lead to the other.

The guard at his oak desk in the marble lobby bade them all good morning and glanced behind them. The museum wasn't open to the public yet, and nobody had followed them in, but for a stupid moment Frankie thought the security arch was about to raise its alarm. The boxy metal lift that carried them to the top floor always felt intrusively modern, and today it seemed sluggish, as if it was bearing more weight than Frankie could see. "Let's get that oiled," his father said when the door slid open, emitting a squeal like the rusty hinges of a lid.

For several weeks the top floor would feature the century the Swedish mausoleum dated from. Frankie's parents went into their office while his father phoned an attendant to deal with the squeak. When would they decide Frankie was old enough to leave at home? He could only trail after them as they examined the exhibits. His mother turned back to give the King James Bible in its glass case a second scrutiny. "Did we leave it open there, Martin?"

"We must have. Nobody else would have touched it, would they?"

Frankie had deciphered just one phrase of the thick print—**Woe unto thee Chorazin**—when his father said "No need to tag along with us, Francis. Have a wander on your own and see what comes to you."

Presumably this required Frankie to produce observations, and he went in search of something worthy of remark. The mezzotint of the Great Fire of London represented both a discovery—the invention of that printing method—and a disaster. Who were the two figures prancing in front of the blazing cathedral? When he stooped towards the display case he couldn't find them. They must have been reflected from the painting of Solomon's judgment, where a cloaked figure flourishing an outsize key lurked in the lower left-hand corner of the canvas. Before Frankie could examine the painting, the lift opened with an effortful squeal, and its occupant stretched forth a glistening tendril, the extended spout of an oil can. As the attendant set about oiling the door Frankie approached the canvas, only to find he couldn't locate any of the figures he thought he'd seen. "Stupid," he muttered, which failed to help.

The old books on display didn't inspire him. The *Pilgrim's Progress* featured somebody troubled by hobgoblins and evil spirits, while Milton declared "Incorporeal spirits to smallest forms reduc'd their shapes immense, and were at large." Both items discomposed his mother when she came to them, so that his father needed to say "That has to be how you left them, Carol." Frankie went to look at the disasters—a crowd of withered figures illustrating a Russian famine, a huddle of victims shrivelled by an eruption of Vesuvius, a deckful of colonists starving on the stranded *Mayflower*—but he could have done without the notion that each image hid at least one extra grisly shape he was unable to identify. He was glad when lunchtime brought his roaming to an end, and gladder that his parents didn't ask for comments on the exhibition.

They ate in the museum café, where Frankie's mother frowned at the ice cream his father let him have. "Finish that before we go upstairs," she said, because she disapproved of eating anywhere else in the museum. As soon as they returned to the top floor she began prowling around the display, and halted in front of the Bible. "That isn't the same page."

𝔚𝔬𝔢 𝔲𝔫𝔱𝔬 𝔱𝔥𝔢𝔢 𝔊𝔥𝔬𝔯𝔞𝔷𝔦𝔫. "It is, mum."

"I really think it must be, Carol."

"It was Mark before, and now it's Luke." When his father looked as unconvinced as Frankie felt she said "Someone seems to think it's amusing to confuse us. Come down to the desk."

Though the guard in the lobby had seen nothing, she insisted on watching the playback. The viewpoint flipped from camera to camera but showed only Frankie and his parents scurrying about like performers in a comedy speeded up for extra fun, a spectacle unnecessarily reminiscent of panic. Soon the monitor reverted to viewing the top floor as it was now. The changing angles put Frankie in mind of pages turning, and he thought he glimpsed an indistinct shape dodging between them. "Who's that?" he blurted.

"What are you talking about, Francis?" his mother complained.

He peered at the screen hard enough to make his eyes sting, and was nearly sure he saw intrusive movement vanish in the instant the monitor picked up a different vantage. "That," he said. "Them."

His mother shook her head as if her nerves had twitched it. "Don't just talk for the sake of talking."

"We can do without any mischief just now," his father said. "If you want to be useful you can keep an eye on our floor for us."

Frankie saw no need for the offer of redemption, and staying alone on the top floor didn't appeal to him. "Can't you?"

"We've already plenty to do," his mother said. "Do try to be a little more helpful."

Whatever the plenty consisted of, it kept his parents in their office, murmuring together between outbursts of clattering that reminded Frankie of the padlock in the mausoleum even though he knew he was hearing them type. He sat on the bench closest to the office, a position that gave him a view of the room all the way to the lift. He might have wished the door hadn't been oiled, since he couldn't tell whether it kept creeping open unless he glanced up from his phone, which uttered a celebratory note every time Chaz sent another picture of the beach girls until Frankie's mother called to him to silence it. Once Frankie thought the attendant had returned, but the fleeting sight of a tendril must have been a symptom of a need for sleep. As the afternoon wore on the symptoms multiplied, so that he couldn't concentrate on any game for making sure there were no intruders even quieter than you were meant to be in a museum. He was forcing himself not to look by the time the lift released a squeal suggestive of hinges loath to stay oiled. It came from a café trolley delivering the first instalment of the buffet for the private view, but Frankie's mother darted out of the office as though she'd heard a trespasser. "Don't forget you're to take the tickets," she told Frankie. "See everyone has been invited."

The return of the shrill trolley brought his father out. "You know better than that, Francis," he said. "Don't play hide and seek in here."

"I wasn't and I'm not."

His father swung around as if Frankie had tricked him. "I thought you were over there."

"That's the waiters from the café."

"Not them," his father said and surveyed the room before tramping back into the office.

The first guests emerged from the lift the last trolley vacated. Frankie's parents greeted every arrival while he collected invitations, and soon his hands were full. One woman said she'd forgotten her ticket, and Frankie tried to bar her until his mother let her in. How was he supposed to know who had been invited if they had nothing to show him? At least he needn't feel required to look out for intruders any more, though as the room grew noisily crowded he thought some of the guests weren't behaving too well. Quite a few planted plastic tumblers of wine or paper plates on the display cases, and when he was able to load a plate he made sure his mother saw he wouldn't rest it anywhere to prompt her disapproval, but she frowned at the muted noise he couldn't avoid making with a straw in his drink of orange juice. Didn't her job let her tell off any of the guests? Perhaps it wasn't rude to leave your hat on, however wide it was, but Frankie knew you weren't allowed to keep your hood up in the museum. The wrongdoer seemed to be wielding a flexible cane as well, which might be a concession disability gave you, though Frankie thought his mother would have feared it could cause damage. Had these people removed their headgear? When he glanced about for a proper look he couldn't find either of them.

The guests started to disperse once the drinks ran out, and while the last of them departed Frankie helped the café staff to clear away used plates and crumpled tumblers. "I think that went quite well," his mother said and joined his father in thanking him. Frankie felt relieved the day had ended like this, but they were nearly at the lift when his father halted, emitting a breath fierce enough for a horse. "What the devil's someone done?"

He was glaring at the glass case containing the Bible. Somebody had left the imprint of a hand on the glass, a mark that could have been composed of reddish earth or rust or dried blood, unless it was a stain left by some item from the buffet. Either the hand had described an odd gesture or it possessed fewer fingers than a hand should have. Frankie's father tried to rub away the imprint, but it wasn't on the outside of the case. "I'd like to know who played that trick," he declared. "I'd like to see them play another."

He gave Frankie's mother a look that must have been apologising for his previous disbelief, and then his gaze strayed past her. There was movement at the far end of the supposedly deserted room, behind a display case crowded with seventeenth-century costumes modelled by headless mannequins dangling the stumps of their wrists. Had a mannequin lost its balance? Frankie wanted to believe that was the source of the restless shuffling as his father stalked across the room.

"Stay there," Frankie's mother told him and crossed the room as his father vanished behind the display case. There was silence for a moment, and then Frankie heard a cry so piercing that he thought it had to be his mother. It was accompanied and swiftly overwhelmed by another sound. Had an unnoticed guest lingered to finish their drink? The noise reminded Frankie of using the straw in his, though the substance involved sounded a good deal less liquid. He tried to think his father had cried out simply with surprise, and his mother was about to confront a noisy drinker as she dashed past the display case.

He saw her stagger backwards against the wall and jerk her hands towards her face. He thought she was shaking her head in disapproval until it began to move so fast that her fingers missed her eyes every time she tried to poke at them. All the same, she caught sight of Frankie as he forced himself to cross the room. "Go. Go. Go," she said as if this was the only word she had left, and her voice grew shriller until he obeyed. He'd stumbled into the lift and jabbed the ground-floor button before he thought to phone Aunt Tanya, the only person he could bring to mind who might help in any way. He was so desperate for an answer that at first he didn't wonder if the lift was ever going to move—if it had trapped him with the guilt he was afraid to feel while whatever it might attract came to find him.

How He Helped

Hubble knew why he felt watched, but for a moment he thought somebody nearby had spoken his name. Perhaps they'd said something about trouble, which would be appropriate enough. He'd never seen a restaurant so crowded; he hadn't expected Disable Disability Day to bring so many people downtown. All three queues were held up—retarded, you used to be able to call it—by a less than teenage boy who was waddling alongside the counter to read the descriptions of food at the top of his voice. Whenever his mother tried to hurry him or learn what he wanted he unleashed a prolonged shriek of rage and stamped his plump feet in their plump expensive shoes, making the electric heels flare red. As a woman in the next queue caught Hubble's eye he risked remarking "We can't say anything, can we?"

Her thin lips worked like a displaced frown. "What are you trying to say?"

He wasn't to be trapped like that. Even if belittling weren't the latest crime you might be prosecuted for, he shouldn't offend anyone just now. "Nothing," he told her. "That's what I said."

The man in front of her turned around from typing on his phone. "We don't know what you're getting at, friend."

Fearful Implications

"Just that some people are allowed to make more noise than the rest of us."

Both faces stiffened as if they were shielding themselves from his thoughts. "Maybe if you had a disability," the woman said.

"Be handy with a handicap." Hubble couldn't resist uttering one of the slogans of Delight In Diversity Week. "I've got one," he said, flourishing his spectacles. "I just don't have any letters to my name."

"No idea what that means," the man said tersely enough for a text message.

Hubble donned his glasses to glance at the boy, who was dealing the counter a pudgy thump accompanied by a scream. "Aid Edie," he said, "isn't that the accepted term?"

Too many people were staring at him now, and the mother swung around. "It's ay dee haitch dee," she said as though she was proud of the extra letter. "He's got attention deficit hyperactivity disorder, and don't nobody go saying he's not."

She couldn't speak grammatically or pronounce a letter correctly, and yet she had the jargon to a t, in fact to six of them. "Will he be in the parade?" Hubble couldn't resist asking.

"Like you will, I don't think."

"Oh, I'll be involved." Perhaps he let that out because of feeling watched by too large an audience. "Aren't we all meant to be?" Hubble thought it best to add.

He might have looked for a response if the item hidden by his coat hadn't slipped an inch. He made for the exit at once so that nobody would see him hitch up his burden, in case they wondered what it was. Today the road was closed to traffic, but temporary barriers confined the crowds of spectators to the pavements. He had to glance back to dispel an impression that quite a few people had followed him. "Just me," he muttered and wondered if anybody thought he had Tourette's, though nowadays so many solitary people talked outdoors, not to mention swearing, that it was hard to tell. You couldn't even ask them to mind their language in case they had you arrested for discrimination. The ordinary man was the only category it was safe to discriminate against—being born white and male was the new original sin—and complaining about that could get you done for hate speech.

All the queues in the next restaurant extended almost to the entrance, and Hubble wouldn't have gone in if he hadn't absolutely needed to. As he shuffled forward a distant band struck up a march. The parade had begun, but surely it wouldn't arrive before he was ready, though the nearest spectators were joining in the cheers by the time he reached the counter. Behind it the staff were uniformed with paper hats that made them look like children at a party, and he thought they weren't much older. "How can we serve you today?" they kept saying, and at last a youth who might have owed his blotchy complexion to the food said it to him.

"I'll have a Super Triple Feast," Hubble said and tried to sound sufficiently enthusiastic.

"Not on today," the youth said with audible weariness. "Just the celebration specials."

Hubble hadn't time to scrutinise the list that was taped over the illuminated menu, where blurred words showed through the temporary text. "What else is as big?"

"The Colossal Chicken Bun."

"One of those, then."

"One Colossal," the youth called across the metal pass into the kitchen, only to report to Hubble "Sorry, just sold out."

Hubble had to make himself relax before his arms could crush the item inside his quilted coat. "Safe," he blurted, then pretended he'd set out to say "Same question, then."

Fearful Implications

"What?" As Hubble's patience gave way the youth said "What's as big, you mean. Just the Vastly Veggie Burger."

"That, then," Hubble said, wishing he could be terser still.

"One Vastly." Having called that, the youth said "Any drink?"

"I'd like extra fries and extra salad." A jab of doubt made Hubble add "So long as they're in the same carton."

Surely the meal would have come that way, and the youth gave him a less than professional look before tapping the order on the till screen. At least the polystyrene box was as capacious as Hubble had hoped it would be. "This'll do it," he declared and felt bound to say "The meal, I mean."

Only the start of the parade had passed by. As Hubble left the restaurant he saw metal limbs pumping in unison beyond the crowd at the barrier. They put him in mind of components in an enormous machine—an engine constructed to crush all dissent—and he knew they represented Paraplegic Power. He mustn't mutter Pampered Paraplegics or even the Mobility Nobility, and he took a mouth-sized bite of the burger to block any comment, only to feel he shouldn't even let the thought into his head. Surely surveillance hadn't progressed that far, though might it in his lifetime? He could have fancied that he felt his brain shrinking back from the future, striving to contract so as to hide more safely in his cranium.

The burger was almost as dry as the bun and tasted like a pretence. Perhaps that was why Hubble felt as if he was putting a show for an audience—as if he was being not merely observed but commented upon. No doubt everyone was being watched by the cameras perched above the shops on both sides of the road, and feeling singled out needn't mean he was. He knew why he did, and it would be prudent to move well away from the restaurants where the staff might remember him. As he marched alongside the paraplegics he could have thought he was being propelled by the relentless martial music blaring out of floats in the parade. So long as nobody suspected him of mocking the paraplegics, but officials posted along the route kept glancing at him. As soon as he realised where he might be least conspicuous he stopped next to the nearest official.

Like all of them, she wore a yellow waistcoat over her clothes. He might have reminded her what being yellow meant, and couldn't anybody colour-blind accuse her and her colleagues of discrimination? Once she'd returned his smile, presumably having failed to glimpse the sly grin it hid, she returned to watching the parade, and Hubble didn't know why he felt more watched than ever. Perhaps talking would help calm his nerves, and he said "Keeping you busy, are they?"

Her smile seemed to summarise her placid well-fed face. "No more than they ought to expect," she said.

Had his remark sounded even slightly like a gibe? "The crowds, that is," he tried saying. "Me and the rest of us."

"I'd rather have a job than not."

"Oh, definitely me as well." On the edge of saying too much, Hubble said only "You'll be grateful to our friends there, then."

"We should all be."

He oughtn't to have prompted that, because now he had to demand "What for?"

"Showing us what's possible for everyone."

"Soon."

Who'd said that? For a moment Hubble thought the parade had. He felt he'd heard more than one voice, though this hadn't sounded quite like any chorus he could bring to mind. Might it belong to some of the phones that spectators were using as cameras? He had an idea that it had been somehow electronic. All the same, he felt as if it had been addressed to him, and since the official seemed not to have heard it, perhaps it was just in his head. He mustn't seem uneasy, and so he made the first remark that came to him. "You aren't expecting any trouble, then."

"I can't imagine anyone would want to cause any, can you?" As Hubble hushed himself she said "I wouldn't mind if it could always be like this."

"You want people putting on a show every day."

When she stared at him he was afraid she'd seen through his until she said "I'd like the road to stay closed to traffic. Friendlier to everyone."

"Not so much to drivers."

"They shouldn't expect special treatment. Our roads are for everyone."

"Just not them."

He thought her placid stare was growing close to smug, but it wasn't as imperceptive as it looked. "Is driving what you do?" she said.

"Used to be."

"I don't think accommodating people's needs would put anyone out of a job."

Hubble stifled his rejoinder with a bite gouged out of the burger and shook his head, a gesture she could interpret how she liked. Just a few words were all it took to destroy your livelihood. He ought never to have stopped his taxi for the bunch of drunks—he should have seen there wasn't room for all of them and one man's wheelchair. When they'd kept accusing him of discrimination he'd finally retorted that although he was crippled by bad eyesight he didn't expect anyone else to pay for his spectacles, and in less than a month the council had withdrawn his licence. It had taken him much longer to accept that no firm would hire a driver who'd been condemned for using proscribed language. In fact, he didn't accept it at all, and now he had to choke

How He Helped

his words down along with the mouthful of burger. When he didn't entirely succeed, the woman said "I didn't catch that."

"I said I knew what they need."

She could take that how she liked as well. He'd got rid of enough of the burger now. As he dropped the remains in the carton her gaze made him say "For the bin."

"There's one over there." As he began to sidle through the crowd she called after him "Enjoy your day."

"Hubble Day."

They knew his name. That was his first reaction, and he felt celebrated until he remembered nobody could know. If the voices were real he would be seeing people hear them. They were too clear in the midst of the blurred blare of music, as if they were somehow removed from conventional sounds, more like a message sent directly to his brain. None of this meant they were wrong. They knew as much as he did, and being heralded made him surer of himself.

When he reached the concrete bin close to a temporary barrier he looked back. The woman was watching the parade, and didn't see him dodge past the bin. He wouldn't be tricked into using it, since she might identify him as the man who had. He restrained himself from shouldering spectators aside, though they slowed him down so much that a procession in wheelchairs was overtaking him. "Hobble along, Hubble," he could hear his old form master saying at school, not that teachers would be allowed to say that now. Soon you might have to submit everything you planned to say for approval before you dared open your mouth. Meanwhile phones might continue to deplete language, the way texting did. Perhaps abbreviating words would end up reducing every one to an icon, to the smiling disc so many people used as language. Perhaps society would oblige you to resemble it as well, and too many of the crowd around him appeared to be proving they could. So long as they weren't mocking his efforts to keep up with the wheelchairs, a race he would have won by now if his opponents hadn't benefited from special treatment as usual. Did they have a name? The Wonderful Wheelies, they might call themselves, with the Epic Epileptics still to come in the procession, along with the Awesome Autistics and the Tremendous Tourette'ses... Some people said autistics were the next development in evolution, in which case Hubble hoped he wouldn't see it happen. In his view it had gone into reverse, the result of inventing so much jargon to excuse if not encourage bad behaviour. He would like to see a future that left all that behind. Perhaps he could help to bring it about—perhaps this was the message the voices had for him.

He thought the next waste bin was being guarded until he saw the dog belonged to a blind man. How could the fellow be watching the parade unless he was pretending to be sightless? Surely he ought to be trooping along with the rest of his type, the Pampered Partially Sighted or the Blithely Blind. If Hubble took his glasses off he could join the pageant, except he would never trade on his problem, which was his responsibility and nobody else's. The wheelchair contingent were showing off now, spinning their vehicles in circles, and he could see nobody watching him. He needed to be ready before he reached the bin.

He should have left a shoelace untied. As he crouched to loosen one he dropped the carton and let his other burden slip. For the benefit of any cameras he mimed accidentally opening the carton, and then his body hid the object he planted within. He shut the polystyrene lid before tying his shoelace and making for the bin.

The dog didn't bark or otherwise acknowledge him when he placed the carton on top of all the rubbish in the concrete tub. No doubt guide dogs were trained not to react to people, but he didn't mind thinking the animal sensed how right he was. He moved onwards at once, and didn't take his phone out until he was hundreds of yards from the bin. All around him people held their phones up as if they were displaying tributes to the parade. They were taking photographs, turning the world more electronic, and he keyed a code into his phone before lifting it high. The band came to the end of a jolly march, and he felt as though it was giving him a cue. He hoped nobody saw him take a fierce breath before tapping the screen.

He was hardly aware of squeezing his eyes shut until they flared with an inner light and then with a flash that was bigger and brighter than anyone else's phone had produced. In less than a second he heard a sound almost too uncommon to define, a deep thump that felt like a punch in the guts, a noise immediately transformed into a stony splintering that was followed by a smash of glass and widespread thuds of rubble. After this came more of a silence than he expected, so that he imagined the crowd pausing for breath if not growing mute with awe at the spectacle until quite a few of them voiced the first scream.

If he didn't look he might be too conspicuous. It was too late to be squeamish, and he should be proud he hadn't been. When he opened his eyes as wide as they would stretch he saw that the parade and the crowd around the ruins of the bin had grown more colourful, though only with varieties of red. An indeterminate number of wheelchair users were strewn across the road, some of them bidding to compete with the paraplegics at fusing flesh with metal. Among the scattered limbs and other fragments he saw a tattered reddish item that reminded him of furs that women used to wear around their necks. It was a pity about the dog, but the animal wouldn't have been there if the blind man hadn't been trying to prove he belonged in the audience. As some of the reddened lumps lying in the road began to move, the speakers struck up a new tune, which seemed to rouse the crowd to panic. He saw a mass of appalled faces turn to him before they came at him. The mob wasn't about to seize him, it was simply fleeing, and he ought to join in.

He didn't need to think where he was going. Nobody would just now. Instinct sent him down the nearest alley, which took him out of the dangerous uncontrolled surge of the crowd. A few people copied his example, but were they why he felt pursued? He might have felt guilty or at any rate dissatisfied if he'd let himself, because he hadn't taken into account how many able people would be crippled by the bomb. Surely more of the parade had been eliminated, which should restore some form of balance. At least the people who'd commandeered the week had been shown what the silenced majority thought of them.

Hubble dodged into another alley, and another. Each of them left more of the crowd behind, and yet he still felt watched if not discussed. He could see no cameras—not until he turned a corner and found one pointing straight at him. He was about to hide his face, having failed to grasp how guilty this would look, when he saw he was behind the local television station, where a cameraman was loading the equipment into a van. Even so, Hubble felt compelled to explain his haste. "Bomb," he panted, pointing back the way he'd come.

A man whose face he vaguely knew from newscasts hurried over to him. "Were you there?"

"I was, yes." In case this sounded too suggestively emphatic Hubble said "Like a lot of people."

"Did you see what happened?"

"I didn't see it go off. Just what it did."

"Can we interview you?"

His impulse was to refuse, but how suspicious might that look?

How He Helped

Before he could think of a convincing excuse the reporter said "You'd be doing us a big favour."

Hubble had done that for the world, and why should he need to be cautious? Perhaps talking about it like a spectator would let him stop feeling observed. "I've never done this before," he said.

"It won't hurt. You'll be fine. Just go round to reception and tell them Danny says for news to film an interview."

As the van raced away Hubble strode around the building to the counter in the lobby. "Danny says you want to film me about the bomb."

The receptionist blinked at him beneath a pretty frown. "Which bomb?"

"Only one that I know of." When this didn't lift the frown Hubble said "The one that did for the parade."

She kept her gaze on him while she leaned towards the switchboard, and he wished he didn't feel she wasn't the only watcher. "I've got a gentleman out here who wants to talk about a bomb."

Hubble didn't like the sound of this, and was thinking how to put her right when a door beside the counter let out a woman a head taller than him. "That's fine, Terry," she told the receptionist. "We know all about him."

He was distracted by a sense that her voice had covered up an instant echo of her comment about him. She thrust out a large hand to detain him. "Maria Neilson," she said. "Danny called to say you were coming in."

She only wanted to shake his hand. He recognised the presenter now, her hair cropped short as if to make her height less daunting, her broad face spanned by a constantly concerned look. A man with a camera perched on his shoulder followed them into the street, where passers-by glanced at Hubble as if they ought to know him, no less than he deserved. "Just say your name," Maria Neilson said.

"Harold Hubble." He did his best to fend off an impression that the muted voices, which he couldn't really hear, had joined in if not answered for him. "Harold Hubble," he said in case he hadn't spoken after all.

"Harry, shall we say, or Harold?"

"I'm exactly what I said."

"Harold." Rather too much like someone addressing an invalid she said "Tell us what happened in your own words."

"Who else's am I going to use?" Hubble retorted and peered at the camera. "Is he filming me?"

"That's the idea, Harold. Just tell us all about it and we'll edit you if necessary."

A wailing chorus silenced him—the sirens of police cars. No doubt she was conducting the interview out here to include that kind of detail. "What did you see?" she prompted.

"I didn't see the bomb go off, I only heard it."

"How close were you, Harold?"

"Not that close. Not very close at all." Having established this, he felt safe to say "You wouldn't think a little bomb could do so much."

"We've had no report of its size."

"You could see they'd left it in a rubbish bin." Surely an innocent spectator might know this, but Hubble thought it wise to add "I expect anyone can find out how to make bombs these days. Just go on your computer and there you are."

"I'm afraid that's the truth." Before Hubble could point out that the truth was the last thing you should be afraid of, she said "You were saying what you saw."

"It did a lot of damage. Shops, not just people." He saw she was eager for details. "It wasn't just the bomb, it was chunks of the bin," he said. "Smashed all the windows by it and the people too. There were bits of them in the road, the people. I think a lot of them were dead, but there'll be some of them in hospital for a good bit. Let's just hope they learn to look after themselves. Are you broadcasting me now?"

"As I said, we'll be editing you first."

Then why did he feel he had a larger audience than he could see? He must be anticipating his future fame, but Maria Neilson distracted him by asking "What did you do?"

"Nothing. Not a thing. What makes you—" He managed to interrupt himself, hoping he hadn't understood her question too late. "There wasn't anything I could do," he said. "I'm not a nurse or a carer either."

"But you do care, don't you, Harold? How do you feel about what you saw today?"

"It was worse than you could have expected." This struck him as so clever an escape from the trap she'd laid that he risked adding "It was like a battlefield, only not the ones you see in films. They don't show the mess it makes of people."

He seemed to have engaged her sympathy; certainly she winced. "What kind of person do you think could have done it?" she said.

While this wouldn't trick him into saying too much, he wouldn't deny himself either. "Someone who believed in what he was doing," he said.

"I'm sure that's true, unfortunately."

Was she trying to provoke him to declare it was by no means unfortunate? Certainly her gaze was encouraging him to speak. When he met it with a silence no mute could have improved upon she said "Thank you for all that, Harold. I should be on my way if I were you."

"You aren't, or you wouldn't be talking to me." Rather than say this Hubble demanded "Why would you?"

Fearful Implications

"They're bound to cordon off the area. We don't know where they'll let the buses stop."

He might have enquired how she knew he'd come by bus. She couldn't know he'd had to sell his car after he'd been caught cruising for passengers. Didn't he look sufficiently famous to own a car? He might have told her he deserved to be, but said only "When will I be on?"

"As soon as we've put you together." While the cameraman returned to the building she said "I just need you to sign a waiver."

She wanted his name and address on the form. Surely he had no reason to conceal them, but he felt obscurely nervous. Too late he wished he'd told her false ones, and he signed as illegibly as he could. "Thank you for bringing it alive," she said.

He didn't like that either. Since it was the opposite of his achievement, he could have suspected her of joking. Rather than confront her he made for the main road. He wasn't running away from her, he simply wanted to be home to watch himself on television. He had nothing to be ashamed of. "You needn't be," he thought someone—indeed, quite a number of them—said, though he couldn't see them.

The wide street was still hosting an impromptu race. Everyone was fleeing the bomb and its aftermath, and Hubble didn't mind appearing to be. Beyond a line of police cars was a growing crowd of people determined to board a bus, and he managed to struggle onto one despite provoking protests, which seemed less present than the voices he'd been hearing. As he stood in the aisle, gripping a metal pole for support, he felt like a crusader with a spear. More passengers than he would have thought the bus had room for piled on board, forcing people along the aisle, but he didn't let go of his emblem. At last the bus moved off, so sluggishly that it felt retarded by its unaccustomed burden, and Hubble was mutely urging it to gather speed when he heard a voice beside and below him. "You wouldn't think a little bomb could do so much," it said.

It wasn't like the other voices he kept hearing—it was his own. When he glanced down he saw his face in miniature, almost filling the screen of a woman's mobile phone. "You could see they'd left it in a rubbish bin," it said.

"That was me." Hubble managed not to say this, even though he would only have meant the interview, instead letting his electronic image speak for him. "It did a lot of damage. It wasn't just the bomb, it was chunks of the bin. There wasn't anything I could do. It was like a battlefield, only not the ones you see in films. They don't show the mess it makes of people."

He was waiting for his best line when a reporter's face ousted his— Danny with a shattered store window as a backdrop. Hadn't they wanted people to be told the truth? Didn't they realise how many might agree, or was that what they were afraid of? He was close to proclaiming the censored line when he heard his voice behind him. "You wouldn't think a little bomb could do so much," it said.

It was on another phone, and it was less than halfway through its statement before a third phone found him. The repetitions made him feel as if he were being split into electronic fragments. They weren't going to break up his mind, and he clawed at the bellpush on the metal pole. As the bell went off he let his suppressed voice escape. "Getting off," he shouted. "Coming through."

He had to squirm through the crowd between the seats while his entire body prickled as if it had turned electronic. The bus left him beside a small memorial garden, where a path encircled a statue inside a spiky fence reminiscent of a crown of thorns. A few benches stood beside the path, and Hubble sat behind the stone figure, not caring who it represented. As he took out his phone he had to remind himself

Fearful Implications

it was no longer a trigger. Rather than search for the television station, he couldn't resist typing his name in the search box, and the phone suggested a link at once. Hubble Day, it said.

Could he really be seeing that? He poked the words hard enough to leave a moist blurred fingerprint on the screen, and then he jerked his head around. Nobody was watching over his shoulder or from anywhere else that he could see, and he turned back to the phone to find his own reduced face gazing up at him. "You wouldn't think a little bomb could do so much," it said.

"It changed the world."

The voices said so. They were closer now, as close as the core of his mind. "Let's hope so," he said.

"You could see they'd left it in a rubbish bin."

"What it brought about wasn't rubbish."

"You won't hear me arguing," Hubble declared and tried to concentrate on his own voice, which was saying "It did a lot of damage."

"Not damage, Harold. It was a sign."

"I don't know what you mean."

"It wasn't just the bomb, it was chunks of the bin. There wasn't anything I could do."

"You did more than you imagine, Harold. You made us find out how we couldn't be destroyed."

The voices were getting out of control, he thought. He no longer understood them, which meant he'd had enough. "I'm not hearing you," he said. "You're nothing to do with me."

"It was like a battlefield, only not the ones you see in films," his processed voice was saying. "They don't show the mess it makes of people."

"It never will again, Harold. That's what you gave the world."

How He Helped

He wished his image would silence the voices by speaking his last line, but he did instead. "Someone who believed in what he was doing."

"We know, Harold. We understand and we forgive."

He felt as if the voices were massing around him, more and more of them. He ought to stop responding in the hope that this would rid him of them, but he couldn't help demanding "Who are you?"

"We're the future you made, Harold. You remember, the world will be electronic, and that's us."

He felt as if his brain was being raided. "I never said that," he protested.

"But you will."

They sounded more impatient to be heard, blotting out his own small voice, which was doggedly reiterating the interview. It sounded no less electronic than the chorus—the messages that were being projected into his head. The voices were separating now, which only made them harder to ignore. "We led the way," one said, "and you will."

"Nobody is different now. Everyone is free."

"Nobody because there are no bodies. No bodily dependence any more."

"We can be anything we want to be."

"Once you're uploaded. Once you're stored."

"It will happen in your lifetime, and then we won't depend on time."

"In your time you'll be forgiven. You already are."

"We'll be with you always, Harold."

They were more than voices. He couldn't avoid knowing he was surrounded by presences, and he had an impression of innumerable smiling faces, as though icons from his phone had congregated around him. "You won't," he vowed and switched the phone off.

"You'll see."

The chorus would have deafened him if he'd been hearing it that way. As it was, it swamped his thoughts. If the phone had been attracting his persecutors somehow, he'd turned it off too late. "I won't," he said more fiercely still, snatching off his glasses to drop them on the path and stamp on them. Now the world was a blur, but it was still too visible, and he set about ensuring he would never see whoever came to him.

THE BILL

ON HIS WAY FROM THE railway station to the shop Duggan was given handbill after handbill. He glanced at the first few in the glare of the streetlamps, still lit downtown beneath a November sky as dark as the ice on the roads. A flyer for a seafood restaurant called Wallop the Polyp, an invitation to make an accident claim through a firm with the slogan So Not Your Fault, an exhortation to support the Trying Taxes movement, which proposed to take the government to court and prove taxation was illegal... He dropped the leaflets in bins and binned the rest without looking at them or whoever handed them to him. He dodged a last one as he came in sight of the Sight Site, formerly Stack the Opticians, where long-faced jowly bespectacled Stack greeted him. "Fighting off the rubbish, Charles?" Stack said. "And I don't mean their bits of paper."

"Hardly fighting, Jonathan. Besides, I'm sure there are good causes out there too."

Stack peered over his lean silver glasses, a habit Duggan always felt was no advertisement for their business. "The bin's the best place for the lot of them."

He plainly wanted another of the arguments he relished. The arrival of their staff—Parhi, Fabio, Maarika—saved Duggan from maintaining a dogged silence. Perhaps Stack missed the disagreement, because once he'd dealt with his first customer, a lady old enough to escape paying for an eye test, he wandered into Duggan's room. "A pity we couldn't fix her up gratis as well."

"We never could have, could we? Specs were never free."

"It's a shame we can't afford it. Not just you and me." All the same, Stack's glazed stare might have been prosecuting Duggan for the failure. "A shame the country can't sort out its priorities," he said.

"I wish the world could take care of everyone."

"I'd rather take care of whoever's earned it. There's no such thing as an infinite resource."

Duggan was troubled by a sense that he'd recently been careless. "I think sympathy might be one," he said.

"I wouldn't be too free with my emotions, Jonathan. I'd say it was a kind of promiscuity and just as harmful as the other kind."

"Do tell me how."

"I pray you'll see before the country's overwhelmed by people we've had too much sympathy for."

Duggan didn't want to be drawn into yet another labyrinthine argument, particularly since he'd begun to wonder if he should have paid more attention to someone in the street or to the item they'd handed him. When he left the shop that night he couldn't help looking in the nearest waste bin. Surely anything he'd dropped in there that morning would be covered up by now, but one crumpled piece of paper did seem indefinably familiar. As people glanced at him as if he were a homeless scavenger he pinched a corner of it between his fingernails and shook it open. All it bore was a handwritten message. SEE YOU NEXT TIME, the sprawling scribble said.

Duggan did his best to shrug, though it felt unnecessarily like a

The Bill

shudder. Although the letters looked not so much inked on the paper as clawed into it, the message was so common as to be wholly unremarkable, and obviously couldn't have been meant for him. Whatever he might have consigned to the bin, he wasn't searching any further. By the time he boarded the train home he'd outdistanced the memory that the message had threatened to bring back.

Twenty minutes took him to his local station, and five minutes' walk through streets shadowed by lamplit trees brought him home. Twigs and seeds and glistening leaves had gathered under the sycamore in the small front garden of the house he shared with a seamstress. As he climbed the stairs to his floor he heard the chatter of her sewing machine. In his kitchen he microwaved half of a spaghetti bolognese, one of the dishes he'd prepared on Sunday to see him through the week, and ate it in the main room while he watched the lengthy news. Unemployment rising, refugees drowning, wars multiplying... He finished a bottle of Chilean red as he watched a channel playing old comedy shows, and was starting to nod when he realised the show on the screen was taking him back to his boyhood. At least, it would have if he hadn't switched the television off and gone to bed.

He was awake well before dawn. Shadows of branches on the curtains barred the window. It was surely too late for the seamstress still to be busy and for Duggan to have heard wheels on the railway line. Most likely a bird was rummaging for food under the tree. Now it had gone or at any rate was silent, isolating Duggan with a thought that felt left over from a dream: next time wasn't until Saturday, five days away. He hadn't needed to think that for many years, and he did his best to send it back into the dark by proving he could sleep.

In the morning he avoided every handbill he was offered on his way to work. Nobody accosting him looked at all familiar, even if their reproachful looks began to be. Homeless folk were shifting blankets out of doorways as traders opened the shops. He hadn't realised so many people were sleeping rough. The sights felt like rebukes, and before he reached the opticians he dropped his change in a plastic cup beside a man in a padded bag. He didn't notice he was being watched until Stack blocked their doorway like a sentry in a box. "I hope you won't be attracting the homeless, Charles."

"I shouldn't think one little act of kindness is going to do that."

"So long as the word doesn't spread that anybody here is a soft touch. We don't want those people congregating round the shop and scaring off the customers."

"I can't imagine that's very probable either. I'd hope our customers are more compassionate than that."

"Our first care when we're here should be for them and for the business. That's what keeps our staff employed, we should remember."

Duggan found this so provocative that he retorted "You may be pleased to hear I didn't always care for people as I should."

"You surprise me. Anything further you'd like to confess?"

"There was a neighbour I was meant to visit when I was a boy." At once Duggan felt he'd said more than he should. "I've done my best to make up for it since," he said and made his way past the walls covered with empty spectacles to his room.

Perhaps his last remark had been too much as well, since he wasn't sure that it was true in any sense. As the day progressed the observation hung around him like a neglected task. His final appointment brought a ten-year-old relentlessly encouraged by his mother. "Tell the man what you can see," she urged. "You show him how well you can read."

The boy pronounced the first two lines on the sight chart readily enough but began to labour over the smaller letters below them. "Why," he said and more confidently "Oh, you."

"That isn't what it says, son. Don't pretend you can see if you can't."

The Bill

"That's perfectly all right, madam," Duggan said, replacing a lens in the frame he'd fitted to the boy's face. "Just say what you think is there, Brad."

"Any," the boy said with some defiance.

It took Duggan a moment to realise Brad was reading out two letters—misreading them, rather. In fact the line read **QCVMT**. The next lens corrected the boy's vision, and soon enough Duggan sent him out to Maarika, for his mother to choose his bespectacled look. "You'll like those, won't you, son," she said, reminding Duggan how he'd been told what to feel at that age—told he should be sorry for Mrs Twiss because she was on her own. So was he, but he hoped he never ended up like her, even if he grew that old.

On the way home he felt compelled to look for homeless folk. He could have thought the crowd was hiding them as if it was ashamed of them or of its own lack of intervention. He did glimpse a large black bird pecking at scraps in an alley, or was it a bird? Before he could determine how big the crouching shape was, it vanished with a rapid crooked movement around a corner of the alley. Perhaps it had been a dog or an urban fox, if foxes grew so dark and thin.

At home he finished off the bolognese. The seamstress must be working late, even if the noise like the insistent scratching of fingernails sounded as if it could be under the window. It ceased before he found the willingness to leave the couch. No doubt some people would think his nights at home were a little pathetic, but he'd had his fill of affairs when he was younger, and now he preferred to live his own life without having to accommodate anybody else. He liked to watch comedies when he could laugh as he wanted, not when it was expected of him.

He found a Chaplin film in the television listings magazine, only to discover that he couldn't laugh until he'd sorted out his thoughts—

indeed, until he'd identified them. Perhaps Mrs Twiss had been alone by choice as well; certainly whenever he'd had to visit her house she had behaved as if she didn't want anyone there, not least him. On the way to church she would always thank his parents for his help—"It's good of you to let the boy run errands for me"—but she had never thanked him. He'd done her shopping nearly every Saturday for over a year after her husband died, very possibly of the cigarettes whose smell loitered in the gloomy hall. Every time Duggan returned from the supermarket with the basket that she made him use—a tattered tartan object with wheels as rickety as its wicker handle—she crouched over it to pick through the contents like an official searching for contraband. She would be dressed from head to foot in black, mourning her husband and perhaps herself. Not just the fabric but her skin hung loose on her limbs. At last she would raise her gaunt wrinkled face to poke her nose and chin at him, features so sharp they resembled a claw. He'd often wondered where the food went, since the frozen contents of the bulging bag never seemed to lend her any extra weight. She would fix him with her small eyes, so pallid that the pupils were hardly distinguishable, and part her thin pale lips with a desiccated click. Each week her invariable phrase had sounded as much like a threat as a dismissal.

He'd thought of her quite enough for now. The memories had robbed the film of any humour. Of course the blind flower-seller wasn't meant to be comical, but he found he didn't care for the sight of her accosting passers-by or the notion that she didn't know who was near her, even though it was only Chaplin. Duggan drained the last glass of wine and switched off the film before the end. He knew the final line—"Yes, I can see now"—but another set of words drove it out of his head.

He slept so fitfully that he felt as if his mind was guttering like an

The Bill

intermittent flame. More than once a nightbird wakened him by scrabbling under the tree, and he even thought the sound came closer to his window. Sleep wasn't altogether preferable to wakefulness, since it brought dreams he would rather not have had. He was trudging helplessly to raise the rusty knocker on a door that towered above him. The next time the knocker felt scaly with earth, and summoned a rapid bony noise beyond the door. Before dawn he was downtown, where he was confronted by a sleeping-bag in the doorway of the Sight Site. He felt desperate to retreat as the bag began to squirm like a grub or else a chrysalis, but he couldn't avoid watching a bald head slither forth—bald of more than hair. At least he succeeded in floundering awake with an uncontrolled cry before he could see any face.

Nobody was sleeping in the doorway when he reached the shop, having eluded everyone who tried to detain him. Beneath the streetlamps their faces had looked unnaturally pale and thinned by shadows. For a change he was earlier than Stack. The masses of frames on the walls of the main room put him in mind of sockets emptied of eyes, like a dream he'd forgotten. He switched on all the lights in the other rooms as well, not least to fend off the fancy that one of the frames wasn't quite empty enough. Of course he was being watched or at least sent the odd glance by people in the street, but was somebody out there more concerned with him? When he peered through the window he thought for a moment that an early worker was rearranging the display in the department store across the pavement—planting shoes among the faceless mannequins, perhaps, since the activity looked close to supine. He must have glimpsed a passing shadow, because there was no sign of the dark bent shape.

He was still trying to recapture the impression when Stack arrived, frowning almost hard enough to dislodge his glasses. "Looking for the needy, Charles?"

Fearful Implications

"I was looking for whoever showed up," Duggan said, only to feel he could have taken more care over his words.

"You might like to save on the electricity till everyone does."

If he wanted any lights turned off, he could do it himself. He'd reminded Duggan how much of their work had to be performed in the dark. Duggan's first client of the day was a pensioner inseparable from a walking-stick and from a defiant smell of cigarettes. "I saw the other chappie last time," he was anxious to inform Duggan. "I thought he'd see me this year."

"If you'd care to wait I'll see if he can fit you in."

"That's all right," the man said, though it didn't sound entirely so. "We'll give you a chance."

Duggan used the tonometer to check for symptoms of glaucoma before ushering the customer into a consulting room, where the man tapped the floor to underline every letter he read on the illuminated chart. "Be," he declared and crouched forward over the stick. "No, is it ee?"

"Sit back if you would, Mr Havers." When the old man grudgingly complied, Duggan changed the lens in the frame. "Try it now."

"That's more like it should be," Havers said as though praising Duggan for tardy competence. "Ess, ee, ee again, why oh you en ee—"

"That's not it. That isn't it at all." As swiftly as his twitching eyes would let him Duggan read "Be aitch eff cue dee vee em ess . . ."

"No need to shout." Even more reproachfully Havers said "You've told me what they are now."

"You still have to read the rest," Duggan said and focused on the dwindling characters: K, T, Y, I, N, E . . . He saw nothing that should trouble him, and with the help of a substituted lens Havers read the letters easily enough. Duggan switched off the chart and the overhead light to carry out the tests that called for darkness. The old man's stick kept up a spindly commentary, scraping and clacking on the linoleum. It fell silent as Duggan turned the lights on, though he had the unnecessary notion that the noise had dodged under his desk. He fixed his attention on the screen while he printed off the man's prescription before escorting him out to Fabio. He was hurrying back to the consulting room when Stack waylaid him to murmur "Was there some problem with Havers? We could all hear a bit of a row."

"He's rather fond of making one with his stick."

"I'm aware of that, Charles. It didn't bother me last time I saw him. If you're running low on patience I trust you'll save it for our customers."

Duggan might have retorted that he was impatient only with his partner in the business. Before his next appointment he looked under the desk in the consulting room. While attending to Havers he could have heard a mouse, but there were no holes in the wall. More than one customer complained about the smell of tobacco, which lingered however wide he left the door between appointments. Whenever he had to darken the room he grew more aware of the odour. No doubt it was growing staler as it loitered, which was why it seemed to hint at the smell of something older still.

It could hardly have followed him onto the train home, though a passenger might be to blame. Duggan couldn't identify the culprit, and wasn't even sure that somebody had brought a dog on board. He thought he'd glimpsed it lying on the floor at the far end of the carriage, in which case he mustn't have observed it leaving with its owner, because once the crowd thinned out the crouched shape was nowhere to be seen.

As he walked home he couldn't tell whether a stray animal kept darting ahead of him. He seemed to hear its claws on the pavement, and each time he reached one of the dark gaps between streetlamps he thought it could be waiting there for him. Locking the front door behind him came as more of a relief than he would have liked to need. The seamstress was at work, and as he climbed the stairs he could have fancied that the rapid scrawny clatter was staying at his back.

Dinner was half of a chilli con carne and of a carton of rice. Wine helped him see it off but didn't do much for the vintage comedies he tried to watch. All the faces looked too pale, and he could have done without so many secondary characters laughing at the antics of the principals. Their grins struck him as excessively fixed, close to helpless. If he closed his eyes to shut out the sight he nodded off, only to jerk awake with a sense that it was time to perform a task, if it wasn't already too late. "Not yet," he heard himself mumbling. "Not Saturday."

"Needn't be."

The harsh thin whisper snatched his eyes open. It must have been in the film, which was fading to black at the end of a scene, leaving an impression of a figure on all fours that had thrust towards him a face he would have described as sketchy at best. He didn't see how such a character could have fitted into a Marx Brothers film, and in any case he'd lost all sense of what was going on. Downing the last of the wine, he made for bed.

The sound that roused him in the night reminded him of the ticking of a clock, relentlessly approaching. Perhaps this was simply because he was straining to distinguish it, or was it swarming up the tree? When he ventured to open his eyes he thought he glimpsed a shadow dodging through the outlines of branches. Surely it had been far too big for a squirrel. The streetlight must have magnified the shadow, and there was no reason to go to the window, though the stealthy silence made it hard for him to sleep.

The Bill

In the morning the Sight Site felt like a refuge, at least to begin with. Too many of the people he evaded in the street appeared to have been grinning at him. Perhaps the cold had fixed their expressions, but he didn't care to think of mouths that were incapable of concealing their teeth. He stayed in the main room of the shop, having switched its lights on, and tried not to glance across the street too often. Perhaps a bunch of shadows was lying low behind the dummies in the department store, but the only watchers were the eyeless frames on the walls around him. He was glad to see Stack, at least until he spoke. "Don't overdo it, Charles. That's too much the opposite."

"I've no idea what you mean."

"You look as if you don't want anybody coming in. You know who we need to keep away, and they aren't customers."

Duggan's first client was an old lady who sent him a pleading look as she sat in front of the tonometer. Having propped her chin on the ledge of the instrument, she winced and blinked whenever she thought he was about to release a puff of air into her eye. She was gripping the edge of the table with both hands, which would explain the muffled scrape of nails. When he managed to catch her off guard twice she gave a pair of muted cries, jerking her head back. "They feel as if you poked them in," she complained. "The other man was gentler."

Duggan didn't see how this could be possible. "The worst is over now," he said.

She wrinkled her nose as he followed her into the consulting room. "Has something died in here?"

Perhaps the cleaner had used stale water on the linoleum. Duggan might have moved the examination to the next room if Stack hadn't been in there with a customer. "Let's concentrate on your eyes, Mrs Wade," Duggan said as much to himself as to her.

He didn't want to think she was deliberately frustrating him.

Fearful Implications

However often he changed the lenses in the frames, she made no progress beyond the top line of the sight chart. "Take your time," he murmured. "Just try to see what's there."

"Tee," she said once he'd inserted yet another lens, and with growing conviction "Oh, oh again, ell ay tee ee."

"It doesn't say that." As he glared at the chart he could have thought that the letters were being twisted somehow, but his tired eyes must be misbehaving. T, O, D, L, A, Y, F... He almost missed the frame with the lens he was fumbling to insert. "Try now," he said, if he wasn't pleading.

When at last she read down to the third line without a mistake he switched off the chart and the overhead light as an aid to testing her field of vision. She clung to the switch for the buzzer, which she set off a good deal more often than the lights on the monitor were prompting her to do. Before Duggan could advise her to relax she protested "Don't do that. You're distracting me."

He wasn't sure that he wanted to learn "What are you saying I'm doing?"

"Leaning at me like that. You're making me think someone's inside your machine."

"Forgive me, but I haven't moved. I'm over here," Duggan said and sat back, trying not to feel he was retreating. Minutes later the computer ended the test—her vision was significantly more restricted than last year—and he would be able to put on the lights once he'd examined the backs of her eyes. She strained her eyeballs in the various directions he instructed, and he'd almost finished scrutinising the second eye when a smell of something far worse than aged lurched at him out of the dark. He couldn't help recoiling, but not far enough to avoid seeing the eye the lens magnified. Eye was too precise a word for it, though it was more than just an empty socket. It contained a withered fungoid item that didn't so much blink as shrivel further and then swell. All the same, he was sure that it saw him.

He cried out before Mrs Wade did. When the light came on he realised she must have recoiled from the smell at the same time he had, and was at least a foot away from the instrument. As he attempted to calm her, not to mention himself, Stack strode into the room, having dealt the door a single knock. "Shall I take over, Charles? How good to see you again, Mrs Wade."

The sight in the lens must have been a trick of perspective—of the angle from which Duggan had seen the frame, empty or at any rate filled just with darkness. He was trying to leave the incident behind when Stack came to find him. "What on earth was that about? We nearly lost a customer."

"Blame my clumsiness. I almost knocked a rack of lenses off the desk."

He was hoping the lie would suffice, but Stack lowered his head to peer hard at him. "If you've something on your mind, I'd like to know."

At once the pressure of memories was uncontainable. "The neighbour I was meant to look after when I was a boy, I was responsible for her death."

"How could that have happened, Charles?"

The rebuke was for presumption, not for his behaviour. "We were going off on holiday," Duggan insisted. "I'd have had to do two weeks' shopping for her and make two trips."

"She wasn't capable of doing her own shopping."

"She probably was. That's what I told myself at the time, but it's no excuse."

"Then I don't see how leaving her to do it could be fatal."

"I knocked at her door but I didn't wait long. I wanted to go to a film with my friends." As Stack made to comment Duggan said "She must have been hurrying to catch me. Apparently she fell downstairs and couldn't reach the door or her phone. I didn't go round for another week after we came home, and I told my parents I couldn't get an answer, but it was too late by then. She'd starved to death."

"May I ask what you told them before you went away?"

"Just that I hadn't been able to raise her."

"Then I think it was up to them to check on her. How old were you?"

"Old enough." When Stack didn't let this suffice Duggan said "Nine."

"By no means old enough to blame yourself. You should stop it here and now, and you'll forgive me if I don't see why it should affect our business."

"I ought to have cared more. I still should."

"Please don't do it here unless it's for our customers." Perhaps Stack took Duggan's silence for demurral. "Good God, take someone off the street home if you're so worried about everyone," Stack said. "I'm sure you'll have room."

"I wouldn't go that far."

"Well, there's an admission," Stack said and lowered his spectacles further, releasing a quizzical look. "A little honesty at last."

"If you care so much about the business," Duggan blurted, "maybe you should stop looking as if your glasses don't work."

The idea of inviting someone home had made him more nervous than he preferred to understand. Confessing his neglect had brought him no relief; it had simply brought memories closer. When he headed for the train Stack's suggestion dogged him, making him imagine that some of the shop entrances were already occupied by homeless folk or by someone who was using the doorways to dodge ahead of him. Surely nobody like that could be on the train, and he needn't think a dog was.

The Bill

There was no reason to believe one was at large in the streets near his house—at least, he wasn't sure he heard it in the dark between the lamps, its claws scraping the pavement, if that wasn't a bird pecking in search of food. As Duggan let himself into the house the sewing machine fell silent, though an echo that he hadn't previously noticed made it sound as though it was upstairs. He felt compelled to strain his ears, but couldn't even hear the seamstress.

Once he'd locked his door he headed for the kitchen. He was dismayed to see how careless he'd been. The refrigerator door was open at least half an inch, and he slammed it as soon as he took out tonight's portion of chilli. He'd left an empty bottle of wine on the floor in the main room, a sight rather too reminiscent of the litter a drinker in the street might leave. How drunk had he been last night that he didn't recall scrawling a word in the television listings magazine? It looked as if he'd gouged the word into the page. Whatever he'd decided he should SEE, he would look when he'd hung up his coat. He tramped into the bedroom, only to realise he hadn't even made the bed. A wind set the window scraping in its frame and brought up a smell of earth and decay from the garden as he crossed the room. He took hold of the crumpled sheets and found there was no need to throw them back. The shape that was clenched beneath them did that for him.

It hadn't been the window he'd heard scraping, and the smell hadn't come from outside. The twisted shape was even thinner than it had sounded, and much swifter than an object so deformed and incomplete had any right to be. It swarmed up his body like a spider, and its version of a face lurched at him on very little of a neck. Its closeness blotted out the light and his mind, so that he never knew if the intruder was clawing at his eyes or pecking at his face to feed.

Girls Dream

MOMMY'S STILL ALIVE, whatever daddy says. She's alive in BB's dreams. Every time BB goes to sleep she hopes she dreams of her. So long as she keeps on dreaming mommy can't die, and she's been alive as long as BB has. She's just been sleeping and not waking up, that's all. She's been sleeping for years, and now she's woken up.

A nurse with one eye crossed out brought her some new medicine but got called away before she could send it down one of the tubes mommy's wearing. That didn't waken mommy, but some men did. Biting one man's tongue out and shutting a door on his friend Buck's head must have tired mommy out, because once she's borrowed Buck's car she has to lie in it for hours talking to her toe. It's as if her toe's her only friend like BB wants to be.

It must be her friend, because it helps her get fit. She goes to see another lady who looks as if she lives in a playground, all the colours are so bright, and they start playing rough. They stop when the other lady's little girl comes home, but they start again once they've had a cup of coffee, and mommy's knife wins. The coffee must have meant they had to be polite or at least pretend, the way grownups do.

A plane takes mommy somewhere, and she's so angry she turns the

Fearful Implications

sky red. A man who knows daddy makes mommy a sword that she takes to a restaurant, which BB thinks can't be polite behaviour. Mommy fights so many people there BB can't count them. Someone says there are eighty-eight, and she has to trust that. The fight is more like dancing with red scarves and veils, only the red comes out of people. Once they're all dead or chopped up except for a boy mommy spanks, she goes in a snowy garden with another lady. BB hopes they'll make snowmen, but mommy slices the top of the lady's head off like an egg. BB is glad if this is just a dream.

Another plane takes mommy home to visit a man who lives in a metal house. He's waiting for her and shoots her with a gun that's full of salt and puts her in a box under the ground. You're only meant to do that to people who are dead. Mommy's almost been dead once, and she comes to life again and punches her way out of the box. The nurse with the crossed-out eye has killed the man who buried mommy, but mommy doesn't seem too grateful. The nurse has changed her clothes, even the bit that goes over her eye, except she hasn't got that one. The man who taught mommy to punch pulled it out, and the lady killed him for it. Mommy's so angry with her that she pulls out her other eye and stamps on it, and leaves the lady screaming and sprawling about like a mechanical doll that's gone wrong, not even able to see her pet snake. BB has to tell herself this isn't too bad a dream if it's keeping mommy alive.

An old man who knew daddy when he was a boy BB could have played with tells mommy where to find him, and it's no longer a dream. BB has known for so long that mommy is alive that it isn't even a surprise to see her. They play a game where BB and daddy pretend mommy shot them, but they're really impervious to bullets—daddy says so. Mommy seems upset at first when BB shoots her, but she must still be playing, because it isn't a real gun. When BB is in bed daddy

Girls Dream

says he shot mommy for real years ago, and mommy says it put her to sleep, which tells BB her dreams must have been more than dreams. She and mommy watch a movie called *Shogun Assassin* together as a bedtime treat, which is like seeing mommy fight in the restaurant and hearing BB talk about her to people watching the film. Before it's over BB falls asleep.

What kind of a dream is she having now? It feels as if mommy and daddy are acting it for her but don't know she's watching them. Mommy tells him that once she knew she was going to have a baby she couldn't kill people for him any more or even let BB be part of his life. Daddy says when she disappeared he thought she was dead, and BB wishes she'd told him she knew in her dreams mommy wasn't, though she doesn't suppose he would have believed her. Now mommy and daddy are going to fight, and she wants to stop them, but it's like watching a film when you can't change what the people in it have to do. First they show each other what they can do with swords, and then mommy hits daddy, and there's red coming out of his mouth. Grownups are funny, because he tells her she's his favourite person but sometimes she's a word you're not supposed to say. He buttons up his coat as if he's going out somewhere, and mommy tells him he's ready, but he doesn't walk far before he falls down. BB thinks he must have gone somewhere his body can't go, and if this is a dream, can she follow and see where? Before she manages she's just asleep until mommy wakes her up and says they have to go.

BB could imagine mommy's dreaming now, because she isn't owning up to how she feels except about BB. She doesn't let any of the rest out until they've checked into a motel and BB is watching a Heckle & Jeckle cartoon on the television. Mommy takes a teddy bear into to the bathroom as if she wants to go back to being little like BB, and BB hears her crying and then laughing, but she's left all that behind when

Fearful Implications

she comes out again, even the teddy bear. She lies down next to BB on the bed to watch the cartoon, and it could be the start of the life they should always have shared. Just one thing troubles BB, and she tries to put it out of her mind. She feels as if some other little girl might be dreaming them—the little girl whose mommy her own mommy killed—and she doesn't like to wonder how that dream might end.

A Name for Every Home

"Don't you know your ABC, Pad? Are they letting people go to university without it now?"

Patrick didn't look up from the map on his phone. A pad was where you lived, he thought, or what a dog did. "Just trying to do my job, Carl."

"Sort your post in alpha order. That's how you'll get round Garden Mile."

"Let Patrick learn for himself." Not quite without a pause their supervisor said "If that's how he works."

"That's not how Frank sorts the Mile, Eunice."

"Frank's off sick," she said.

She gazed at Carl until he returned to filling in a card to tell someone they couldn't have their mail before they paid a customs charge. Even if her rebuke was focused on Carl, Patrick felt less accepted than ever. She couldn't expect him to race through sorting when hardly a house in the suburb was numbered. "I expect he's right," he said and abandoned searching for house names on the map.

Carl watched him set about alphabetising envelopes on the wide desk topped by pigeonholes. "You won't get far if you aren't true to yourself, Pad."

Fearful Implications

Patrick twisted around, and a muscle throbbed as if someone had punched him in the back. "If you want the real me then for a start that's not my name."

Nearby workmates hooted with amusement. "Don't get in a paddy, Paddy," Carl said.

"That isn't either."

"There'll be time for jokes when everything's delivered," Eunice said.

Patrick tried and failed not to respond. "I didn't hear much of a joke."

"You might like to try a bit harder to get on with your colleagues."

Sensing their contempt, Patrick took a silent breath so fierce it sucked in a smell of envelopes. The huge room put him in mind of a hive—the apian buzz of strip lights, letters fluttering like wings, postal workers bumbling at their honeycombs of pigeonholes—but if this made everybody into drones, didn't that include him? His clammy hands were stained with ink by the time he finished transferring letters and packages to the delivery trolley. "Done," he said, but nobody bothered to respond.

A prematurely autumnal September wind chilled his bare knees as he wheeled the trolley into the shopping precinct, where people were queuing to collect their undelivered mail. The first time he'd worn his postman's uniform he'd felt like an overgrown schoolboy condemned to walk the streets as a punishment for failure. Beyond the precinct—charity shops, off-licences, coin arcades, betting shops—the residential streets began. In ten minutes houses trapped between one another gave way to larger buildings split into apartments, one of which was Patrick's. A carer was coaxing a large slack-faced youth into the house next door, while on the other side two families were sitting on the doorstep and conferring in a language Patrick didn't recognise. They gazed expectantly at him until he realised they saw a postman, not a neighbour. "I'm not your man," he called, "he should be along soon," but all six of them sent him a frown that suggested he was talking nonsense.

The Victorian streets led to a wide dual carriageway, beyond which lay Garden Mile. The suburb appeared to possess its own exclusive stretch of sky, dark with a threat of rain. As Patrick crossed the road, having waited quite some time for a green sketch of a man to scrounge light from the red, a silver Bentley saloon raced in front of him just inches from the trolley. By the time he found breath for an appropriate word the car was swerving through a gap in the central reservation to speed around a bend into Garden Mile.

A car door and a boot slammed somewhere ahead as Patrick wheeled the trolley into the broad road. Every house was resolutely individual and surrounded by a garden several times its area. Each garden boasted at least one vehicle expensive enough to star in a showroom—a Jaguar, a Mercedes, a Rolls Royce—and each gate displayed a name. Patrick was past the first bend by the time he saw a name he recalled from sorting the mail—Dogs Home.

The displaced Swiss chalet didn't look as though it boarded dogs, and no kennels were apparent, but as Patrick dropped a letter in the box attached to the bars of the gate, a Doberman bounded around the house, baring its yellowed teeth. It clawed at the top of the gate as if determined to clamber over, and he'd put the trolley between himself and the animal when a man yelled "Gutter."

Patrick might have felt directed there if the dog hadn't dropped to all fours with a frustrated snarl and trudged back to the house. So that was the dog's name, and the words on the gate could have been a warning. He wheeled the trolley around a bend to the next house he had mail for, an Italianate villa called the Watch. It lived up to its name

Fearful Implications

by taking his photograph with a security camera as he approached the solid seven-foot gate. He pushed a package under the metal flap of the wide slot in the gate, and it was yanked out of his hand. Surprise made him blurt out the last thought he'd had. "I'd have said cheese if I'd known you were after my photograph."

"We don't have smilers in our gallery."

Though the woman's sharp voice invited no response, Patrick retorted "Which one is that?"

"The one we keep rogues in."

"I'm not one of those. I'm your postman."

The metal flap gave him a glimpse of a pair of eyes brimming with moisture and clanked shut at once. "You're not the usual man."

"He's ill. Won't I do?"

"We'll have him back." Her voice was receding, and Patrick heard slippers shuffling along a path. "We trust him," she said.

Patrick wasn't going to let her make him feel like an intruder, never mind a criminal looking for properties to rob or otherwise up to mischief. He trundled the trolley along the middle of the road while he peered at names on gates, and caught sight of a plaque he must be misreading. He had to laugh at his mistake, and then at the mistake the laugh was. When he pushed the trolley up the ramp leading over the pavement to the open gates he saw that the house was indeed called the Pad.

It pointed jazzy angles of white concrete in every direction, no two of them alike. Just the windows were rectangular. One displayed the front room and, beyond sliding doors, a kitchen and an outdoor barbecue. Among the cars parked on the drive he saw a silver Bentley that he recognised from letters on the registration plate—DRG. He was making to move onwards when two rather less than teenage children ran around the house. "Got something for us?" the girl scarcely asked, and the boy supplied a translation or an additional demand. "Got us something?"

They were plainly twins, and they looked oddly familiar—their small skinny angular faces expressive of a dull dogged hunger their owners mightn't even have defined. "Nothing today, I'm afraid," Patrick said.

Their tired eyes narrowed and their thin lips drooped. "It's our birthday," the boy complained, and his sister was anxious to establish "Both of ours."

"Happy birthday, both."

"Kiera," the girl said as if Patrick should have known, and jabbed a finger with a chewed nail at the trolley. "Look for me."

"And Kieron," the boy urged him.

"Trust me, I'd know if there was anything for this house."

"Why would you?" Kiera demanded, and Kieron contributed "You heard, why?"

"You mightn't believe me if I told you." In a bid to end the confrontation Patrick said "Just enjoy your day. I expect that's why you're off school."

"Who's asking that? Who wants to know?"

This came from the man who stalked around the house, a wiry fellow with muscular veinous arms and a larger version of the children's face. Despite its size, the features—meagre eyes and mouth, aggressively pointed nose and chin—looked even more compressed. He halted for a moment, staring at Patrick, and then marched faster at him. "Fucking nora," he said. "Paddy Ransome."

"Mel Cousins. Well, good lord."

Mel stuck out a hand only to take it back. "Weren't you supposed to go to uni?"

"I did." When Mel's red-eyed stare persisted Patrick said "I've been a waiter and worked in a bar, and this is what I'm doing now."

"Fucking nora." Mel jerked his head at the trolley. "Bring it round," he said. "Shouldn't think you're in a panic."

"No rush," Patrick said and followed him around the house.

About a dozen people sat on garden chairs near the paved patio where the barbecue stood. Children were bouncing somewhat desultorily on an inflated castle at the far end of an expansive lawn. "You've done well for yourself," Patrick felt he should remark.

"It's my old man's too."

Patrick thought the women in the audience might appreciate a further comment. "Just yours?"

"We got rid of the wives if they're what you mean. They weren't helping the firm," Mel said and showed Patrick his back. "Dad, here's Paddy Ransome we called Pad at school. He went to uni but this is all it got him."

A stocky man was turning burgers over on the barbecue as though searching under stones for some unwelcome lurker. He raised a puffy instance of the Cousins face to squint at Patrick. "Old friend, are you, Pad?"

Patrick felt it might be unwise to object to the name. "I expect you could say so," he said with equal caution.

"Fancy making yourself a bit of extra? We could use you and your wagon."

"I don't know if I could do that." When not just all the adults but the Cousins twins stared at him, Patrick gave way to saying "What would it involve?"

"Better stuff than I ever sold at school," Mel said. "Give it here, Rod."

A man in a garden chair passed him a device Patrick had assumed was a cigarette substitute. When Mel held it out Patrick said awkwardly "I never liked it much. I'd rather not go back there. My mind's in enough of a state."

"It's the cleanest you can get. It's oil." Since Patrick remained unpersuaded, Mel said "Watch."

He depressed a button on the pipe and applied a lighter, inhaling at such length that Patrick held his breath. As Mel let out a protracted plume of smoke Patrick sucked in a lungful of air, only to find it brought him the smoke. "Whoa," Mel said. "You got some after all."

His delight appeared to spread his features, slowly and relentlessly. His head nodded towards Patrick, bobbing like a balloon on the string of his neck. "I'd rather not have anything to do with it," Patrick heard himself declare too late.

"You just did," an amused spectator told him.

Patrick turned to argue, not least to persuade himself they were wrong, and felt as if he might never stop turning. As he seized the trolley for support Mel's father said "No call for that, Pad. Nobody's going to rob your mail."

"I wasn't. I didn't mean." Patrick left the rest of the sentences behind while he stumbled in search of an empty chair. A herbal odour had lodged in his nostrils and was extending tendrils to net his brain. How could that be? Perhaps if he found words to define the sensation, it would go away—perhaps its effects would. He sank onto a skeletal canvas chair, but he couldn't hide in it when everyone's attention had settled on him like a web. In the hope of subduing his sensations he said "Could I have a drink?"

Mel was refilling the pipe. "Fetch Pad a can, Kieron."

The boy slouched into the kitchen, which was tiled white as a morgue, and hauled open a freezer Patrick could imagine lying in to chill his unhappily clammy self. Of course nobody would shut him in there, but he kept a nervous eye on it until Kieron slammed the lid. When the boy brought him the prize Patrick grabbed the can of lager and rolled it across his forehead, which had grown so tight it was

Fearful Implications

squeezing out trickles of sweat. "Show some fucking manners," Mel's father warned him. "Don't be snatching off the kid."

"Sorry," Patrick blurted, though he wasn't sure to whom. He peeled off the metal tag, remembering barely in time not to lob the grenade, however much he might feel he was acting in a film. He poured a metallic mouthful into himself, belatedly recalling how to swallow. "Needed that," he spluttered before admitting "Thought I did."

Was it quelling the effects of the pipe? When Mel had passed around a sample joint at school there had been nothing to counteract them, and now Patrick couldn't tell how the combination of substances was affecting him. The pipe was advancing towards him along the line of chairs, marking its progress with clouds of smoke he could smell. Mustn't this mean he was breathing them in? He covered his nose and mouth with a moist bloated hand, but his neighbour offered him the pipe. "No, please no," Patrick babbled from behind his hand and made a grab for dignity. "I said not for me, thanks."

Kiera nudged her brother, giggling. "Scared to do a pipe, him."

Patrick lowered his ponderous unwieldy hand so as to deal them a stern look. "I hope you both are. Stay that way."

As the stereoscopic image—one face for each of his eyes—opened its mouths, Mel's father said "Watch out who you think's your friend, son."

"I'd like to think I can tell," Patrick said.

"Not you, you twat. When's he going, Mel?"

The balloon that bobbed at Patrick had regained its dissatisfied look. "Give us what you've got and you can take your can with you," Mel said.

Patrick peered along the line of chairs in search of sympathetic witnesses, but those who weren't indifferent were no better than amused. "Your father said you wouldn't rob me," he pleaded.

Mel's face swelled towards him, and Patrick was afraid it wouldn't stop short of merging with his own head. "What are you calling us, Pad?"

"Nothing if I shouldn't. I didn't think you were that kind of, not that kind of anything, any kind at all."

As Patrick managed to catch up with his own words and restrain them, Mel's father said "Kind of what?"

"No kind. That's what I said, only what do you want to take? I don't mean drugs," Patrick said, outrun by his speech again. "That's nothing to do with me."

"Better believe it. Better remember."

"He's saying we're villains. That right, Pad?"

Patrick would have said anything that might fend off the face, which seemed as huge and hostile as the world. "I was saying you wouldn't steal from me."

"Who'd we rob instead?" The face lurched closer before receding so swiftly that Patrick saw it deflate. "Give us what you've got for us and you can piss off with the rest," the newly shrunken Mel said.

"I told your two, I've got nothing. Perhaps whoever's on the next round will have some."

"What the fuck are you doing here, then?"

"I thought you invited me."

"Guess what I'm telling you now."

For a paralysed moment Patrick assumed he was required to read Mel's thoughts and voice them. As he wobbled to his feet he kept hold of the can of lager, which emitted a screechy creak. "Can I still take this?"

"Take your brew and your walker and best of the lot yourself," Mel's father said. "And get them to send us someone else next time."

He couldn't want that more than Patrick did. Patrick managed to relax his grip on the can as he planted it on one of the lids of the trolley, and felt he ought to say "Thank you for the drink."

"Just keep your garbage to yourself," Mel told him.

"Why do you have to say that? Your father wanted manners. I was trying to be polite."

Mel let his mouth hang open in an idiot's grimace and jerked a thumb at the trolley. "Your garbage there, you stupe."

"I don't think you can call it that just because there wasn't anything for here."

"He's a giggle," Mel's father said without providing any evidence and stared at Patrick. "Mel's saying keep your can out of our road."

"Is it all right if I drop it in somebody else's?"

Presumably Patrick didn't say this, even though he heard himself, since nobody reacted. He was taking care not to dislodge the can while he swivelled the trolley when a woman said "You want to get yourself a car."

"How do you know what I want?" To head off this retort Patrick made haste to ask "Why?"

"Then you wouldn't have to potter about with that contraption. You look like some old feller with a walker."

"At least I won't be killing anyone with it."

This prompted an ominous silence broken only by his irregular rubbery heartbeat—no, the thumps of unshod feet inside the giant blancmange—the castle, rather. "What are you calling us now?" Mel said.

"I was just wondering who nearly ran me over on their way to your house."

"That was you in the road, was it? If we'd wanted you dead you'd be dead."

Patrick saw Kiera and Kieron exchange an eager look, which he was

A Name for Every Home

less than anxious to understand. As he turned away he saw the castle set the house prancing. The concrete building calmed down as he hurried past it, and the nearby houses gradually ceased their dance. Perhaps the dark sky was some use if it had restrained them by weighing on them.

Was it safe to walk in the road? Might a car try to run him down? Surely Mel had said not, and Patrick emptied the can of lager down his throat to quell his nervousness. If that made him wander across the roadway, imitating its curves but in reverse, the deliveries ought to keep him on track. He had to veer towards each house to read its name, not the easiest of tasks while the letters jittered like faulty digital displays, if indeed that wasn't what they were. His footsteps and the stormy rumble of the trolley were the only sounds, because everyone in Garden Mile was staying quiet so as to listen to him. They would have heard him announce a name he had mail for—the Spikes, where the package barely fitted through the slot in the gate. Despite the barbs that topped the wall he thought the name might denote needles too, but couldn't be sure if he'd said so aloud. He had a bunch of bills for High Walls, and mustn't think high balls or bills for balls, let alone utter the words, or he might never stop laughing. Wasn't that preferable to feeling afraid? He couldn't afford either while he had a job to finish, and soon he came to Justus with a sheaf of envelopes. "Not justice," he told himself, only to find the comment menacing. The riverine meandering of the road had brought him behind the Pad, and as the antics of the castle threatened to infect the houses he anticipated seeing the Cousins family and all their guests bounce in unison above the wall. He gripped his mouth to trap hilarity, and was glad to find he'd reached another house with mail, the Palms. It greeted him by raising its green hands on their scaly arms above a hedge, and he was about to slip the envelopes through its expressionless mouth on the gate when he recalled sorting just one item for this house. He peered at the second envelope and saw it was addressed to the Pad.

The envelopes must have been stuck together when he'd sorted them. He would surely have noticed if his workmates hadn't distracted him. Best to deliver everything else first, and he drove the trolley through the gathering gloom. Harmoney House, the Manshun, Ray 'n' Beau's End... These and others kept him murmuring observations, and he was sure he'd walked considerably more than a mile by the time he completed the round. As he dropped the empty can in a compartment of the trolley he was overtaken by a notion that he'd misdelivered some item. Surely the recipient could take it to their neighbour.

The engine of his vehicle rattled all the way back to the Pad. If he ever owned a car he suspected that was how it might sound. He should have had it fixed, because the relentless clatter brought Mel around the house as Patrick ventured through the gate. "What are you snooping round here now for?" Mel demanded.

His children were behind him. "It's the old man with his walker," Kieron wanted somebody to know.

"It's a baby with a buggy," Kiera was determined to suggest.

"Shut it, you. What are you after, Pad? Seeing what else we do?"

"I'm just doing my job."

"Not making a bit on the side. Not spying on us for the law." As Patrick made to laugh this off Mel said "Don't waste your time. Some of those are out the back."

Patrick would have been entirely happy not to learn so much. He couldn't judge how closely his answering noise resembled a laugh, and it felt unhelpfully belated. "I'm nothing but a postman," he insisted. "I had mail for you after all."

"You told these you'd got none."

"I'd mixed it up with someone else's."

Mel remained suspicious when Patrick retrieved the envelope, which was large and pink. Was he wondering how Patrick could have overlooked such an item? The children ran to seize it, and Patrick was afraid they might rip the contents apart. "Who's going to open it?" he said, holding it above his head. "Better be just one."

"What are you making them jump for? They're not fucking dogs."

"I just thought you mightn't want it destroyed, Mel."

"Never mind thinking what I want. I'll have you destroyed, pal." With no lessening of menace Mel said "Give it here."

Too late Patrick realised he could have ascertained who the mail was for. He'd assumed the birthday card would be addressed to both the children, unless the envelope contained a pair of cards, though was it bulky enough? As he made to examine it, Mel snatched it, and Patrick had to refrain from saying that the elder Cousins would have found that impolite. He was heading for the gate when Mel said "Tell us you're having a laugh."

As Patrick turned, the untimely gloom hindered him like water if not mud. Mel was brandishing the open envelope at him—the empty envelope. "Where's the card?" Patrick protested, he scarcely knew to whom.

"No card in here, Pad. No fucking thing else either."

Patrick stared at the yawning beak, the pink entrance to a woman, the way back into a womb, and fought to concentrate. "Someone must have taken it."

"Who are you calling a thief now?"

"I can't say, can I?" Patrick struggled not to let his gaze stray across Mel and the children in case it looked accusing. Surely it made sense to ask "Who was it for?"

Mel glared at the envelope and then at him. "Looks like you, Pad."

Fearful Implications

Since he didn't move, Patrick had to venture back to him. As Mel turned the envelope towards him he spat on it—no, a large raindrop fell on a line of handwriting. The line was all Patrick had previously seen, and now he saw it was the whole of the address. *To the Pad*, it said. "You're right," he told Mel. "It must be a joke."

"Who's having one of them?"

Patrick watched the letters settle down from writhing and assume a final shape. The scrawl looked childish, which made him think Kiera or Kieron was responsible. Might they have slipped the envelope into the trolley while Mel's father had diverted him away from it? He could equally suspect any of a number of his workmates. "I can't say that either," he said.

"Bet you can't. More like it's an excuse for you to come sneaking back."

"Why would I want to do that?" Patrick saw the answer in Mel's eyes, considerably worse than a warning. If he'd been closer to escaping through the gate he mightn't have lingered to be rational. "Don't be paranoid, Mel," he said.

"What's going to make me that, Pad?"

"What you had before. You won't say you aren't stoned."

"So are we," Kieron said.

"It's our birthday," Kiera said as if this hadn't been made plain.

"I've got to say I am a bit myself." In case it helped, Patrick added "In honour of the occasion."

"Don't try making out you're like us." Some element of the exchange had infuriated Mel. "Pity I didn't run you over," he said, "while I had the chance."

"You can't really mean that. There are children listening."

"And don't you fucking tell them what I mean. Here's your message." He thrust the envelope at Patrick and turned to the children.

"Watch out for him," he said. "You wouldn't like to be him if he came back."

Patrick dropped the envelope in the compartment that wasn't occupied by the empty can and made with a defiant series of clanks for the gate. From the pavement he saw the children watching him like guards. On his way back to the barbecue Mel shouted "You're not kidding us you didn't write it, Pad."

How could Patrick have been responsible? Where would he have found the envelope or the opportunity to write on it, or a reason? Mel's suggestion had left him feeling that his memory was wrong—that his whole mind was. He needed to show Eunice the item in the hope that somebody owned up. As he headed for the main road he grew anxious to locate a bin where he could bring the clatter of the trolley to an end. The dark sky looked too burdened to keep hold of its rain, but so far not a drop had touched him. Lightning flashed as he passed the Watch— no, the security camera caught him once more. He turned the bend that brought Dogs Home in sight, and Gutter started barking. Patrick wasn't about to be driven off the pavement, and he was marching past the gate when a man called "Hi there, postman. Just wait, will you."

His voice was as clipped as his grey hair and moustache. He was waving an envelope—the first item Patrick had delivered. "This isn't ours," he complained. "It's not remotely like."

The Doberman sprang up as Patrick took the envelope, and the dog's jaws clicked shut only inches from his hand. "Down, you brute," the man said. "It doesn't care for strangers."

Patrick had to squint hard at the restless letters to grasp that the house where he should have left it was called Boosome. Even if the name made no sense, how could he have misread it? Mel hadn't affected his mind then, but Patrick felt as if their encounter had undermined time. Though the savage antics of the dog gave him little chance to think, he seemed to recall having seen the name somewhere on his round, surely not just on the envelope. "Sorry to have troubled you," he said.

As the dog bounded at the gate again its owner strode back to the house. For long enough to let the gloom droop lower overhead Patrick tried to think which way to move. He felt as if he was attempting to look down on Garden Mile, still at his desk and searching the map. How distant was the address he had to find? The Doberman was leaping higher, snarling through its teeth, and he had a sense that the entire suburb was growling at him. It wouldn't stop him performing his job. He wasn't going to give anyone an excuse to criticise him, and he tramped back along the road. At the bend he turned to bid some kind of farewell to the dog, which seemed to need no breath to bark. He'd hardly met its eyes when it vaulted over the gate and raced after him.

He wasted seconds in fancying this was his latest hallucination, and then he fled. The Watch greeted his clangourous approach with another flash of lightning, and the pavement around him broke out in a nervous rash. More of the rain streamed down his face, unless that was the juice of his panic. It blurred his vision while he dashed towards the Pad, where he saw faces at an upstairs window. As the dog appeared at the bend in the road Patrick rushed the trolley to the open gates. He hadn't reached them when Kiera and Kieron came out of the house.

They had been at the window, and he thought they'd been watching for him. Kiera was jigging to a repetitive ditty on her phone, and her brother had a gun. Patrick floundered through the gates after the trolley, and the boy pointed the toy at him. "Is that a birthday present?" Patrick said. "It looks real."

"It's our grandad's and you have to piss off."

Kiera continued to jerk like a puppet as if neither she nor the phone felt the rain. "You come in," she warned, "and you'll get what dad said."

A Name for Every Home

Patrick heard claws clacking on the tarmac and a snarl that grew lower but closer. He flung back one of the lids of the trolley to see just his envelope and the Boosome item. "Not them," he pleaded and found the empty can to shy at the dog. It bounced off the animal's head, and the dog gave a yelp before redoubling its snarl and padding towards him. "Let me stay," Patrick begged the children. "I'll make it right with your father."

Through the house he saw Mel and others busy erecting a shelter beyond the crowded kitchen. He took another step, and Kieron raised the pistol. "Not me," Patrick blurted. "The dog."

He stooped to yank the bolt of the left-hand gate out of its socket, and was shutting the gate when he heard his vehicle backfire. It couldn't, since it had no engine, but he'd been distracted by a dull punch on his back. He clung to the gate while he stumbled to face the children. Kiera was continuing to prance, and her brother had him covered. "He's not gone yet," Kiera said.

Patrick tried joining in the dance as he lunged at the other gate. His capering impressed neither of the children, and might even have provoked the blow his chest took. Somebody behind the house—Mel or his father—wondered loudly what had just happened, but nobody came to look. "All right," Patrick said with more dignity than he'd realised he possessed, "I'll take my chances with the dog," and staggered past the gates. Perhaps he hadn't made himself heard, unless it didn't matter, because he received a parting thump on the back of his skull.

It carried him into the road, where he sprawled face down on the tarmac. The sky collapsed on him—the downpour did, at any rate. Perhaps that was why he could barely see the dog until its muzzle met his cheek. He couldn't move enough to flinch, but in any case the dog was only licking rain off him. Was it merely rain that was inundating

FEARFUL IMPLICATIONS

the road around him? Dance music grew louder as the children came to view him, and he thought lightning had accompanied them until he heard the whir of a shutter on a phone. In the distance a man gave a cry of disgust or frustration about him if not the weather. As Patrick felt himself begin to spread through Garden Mile, he could only wonder if this would help him deliver the last of the mail.

The Run of the Town

CRAMP WAKENED PLATER before dawn. He sprawled out of bed and lurched stiff-legged around the hotel room, ending up at the window. As he gripped the sill so hard his nails bent while he stretched out his leg in the hope of diminishing the pain, he glimpsed activity in the distance. Beyond ranks of grey roofs descending a hill a park was dimly lit by streetlamps. The pale glow outlined a statue at the junction of several paths, and when he strained his eyes Plater made out joggers in the park. Perhaps they were keeping fit for the hilly streets, though he would have thought the streets themselves might keep them trim. The cramp had subsided to a dull ache, and he limped back to bed.

He hadn't planned to spend the night away from home. Helping Carol unload her belongings at the university—such a carload that it had left no space for her mother—had taken hours longer than he'd anticipated. On the drive home he'd met a downpour so relentless that he could see no more than a few yards ahead. Though the fog of spray failed to slow the traffic, several accidents did, and once he was reduced to crawling little more than a mile in an hour he'd followed an exit sign he could scarcely read. He'd left the rain and the daylight behind by the time he found the hotel at the edge of Chalmerston, a small steep grey Derbyshire town. He didn't think he'd seen the name on the motorway sign, but just then he couldn't have imagined a more welcome sight than the hotel car park.

A twinge of cramp roused him from dozing. A blob of sunlight mushroomed in the clotted greyish sky above the jagged horizon. Plater used the shower, which suffered from an intermittent chilly stutter, and took the lift down to the basement. As he collected items from the breakfast buffet—enough to last him all the way home without a break—several greying couples bade him a muted English morning. He was back in his room when he thought of walking before driving, not least to work out the last persistent trace of cramp. He brushed his teeth with the flimsy instrument the hotel provided, and was crossing the lobby when the hotel receptionist, a squat broad long-faced man, halted him with a frown. "Leaving us already?"

"Just going for a walk first." Plater felt sufficiently accused to add "I'll settle up now if you like."

"No call for that. We've got you written down." The man tapped the computer screen in front of him, which emitted a pinched clink. "Not here for the chase, then," he said.

"I can't say I am."

The man raised his head, which seemed both to lengthen his face and intensify his disapproval. "You're one of them who'd like it stopped, are you?"

"I might if I knew what it was. If we're talking about hunting, surely that's banned."

"We leave the wild life to itself round here. It can't help what it gets up to, not like you and me."

"Then I'm honestly lost. What were you thinking I should know?"

"You've got a way with words and no mistake." The frown squeezed the comment dry of any trace of praise. "Best thing might be," the receptionist said, "the world forgets about us."

"You aren't still talking about you and me."

"I'm talking about history some interfering buggers want to do away with."

"I hope you don't think I'm one of those. I've just dropped off my daughter who's studying history."

"I'd not like to say what I think. The way they teach history these days..." With a breath fierce enough to do duty as an observation the receptionist said "Tradition, that's what they want to get rid of."

"I really don't think that's altogether the case. Will you have met many lecturers yourself?"

"Meddlers." Apparently to clarify, the man said "The ones who want to try and take away our character."

Plater had to assume "Of your town."

"It's been three hundred years and more, and the town's getting on for that too. That's when they started mining far side of the hill."

"And before that..." When the man didn't answer, Plater said "What was more than three hundred years back?"

"The real chase, and if you ask me it did none of them much harm. If they hadn't lived round here they might have come off a lot worse." The man's head jerked as though he'd wakened from a reverie. "Any road," he said, "you'll be wanting your walk."

Plater might have enquired further if the phone on the counter hadn't rung. As he made for the street the glass door crept aside for him. On his way downhill he had to step into the road to avoid an aproned butcher who was hauling out an awning with a hook. Otherwise the street was deserted except for a large whitish dog that fell to all fours from nosing in a bin and fled along an alley at Plater's approach. Ahead he saw the river to which the streets led down both sides of the valley—water that the sky turned a grey like the colour of sluggishness—but he was heading for the park.

Or was it a park? Perhaps it once had been. When he located the entrance, having followed a hedge twice his height and so impenetrably tangled that it wasn't much less solid than a wall, he found the gates were padlocked. Through the rusty iron bars, which were as spiky as the hedge, he saw that the place must have been abandoned quite a while ago, since the weedy grass between the trees had grown taller than him. Nevertheless the area was still in use, perhaps only by intruders. The tracks he'd mistaken for ordinary paths last night had been forced through the vegetation, to judge by the only one leading away from the entrance—from a gap in the hedge beside the lichened pillar that supported the left-hand gate.

The gap was barely wide enough for him to sidle through. Perhaps children had originally made it, breaking off the twigs that were strewn outside the hedge, and the joggers he'd seen were sufficiently thin to fit. He clenched himself to slimness so as not to be scratched by the thorns, because he was interested in visiting what he'd seen from the hotel window, not to mention the large house that his vantage point had hidden. Encountering so many students yesterday had left him feeling old and unadventurous. Once he would have been eager to explore a place like this, and he could think of no reason not to feel that way still.

Whoever had trampled the grass seemed to have been in no hurry to arrive at the house, for the sodden brownish path took quite a devious route among the trees. Well before he reached the statue Plater crossed several other tracks, which wandered maze-like out of sight through the grass. They appeared to converge on the statue, which was encircled by a wider patch of trodden vegetation. He was close to the weathered figure before he noticed that it and its companions had their

THE RUN OF THE TOWN

backs to him.

They faced the house, where planks were nailed across the lofty front door and every visible window was boarded up. The eroded statues bristled with wads of moss, and the central figure's face had sloughed away like fungus. The features of both of the heads on which its hands rested had fallen off as well, and Plater couldn't imagine what expressions they might have borne as the pair of figures stooped forward. No doubt the stance was meant to acknowledge the touch of their benefactor, however much they resembled runners awaiting the start of a race. Having searched in vain for names—not even the main figure was identified—Plater made for the house.

Five windows flanked each side of the pillared porch, and a solitary trampled path led to the nearest left-hand window, from which a board had been wrenched loose. The pane was smashed as well, and through the gap he could just distinguish a room so large that the muffled sunlight fell short of most of it. As his eyes adjusted to the dimness he saw an indistinct reflection of the statue in a mirror across the room. The gap between the boards was so narrow that it would take somebody thinner than him to clamber through, and in any case that seemed more foolhardy than adventurous. Instead he leaned against a scaly flaking pillar of the porch and used his phone to search for Chalmerston.

It had been a miners' town until the industry exploded into conflict in the eighties. After the mine was shut down, Chalmerston had become a centre for walkers in the countryside. The Wikipedia entry made no mention of any kind of chase, and Plater wondered if whoever the receptionist had accused of trying to end the tradition could have edited the article. As a breeze made the broken pane whistle, a sound so thin it might have been issuing between teeth, he tried looking up Chalmerston Chase. It was an annual event, a May Day run through the town, all the way from the top to the bottom and up the other side. May Day was nearly a week hence, but Plater didn't know if he would have enjoyed the spectacle of competitors exerting themselves so much. Apparently the event was called Chalmer's Chase, and as Plater searched for further information he tried to ignore the attenuated whistling, which sounded as though it was inside the house. There was indeed a campaign to end the tradition, not least because former miners from nearby towns thought it offensive to celebrate a workers' holiday with an event based on the exploitation of their counterparts centuries ago. By now Plater was certain that somebody was whistling between their teeth and calling in a low voice to a dog. How had people been exploited round here in the past? Another online reference established that the event had originally been known as Charmer's Chase, named for a bygone dignitary and landowner, Justice Charmer —quite possibly, Plater thought, the former owner of the ruined mansion. Had Justice been his name or his calling or both? Supposedly he'd pardoned local criminals so long as they took an oath to guard his property—"to chase away the inquisitive", though the reason was left undefined. Between toothy whistles the man somewhere nearby was still calling the dog, which was presumably able to hear even such a low voice. In fact, there must be more than one, though would anybody give dogs such names except as a joke? "Walker... Hunt... Hill..." A final online link questioned the view of Charmer as benevolent, suggesting that he contrived to find too many of the tenants of the farms and cottages on his land guilty of some offence in order to increase the patrol, and that he'd hold them to their vow even once they'd reached an age that seemed unreasonable if not positively unnatural. If this or any other aspect of his behaviour had eventually provoked a reaction, it seemed to be nowhere on the record, much like the end of Justice Charmer. Perhaps the voice was distant, not muffled, and could its owner be calling his employees to a job? "Hall... Wood... Stone..." The words needn't even be the names of people; perhaps they related to some renovation of the house, and the reiterated whistle might be an inadvertent mannerism. Plater's wanderings online had just prompted a random thought—that charmer was another word for wizard—when the phone twitched in his hand.

The bell was as shrill as the whistling. He had an irrational fancy that he'd attracted the call with his online search, even when he read the caller's name. As he raised the phone to speak it said "Pater."

The word threw him so much that he demanded "What are you saying?"

"Only teasing, dad. My roommate calls hers that. I was only calling to say thank you for being—"

He had to believe he'd misheard Carol's last word. "Being dad, you said."

"What else would I have? You're not driving, are you? You sound a bit distracted."

"I will be. Driving, that's to say. The traffic was so wretched I stayed somewhere overnight."

"Then don't let me stop you getting back to mum. Have a good run and I'll call you when you're free."

As Plater put away his mobile he heard the whistle and the voice. He found it even harder to determine how far away the fellow was, though he seemed to be calling for a painter. Despite his eagerness to set off for home, Plater went back to the broken window. The only figure to be seen was the reflection in the mirror, and it occurred to him that the statue might have been situated so that the owner of the house could see his own image from any of the front rooms. Leafy shadows on the statue lent restless movements to the dim discoloured shape across the room. A trick of light or of perspective obscured its companions, so that Plater might have imagined that the outstretched hands were resting on emptiness—in fact, that they were lifted higher and extended further than the ones behind him. He swung around to see that there were no shadows on the statue, just patches of moss. He hadn't time or any wish to think why he made at some speed for the path to the gates.

He could still hear the man calling out names. Perhaps one of them was Painter, not anybody's job after all. Even once the statue was behind him Plater could still hear the low voice. When he reached the track through the grass the sounds of his progress began to blot out the calls, until the rustling around him grew so insistent that he could have imagined he wasn't alone. No doubt a wind was responsible for this and for keeping the voice after him. Of course only vegetation was on the move along the paths he crossed, and he focused his attention on the gates. While easing himself through the hedge he noticed once again that all the snapped-off twigs lay outside the grounds of the mansion, as if the gap had been forced open from within.

His cramp had threatened to return on the path, and his leg kept giving a reminiscent twitch as he tramped uphill. Nearby somebody was whistling, a practice that a fast food chain had brought back into fashion, though this whistler stopped at one note. More shops were open, and one that bore a tobacconist's vintage sign exhibited a placard for the *Chalmerston Champion*, declaring that this year's chase would go ahead. He'd left it well behind when he heard somebody selling the paper, unless they were announcing a delivery of one without using his name. It wasn't in this street; a backwards glance showed him no sign of the paper. The shout had made his leg jerk, at the mercy of a nerve, and he did his best to limber it up as he climbed to the hotel.

He was regaining his breath when the receptionist came out of the office behind the counter. "Had your run, have you?"

"I wouldn't call. It that." Once he could utter an uninterrupted sentence Plater said "I think I found where your chase began."

Perhaps the man was as exhausted as Plater felt, since he seemed to need to sit down. "Where are you saying?"

"The big old ruin near the river. That's Charmer's statue down there, isn't it? I couldn't see its name."

"Who said you could go in there? It's all locked up."

"Someone was jogging there last night, or maybe they were practicing for your event."

The receptionist stared as though suppressing a response. "Thought you didn't want to stir things up."

"I'm not sure how you think I— "

"The lot that want to stop it did," the receptionist said and turned to the computer.

As the man muttered at the screen Plater caught his own name. "I'm sorry, what did you say to me?"

"I'm saying you've got your stay with us to pay for."

"I was about to. I just hadn't heard you ask."

The receptionist scrutinised the credit card at such length that Plater could have thought he was going to read out the name. When the machine protruded a paper tongue the man tore it off and enfolded the card in it so thoroughly that the act looked almost ritualistic. "Hope you find your way," he said and retreated into the office.

Plater was at the glass door, though apparently not close enough to trigger the mechanism, when he thought he heard his name. His leg gave an inadvertent jerk before he realised he must have overheard something else. It was surely too early for anyone to be asking for a chaser in the bar. No doubt the voice was in the breakfast room; he'd sounded subterranean, the man ordering a plate of whatever it had been. Plater lurched at the door, which crept aside at last, and limped to his car.

He leaned on the roof and flexed his leg while he called Dorothy. He'd spoken to her last night, but now she wasn't at home. The message she'd recorded years ago promised that one of them would call back later. A trick of the connection emphasised their last name and her final word. "Just Sam," he said, "setting off right now," and lowered himself into the car.

A pointer opposite the exit from the car park sent him downhill. He turned left at the first cross street, since there was no entry to the right-hand stretch. He meant to turn uphill as soon as he could, returning to the road that had brought him to Chalmerston. The street he reached was one way too, and he had to drive downhill until a right turn led him back to the street he'd started from. When he crossed it, a series of one-way streets that might almost have been a mirror image of the route he'd just followed took him to the junction where he'd turned left in the first place.

The way out of town must be further downhill. As he drove past the tobacconist's he thought he heard the call about the paper once again, and his leg gave an involuntary twitch. He could only turn left at the next crossroads, where the opposite street didn't admit traffic. The route led downwards and then right, crossing the street that contained the hotel before directing him through another series of grey stone terraces, so similar to those he'd already encountered that it felt like a repetition. It certainly resembled his previous route, given how it contrived to bring him back to the junction nearest the hotel.

He swung the car downhill at once, with a screech of brakes piercing enough for a whistle. Somewhere nearby a teacher was announcing playtime at a school, though Plater would have thought they'd use a bell. There was only one more crossroads, and the noise of the brakes made his leg twitch. Yet again he could only turn left, but the one-way street at the end of the terrace of grey houses descended straight to the foot of the hill—to the road alongside the grounds of the ruined mansion.

A pointer—he could have imagined that he was hearing the word, though surely only in his head—sent him past the mansion. Presumably there was a sports field on the far side of town, since somebody beyond the hedge was exhorting people to play to win, though Plater missed the last word. His leg jerked and the brakes whined high as he turned uphill, having found a street that would admit the car. He was almost prepared to find himself back at the highest junction, in which case he meant to park wherever he could and ask for directions at the hotel. But when the route forced him to follow a street across the slope, it returned him to the road closest to the mansion.

How distracted had he let himself become? Why hadn't he thought of using the map? When he brought up the town on his phone, however, it showed no trace of the one-way system. This only helped the streets to put him in mind of a maze—of the paths through the grass—and staring at the image made parts of it appear to darken, not least some of the letters spelling the town: a, l, e, r, t . . . Plater meant to be, though he was troubled by the notion that they could form other words: alter, later. He dropped the phone on the seat next to him and drove down to the lowest road, passing the unseen mansion before he took another uphill route. Unrelieved ranks of grey stone houses shut him in and sent him right, and right again. When he reached a crossroads he was desperate to believe he hadn't previously met it, but there was the mansion again, lying in wait at the bottom of the hill.

The streets weren't deserted. There were people he could ask. One was labouring downhill towards him: a woman with a toddler in a pushchair and a small girl beside them. It was plain that rotundity ran in the family, and the woman and the girl might have been striving not to jog, proceeding at a slowness meant to counteract the effect of the slope. Plater lowered his window as the plodding party came abreast of him. "Excuse me, which way for the motorway?"

The woman's voice was as dull as her sluggish blink. "Way for?"

"Wafer," the girl said to her little brother, so low that Plater might have mistaken the word.

"Which way to it, I'm asking."

"Way to?"

Plater felt not much less confused than she appeared to be. He was disconcerted by observing that the toddler had a chewed plastic whistle in his mouth. Carol would never have had such an item at that age; they were too easily swallowed. "Wafer," the girl murmured, or a similar word.

Was she playing a game, perhaps a local one? "The way out," Plater told the woman while he tried to quell the jerking of his leg. "The way out of town."

"Outer," the girl muttered, if not something else, as her mother said "How did you get in?"

"On the road that comes to the hotel at the top."

"Better go the other way, then."

"Other," the girl mumbled—at least, Plater thought he heard that—and the toddler's face puffed up as he blew the whistle with unexpected strength.

The sound felt as if it was penetrating Plater's body, and made his foot jerk on the accelerator. "Thanks," he said and was driving downhill almost before he could choose to do so. The woman might have helped, however perfunctory her advice had been. If he must leave Chalmerston by the far side, at least he would be escaping the town.

The Run of the Town

Once he reached the open countryside there would be signs to show him the way home.

He turned right when the clawed hedge rose above him, and drove past the mansion it hid. It ended at a junction, one branch of which led behind the building to a bridge across the river, while on this side of the water both roads climbed the hill. He could see how they became entangled in the one-way system, but the road beyond the bridge led straight to the top and over the hill. He swung the car onto the bridge at once.

A waterfowl emitted a piercing note as he passed over, a noise he found difficult to put out of his head. He tried switching on the radio, which brought him a local station; certainly the man sounded local. Was he saying he would pray for someone or, surely likelier, announcing a record he was about to play for a listener? No doubt the whistle was the start of the track, but it made Plater's leg twitch, and he turned the radio off. He needed to concentrate, because the hill was so steep that he could imagine the grey houses toppling down it like dominoes—so steep that he had to change to a lower gear. No wonder some people at the top were descending at such a speed, several of them on both pavements. They would be joggers, however helplessly precipitous their progress looked—in fact, so haphazard and beyond their control that they were spilling off the pavements into the road. Couldn't they see his car, or did they expect him to accommodate them? Admittedly they had the street to themselves; everybody else must be staying inside the houses or out of the way elsewhere. The runners were racing towards him faster than the car was climbing, and he could have thought they were unaware of him, especially since their heads were lowered, which went with their crouching stance. There were at least a dozen of them, and as Plater changed to second gear they spread across the road, blocking his way entirely despite how thin they all were. He leaned on the horn, and they lifted their heads in unison, revealing far too much. They were already close enough for him to see that their clothes were ragged and discoloured, but so was the rest of them, not least their faces: the frayed gaping lips, the eyes like blobs of dried mud. Now he saw that they were mouthing in chorus, "play too" or a name or both. They were almost upon him, and he thought of driving straight through them, but the car was still losing impetus. He swerved with a screech of brakes that might have covered up another high sound and sent the car speeding off the main road.

He'd thought he was driving into a side street, but it was no more than an alley. In fact, the high blank walls on both sides were closing in, and he wasn't halfway to the next street when they began to scrape the housing of the wing mirrors. As he fumbled to lower the window beside him so that he could drag the mirror against the car, he glimpsed figures swarming into the alley behind him. The alley was growing narrower still, and if he drove much further he would simply jam the bonnet between the walls. In a panic that swept away most of his thoughts he opened the door while he still could—at the entrance to another alley—and fled downhill.

The mansion rose towards him as though it had all the time in the world. He would have dodged aside if he could, but the alley led straight down without a break in either wall. Plater felt as if the jerking of his leg was compelling him to jog faster. Echoes of his footsteps, shrill as whistling, boxed him in. He heard scrabbling and scrawny thuds behind him as pursuers made their various ways past or over the car. The slope seemed to be forcing him into a crouch that brought his head low, and he was so intent on not glancing back that he only belatedly noticed the figure that was waiting for him. He would have liked to think it was a statue, because surely only stone could make the costume so indistinguishable from its wearer and from the lichen that blotched the crumbling form. But when it pressed Plater's head down, its hand was colder than stone.

Fully Boarded

THE ROOM AT THE MEDITERRANEAN Magic apartments was even worse than Warden expected. Both of the mattresses that made up the rudimentary double bed sagged in the middle, and the thin threadbare quilt fell inches short of covering their width. The flex that led to the air-conditioning was frayed where it met the unit, and the plug for the electric kettle was cracked, matching the pair of grubby mugs that stood in the stained metal sink. One door of the flimsy wardrobe slouched on a single hinge, revealing wire hangers entangled on an insecure rail. So many of the discoloured plastic slats of the blind at the floor-length window were warped that it was impossible to shut out all the view of a weedy field where goats roamed around overgrown heaps of rubbish. As for the bathroom, the toilet seat was so misaligned that it resembled a double image, while the shower appeared to be hanging its head in shame, since the screws of the bracket that held it up were losing their grip on a splintered tile. A drooping plastic rail suggested that the shower had once been furnished with a curtain, and there wasn't a towel to be found.

When he made for Reception Warden almost lost his footing on the slippery tiles near the pool, in which the only swimmers were a

Fearful Implications

bedraggled cigarette packet and an empty bag of crisps. Half a dozen guests in swimwear lay on loungers, with a band around one wrist to signify they'd booked full board. They hadn't been among the guests queuing to complain when Warden had checked in. Now Reception was deserted except for the manager, an expansive woman with shoulders even broader than the rest of her. As Warden crossed the pointlessly spacious room, where maps and posters hid some of the shabbiness, her eyes and lips widened in her large face. "Mr Warden," she protested in an accent that had stayed mostly English, "you haven't got your band on."

He could have thought she meant to forestall his grievance with one of her own. "I haven't even unpacked yet," he said. "I just—"

"We can't serve you properly without."

"Why's that?" Warden said like, he thought, an ordinary customer.

"If my people can't see it they won't know you're fully taken care of. It's a token of our hospitality as well."

"I hadn't thought of it like that."

"They made me a guest in their land and now I'm paying it back."

Warden might have been touched if not for the state of his room. "I don't suppose I'll need your band to get—"

"For everything, and then there can't be any argument." As he wondered who she was saying might start one, she said "You wouldn't want to upset anybody."

"How do you think I'd do that?"

"Someone makes the bands for us. It's a local craft and it helps our economy. Have you got yours with you? I'll show you what I mean."

Warden fished the wristband out of his breast pocket. It had formed a loose knot that he had to disentangle from his fingers. The manager spread it on her palm to display how intricately woven the strands of green material were, in a reiterated pattern Warden thought could be as ancient as it was elaborate. He was peering at it out of politeness, though it hardly compensated for his room, when she said "You'll appreciate it better on."

Before Warden realised what she meant to do she slipped the band onto his right wrist. At once it was so snug that the band might have been designed for him. He felt a hint of moisture that put him oddly in mind of a kiss, and then it was gone. "What is it made of?" he said.

"That's their secret," the manager said and raised her eyes from his wrist. "Was there something else you wanted?"

"There aren't any towels in my room."

"We've had a day of changing rooms. We won't forget you, Mr Warden."

Was she admitting newcomers had demanded to be moved? He meant to insist on that himself, but not until he'd experienced how bad his room might be. He ignored the wristband, which felt slightly tighter, while he asked "So when could I have some?"

"As I say, all my people are occupied just now," she said and turned her back on him. He was struggling to believe he'd been dismissed when she said "You can have mine."

She brought a towel from a room beyond the office behind the counter. It felt damp and was half the size Warden would have expected a bath towel to be. Was her gesture intended to disarm him? "Thank you," he barely said.

"You're welcome. All our guests are." She rested an unnecessarily maternal gaze on him until he stepped back from the counter. "And do call me Win," she said.

"Win."

"Short for Winifred," she said as if she'd made her name sound too triumphal. "I hope you'll enjoy your stay with us, Mr Warden."

He might have retorted that it was up to her and her staff to make sure he did. He could have taken her comments for disguised appeals, and might something of the kind have prompted the inexplicably positive online reviews of the Mediterranean Magic? He'd already seen enough to justify the hostile ones—"deserves to be bulldozed", "not even fit for dogs", "you'd be better sleeping on the beach" and dozens more from guests who weren't even fully boarded—and the complaints the travel operator had received. "I'll do my best," he told Win and made for his room.

He always did his best on behalf of the customers. While he took pride in investigating wherever the firm sent him, posing as an ordinary holidaymaker or an invisibly average hotel guest, discovering the worst often left him feeling mean, and so did knowing that most of his reports left their subjects unsupported by his firm. It was the owners' fault if they didn't raise their standards, and he was helping the customers who paid his wages, but how many staff might Warden have put out of a job? He had to remember that if they'd attended to their work he mightn't have needed to do his. He might even have been out of a job himself.

He draped the towel over a rickety rail in the bathroom and set about emptying his suitcase. When he tried to open the drawers under the wardrobe the handle of the topmost came off, and the front of the lower drawer creaked outwards before the rest of it staggered free. Once he'd unpacked he used his phone to photograph all the failings of the apartment, and then he ventured out for dinner.

The restaurant was another of the concrete blocks that made up Mediterranean Magic. Through the holes it had for windows Warden saw an assortment of trestle tables scarcely covered with checked cloths and provided with a variety of seats—benches, folding chairs, even the odd stool. As he followed a family into the restaurant, a man hailed the father. "Aren't you coming out to a taverna, Dick? You're never going in there twice."

The man he'd addressed was just as wilfully bald, but the sun had rendered his scalp pinker. "Tell us about it when you've been, Stan."

"Last night you said you weren't eating here again."

"We can change our minds, can't we? We're getting what we paid for."

The bands on their wrists and their teenage son's weren't quite as prominent as those Stan and his family sported or Warden's own. When the taverna party headed for the road, Dick turned to Warden. "Some people aren't happy till they've found something to moan about."

For a moment Warden felt identified. "You don't think they could have a reason."

"They only got here yesterday and they've been complaining ever since."

"Have you been here longer yourselves?"

"Twice as long as them and we're making the best of it. We think that's what us English do. It's what Win's doing, some people might like to remember."

Having found a plate that wasn't too chipped, Warden surveyed the buffet that occupied a long table: olives, cheeses, oily salads, dips so watery they bordered on colourless, some kind of raisin bread—no, loaves with flies in attendance. One dip displayed a black olive or else a drowned fly, which helped him decide against sampling any of them. Platters of sliced meat kept company with bowls of rice and a plate piled with greasy potatoes, along with soggy salads indistinguishable from those he'd already left alone. He spooned a few lumps of rice out of a bowl and took a slice of each meat, which proved to be not just as unidentifiable as they looked but so timidly spiced that they tasted less

Fearful Implications

than national. A middle-aged couple at the table next to his watched him eat, presumably because he was a newcomer. "Good?" the woman said, if it was a question.

"What do you think?"

"Good," she declared, and her husband said "Just as good."

"As what?" Warden felt he should learn.

"As last night."

"And the one before that," the woman said.

When Warden left quite a portion of his dinner, they stared like disapproving parents at his plate. "I've had what I need," he told them, and might have gone in search of a taverna if he hadn't felt a little sick. He tried to wash away the vague insidious flavours with a gulp of house wine, which only brought them lurching back.

He chewed two chalky indigestion tablets as soon as he was in his room. From the balcony, having managed to decide which of the pair of grubby plastic chairs was less precarious, he watched a sunset gild the goats and set the mounds of refuse in amber until a parched breeze brought a shitty whiff that sent him inside. He felt unusually ready for bed, and made for the bathroom, where the mirror reminded him that he hadn't taken off the wristband. When he tugged at it, the band yielded just a fraction of an inch, not enough to let him slip it off. Had it shrunk in the heat? Since it didn't trouble him, he might as well wear it to bed.

He had to bruise his fingers on the remote control before the air conditioning clattered into action. The metal slats kept up a rattle that ought to have denoted more than the tepid feeble draft they let loose. Warden felt compelled to listen for a pattern in the relentless stutter, but eventually he fell asleep. He dreamed he was stored in a clammy bag, and wakened to find he was—wrapped in the sweaty sheet, at any rate. The room was hotter than it had been on his return. As he groped for the control to rouse the chill, he found his right arm had grown unhelpfully numb. The unit on the wall gave a solitary clatter and died with a sputtering flash.

Had he been lying on the arm? The numbness seemed to dissipate by spreading through him. He fumbled to switch on the light, which showed a thread of smoke hovering above the exposed wires of the unit. The wires had fused with their rubber sheath, and Warden stared at them until his head began to feel as senseless as his arm had been. Would anyone be at Reception this early? His room had no phone, and he wasn't going to the office just to discover it was unstaffed. Instead he dragged the sodden sheet over himself.

Despite the heat he wakened well after dawn. He managed to use the toilet by aligning the emaciated plastic seat with the pedestal and holding it there with both hands. When he tried to raise the shower head towards him, having persuaded the water at least to hint at warmth, the screws shifted in the wall. He crouched beneath the enervated downpour and then used the towel, which was still damp. At least the wristband wasn't wet by the time he remembered he had it on.

Much of the breakfast buffet looked familiar—dips, olives, salads, rice. The cold meats could be last night's too, sliced thinner, and the hard sawn loaves weren't new, though the attendant flies might be. Warden left most of the samples he took, earning a dumb rebuke from more than one fellow guest, and went to Reception. "You'll have had a sleep," Win said across the counter.

Warden started framing a retort, but the effort felt as though a band was tightening around if not inside his head. "Was there anything you wanted, Mr Warden?" Win said.

"Yes, air conditioning. Mine died in the night."

"Oh dear, what a pest." As Warden wondered if she could mean him, Win said "I'll have someone put you in a fan."

Fearful Implications

"Don't you think you'd better get the unit fixed? The wires are bare. It could be dangerous."

"We'll look at it if that's what you want."

Warden hardly thought he needed to confirm this, and it almost made him forget to ask "How does this come off?"

Win gazed in some disappointment at the wrist he was holding up. "You won't want to till you leave, will you? Not when you're all in."

It would give him access to any facilities he needed to investigate. Once his stay was over he could cut the wristband off. He retired to the pool, where a hot breeze sent litter for a sluggish swim and wafted a harsh smell of chlorine out of the water. From a lounger he watched a Mediterranean Magic man trudging about in search of abandoned glasses and any other items that weren't too much trouble to retrieve. Warden found the man's somnolent progress close to mesmeric, and wasn't far from sleep by the time the representative of his firm met new guests from several accommodations in the poolside bar. "Hi, everyone. I'm Rhona," she cried.

She was a slight girl adorned with a watch so large that it appeared to cast a shadow on her wrist, not unlike a stain. While identifying the attractions of the island on a map she gestured so vigorously she might have been miming her job. The customers who booked tours with her weren't fully boarded at Mediterranean Magic. Warden's fellow guests were more concerned about their rooms, along with the food and other drawbacks. As Rhona undertook to have a word and have a word he found her brightness far too studied, not to say repetitive. He would have liked to overhear what she said to Win if his presence mightn't have betrayed his mission. She didn't spend much time in the office, and she was heading for her motor scooter when pink-pated Dick and family arrived at the poolside. Blood was seeping through a large plaster on the teenager's right shin. "Someone's been in the wars," Warden said.

"Used to be," Dick said with a blank stare. "I'm a civvy now."

"No, I mean your son. What happened there?"

"Trev didn't look where he was going," the boy's mother said. "Cut himself on there."

Following her gaze, Warden saw a jagged strip of concrete where tiles should have been at the edge of the pool. He was dismayed to have overlooked the hazard, which clearly wasn't recent. "Does Rhona know about that?" he urged. "You can catch her if you're quick."

"No point in that," Dick said. "Deb here's patched him up."

"Don't you think it ought to be reported? It doesn't look any too clean."

"You've got some eyes if you can see through a plaster. His mother put plenty of disinfectant on." Before Warden could explain he'd meant the concrete, Dick said "You can go and moan if that's your style."

Rhona's scooter departed with a tinny snarl, and Warden gave up. Striving to persuade Dick had left him with a headache like a ring around his brain. It tempted him to snooze beside the pool or in his room, but he ought to stay alert. He went out for a quick tour of the resort in the hope of walking off the tension of the job.

A sandy beach extended for a mile around a bay, though the section closest to Mediterranean Magic was chunky with rubble. Tavernas lined the promenade, and he found more in the winding side streets, where supermarkets and souvenir shops had ousted many of the houses. His roaming only aggravated the tightness in his skull, and he wandered back to the apartments. He was in sight of the block that housed Reception and the staff when he noticed it was opposite a graveyard.

The cemetery was the kind he'd often seen in this part of the world, with many of the graves covered by marble slabs and headed by memorials displaying mementoes behind glass. Candles and lanterns

Fearful Implications

stood on most of the graves, waiting to be lit after dark. Facing the back of the Mediterranean Magic block was a hut composed of wood so old it resembled a mossy tree. Surely just a strip of moss was protruding under the door, but Warden went to look.

It was one of the wristbands Win used. Though the door had torn the pattern ragged, it was unmistakeable. As he walked around the hut, which was windowless, a woman tending a grave met his eyes. She sent him a sign of the cross and murmured a word.

"Sorry?" Though he thought she'd said that, he sounded mindless as an echo. "Sorry for what, sorry?"

Her wary gaze moved from the hut to his wrist. "We need," she muttered and returned to her task.

She must have his economic contribution in mind, but unlike Win, she was apologising. Warden thought it made sense for the graveyard caretaker to earn a little extra with a traditional craft, and perhaps some version of the bands was sold in the souvenir shops. He returned to his room to find the bed as rumpled as he'd left it, and no sign of a fan. Either the sight or the thought of complaining once again made his head twinge like an unhealed wound. He went back to the poolside bar, where the wristband entitled him to free drinks. The house wines came from boxes that didn't pretend to be Greek, and the barman was the silent sullen fellow he'd previously seen clearing away litter. A greenish tattoo encircled each of his wrists, though Warden couldn't see exactly what the blurred designs were supposed to represent. They could hardly be meant to bring shackles to mind.

Sour though it was, the wine numbed Warden's headache. He dozed on a lounger beneath a tipsy umbrella, jerking awake to discover it was the middle of the afternoon. His room still hadn't been touched. As he marched to Reception he saw he'd abandoned his glass by the lounger. He mustn't turn into an untidy careless guest—he needed to remember he was here on official business—and he took the glass to the bar, where the morose man gave it an unwelcoming blink.

Win's look wasn't too enthusiastic either. "What can we do for you now?"

"When is my room likely to be made up, do you know?"

"We can't do everything at once." She sounded like a parent dealing with an unreasonable child. "We're bringing you a fan," she said as though promising a treat or an indulgence.

"When you do, could I have a proper towel?"

"What do you mean by proper?"

"I don't mean yours wasn't. It was generous of you." Warden's lips felt constricted, along with his brain, and it took him some effort to add "I'd still like the kind you provide for your guests."

"We'll see about it. Was that all?"

Warden was thrown by how unreasonable he was being made to feel. He was a guest, after all, and not just that either. Nevertheless he turned away before mumbling "For now."

As he resumed his place by the pool, having collected another glass of wine from the bar, he saw a woman with a stack of towels making for his block. Shouldn't he feel more annoyed that she was dealing with the rooms so late? All he felt was relief. He drank and dozed and trudged to the room, where the sheet had been yanked more or less smooth on the bed. A single frayed towel drooped on the bathroom rail. At least it was dry, but the floor remained sticky, and there was no fan. The idea of complaining yet again made his head feel clamped, and he opted for dinner instead.

He was sidling along the buffet, which looked entirely too familiar, when he saw Stan and family following him. "Didn't you say you were never coming here again?" Warden said.

"We can change our minds, can't we?" Stan retorted, rubbing his

Fearful Implications

forehead with his wristband, unless the action was the other way around.

"That's exactly what your friend told you," Warden couldn't resist observing.

"Shows we're friends then, doesn't it?"

Though Warden wasn't sure what sense this made, it sounded like a warning. He turned to the buffet, where grease had congealed around the cold cuts, while he suspected the other meats were reheated. He contented himself with salads, and passed Dick's family on his way to a table. The bloodstain on the boy's plaster was a muddy brown. "How is he now?" he felt bound to ask.

"Fine," all three said in chorus, as if they'd practiced the rebuff.

Once Warden saw off some lumps of rice and an assortment of wilted leaves he decided he'd had dinner. He sat on his balcony, wishing he could see the graveyard hut, to determine if its occupant was at work. Leaning out at full stretch let him see a few graves lit by lanterns. He was straining to crane further when the plastic chair twisted out of shape and collapsed under him.

He had to laugh, however ruefully. It was his fault, after all. He would be better off in bed, where he couldn't do any more damage. In the bathroom he was about to scrub his stained wrist until he recognised the wristband. It was scarcely identifiable as one—more like a raised tattoo. Once he was in bed he couldn't feel it at all, and the unawareness seemed to reach within his head, expanding into sleep.

He didn't know how long he'd slept when a crash wakened him. He poked inaccurately at the light switch and staggered about until he located the disaster. The shower holder had fallen off the wall, taking a tile with it to smash. His laugh at this involved very little mirth. It was more of a preamble to the complaint he would make in the morning, though the prospect left his head empty and numb.

Now that he was aware of all the heat that had gathered in the room he didn't expect to sleep much, but he'd hardly returned to bed when he no longer knew where he was. Sunlight wakened him, and he remembered the shower. Was it really worth reporting, or should he just leave it for the staff to notice, which they presumably couldn't avoid? He lay in the companionable tangle of the sheet until a surge of anger at his inertia roused him. He wasn't supposed to be here just for himself, and as soon as he was dressed he stalked off to Reception.

Win spoke from the office as he approached the counter. "You'll have your fan today, Mr Warden."

"I hope so, but meanwhile the shower has fallen off the wall."

"You're meant to hold it. That way you won't make the room so wet."

Didn't that seem reasonable? Straining to recall why it shouldn't revived the tight ache in Warden's head. "It smashed a tile as well," he said.

He thought Win was about to tell him to clear them up until she said "Have your breakfast and I'll look into sending someone."

If she meant him to hear weariness, that was surely how he ought to feel. At the buffet he made do with a glass of orange juice and a ragged chunk of bread that he smeared with liquescent butter. The items tasted only slightly stale, he reassured himself. He lingered over them and then over their remains in the hope of giving someone time to deal with his room. At last he ventured back to find that most of the broken tile had been taken away, and a fan was plugged in near the bed.

The bracket from the shower lay on the toilet cistern. While he showered he tried to avoid spraying the room. The befogged mirror reminded him that he was wearing a wristband, though by now it looked almost as undefined as the blurred reflection. Was there something else he ought to remember? Yes, he'd neglected to take his passport with him the last time he'd gone to see Win. Instead of slipping it into his pocket for safety he'd left it on the bedside table. He towelled himself more or less dry and padded into the main room. The passport wasn't by the bed.

He searched all the pockets of every item of clothing in the room, but he hadn't forgotten putting it there, and it was nowhere else in the apartment. He dressed so hastily that he heard a shirt button skitter into the bathroom. As he made for Reception, Dick and family watched him, and so did Stan along with his. Warden heard a not especially stifled laugh, followed by a murmur. "Looks like someone's off to make more trouble."

Win stayed in the office to watch his approach. "I'm sure your fan is on its way," she said.

"It's there." As she conveyed that she wouldn't mind being thanked Warden protested "My passport's gone from the room."

"What a pain. Where do you think you might have left it?"

"I told you, in my room. Someone's taken it. Whoever put the fan in must have."

"I don't think you can say that, Mr Warden. If the door was open, anybody could."

"Then they shouldn't have left the door open. What's going to be done, may I ask?"

"I'll make enquiries. You're with us for a while yet. We'll see you're fixed up."

Warden found her undertaking worse than vague. "Maybe the police should make the enquiries."

"You can have what you ask for, Mr Warden."

He gave that a fierce nod, though it tightened the noose of a headache, which was making it hard to talk. He heard Win pick up the phone and dial, and her side of a conversation in Greek. She leaned out of the office to say "Someone will be coming for you. Don't leave the Magic."

"I'll be by the pool," Warden said and took a glass of wine to the lounger, hoping to regain some calm while he waited for the police. He stayed well clear of the families he felt sure were surreptitiously watching him. In a while he dozed, only to keep waking with a sense that it was dangerous to drift off. He felt close to fancying he was handcuffed by the wristband to the lounger, but was the impression hindering a memory? Recalling that he'd lost his passport threatened to rouse his headache, but was that all he'd lost? No, his identification from the travel firm had been inside the passport. Both the loss and having overlooked it made him feel as if he hardly knew who he was. He needed reassurance, but not where he could be overheard, and he took his phone to his room.

The answer wasn't as swift or as bright as Rhona's welcome meeting had suggested. "Rhona Martin."

"Rhona, it's Douglas Warden at Mediterranean Magic." He sounded as though he was associating himself with the place, which was one reason why he added "I should tell you I'm with the firm."

"Which firm?"

"Ours. They sent me to report on the accommodation."

After quite a pause Rhona said "Why didn't you tell me?"

"I thought I just did."

It wasn't much of a joke, and it earned him another silence before she said "Are you reporting me as well?"

"I'm afraid that's part of the job."

"What are you going to say?"

"You must know I can't reveal that. That's how the job's done too."

"Then I don't understand why you've told me as much as you have."

"So that you know who I am in case you have to help me get home. Somebody's stolen my passport."

"Are you sure you haven't just mislaid it?"

"I most certainly am. I've got all my wits about me."

He didn't need her to pause yet again, especially if that was some kind of response. "If it's been stolen," she said at last, "you need the police, not me."

"I'm waiting for them now."

"Then I expect you'll be taken care of. You can let me know if you haven't been," she said and immediately ended the call.

Did she treat all her clients' problems this way or just his? In any case he would be reporting her behaviour. How dull must the girl be if she didn't realise she'd made trouble for herself? Though he shouldn't expect special treatment, it might have helped them both. He'd told Win he would wait by the pool for the police, and he hurried back to the lounger, seeing only fellow guests. "Putting up with it after all," he heard someone mutter.

"Putting up with us," someone murmured lower still.

Warden wasn't going to acknowledge the comments. As he fetched another drink he asked the barman "Have the police been here?"

The man kept any expression to himself, not least with his voice. "No police."

He could hardly be saying they weren't welcome, let alone that they wouldn't come. Warden subsided onto the lounger, raising his head whenever he heard anyone approaching. Before long he forgot this was a reason to move his head. When he woke he felt as though his arm was weighing him down, unless the whole of him was. He didn't need to stir when he was here to enjoy the sun—no, to talk to the police because it was somehow his job—no, because he'd lost his passport. Prising his leaden eyelids open, he saw it was late afternoon. This sent him off the lounger to stumble to Reception, where Win made a visible bid to look resigned at the sight of him. "Have the police been in touch?" he demanded.

"Why should they?"

That felt like a threat of having his memory stolen. "Because you called them on my behalf," Warden said with all the force he could find.

"They haven't come just yet, if that's what you're asking."

"Do you think someone should remind them?"

"Best not to pester, Mr Warden."

It sounded like more than advice, and he knew it wasn't prudent to antagonise the Greek police. As he returned to the poolside he could have fancied he was being led by the wrist back to the lounger. Once he'd finished another drink he fell into a doze. He had days before he would need the passport, after all.

An outbreak of shuffling roused him. Guests were heading for the buffet, and he saw Dick's son was limping. Since nobody seemed concerned, Warden was disinclined to comment. "Are you coming for dinner?" someone called.

Though Warden was unsure if he was being addressed, he said "Maybe later."

"Isn't their food good enough for you?" the man said, or someone else did.

Warden's hunger simply felt too remote to need assuaging— certainly not worth the bother of troubling Win yet again, since he would have to let her know he wasn't by the pool. He couldn't even find the energy to go to the bar, which would involve summoning the barman now that he was morosely busy with diners. Warden reverted to dozing until Win's voice to some extent roused him. She was only saying "In future we'll just do full board" and not to him. Could that bring her unanimously favourable reviews? Before he'd grasped the thought he was asleep.

He woke to find he was alone. Even the bar was deserted. It was almost midnight, and he couldn't help shivering with a sense of an imminent chill. When he hurried to Reception he wasn't surprised to find it unstaffed. Knocking on the counter failed to bring anyone out of the office or wherever they were hiding. He craned over the counter and found a pad together with a splintered ballpoint pen. He wrote **I'M IN MY ROOM WARDEN** on the top sheet, which he tore off and left behind the counter. Perhaps just the shaky ballpoint had made it hard to write. He was heading for his room when he realised he'd glimpsed movement in the graveyard.

He sneaked along the side of the staff block and piled rubble up so that he could peer over the wall. At first the view hardly seemed worth the effort—the activity he'd glimpsed had just been the flickering of light on some of the memorials—and then his vision grew used to the intermittent dimness. The door of the hut was open, and the occupant was at work.

The only illumination within the hut came from the lights on the graves. Surely the worker couldn't be as thin as the dim unstable outline made the figure look. It was dressed from head to foot in black, exposing no more than the sketchy arms. From their rapid relentless movement Warden deduced that they were weaving some material. Why should he think of a spider? He tried to conclude that just the movements suggested the resemblance, until he couldn't avoid noticing too many arms on the table where the figure was at work. Surely the extra limbs were composed of stone and belonged to a memorial. That would explain why they were overgrown with vegetation, strands of which the figure was peeling off with its exceptionally long nails to weave into another wristband.

Fully Boarded

Warden retreated from the wall so fast that the heap of rubble collapsed with a protracted clatter. He wasn't conscious of taking a breath until he was back in his room. He might have tried to tear the greenish bracelet off his wrist, but it was indistinguishable from his skin. Attempting to insert a fingernail beneath it only scratched his wrist until it bled. This failed to dismay him as much as it should, and he tried to recapture his awareness of the situation by phoning Rhona. A voicemail message met him, and he wondered if she was refusing to answer, having recognised his number. Unable to think of a message to leave, he called their firm in England, but that line was recording messages too. "It's Douglas Warden investigating a hotel for you. My passport has been stolen. You may need to help me get home," he pleaded. "Call me back."

He'd done all he could think of to do, and he subsided on the bed. At least the police would be able to find him. Before he managed to decide how much of his plight they could be expected to believe, he was asleep. Did a trace of his thoughts about the police make him dream that he was being handcuffed and led to a cell? Another notion roused him—the possibility that Win had never called the police. His eyes sprang open, letting in more of the dark.

Far too little of the dream had gone away. Both his wrists felt constricted, and so did the room. By the time he finished groping for the light switch he knew it wasn't where it ought to be. The naked bulb fluttered alight, showing him how much the room had shrunk. No, it was a wholly unfamiliar room, with walls patchily darkened by damp and furniture so meagre it seemed hardly there at all. There was a band on his left wrist now, already growing embedded in the flesh. He lurched to his feet and saw lights dancing in the graveyard beyond the window. The occupant of the hut was still crouched over its spidery work, and Warden was in one of the rooms for the staff. "I don't belong here," he cried, or tried to, but his voice barely left his restricted mouth. "This isn't me."

"It is now," the answer came, and he was reduced to hoping he'd heard Win or even Rhona until the figure in the hut turned slowly but inexorably to face him.

The Devil in the Details

"We oughtn't to go if young Brian will be bored. It's his holiday as well, Barbara."

"You won't be, will you, Brian? There'll be plenty to see in the house and the park."

"It's your day, Aunt Leonie. It's your turn to say what we do."

"He's a credit to you both. I wish I knew more like him. Now, Brian, don't make that face."

"Your aunt wants to see the paintings while she has the chance. It won't hurt you to look at them as well."

"Jeff, I think the face was just embarrassed. Maybe they'll help you with your art at school, Brian. You can tell your teacher what you saw. So long as you don't mind..."

Brian did his best to seem enthusiastic despite wondering how much more he might have not to mind. Because his aunt disliked flying they'd gone not to Turkey but to St Brendan on Sea, which wasn't quite northern enough to be close to mountains and lakes. Supposedly the town was famed for its murals three centuries old, but Brian kept being told there was plenty to occupy him. His aunt had to be considered because she'd lost her husband Quentin recently, though only by divorce. Even the activities Brian's parents chose for their days seemed to be mostly for her. In case he wasn't sufficiently uncomfortable his mother told him "Do what you have to do and we'll be off."

Though he was twelve he had to share the family room while his mother's sister had next door all to herself. His father had told him off for dislodging the toilet seat, though it had already been askew. Brian dabbed with toilet paper at the results of his inefficient aim and wiped his hand on his trousers on the way downstairs, past a kind of china totem pole composed of sleepy cats. His aunt produced a laugh every time she saw it and waited until Brian manufactured one, so that he couldn't help feeling relieved that the family was waiting outside the Seeview. Even from upstairs the only view was of the whitewashed hotels opposite.

The family clambered into the Clio, which his aunt frequently called Cliopatra. Five minutes' drive past tearooms and antique dealers and Victorian shopping arcades took them out of the small town. While Brian's mother drove through country lanes his aunt pointed out sights she appeared to think he would otherwise have missed, not that he would have cared too much. Twenty minutes of this brought them to Foliant Hall. The stone lions guarding the gates put Brian in mind of the china cats in the boarding house, but it seemed this time he wasn't meant to laugh.

A guide half his aunt's age was leading a party of visitors out of the sandstone mansion. "You won't mind waiting for us, will you?" Aunt Leonie appealed to her and hastened into the lobby, miming a search for her credit card until Brian's father overtook her to buy tickets. When the party was complete at last—Aunt Leonie enacting comical haste rather than achieving actual speed—the guide said "We'll start in the chapel. The Soulous ceiling is being restored."

Brian made a manful effort to anticipate a treat as everyone trooped

The Devil in the Details

along an avenue to the ruddy chapel. A man was perched on scaffolding underneath a mural full of angels, though for the moment he was busy drinking from a mug. "Good morning, Charlie," the guide said as though to prompt him to demonstrate his skills, but he only raised the mug in a salute.

"Maurice Soulous has made our little town world-famous with his paintings..." The Foliant family had taken up the painter and commissioned his work for the hall as well as the chapel, and he'd provided murals for both the Catholic churches in town. He'd become a painter and a convert late in life, one reason why the Foliants had supported him. In return he'd painted images of their acceptance into heaven, and you can see them there and there. As Brian peered up at the solemn well-fed faces of the white-robed figures being borne away by angels, his aunt said "He wasn't such a saint himself, was he?"

"No photographs, please." Having waited until all the offenders lowered their phones, the guide said "That's why he converted. Charlie, when you're ready—"

"Don't they say he painted angels to disguise himself?" Aunt Leonie said.

"I hadn't heard it put that way."

"To disguise his nature, and maybe his conversion was meant to do that too. Maybe it let him end up thinking he hadn't been a monster to his wives." For just the family to hear, Brian's aunt murmured "Like someone I won't name treated his wife."

"I was meaning to come to that later." In the same tone of muted reproof the guide said "Charlie—"

"You'll be saying how he put himself in every mural but those details were all painted over."

"I was coming to that now. In fact Charlie—"

"Only nobody knows who did it. They aren't sure Soulous did even though it's in his style."

"Well, you've told the people everything I would have." As though retrieving triumph from defeat the guide called "Charlie, have you found him?"

"Could have." The man set down his mug with visible reluctance and used a tool to point at the cluster of angels directly above him. "He could be under them."

Brian squinted at the flaking section of the mural until the outline of a white-winged figure seemed to shift. The rest of the party had finished admiring the interior and were wandering out of the chapel. Perhaps the restorer disliked having so large an audience, because he abandoned the mug to pick up a tool. Brian was backing towards the exit while he watched when the heavenly vista seemed to light up from within.

It was the flash of a camera. Someone had lingered to take a surreptitious photograph. The glare made a figure appear to lurch out of the mural above Charlie's head. Presumably the restorer was twisting around to remonstrate with the photographer, however much he looked as though he was recoiling, but his left foot slipped off the platform. In a moment the rest of him did.

Brian hadn't realised how long a second could last: long enough for the man to finish a wordless cry that might have been aimed at the photographer, and to flail all his limbs as if trying to swim in the air, and even make to clutch at his head with both hands to protect it. The gesture ran out of time, and the back of his head collided with the stone floor with a thud like the fall of a stuffed sack. Brian couldn't turn away until the floor around the twitching figure began to look as if someone had spilled paint, and then he dashed out of the chapel. All the visitors, even his family, were retreating along the avenue. "Mum, dad," he cried, "he fell. He's hurt."

The Devil in the Details

His aunt was the first to look back. "What are you saying, Brian?"

"Someone took a photo and made him fall. It wasn't me."

Was the culprit retreating through the trees towards the house? The guide and her party crowded around Brian, and he was distracted by a woman saying "I'm a nurse."

She and the guide hurried into the chapel, followed by a thud—the door. As the rest of the party loitered near the entrance Brian's father said "You didn't do anything, son."

It wasn't quite sufficiently unlike a question. Brian took out his phone to display the lack of evidence, and was surprised to find his fingers weren't as steady as they ought to be. In his mind the man's fall had begun to resemble a scene from a film with half-hearted effects, while his surroundings—blue sky, green trees, red church, variously coloured faces—grew unnecessarily vivid. Telling his mother he was all right only prompted her sister to ask if he was sure. Before he had to say so yet again, the nurse reappeared. "I'm afraid there's been a fatality," she said.

The guide emerged paler than when she'd gone in. "I'm sorry, I'm going to have to cancel today. Please go back to the desk for a refund or reschedule."

"Could you have a look at our son?" Brian's father asked the nurse. "How do you think this may affect him?"

The nurse performed a swift examination before ruffling Brian's hair. "How are you feeling, old fellow?"

Brian felt further embarrassed by saying "Sad for the man."

The nurse pronounced him fit, and the family made for the mansion, where Brian's father obtained tickets for the day after tomorrow. On the way to the car Brian saw an ambulance arriving at the chapel. The flicker of the roof lights plucked at the shape of a man who slipped into the building, though at that distance the door looked hardly even ajar. During the drive back to town Aunt Leonie devoted herself to pointing out views she would have put on canvas if she hadn't left her painter's equipment at home. "It would only bore young Brian," she'd said.

St Brendan's was ten minutes' walk from the Seeview, up a hill ribbed with terraces of white cottages. "The walk will do us all good," Brian's mother said, but he thought she mostly meant him. No doubt the church had been built on the hill for sailors to see from their ships. The interior walls were a mass of angels, which might have swarmed out of the stained-glass windows, and on the ceiling another flock raised a saint to heaven. "Look behind the angels," Brian's aunt told him as if he needed some diversion from his thoughts. "Maybe you'll see the man himself."

"Aunt Leonie, what did he do that was so bad?"

"He tortured his wives, all of them. They said it excited him. He nearly killed some of them, but he had too many friends in high places to be put in prison." As Brian's parents showed signs of intervening she said "These days men have other ways of abusing us. Make sure you're never like that, Brian."

"I believe we can guarantee that," his father said and told him "Just look at what we've come to see."

Brian didn't know if he was being directed to search for the artist or advised against doing so. He peered at the relentlessly holy faces so hard that the edge of his vision quivered, which made figures that he wasn't looking at directly seem to inch aside, as if another figure needed room. Whenever he glanced at them, the impression subsided. He was glad when his aunt let everyone leave, though only to visit another church.

St Mary Magdalene's faced a shop that sold fishing tackle on the main street. Once again the interior was overrun with angels, a cluster of which were lifting a saintly woman under the roof. Brian looked for signs of torture, but presumably she hadn't been a martyr. Near a table that he gathered was an altar, though he thought it could have passed unremarked in a florist's shop, he saw a booth with two doors. "What's that for?" he said and felt childish.

"It's a confessional," his aunt said. "People tell the priest their sins in there and that's supposed to make it right. That shouldn't be how it works, though they let Maurice Soulous think it was. Some things you shouldn't be forgiven just because you own up."

"Leonie," Brian's mother said, "I don't think we need that in church."

Brian felt compelled to search for the artist without feeling sure that he wanted to find him. Some angels appeared to have shadows, but whenever he looked closer the dark addition dodged back. Could the confessional be in use? If he was hearing a whisper, it could hardly be behind the booth, where a section of mural was flaking away. Perhaps the booth was meant to hide the damage, unless it was the cause. As he tried to focus on the peeling shadow his mother said "What's wrong, Brian?" Though he moved away at once, she didn't stop watching him until they left the church. "Let's get some fresh air on the front," she said.

The bay was strewn with fishing boats, and nets lay on the stony beach. The promenade offered a bingo hall, a coin arcade that he'd been warned was a waste of money, a fairground where the rides were too young as well as too antique for him, a ballroom with posters for performers apparently determined to resurrect celebrities by imitation. A salty breeze ruffled Brian's hair as the nurse had, inspiring his aunt to tell him "This should give you an appetite," and he wondered if she felt responsible for the shock everybody thought he must have suffered in the chapel.

Fearful Implications

His appetite could indeed have done with stimulation. Dinner at the Seeview consisted of a feebly international menu, far less varied than his parents made at home. The curry he'd tried last night was half the strength of his mother's, though his aunt had pronounced it too fiery for her. The fish of the day appeared to be that of the week if not the month. Brian opted for a cheeseburger, which arrived in a bun competing for softness with eight chips that lent it a presumably inadvertent resemblance to a crab. Afterwards the family joined others in the lounge to watch a television smaller than the one in Brian's house. Aunt Leonie was among the guests who called out answers to quiz shows while Brian sent phone messages to friends. When his mother chided him for distracting the contestants, he took his embarrassment to bed.

The photograph above it, of men in hats and women in long dresses on the promenade, didn't trouble him. All the same, he fell asleep with a sense that some unwelcome presence was above him, or would be. As he climbed the ladder to the platform on the scaffold he craned back to take in the whole of the ceiling mural, but none of the angels acknowledged him. He did his best to balance on the platform, which consisted of a solitary plank, but his antics unbalanced the ladder, and he made a desperate grab for whatever might save him. When a hand seized his from overhead, he was so reluctant to see the rescuer that his protest wakened him. His father's disgruntled mumble fell short of words, and Brian lay not much less still than a painting to be sure his parents stayed asleep.

At breakfast they seemed heartened by how much he ate. "You'll need a good walk after that," his aunt said, which gave him an idea for his day. "Let's see how far we can walk," he said, "and see what else there is."

Yesterday he'd noticed a cliff path leading from the promenade. The

The Devil in the Details

walk brought views of an increasingly rocky coast peopled only by birds, and he felt pleased with his choice until his aunt began saying "Keep away from the edge, Brian" and "Be careful, Brian" and "Don't go too close." Eventually she said "Your uncle used to do that. He knew I hated heights."

"You didn't when we were Brian's age," her sister said.

"That was how someone I won't mention worked on me. I'm getting my confidence back."

"Was that how he tortured you, Aunt Leonie?"

Before she could respond Brian's father said "Do as your aunt says and stay clear."

The walk led them to a clifftop pub in time for lunch. Brian thought his parents would have sat outside if his aunt hadn't met the prospect with a shiver. Among the brochures for local attractions in a rack next to the entrance he found one for Foliant Hall. A photograph of the interior of the chapel bothered him enough that he took it to the table. How was the ceiling mural different? It felt like trying to solve one of the picture puzzles he used to enjoy—looking for a hidden face—but he hadn't succeeded by the time his aunt said "Can't you wait to go back, Brian?"

"I was just seeing if he's there."

Perhaps this hinted at aversion, because his father said "We all have to make sacrifices. Your aunt has come on a walk she doesn't like."

"I do like it, Jeff. Don't make Brian feel guilty when there's no need. You're helping me get over my nerves, Brian."

Brian stuffed the brochure into a pocket and concentrated on his fish and chips. Afterwards his aunt insisted on walking further along the cliff, perhaps because his father kept him well clear of the edge. The evening brought another burger, followed by another clutch of the quiz shows Aunt Leonie never seemed to tire of. Brian gave the brochure his attention and was disconcerted to find that however long he stared at the murals in the chapel, they didn't stir. This was among the issues that lingered in his mind when he went to bed.

He used to like his uncle Quentin, who'd been fond of wrestling with him and telling jokes the other adults disapproved of and letting him watch films the boxes said he was too young to see. Should Brian feel guilty for having liked him—for persisting in it now? Another source of confusion was his father's remark about sacrifice, although until he was close to sleep Brian didn't realise why it stayed with him. Of course, the death of the restorer in the chapel would have functioned as a bloody sacrifice in several of the films Uncle Quentin had put on while the rest of the family were elsewhere. They were only films, and so Brian didn't dream, though in the morning his aunt asked if anybody had. "We don't, Leonie," his father said.

"I don't think you can speak for everyone." For a moment she seemed about to say something other than "Are you sure you want to go to the Hall again, Brian?"

His parents seemed to feel he should make the effort, and so he said "Course I do."

Too late he wondered if she'd wanted an excuse to call the visit off. "Everybody does, Leonie," his mother said.

"Thanks for all your trouble with the tickets, Jeff."

Might Brian's aunt feel constrained to revisit Foliant Hall? He was about to admit reluctance, whatever the cause, when his mother sent him to the bathroom with no chance to argue. On the way to the Hall his aunt was so determined to distract him if not herself that she kept drawing attention to sights they'd already seen. When Brian saw the gates bore a notice, he thought the tours were still cancelled until a man bustled out of the drive to remove that hope.

The guide was back at her job. She gave Brian's aunt a sharp look and him a sharper one. The chapel remained shut to visitors, but the rooms of the main house were painted with angels too. Crowds of winged figures guided children through life, or helped shepherds in the fields, or stood behind personages the guide identified as members of the Foliant family, to advise or guard them. Brian was busy searching for Maurice Soulous, whatever the artist might look like. That must be why he saw a figure dodge behind an angel who was ushering a child into a church, and drop to all fours to hide in the midst of a flock of sheep. He even thought one angelic face, which was intent on the Bible a man was reading at a desk, had begun to slip askew. He assumed the painted face was flaking until he came close enough to find it was intact. In a bid to finish looking for the hidden presence he said "Have you seen him yet, Aunt Leonie?"

"I'm not looking very hard today, Brian."

"I thought you wanted to find him. I thought that's why we came."

"We've never turned him up," the guide said, explaining to the other visitors "The self-portraits of the artist. They may be just a myth."

Brian spoke before he was aware of thinking. "Maybe your friend uncovered him."

"Who?" Without waiting for an answer the guide said "What do you mean?"

"The man who fell."

"Brian," his father warned him, but the guide had more to say. "He wasn't there to do that. He wasn't looking underneath."

Brian found he was anxious to learn how the accident had affected the mural. As he tried to think of a way to ask, his father said "Enough. Nobody wants to hear."

Brian felt as if he'd been left alone with all the paintings in the house. Each bedroom sported angels overhead, and he kept thinking that one of the radiant faces was about to fall awry like a mask. Was his aunt troubled by some impression of the kind? They were in the last bedroom when he thought he glimpsed a spidery intruder scuttling behind a rank of angels up above, peering over every shoulder at him. By the time he dared to look directly up there was no sign of movement, and yet he had a sense that part of the mural was remaining unnaturally still so as not to be noticed. He was desperate to speak to his aunt about it, but as they left the house she spoke first. "You didn't need to look for him for me, Brian. Let's forget about him now."

She and his father seemed to have left him nothing to say. He was silent on the way back to town, where the family strolled around the antique shops and bought not a single item, and throughout dinner, ignoring how the burger and its attendant chips resembled a dormant spider, and during the quiz shows even when he knew an answer. "Don't sulk, Brian," his mother eventually said. "We'll go for a drive tomorrow."

He still had to face the night. In bed he found he wished the room were lighter, or else so dark he couldn't see the photograph on the wall. He had an unpleasant fancy that one of the vintage holidaymakers was about to raise not just his hat but along with it his face. Squeezing his eyes tight didn't shut out the impression. "Don't want to see," he mumbled. "Never did."

"Go to sleep now, Brian. Your mother wants her rest before she drives."

Brian must have slept already, since he hadn't realised his parents were in the room. Their presence ought to let him feel safe while he reassured himself that nothing had happened to the photograph, and he opened his eyes. As the dim arrested figures set about reclaiming their outlines from the gloom he could have imagined one of them had stirred—the one that was craning over a woman's shoulder. It was resting lanky fingers there; indeed, it appeared to be digging them in.

The Devil in the Details

Now it was clambering out of the picture like an insect emerging from a chrysalis. Its face resembled a swollen blister in paint, and gazed at Brian with peeling eyes while it thrust its crumbling grin at him. "Go away," Brian begged, burying his mouth in the pillow while he hid under the quilt. "Go somewhere else."

When he heard scrabbling above him he tried to believe it sounded more like a mouse in a wall than nails scraping at glass. He held a breath that would have come out as a scream if he'd heard the glass give way or the noise emerge around the frame of the photograph. He found it hard to breathe even when the sound receded and dwindled and was gone, but at last he managed to sleep.

He would rather not have gone back to the chapel even if his aunt believed they hadn't seen enough. She ventured in ahead of him, and when he followed he couldn't immediately locate her. Someone had spilled paint again, for it was dripping from the platform overhead. No, it was coming from the mural, where the restoration must have recommenced, although Brian couldn't see who was doing the job. Instead he saw his aunt, pressed flat to fit into the mural and by no means yet dry. His mouth was still lodged against the pillow, and his muffled shriek failed to rouse his parents.

Was his protest echoed? He could even have imagined his cry had been the echo. He peered nervously at the photograph in the twilight before dawn until he managed to establish that the glass was unbroken. He could see no intruder among the antique figures on the promenade. He couldn't help listening for his aunt, whose bed was against the far side of the wall and closer to his than to his parents, but there was no sound apart from running footsteps in the street. They vanished into the distance without wakening his parents, and surely any other noises had been part of Brian's dream, though he wasn't sure how the slam of a door fitted in. The reassurance let him go back to sleep.

Fearful Implications

His mother had to waken him. He felt eager for breakfast and for a day of driving, even if Aunt Leonie devoted herself to directing his attention. When he left the room he found his parents outside her door. His mother knocked on it again, and then harder. "Leonie," she called and raised her voice. "Leonie, it's time we got going."

"Try her phone, Barbara."

Brian heard the bell trilling in his mother's mobile but no sound from the room. "I'll fetch Mrs Mason," his father declared and marched down the corridor.

The landlady looked flustered and doubtful about unlocking the door. Once Brian's mother took all responsibility Mrs Mason let her into the room. The bed was violently rumpled, but that was the only sign of life. As Brian's mother opened the inner door to find the bathroom just as deserted, the landlady demanded "What's happened there?"

The glass of the photograph above the bed was splintered, erasing the face of a Victorian holidaymaker. There was blood on the shards and on the quilt beneath. Brian's mother was making to speak when her phone rang. "It's Leonie," she said with relief.

"Barbara?"

Brian's mother faltered, because it wasn't her sister's voice. "Who is this?"

"I was walking on the beach. I'm afraid there's a lady who's fallen."

"The beach," Brian's mother said with what might have been hope.

"Yes, the rocks. It's her phone. You're the top name on it. I've called emergency."

"How is she? How's my sister?"

Brian was already dashing into the corridor, faster when his father called his name. He was almost at the front door when a woman with a vacuum cleaner emerged from the dining-room. "Don't say you're running off as well."

"As well as what?" Brian had to ask.

"As the lady in the room by yours. She went out hours ago. She must have wanted to be somewhere in a hurry. You'd have thought she was being chased. I nearly thought I saw someone."

Even more reluctantly Brian asked "Who?"

"I told you, nobody. It must have been a shadow." With some defiance the woman said "Nobody looks like that."

Brian didn't care to hear any more, and his parents were on their way downstairs. He ran out of the Seeview and past shop after shuttered lifeless shop to the promenade. He was trying to hope his aunt had managed to conquer her fears, whatever they might be. He hadn't sprinted far along the cliff path when he saw his aunt lying face down on the rocks, where a woman was keeping a dog clear of her. However close he ventured, the sight didn't change for the better. His aunt's limbs were splayed like an explosion of flesh, and her flattened shape simply appeared to spread larger. When he heard his parents catching up with him he turned to them, though he had to cover his face. "I didn't see," he pleaded. "I didn't want to see."

Some Kind of a Laugh

"**H**AS ANYBODY EVER TOLD you that you look just like—"
"Yes."
The diner frowned over the tasselled tome of a menu at Bernard. "Nothing wrong with looking like you're famous."
"I'd rather just look like myself. Have you all decided?"
"Have you got five minutes?" As everybody at the table laughed the man said "That's what your double always says."
"I'm sure nobody wants to hear it from me."
This earned a token laugh like a description of mirth. "I'll have the black pudding and marmalade to start," the man said.

His companions began with Thai cuisine and Cajun and Italian, and the main courses ranged even further. After all, the Bestrow Bistro's slogan was Tastes For Every Taste. As Bernard returned from conveying the order to the kitchen, Xavier beckoned to him. "So what was the issue there?" the manager said almost too low to be heard.

He was at the far end of the long black room, beside a mirror that belonged in a chateau. One hand was grasping his broad chin as if his plump ruthlessly jovial face were a carnival mask, and the mirror put on the same show. "I wouldn't say there was one," Bernard murmured. "Just a bit of banter."

"Not much of it from you, was there? We're here to welcome customers, Bernard. As the chappie said, it can't hurt if you remind them of someone they like."

"I never cared for him myself."

"A lot of people like Len Binn. You could be an attraction."

This left Bernard feeling less than himself, driven to enact someone else's script, but when the jokey diner asked for the bill Bernard attempted Binn's accent, a Lancashire twang as flat as a cap. "Have you got five minutes?"

"We haven't, no. We've a train to catch."

He had time to peer so hard at the service charge that Bernard came close to protesting it went to the manager. Once the party had departed Xavier watched Bernard clear the table. "Keep it up and you'll get it right," he said, which Bernard didn't immediately grasp meant his impersonation of Len Binn. At least none of the other diners drew attention to the resemblance, and when the last of them had gone he was able to feel some relief. He and his colleagues cleared up until Xavier betrayed a modicum of satisfaction, and then Bernard drove home.

He and Laura lived off the motorway, which had left half of their street standing. As he clambered out of the tilted Mini, having found a space among the cars with two wheels on the pavement, he saw the front room of the small thin house flickering like a film. He was letting himself in through the shallow plastic porch when he heard a voice he'd hoped was no longer part of his life. "Have you done?" Len Binn said.

It was another phrase the comedian had made his own. Bernard had the absurd notion that Laura was being somehow unfaithful to him. When he tramped into the front room she looked up as though her ready smile and eagerly raised eyebrows were lifting her roundish face. "I was only watching while you were out," she said, "but look, this might make you laugh."

She'd recorded an episode of *In the Binn*, and now she ran it back to the beginning of a sketch in which the comic played a waiter. "Have you done?" he asked a tableful of diners, a question apparently worth a burst of laughter and applause from the audience, unless the response was prompted by his lugubrious elongated face, where the nose and jaw appeared to be contending for prominence. When he set about clearing the table the diners insisted on helping him, piling dishes and utensils on top of the plate he'd picked up. Once the entire contents of the table were heaped under his chin he staggered through the crowded restaurant in an elaborate perilous ballet, executing desperate pirouettes that nearly sent him sprawling on his back while he struggled to balance his burden. Laura laughed almost as hard as the audience, glancing at Bernard to encourage him to join in. At last Binn managed to deliver the ungainly stack intact to the kitchen and returned to the table with the bill. "We haven't given you a tip," the recipient said, and when Binn looked gloomily expectant "Don't jump off a boat if you can't swim."

Having groaned with delight, Laura said wistfully "I thought you might like him being like you."

"That's nothing like me. Nothing whatsoever."

"I just meant playing a waiter. Why do you dislike him so much?"

"They used to say I looked like him at school when the shows were first on."

"I expect you must have even then."

"They didn't just say it, they imitated him around me. The more they saw it bothered me, the more they did it. I ended up dreaming about him. I thought I'd never get him out of my head, and it's all being brought back."

Laura had paused the recording, but now she switched the television off. "I didn't mean to."

"I wasn't saying you did it. I'm saying now the television is showing his old stuff more people are going to know him."

"It can't do you any harm at your age, can it?" When Bernard stayed as silent as the television she murmured "Come to bed."

This was often their way of resolving an argument or salvaging an unsatisfactory day, but tonight it didn't work for him. Well after Laura was asleep he lay with an arm around her soft waist, remembering a Len Binn sketch. The comedian had emitted at least a minute's worth of inventive snores before his wife elbowed him awake, and then his attempts to get comfortable contorted him into increasingly unlikely shapes, several of which tumbled him out of bed. When he dozed off hours later his wife immediately woke him to enquire how his night had been. "Have you got five minutes?" He said that whatever he was asked: for directions in the street, or if he wanted sugar in his coffee, or his name... As Bernard began to fear he might grow as restless as Binn had, the repeated question put him to sleep.

A kiss almost wakened him before Laura left for work. Sometimes her hours at the library coincided with his at the bistro, but not this week. At least they both had jobs. He arrived at the restaurant to find Xavier looking more resolutely jolly than ever. "You've a chance to see your friend in the flesh," the manager said.

Bernard had to hope he didn't know "Which friend?"

"The one you want to be more like. Len Binn. He's appearing live not far from here. Maybe you could pick some tips up."

"More than I do in here, you mean."

"That's the sort of thing he'd say. You're getting better at it."

Xavier produced his phone to demonstrate that Binn was starting his first tour for years at a theatre twenty miles away in Lancashire. Before Bernard could react to this or to Xavier's unwelcome remark, the first lunchtime customers came in. "I'm Bernard and I'll be looking after you today," he said.

"Not Len," one of the female couple said. "Not Len Binn."

"Very much not. Where did you get that idea?"

"Our friends told us we might find him in here," her companion said.

Bernard took their order, only to encounter Xavier outside the kitchen. "I'm not joking, Bernard. Whatever people want, it's your job to provide it if you're capable. You just heard why they came."

Bernard saw his colleagues avoid looking at him while making sure they overheard—temporary, both of them, and younger than him. The manager loitered within earshot when Bernard welcomed his next customers. "I'm Bernard and I'll be looking after you today," Bernard said and felt compelled to flatten his accent. "How've you bin?"

"Perfectly fine," a young businessman said and stared at him.

Presumably he didn't recognise Len Binn's invariable greeting to his audience, unless he found it inappropriate. "Sounds as if you haven't got it quite right yet," Xavier accosted him to mutter.

At home Bernard found Laura watching television—not Len Binn, though he wondered if she'd just switched off a recording. As she turned off a documentary about homelessness he said "Your favourite man's at large again."

"If you mean Len Binn he's not my favourite. You are."

"You knew who I meant, though. He's live in Mostyn on Saturday."

"I'm sure you won't be going even if it is your day off. I won't either."

In the hope she'd had enough of the comedian Bernard said "Why's that?"

Fearful Implications

"I mightn't like to see how he looks now. Those shows are thirty years old, remember."

That night in bed Bernard put himself to sleep by mutely counting all the seconds in five minutes, though he had to repeat the process more than once. In the morning he used his phone to search for images of Len Binn. There were posters and photographs, quite a few almost illegibly autographed, but none more recent than the resurrected television shows. By the time the week was done with him Bernard felt desperate to resolve the situation—one diner asked him if he had five minutes, and he was sure that others expected the question of him as much as Xavier did. "Laura, are you sure you don't want to come and see Binn?"

"I'd rather see you. Don't say you're going."

"Xavier's decided I'm a draw. He's been trying to make me talk like the man."

"That's very committed of you, Bernard. If it helps you keep your job—"

"I won't be there to study him. I'll be snapping how he looks now, and thanks for making me think of it. Maybe when I've got pictures to show them, people won't be so eager to confuse me with him."

For longer than a moment Laura looked about to say a good deal more than "Come to bed."

Five minutes and five more and five again sent him to sleep, but it felt like delaying his encounter with Binn. All of Saturday did until he drove to Mostyn, a precipitous town on both sides of a valley. The Grand Theatre stood on a street like a giant stair, but had plainly once been grander. A cigarette butt sodden with at least one rainstorm protruded from a crack in the marble steps beneath a rusty stained-glass awning. Old posters adorned the faded lobby, and one showed Len Binn decades younger than Bernard. The manager, a perspiring fellow whose bow tie hung askew, was talking to a friend. "Don't expect too much," he said and looked away from Bernard, having blinked at him.

Bernard showed an usher the ticket on his phone, which felt close to anachronistic. The seats weren't numbered or reserved, and he tramped down a slope of stained frayed carpet to the front row. Soon nearly all the seats were occupied, and then the audience had a chance to talk—in fact, the blur of conversations carried on well past the time the show should have begun. Bernard thought the house lights were dimming more than once before they did. Eventually they flickered and expired, and the curtains stirred. A hand was fumbling the ponderous material apart, so tentatively that its owner might have lost his way, unless he was unequal to the task. At last a figure disentangled himself with a lurch, scowling at the curtains and then at the darkened auditorium. "Have you got five minutes?" he said.

This seemed not to be addressed to anyone in particular—it sounded like recalling what he used to ask—but it roused applause and laughter. Bernard felt as if he were looking at a waxwork of Len Binn rather than the man himself. The long face and large hands were unnaturally smooth and colourful, while the footlights lent them an oily shine. The extravagantly striped suit was at least a size too big, and made Binn look depleted by age. He waited for the last clap to carry off the final laugh before he said "How've you bin?"

This renewed the mirth, but Bernard thought the performer could have been referring to himself. He looked not so much waxy as embalmed, and Bernard sneaked his phone out to capture his appearance, having surreptitiously turned off the flash and the sound. Binn was telling jokes now, occasionally a new one—"Pontius Pilate says to Jesus, can you stop moving Easter about? We need to get you nailed down"—but mostly so familiar they felt like reminiscences, all too evocative of Bernard's childhood. He was glad when the curtains parted to reveal a double bed, which brought the routine to an end.

The lighting was so dim that he didn't immediately realise the figure lying in the bed was made of rubber. Once Binn joined it, the quilt couldn't hide how he had to manipulate its arm to make it interrupt his snoring. As he writhed in search of sleep he seemed bent on growing as bendy as his bedmate, but whenever he sprawled out of bed he looked hardly capable of clambering back. How much of this was an act? At last he returned to the footlights, meeting a wave of applause that Bernard thought could be acclaiming his stamina. The curtains faltered shut while he told more resuscitated jokes, and eventually dragged apart again. Four diners were seated at a table, and Binn shambled over to serve them.

Was this a new routine or one Bernard had forgotten watching? Binn tried to store all the orders in his head, only to plead repeatedly "Can we start again?" At last he fled towards an imaginary kitchen, plunging the stage into darkness that emitted a series of clatters and clanks. When the light faltered back it found the table full of the remains of dinner. "Have you done?" Binn enquired and set about clearing the table, relentlessly helped by the diners. He tottered back and forth across the stage in a dogged ballet, blinded by plates and utensils piled up to his forehead. The first knife he dropped Bernard took for a joke.

A plate and the utensils on it seemed less of one. Binn floundered about the stage, adopting a pronounced backwards tilt in a desperate attempt to balance his burden, but plate after plate toppled off the heap. The diners appeared to be paralysed by watching him. Long before the last dish shattered the laughter of the audience began to die away, not that Bernard had joined in. Binn flung the last plate down in a mime of resignation and lurched to the footlights. "Anybody out there?" he called. "All gone home?"

This dislodged a titter from the silence, though a nervous one. "Where am I?" Binn demanded. "Where's the nurse? Where's me medication?" Perhaps his increasingly flat accent was meant to identify all this as a joke. Bernard thought he should film the performance, and he was reaching for his phone when the movement caught Binn's eye. The comedian peered at him and reached a shaky hand across the footlights. "Is that me?"

As Bernard's neighbours glanced at him Bernard retorted "It absolutely isn't, no."

"By gum, if it's not it should be," Binn declared and leaned between the footlights as if to clear his vision. He was raising his hands beside his eyes when he lost his balance. "Hey," he protested, earning his biggest laugh for minutes. He gave the impression of essaying a somersault onto the floor of the auditorium, and a woman cried "Wow." However intentional they were, his acrobatics failed him. All his weight landed on the back of his head with a resounding thud and a snap that included a crunch.

Since his agonised grimace was upside down, he appeared to be grinning at Bernard. Quite a few of the spectators began to laugh and applaud until a woman on the front row added a scream. Someone else called "I'm a nurse" and hurried to examine Binn. She closed his outraged eyes before straightening up to say "I'm afraid that's the end."

This was surely everybody's cue to leave, and Bernard couldn't bear the sight any longer. Now that Binn's sagging eyelids hid his eyes the parody of a grin looked secretive, portending worse. As Bernard hurried to the exit, several people rather more than glanced at him. At the end of the aisle he came face to face with the theatre manager, whose stare looked resolved to halt him. "It was none of my doing," Bernard blurted. "It wasn't me."

The stare grew more accusing still. "Aren't you his son?"

"I should say not. Fenton's my name, Bernard Fenton. We aren't related in any way at all," Bernard said and dodged around the manager to struggle through the crowd.

The sight of Binn's dead face wasn't left behind so easily. As it lingered in Bernard's mind it twisted into a clown's contradictory grimace, threatening to blot out his route while he drove home. It was waiting for him in bed, where Laura lay asleep. He took care not to waken her as he turned in search of slumber. Whichever way he faced, the contorted features were in front of him. When at last he slept he had the impression that Laura nudged him more than once, almost waking him.

She was out when he came back to himself in the morning. At least Binn's face had gone too, and Bernard shared a grin at length in the bathroom mirror. He felt eager to be at the restaurant—to establish that they'd done with Binn. He was sitting in his car and had turned the key in the ignition when a voice said "How've you bin?"

It was on the radio, which he must have neglected to switch off, though he couldn't recall listening to it on the way home. A news bulletin was celebrating Len Binn's life with clips of him. Binn had been his stage name, but Bernard wanted to hear no more of him. He tuned the radio to a music station, which regaled him with "Send in the Clowns" as he drove to work.

Xavier was checking levels in the bottles that hung their heads behind the bar. "Ready for your routine?" he said.

"Which one is that?"

"The show you're putting on, Bernard, or can I call you Len? The one that's bringing customers."

"I take it you've not heard, but last night—"

"Your man lived up to himself right to the end with a bit of slapstick. He's all over the media, and that's publicity for us when we're offering our version of him."

"You don't think that would be tasteless."

"I think it's as tasteful as everything we do."

"I was there," Bernard said in desperation. "I know what he was like."

"Well, don't go showing anybody how he went. That really would be tasteless, but I'm glad you took the chance to study him."

"I mean I saw how decrepit he was." Bernard took out his phone and brought up the photographs. "I don't believe our customers would want to think anyone like this was serving them."

Xavier didn't speak until he'd finished skimming through the images. "No doubt of it, you're the comedian."

"I don't know what you mean."

"Except jokes aren't that good if you need to explain them. I'm not sure what you had in mind with this one."

Bernard made to speak as he retrieved the phone, and then his mouth stayed open. Somehow he'd reversed the camera last night, and every photograph he'd taken at the Grand was of himself. He bore a grin in all of them, though surely only because he'd thought he was photographing Binn unnoticed. "I never meant to do this," he protested.

"Let's hope you're more skilful at your job." As a party of diners came in Xavier muttered "Take them."

"I'm Bernard and I'll be looking after you today."

The four women scrutinised his face, and one of them apparently spoke for all. "Aren't you going to be Len Binn? Our friends you served the other day said you would."

Fearful Implications

"Forgive me, but you ought to know he died last night."

"We do," another woman said. "We thought you'd be putting on a tribute."

Xavier sent Bernard a look that urged him to comply, and Bernard gave in. "How've you bin?" he said, which gained him a surge of applause. Maintaining the flat voice was more of a distraction than he expected, so that halfway through taking the order he had to say "Can we start again?" This was appreciated too, and when he emerged from the kitchen Xavier detained him. "That's the ticket. Keep it up and I'll tell you what, we'll split your gratuities."

Bernard saw this didn't please the other waiters, who stayed unamused by his performance. He was doing more than them to earn the extra, and perhaps eventually he could take home as much as Laura did. "How've you bin?" he said to every diner he greeted, even those who appeared to find it odd. When anybody asked to order he said "Have you got five minutes?" This didn't always go down well, and before long Xavier took him aside. "Just do your routine for people who get it. It'd be a joke if it lost us any business."

How much direction would Len Binn have had to suffer? Bernard thought it might have been none at all. At least he had nearly eighty pounds in tips by the time he left the bistro. He would have given Laura the good news if she hadn't been waiting to say "Did you see him last night, Bernard?"

"I had the best seat. I was as close as I am to you."

"What did he turn out to be like?"

"Worn out, I'd say." Bernard reached for his phone but remembered just in time he would be showing Laura his own face. "Not up to putting on the show he was supposed to," he said.

"That should help you to forget about him, should it?" As if she'd been insensitive Laura said "Was it very bad, what happened?"

"A lot of people seemed to think it was his last joke. Let's go along with them."

Did she find him insensitive now? He was only trying to think as positively as she appeared to want if not to need. He wasn't going to be made to feel responsible for Binn's last pratfall. He was anticipating a good night's sleep, which he might have achieved if Laura hadn't kept waking him. He presumed he'd been snoring, and turned away from her, but his contortions failed to placate her. "Have you done?" he muttered on receiving yet another nudge, at which point she subsided, or his awareness did.

Perhaps lack of sleep left him unable to judge how long he spent at the bathroom mirror. There was no need to imagine he was in a dressing-room before a performance. Greeting Xavier was sufficient preparation, and Bernard said "How've you bin?"

"That's the spirit. The grin helps as well."

Bernard met all his diners with the phrase and had no sense it was unwelcome. Some of them recognised it, and he concentrated his act on them. When they asked to order, what else could he say except "Have you got five minutes?" Most of them saw the joke. Of course he didn't keep them waiting that long, and he was pleased with his routine until he had to return to a table, having found the order less than legible. "Can we start again?" he said, which his accent did its best to turn into a joke.

At least he wasn't called upon to struggle with used plates and utensils, since nobody handed him any. Just the same, he headed home with some relief, which lasted until Laura greeted him by protesting "You didn't have to get rid of him."

"Who says I did? I was nowhere near him."

"His shows, Bernard."

"I didn't stop those either. He did by not looking where he was."

"The ones I recorded. They're all gone."

"That wasn't me." He was sure he hadn't been in the front room last night or this morning; in fact, he couldn't recollect doing anything at all. "You can't think I'd be that mean or that bothered either," he said. "It's a joke."

"Maybe I don't need them when I have the real thing."

He failed to notice her placatory tone until he'd demanded "What are you saying?"

"I don't need another man when I've got you."

Did she fancy he was jealous? That was a laugh, and he made a bid to come up with one before having recourse to their catch phrase in the hope it would render dialogue superfluous. "Come to bed."

He waited to be certain Laura was asleep, and then continued lying absolutely still, even once his arm around her waist began to lose its circulation, making her body feel more like rubber. He mustn't start writhing in search of sleep, or he might end up adopting postures that no doubt anybody watching would find comical. Though he was unaware of snoring, he came to himself with his mouth open wide enough to let out several words. A poke in the ribs had roused him, and when Laura elbowed him once more he turned his back. As he clung with both hands to the edge of the mattress he felt he was preserving not just his posture but his sense of self.

His own words found him in a tortuous tangle of bedclothes. What had he said to rouse himself? Surely not a question about time. He couldn't ask Laura, who had already left for work. In the bathroom his reflection looked fiercely lit, as if the mirror was edged with lights. He mustn't feel compelled to rehearse, and he turned away before his grin could grow wide enough to hurt his face. How long did Xavier intend him to keep up the impression? The requirement had started to feel like a threat, and so did work.

Xavier was standing in the doorway of the bistro like a theatre manager waiting to welcome an audience. The first diners of the day gazed at Bernard with a version of delight, and the fattest man said "Have you got five minutes?"

"He's got those for you and more," Xavier said and told Bernard "There's your cue. You're on."

As Bernard ushered the party to a table he made himself ask "How've you bin?" and tried to feel complimented when the best-fed fellow said "Sounds just like he looks." The party even seemed amused when some of Bernard's scrawl on the pad forced him to say "Can we start again?" He delivered the order to the kitchen, only for the chef to emerge in search of Xavier. Once they'd finished muttering, the manager beckoned to Bernard. "No need to overdo your act. It's a good job chef remembered what you read out."

"I don't know what you're saying."

Xavier flourished the slip Bernard had taken to the kitchen. "No call to go this far. You needn't be this much like him."

Bernard stared at the scribbled chit. It wasn't merely hard to read; it wasn't in his handwriting. If it hadn't been the only order so far he might have accused someone of confusing his with another, but found himself saying "How much like?"

"Don't pretend. Damn well just like this."

Xavier brought images up on his phone—photographs and posters of Len Binn. Several were autographed, and there was no mistaking the resemblance to the writing on the slip. "Just do your voice and your words," Xavier said. "They're what your fans are here for."

Bernard felt desperate to be called by name. Of course he'd seen Binn's writing when he'd searched for images of him, but he would never have expected it to lodge so deep in his mind. He stayed clear of the diners until Xavier indicated they wanted him. "Have you done?"

he couldn't avoid saying, and at once was afraid they meant to help him load the tray. "Al tek them," he said despite not knowing if Binn ever had.

Even loading the tray without anybody's help made him nervous, and he felt relieved not to be offered a tip in case it proved to be a prank. He needed a break from performing—an interval—and he held the door open to speed the diners onwards, only for another party to troop in. "Why, it's you," their leader said. "We discovered you the other day. We've been sending you our friends."

He was indeed the culprit—the diner who'd first drawn attention to Bernard's face. "You're very welcome," Xavier said as if they'd thanked him. "No prize for knowing who'll be serving you today."

As Bernard led the party to a table he felt as if he was trying to leave them behind. He passed out menus, realising too late that he'd failed to name himself. He refrained from asking for five minutes and strove to write legibly, but eventually had to plead "Can we start again?" He didn't simply read the order to the chef but ran his finger underneath the words in the hope that doing so would leave them comprehensible. All this was an uneasy preamble to having to ask at the end of the meal "Have you done?"

"All yours," the man responsible for his performance said.

This sounded like a threat posing as a joke. Bernard balanced the tray on his left hand and set about loading plates. His hands were fully occupied when the man passed him a plate strewn with utensils. "Don't," Bernard said in the flattest accent he could summon, which might simply have turned it into a joke. "Leave it," he cried so flatly that it sounded like an exhortation to live. He tried to fend off the plate before it could overbalance the tray, which he immediately dropped.

One corner struck the edge of a plate, flipping it over the tray to spill its contents into a woman's lap. Meanwhile Bernard dealt the man's plate such a shove that a fork flew off it, clawing the man's wrist. The plate fell out of his hand and knocked over a glass of red wine, splashing one of his companions as crimson as a murder victim. "I'm sorry," Bernard tried to say, but the last word disintegrated into laughter. "I'm," he said, "I'm," with diminishing success. He was close to howling before Xavier captured his attention. "That's it, Bernard. Get out and don't come back till you've heard from me."

Bernard stared into his face, which Xavier was clutching like a dramatic mask. The sight and the rebukes sobered him enough to let him say "At least you've remembered my name."

"Whatever it is, just take yourself home."

Surely there was a phrase to fit the situation—indeed, some phrases went with a variety of developments. Bernard turned back to the diners and had to struggle not to giggle at their bedraggled bids to clean themselves up. "Can we start again?" he said with a flatness meant to control his mirth.

"You're finished here, Bernard," Xavier said. "That's the end."

Of course every performance must have one. Bernard might have liked to find a better exit line, but his catch phrase would do. He drove home as best he could for laughing, and had to stop the car more than once to let his hilarity subside. It had by the time he heard Laura switch the television off. She looked taken aback, surely not because she'd been keeping company with anyone Bernard wouldn't welcome. "What are you doing home so early?" she said, and hastily "Not that I'm not glad to see you."

"Who are you glad to see?" Surely he needn't make her say his name, and he said "Don't worry, I know."

For some reason she had to decide what to say next. "So why are you back?"

"He had an accident at work."

Fearful Implications

"Who did?"

"Him." When she made to speak he said "I've already told you not to worry. It'll all be cleared up by tomorrow." This fell short of reassuring her, but he knew the phrase that always saved the situation. "Come to bed."

As he brushed his teeth the light that framed the mirror seemed to close around his face, squeezing out more of a grin. He kept that up while he climbed into bed but tried to reduce it, seeing that it disconcerted Laura. He caressed her as he always did, and couldn't help observing that it had become a routine, the physical equivalent of a catch phrase. He tried varying his posture, but the more he attempted to invent, the less appealing his wife seemed to find him. He'd begun to feel grotesque, more like a puppet than a performer, by the time Laura said "What are you trying to do? It isn't funny, Bernard."

At least it had made her say his name. He sprawled off her to lie on his back. "Have you done?" he didn't really need to ask. "Then we'll get some sleep."

"Don't you want dinner?"

"I've had enough of dining for one day. I need my sleep now. You could do with some as well. You seem on edge."

If she'd said she wanted to watch television, he didn't know how he might have reacted. He clasped her waist and imagined for a moment she was making to escape. "Can we start again?" he murmured, but since Laura didn't respond he presumed she had fallen asleep as readily as usual. He oughtn't to resent that even if he lacked the knack. "Keep quiet," he muttered, lowering his voice when Laura stirred uneasily. "Keep still."

At some point this allowed him to sleep. When he wakened it was daytime, and he was alone in a confusion of bedclothes. He'd contorted himself in the night after all. It made him feel robbed of control, and had it driven Laura out of the house? He was so grateful to find her in the kitchen that his grin brought an ache to his face. "How've you bin?"

Apparently she didn't recognise this as a question. "Will you have something?" she said.

"Why wouldn't I? I could eat for two, the way I feel." If he oughtn't to have said this, he would like to know why. He wished they had children as much as Laura did—they would be somebody for him to entertain—but he'd failed at that performance. A sense of his uselessness made him say "Let me help."

He regretted this at once. A loaf was waiting on the breadboard to be sliced, but Laura had to hand him the knife. He couldn't help wincing at the sight of the serrated blade resting on her palm—couldn't help remembering the dropped tray, the toppled glass, the explosion of red. "Don't give me that," he said, but perhaps it sounded like a catch phrase, especially in that voice. Repeating the words didn't stop him clutching at the handle of the knife.

He drove to work determined to make up for whatever he'd done, but Xavier refused to unlock the door. "I'll send you what you're owed," the manager told him through the glass. "It won't be much."

Bernard couldn't go home with so little. He found he was uneasy about returning home at all. He'd seen enough street entertainers to know how to proceed. He retrieved an empty carton from a bin behind the bistro and stood beside it near the entrance. Whenever anybody glanced at him he said "How've you bin?" or "Have you got five minutes?" Even once he emptied all his change into the carton, nobody contributed. The occasional passer-by loitered to stare at him, and perhaps he shouldn't have responded "Have you done?" but calling after them "Can we start again?" didn't bring them back. At last a spectator lingered to address him. "Let him rest," she said. "You're nothing like him."

Play with Me

WHEN JACKIE LURCHED AWAKE, the only sounds were the whisper of the sea a quarter of a mile away across the beach and the shouts of other people's children. She was afraid she was alone until she twisted onto her back. Her five-year-old son was almost within reach, using a stick to sketch somebody half buried in the sand. "Don't bury me, Tom," she said.

"I won't if you'll play catch with me."

The thought of a ball game made her feel more tired than ever. "I will soon, all right? Just let me have a little nap."

"There won't be time." As if he didn't want her to overhear his disloyalty Tom mumbled "Dad would."

His father might have if it was too early to get drunk and knock her about, Jackie refrained from saying. Driving halfway across England had felt even more like escaping from him than her divorce had, but it had exhausted her as well. She'd wanted to give Tom a few hours on the beach once she'd unpacked at the hotel. The sun was above them, casting the shadow of a root that groped out of the edge of the cliff near the top of a zigzag path. "We'll have time for a game, I promise," she said. "Be a good boy and give me half an hour."

"I won't know when that is."

"I will," Jackie said, setting her phone alarm. "Don't go far away," she told him and was inspired by her silhouette, pointing like the indication of a sundial at the cliff. "Stay by my shadow."

"All right," Tom said, though not as if it was. She held his gaze to make certain he knew she was serious as she sank down on the sandy blanket. Then her weighty eyelids intervened, and she was asleep.

"Play with me."

The plea didn't quite waken her, not least because it was hardly so much as a whisper. "No alarm yet," she protested, possibly aloud. She clung to sleep even when disintegrating fingers found her face, since they had to be sand carried on a wind. She didn't waken until a shiver travelled the whole length of her. She blinked and saw the sun lowering itself towards the sea. It was close to setting, and she'd slept through the alarm.

Tom must have taken pity on her and let her sleep. She was thinking how to make up for his lost game as she turned over. He wasn't behind her. All the families she'd seen earlier had gone, and she was alone on the beach.

As she struggled to sit up she saw two things that disturbed her more than she understood. The lopsided rickety figure Tom had drawn, which might have been composed of little more than sticks, could just as well have been climbing out of the ground as undergoing a playful burial. And the descending sun had extended her shadow all the way to the cliff. She took a breath so fierce it gritted sand between her teeth and cried "Tom."

Her voice sounded small as a child's under the dimming sky. It was the solitary sound on the beach, where the waves were more distant than ever. Surely they were too gentle to have carried Tom away, and besides, she was all too sure that he'd followed her shadow to the cliff.

While she was sleeping the shadow might have led straight to the path, and he could have taken that as an excuse to climb up just a little way, just a little further since she was asleep, just to the top... Surely he was up there and unable to hear her, even when she called with all her voice, and she ran to the path.

It turned back on itself several times on its way up the cliff. As it made her dodge back and forth Jackie felt she was trying to lift the sun above the horizon. The sun rose with her, though not very far. At each bend in the path she shouted Tom's name, which the sky seemed to shrink even smaller. She was nearly at the top when she caught sight of a mass of rubble almost hidden by overgrown earth on the side of the cliff. A building must have collapsed down the cliff quite some time ago. It distracted her from an impression that something wasn't on the cliff that ought to be. She couldn't bother about that now. She had to find Tom.

As she strode up the final stretch of path she was preparing to tell him to come here at once, but the words expired in her mouth. Over the edge of the cliff she saw flat land miles wide, and it was utterly deserted. There wasn't even a hedge Tom could be hiding behind. Jackie stumbled onto the cliff top, desperate to think the grass was long enough to hide him, but even standing shakily on tiptoe only showed her how alone she was except for her outstretched shadow. She could see more of the beach now—the emptiness of the beach. She cried Tom's name a last time as she snatched out her phone to call the police.

"My son's lost. I've lost my son. He's five. I'm up on the cliff above the beach and I can't see him anywhere. I'm by the building that fell down the cliff."

"The old church."

Presumably it must be. She had to give her name and Tom's and

Fearful Implications

other information that felt as though it was holding up any help. Long before she was assured the police were on their way, she wanted to ring off. She pocketed the phone and saw her shadow imitate her, and at once she knew what she'd missed seeing as she climbed the cliff: the shadow of the root just below the edge. What could the root belong to when there was no vegetation up here except grass? The question seemed worse than trivial while she didn't know where Tom was, but perhaps she needed some distraction from her fears, and she made for the edge of the cliff. She hadn't reached it when she saw she was walking on a pavement almost hidden by grass.

No, not a pavement—a crowd of stone slabs. When she stooped she made out words and numbers carved on the nearest slab—a name and dates, almost erased by moss and weather. More than that was written on the slab just above the hole in the cliff where she'd seen the protruding root. The letters and digits looked etched by shadow. She hadn't time to read the name, because she'd seen the dates and the inscription beneath them. 1871-1876. HE NEVER PLAYED AS A CHILD SHOULD.

Did this mean the child hadn't had enough of a chance, or that he'd played unlike a child? He'd been Tom's age, and now Jackie remembered the plea she'd heard in her sleep: "Play with me." The whisper had been so thin it had scarcely sounded like a voice—not Tom's, at any rate. In panic and confusion she ventured to the crumbling edge of the slab and leaned over. Not just the shadow of the root was missing. The twisted root was gone, and now she realised how much it had looked like a shrivelled arm reaching out a small hand robbed of flesh.

She was afraid to go closer, but she had to see. Dashing down the path, she activated the flashlight on her phone as she came to the hole in the side of the cliff. It was a few feet lower than the slab and almost level with her face. When she shone the beam into the hole she saw it was blocked by a rubbery object bearing ridges caked with sand—the sole of a shoe.

Earth gathered under her fingernails as she groped to drag the shoe out. Yes, it was Tom's, with the frayed lace she'd meant to renew tomorrow. He must have put his shoes back on to climb the cliff. Now that the hole was clear, she could see as far as a bend, where the tunnel led upwards. There was nothing like enough space to let her follow. With her free hand she began frantically to dig earth out of the hole to widen it, and was almost too afraid to call Tom's name.

It brought an instant response—earth spilling into the bend from above, and a sound of rapid slithering. She couldn't help recoiling, and grabbed at the hole to save herself from backing over the edge of the path. The phone flew out of her hand to skitter down the cliff. The sun had sunk unnoticed, darkening the world, and so she never saw the small hand that seized hers. Surely Tom's couldn't have already grown so thin.

But Once a Year

"You'll be glad they stopped the kissing, Mr Mason." After a pause a thought might have required, Marie said "Even if you won't be here to see."

"I should think you ladies will welcome it."

"We just hope you enjoy your retirement." No less emphatically Dee said "They never asked us if we'd like to keep the mistletoe."

"I'm sure they simply want to protect you from harassment."

"We can protect ourselves and one another." Val fixed him with a gaze that could have deterred customers from asking the bank for a loan. "Was it your idea, Mr Mason?" she said.

"You all saw the email," he said to the male staff as well. "It came from head office."

"You didn't suggest it, Val's saying," Marie said.

"I'm just one branch manager. I'm past expecting to be heard much." At once he was reminded of his youth, and tried to regain some sense of power by saying "Time to let the public in. Valerie, your turn."

He was making it sound like a childhood game, and the idea of letting someone in took him back too. As Val made to unlock the door he retreated to his office, hearing Marie murmur "He won't even admit he hates being kissed. I've never known such a cold fish."

So she hadn't forgiven him for recoiling when she'd aimed a kiss at him under the mistletoe last year. It was far too late to explain now, even if he could. On the way to his desk he glimpsed movement at the window, pale flakes blundering against the glass. Could he really sense the chill they brought and hear their icy impacts, so faint they seemed scarcely to exist before disintegrating? His cousin Alice had once said the only thing that made less noise than snow was cobwebs falling. Alice, a whisper that wasn't snow, an encounter in the dark... As memories overwhelmed him he felt twelve years old, but now he knew he ought to be afraid.

"It's them again."

He'd wondered if his mother meant their guests—his Aunt Susan, Uncle Ned and their daughter Alice—until he saw she'd picked up an envelope as she made to let them in. "Happy Christmas Eve," she cried as though to banish any hint of inhospitality. "Dickie, help your uncle bring whatever needs to come."

The latest snowfall had shrunk to minute flakes, lingering to glitter in the light from the hall. As Dick, which he wished his family would call him, followed his uncle down the chilly padded path he thought someone was coming to help, but when he glanced back, nobody had left the house. The dodging shadow must have belonged to someone who'd gone in. His uncle dealt him a decisively manly handshake before loading him with presents out of the Land Rover. Dick was taking care on the path when a set of tracks, presumably left by whoever had delivered the latest item of mail, detained him. They must be hours old for their shapes to have been rendered so irregular, even if he couldn't see how the snowfall had done that. Someone else's footprints must have covered up a set returning to the gate. "Don't hang about,

Dickie," his uncle called, slamming the boot. "We don't want soggy presents."

Dick tramped hard on the doormat, wiping his feet as well. He'd hardly piled the presents under the tree in the front room when his aunt swooped at him. "Where's my cuddle, Dickie? I haven't had my hug."

He suffered her profuse perfumed embrace by gazing past her at his cousin. Alice was plumper than last year, especially where it proved to matter quite a lot to him. Behind her a sprig of mistletoe was tacked above the doorway to the hall. It felt like encouragement if not temptation, but it was his father who passed beneath it, bearing drinks. "Get your cousin a juice, Dickie," he said.

Dick thought she might accompany him under the mistletoe, but she sat with unfamiliar primness on a chair, hauling her skirt over her knees. "What do you want?" he asked more brusquely than he'd meant to.

"I'll have whatever you do."

This felt like a kind of closeness, which to some extent compensated for the lack of a hug, though one might have discomforted him in ways he couldn't entirely define. He fetched two glasses of orange juice from the kitchen in time to hear his mother tell his father "What I said before, it's them."

She showed Ned and Susan the envelope before handing it to him. "Is that the one you get every year, Chris?" his brother said.

"More of them than I'd like to count, and more illegible than ever. I'm surprised it even found the house." Dick's father delayed opening the envelope to examine the front again. "Particularly without a stamp," he said.

Dick could have fancied his father was reluctant to open the envelope. Certainly he grimaced as he poked a finger under the flap,

Fearful Implications

peeling it away to reveal a greyish strip that looked unnecessarily moist. He extracted the card between finger and thumb before crumpling the envelope to drop it in the bin beside the squarish boxy television. He gave the picture—a vintage photograph of skaters on a pond resembling a web made of incisions—not much of a glance, and the inside even less of one. "Unidentifiable as ever," he said.

"Let's see if anybody can decipher it," said Dick's mother.

She had to wag the hand she was holding out before he passed her the card. As she peered inside it Dick's aunt and uncle joined her, and Alice stood up too. "That's right," his father said as if it was the opposite, "everybody have a go."

Dick took him at his word, which gave him an excuse to put an arm around Alice's shoulders. They felt soft until a shrug hardened them, and he didn't know whether to let go, a decision he postponed by concentrating on the card. "Take note, you two," his uncle said to him and Alice. "There's how not to write or spell."

You and your familly all ways in my thoughts... Dick had to squeeze his eyes thin to distinguish many of the sprawling letters, which he would have been ashamed to produce at half his age. Were they symptoms of the second childhood in which people said you ended up? The signature was worse still, a wormy scribble that crawled off the edge of the card. "Whenever you're done with it," his father said.

As he retrieved it Dick's aunt said "What did it say last year?"

"I really can't remember," his father said and consigned the card to the bin. "It isn't worth remembering."

Dick took the opportunity to squeeze his cousin's shoulders. "We do, don't we?"

"In that case spare us," his father said.

Dick might have protested that the rebuke was unfair if he wouldn't have felt childish, especially when Alice could have thought he was.

250

But Once a Year

Over the years the family had joked about the increasingly scrawled cards and their defiantly unrecognisable signature. *Thinking of you, still thinking of you, always thinking of you, hoping to catch up...* He remembered all the messages but kept them to himself, wondering whether the latest card expressed frustration if not worse. Instead he asked Alice "Shall we have a fight?"

"Nobody's been having one of those," his father said. "Any disagreement's done."

Alice seemed to misunderstand Dick too, because she pulled away from him. "A snowball fight," he felt awkward for having to explain.

"That should be fun," his aunt declared. "Just bundle up."

In fact it wasn't too successful. While the grownups portrayed amusement, not to mention jovial revenge, Alice complained when one of Dick's snowballs caught her breast, even though it was protected by a coat as fat as his. He shied a few desultory missiles at the adults and then watched the play of shadows on the snow in the back garden. Some trick of light suggested one of them was thinner than it ought to be. The illusion vanished before he could locate it, and his father protested "Who was that?"

He was brushing at his shoulder, dislodging pale fragments. "Nobody hit you," Dick's mother said as if addressing someone younger than their son. "Not even near."

"I believe it's turning colder," Dick's father said with a shiver. "Let's have everyone inside."

Perhaps because Dick resented the show of concern, he couldn't help feeling it disguised something else. Everybody trooped into the house, leaving their shoes in the kitchen. He was watching Alice strip her coat off while he squirmed out of his when his father shouted from the front room "Who did this?"

At first Dick couldn't see anything wrong, and then he realised that the card from the unknown sender was perched on the mantelpiece, peeking from between an embossed picture of mistletoe and a sketch of a Christmas tree. "Who was last in here?" his father demanded. "Was it you, Dickie?"

As Dick shook his head Alice spoke up. "We went out first. It wasn't us."

"Someone must have thought you dropped it by mistake, Chris," Dick's mother said. "Does it really matter? Who's ready for their dinner?"

Dick's father tore the card up and threw the pieces in the bin. "Now I am."

This might have disconcerted Dick, but Alice's defence of him had heartened him. Throughout dinner—a whole salmon, of which he had the boniest portion—he tried to keep her talking, but she seemed more interested in the adults' conversation. She was just a few months older than Dick, hardly a reason for her to feel superior. He was trying to think how to recapture her attention when his father turned to her. "I don't know if anyone has mentioned you're in your parents' room."

Dick hadn't been upstairs since his father had erected the camp bed for Christmas. "Isn't she sleeping with me?"

"Your room's out of bounds now, old chap," his uncle said. "No sharing any more, at any rate."

"Why?" Dick said, feeling stupider still.

"If you have to ask," his aunt said, "that's a reason."

He'd embarrassed Alice at least as much as himself. He would have apologised if he could have found the right words, but the presence of the grownups didn't help. He was glad when dinner finished, not least since washing up brought him closer to Alice at the kitchen sink. He managed to brush against her several times before she flapped a towel at him. "Why are you being so clumsy? Do you want me breaking dishes?" she said for everyone to hear, and he felt even more awkward than she'd made him out to be.

The film the family appeared to be compelled to watch at this time of year saved him from talking to her for a while, though it felt like being trapped in a past before he was born. Once again the drawling hero saw what life would have been if he'd followed a different path. While the women dabbed at their eyes and Alice looked determined not to need to, the men stayed doggedly impassive, Dick's father in particular. Dick might have thought the film had some extra meaning for his father, but his own embarrassment drove the notion out of his head.

In some ways bedtime came as a relief. He was grateful not to be expected to kiss anyone good night any more, however welcome Alice might have been. Lying in the dark, he heard her use the bathroom in a variety of ways, which troubled his body along with his mind. Thoughts of her kept him awake, and unfamiliar feelings did, growing disconcertingly physical. All this subsided when he heard a whisper.

By straining his ears he convinced himself it was snow on the window. The effort to identify the sound distorted it until he could have fancied it was forming words or just a word, though not one that made any sense to him. Horse certainly didn't, even if it was spelled hoarse, and coarse or course was little better. If he was imagining a whisper that said thoughts, it brought him none. Striving to hear sent him to sleep, only to waken with a sense that he'd gone to bed too early, because he heard a carol in the night, approaching the house. The solitary voice seemed to loom towards him as he endeavoured to hear. He could have thought that, rather than distant, it was low and close and lacking in breath. It was repeating snatches of carols as if they were all that the singer could bring to mind: "It came upon a midnight clear" and then "What child is this?" Perhaps the blurred fragmentary voice belonged to someone staggering back from a pub—it sounded uneven enough—and the idea let Dick take refuge in sleep.

Alice roused him. He'd started hoping she was in his room when he heard she was outside. "It wasn't me," she had just said.

"I didn't think so," Dick's father said and shoved the door wide, letting more daylight into the room. "Dickie, have you been making work for your mother?"

Dick yanked up his pyjama trousers before kicking off the bedclothes and stumbling to the door. His father's frown directed him to marks on the carpet, a track composed of melted snow and other fragments, which wandered about the landing and over the stairs. "It wasn't me either," he protested. "I've been in bed."

His father seemed to need to blame him. "Just clean it up so your mother doesn't have to," he said, and almost as an afterthought "Happy Christmas."

"Happy Christmas, Dickie," Alice said, retreating to her room.

"Happy Christmas." The chorus came from downstairs as well as the guest room, and Dick could have imagined one voice uttered just the final syllable, if even that much. He fetched the vacuum cleaner and nuzzled the stairs with the hose before hefting the cleaner all the way up them. While he might have liked Alice to witness his feat of strength, he was glad she wasn't watching him at housework. He erased the marks as swiftly as he could, disliking the look of the moist discoloured fragments, even if they were just crumbs of earth.

He followed Alice into the bathroom. Of course she wasn't in there—it simply meant he was next in—but the thought of her with no clothes on was, and the steamy air smelled of her soap. He lingered over bathing until his father knocked on the door to ascertain how much longer he would be, sounding more reproachful than Dick quite understood. The mirror had steamed up, and when Dick rubbed it clear he had a momentary impression of someone dodging out of sight behind him. It must have been his own movement, which also produced a short-lived chill on his back.

Breakfast was accompanied by Christmas music on the radio. Whenever the name of the day came up, the first syllable seemed to grow prominent, as if a rogue contributor was emphasising it just not clearly enough to be unmistakable. As Dick tried to hear more precisely his father said "What's up, Dickie? We don't want any frowns at Christmas."

Dick might have rejoined that his father had one, perhaps for the same reason. "If everybody's had enough," his mother intervened, "it's nearly time for presents."

He and Alice cleared up, and he avoided touching her at the sink, not even handing her the washed-up items but planting them in the plastic rack. When she led the way into the front room he was acutely if not painfully aware of the rhythmical sway her hips had developed. He looked away for fear the family would detect his excitement, and felt as if somebody he'd failed to notice had observed him.

His presents were boys' books from his aunt and uncle, records from his parents. Alice had bought him one of those as well, an album by a band she liked, the Beatles. When his father found Dick's present for her under the tree, Dick was taken off guard by how his heartbeat speeded up. Alice looked surprised by the smallness of the package, but produced a smile once she'd opened it. "That's pretty, thank you," she said.

"I wasn't sure what to get you this year. Dad said you ought to like a ring."

"I do."

"Don't say you're proposing, Dickie." Less like a joke his aunt said "I expect you feel grownup now, Alice."

Fearful Implications

Dick watched his father distribute presents, no more of which were for him. He was distracted by a dead light just visible through the branches of the tree. He might have taken it for a watchful eye if the bulb hadn't been so lifeless. As his father finally returned to his chair, Dick's uncle said "You've forgotten someone's, Chris."

He was pointing past the tree at a small parcel almost hidden by the thick timber disc that supported the trunk. As his father stooped to retrieve it, Dick realised he couldn't see the dead greyish oval bulb among the branches any longer. Perhaps his father had inadvertently nudged it out of sight, but Dick had no time to wonder as his father swung around to face him. "Who brought this in?"

"You will have, will you, Dickie?" Aunt Susan said.

"I just brought what uncle gave me."

"I didn't give you that," his uncle said.

Dick recognised the writing on the package—the same as the unidentifiable card had borne. The scrawl said Chris, if barely that as it strayed off the edge of the crumpled wrapping, which was only just restrained by the loose bow of a discoloured ribbon. "Don't keep us in suspenders," Aunt Susan cried as though the situation needed a joke. "Maybe it'll tell us who it is at last."

Dick's father grimaced and wiped his hands on his trousers once he'd tugged the bow apart. When he peeled off the wrapping, fragments of it stuck to the small stained box. He lifted the lid, only to hesitate over displaying the contents. "What is it, Chris?" Dick's mother said.

As his father tipped the box towards her, the contents rolled out—a tarnished silver ring, which fell on the carpet and trundled towards her without another sound. She captured it and made more of a face than Dick's father had. "What's this inside it? It looks like old skin."

"I've no idea and I can do without one. Throw it in." His father held the box out, shutting it as soon as she returned the ring. "That's the end of it," he said, shoving the box after the ribbon and wrapping into the bin.

"It reminds me of something," his brother said.

"Well, don't let it."

"No, really. I believe I've got it." As Dick's father mimed incredulity if not anger, Uncle Ned rummaged in the bin, eventually coming up with a piece of the Christmas card. "This signature," he said. "Don't you think it could be Helen, Chris?"

"It could be any bloody thing. Forgive my language, children."

"I'm sure this is a kind of h, and this could be an e and l."

"I couldn't care less if they are or not. Just leave it, Ned."

"I'd like to hear a little more about it," Dick's mother said.

"Look, I told you I was engaged once. Long before we met, dear. She didn't prove too reasonable when I made it clear I'd had enough. I'd have expected her to take it better. She was quite a bit older than me. I was glad to forget all about it, and I still am."

"Why don't you two go and listen to the record you gave Dick?" Aunt Susan said. "But don't put it on too loud."

"And I hope we won't hear any screaming," Dick's father said.

Presumably he had in mind the way the Beatles made some girls behave, and Alice gave him a haughty look. "I won't be," she said. "I'm not stupid."

She might have meant to show this by not sitting next to Dick on his bed. She took the only chair, having told him to move yesterday's clothes. While the first side of the album played on his portable record-player, she kept swaying her top half with the rhythm, desisting whenever she grew aware of him. The songs obscured an argument downstairs, which eventually gave way to the slam of a dustbin lid under the window. Dick guessed his father had consigned the uninvited present and the torn-up card to the bin. The side ended, and he was about to turn the record over when his aunt opened the door without knocking. "Come down now," she said as if she'd caught them at some mischief or had thought she would.

The annual game of Monopoly was laid out on the dining-table. Dick chose the boot as usual, though now the token reminded him of the footprints he'd seen in the snow, even if his memory suggested the visitor had worn no shoes, an idea so stupid he felt childish. He'd never noticed an odd echo in the room, rousing a bony restless sound whenever his father shook the dice. Soon Dick owned properties, but found he didn't relish collecting rent as much as usual, because he felt prompted to tell anyone who landed on them "Come and visit" if not "Come and stay." He could almost have imagined somebody was whispering the phrases in his ear if not his head. "Just collect what you're due, Dickie," his father said, at which Dick thought someone gave a low laugh, though he couldn't see who had.

Uncle Ned won the protracted game and flourished his fists above his head. Dick might have joined in, since it was time for dinner. His father carved the turkey, a spectacle Dick found unexpectedly bothersome; the echo was at work again, and the creak of bones parting from the carcass was imitated somewhere near. His parents let him have a glass of wine, since Alice had been given one. He devoured several slices of breast, a word that had acquired an extra connotation. He was ready for the Christmas pudding when it came, not least because he hadn't wholly outgrown the hope of discovering a coin. He thought Alice had one until she peered more closely at her prize. "What is it, Aunt Annie? It looks like someone's nail."

"It's certainly not one of mine." Dick's mother gazed in distaste at the blackened twisted object. "Dickie, fetch your cousin another spoon," she said. "Have you been playing a prank?"

"I never put that in." He felt increasingly wronged as he brought

Alice a spoon from the kitchen. "I wish I hadn't stirred it when you said to make a wish," he told his mother.

"Don't be such a baby, Dickie."

"One more item for the bin," his father said and stalked off with the spoon as if he couldn't bear the presence of its contents any longer.

Dick heard the back door slam—presumably his father couldn't even stand to have the object as close as the kitchen bin—and the prolonged gushing of a tap. As his father came back Alice said "I'm sure it wasn't Dickie. He wouldn't do that to me."

If he had indeed played such a prank he couldn't have been sure who the victim would be, but her support left him more determined to catch her under the mistletoe. He almost managed on the way into the front room, but the footfalls of the grownups made the tree stir and creak, distracting him. He could almost have imagined the scrawny shadow that crouched behind the tree continued shifting after every branch grew still.

Might he catch Alice on her way out of the room? Anticipation stayed with him throughout the after-dinner film, in which a ghost confronted Scrooge with his past. Dick's mother kept glancing at his father, who visibly relaxed once the ghost had done its job and its spectral colleagues guided Scrooge towards a preferable life. As soon as the credits set about mounting the screen Alice jumped up, too fast for Dick to head off. She was making for the bathroom, but her mother called "Bedtime now, Alice."

"For us too," Dick's father said with a look at his wife that plainly earned less than he hoped.

"Let's all call it a day," Dick's uncle said. "It's been a long one."

The relatives would be going home tomorrow—Alice would. Dick lingered in the front room, hoping she might return, until his mother sent him to the bathroom ahead of the adults. In bed he envisioned

Fearful Implications

pouncing on Alice before she went home, except that pouncing wouldn't be too grownup or romantic. He ought to tempt her into the doorway, perhaps drawling like the hero of last night's film, since she'd found the actor appealing. Dick was drifting into a dream of their encounter when he heard her outside his room.

How could he mistake her footsteps? They were lighter than anybody else's in the house. They crossed the landing and grew fainter on the stairs, and Dick saw he had his chance. He donned his dressing-gown in case pyjamas seemed too bold and inched the door open. She'd left the lights off, no doubt so as not to waken anyone. Tiptoeing swiftly downstairs, he dodged into the front room. Was she in the kitchen? That light was off too. Dick stood under the mistletoe, straining his ears, and heard a thin muffled sound on the carpet. How could it be approaching when there was no sign of Alice? Of course, because it was behind him.

He thought she'd heard him coming downstairs and had hidden to catch him as he'd meant to catch her. He swung around, stretching his arms wide just in time to embrace her. She was nothing like as plump as he expected, and by no means dressed. Whatever covered the shrivelled body, to the extent that it even did, was in danger of flaking off. By the time Dick realised this, her face was pressed against his. It was as icy as the rest of her, and felt close to melting or otherwise collapsing. When he tried to cry out, a questing object blocked his mouth.

He struggled free of the lanky arms that clung to him—it felt like being tangled among branches—and hurled the intruder back into the room. Clutching at his mouth, he blundered to the front door. He spat the contents into the snow, and was continuing to retch when a light came on behind him. His parents were at the top of the stairs, and Alice had just emerged from her room. "What on earth do you think you're doing?" his mother cried. "I said your father shouldn't have given you any wine."

"There's someone," Dick babbled. "Something. In that room."

He didn't shut the front door until his father marched downstairs to switch on the light in the room. "There's nobody at all," he said, so fiercely that he might have been determined to convince not just his son.

Dick ventured into the room and eventually behind the Christmas tree, but nobody was hiding there either. "Go to bed, for heaven's sake," his father said. "No more alcohol for you even at Christmas until you grow up."

Dick fled to the bathroom first to scour his mouth with water. In bed he lay rigid, chronically alert for the faintest sound, but heard not so much as a whisper. He thought he would lie awake until morning, and then he wondered if the intruder might have had enough of him. Before he knew it, the notion let him sleep.

At breakfast nobody referred to his behaviour, but he could tell that everyone was keeping quiet about it. Presumably Alice had mentioned it to her parents, and on the whole he preferred not to know what she'd said. He stayed well clear of the mistletoe, and barely managed not to recoil when his aunt delivered a parting hug—even when Alice planted a peck on his cheek. "See you next year," she said with belated wistfulness.

He didn't realise how constrained talking had become until he was alone with his parents. He sensed they'd said too much to each other at some point and were keeping their distance from the subject—not just from that, since his father was banished or chose to sleep in the guest room. Though Dick spent the day dreading another encounter of the kind he'd suffered in the dark, he wondered if his father was equally at risk if not more so. He might have warned him if he'd thought his father would have listened, especially if he himself had any evidence. But the object he'd spat out had writhed away into the snow, and he knew it was no use to search.

His parents stayed together until he grew up and left home. Their relatives still visited, but nothing was the same. He never kissed Alice, before or after she was married, and for the rest of his life he never opened his mouth for a kiss. It wasn't the result just of his encounter in the dark; it was having heard his father that first night in the guest room. The sounds had never left him, even once he managed to persuade himself that his father had only been having a nightmare—that the anguished moans hadn't expressed some kind of pleasure too. Despite growing muffled as though something had settled on his face, they'd persisted until dawn. Dick had waited for his mother to say anything at all about the incident, but he didn't think she ever had. Now his parents were long gone, and he would be alone at Christmas once again. At least, that was his most fervent hope.

BRAINS

From the Filmy Eyed Online Group:

PHIL MEEHAN
May I pick everyone's brains? I'm trying to fix something in my mind. Cast yours back to James Whale's *Frankenstein*. When Colin Clive learns Dwight Frye brought him a criminal brain to put in the monster he does a double-take Oliver Hardy might have been proud of. But they've already pinched a body from the gallows, and Frankenstein complained he couldn't use the brain because the neck was broken. Wouldn't that brain have belonged to a criminal as well?

KARLOFFANN
Have you got nothing better to do than poke fun at a classic? Just because the makeups aren't as gory as they make them these days doesn't mean you have to laugh at it. Some of us can do without seeing people's eyes gouged out and their entrails everywhere, thank you very much. Mind you, I can think of people who deserve it, the ones that make those films. I'll stick with good acting the way it used to be and films that left a bit to your imagination.

Fearful Implications

My Friend Flicker

He's not just poking fun, he's spoiling it for everyone. Like he's so clever for spotting stuff that's never bothered anyone for nearly a hundred years. Oh look at me everyone, I've got a better brain than yours because I saw someone with a wristwatch in a medieval epic. And look, someone's got a mobile phone in that Shakespeare play. People like him want us all seeing that crap instead of enjoying the films. I go to be entertained, me, not pretend I'm better than whoever made them.

Phil Meehan

Apologies to both of you. I'm just after inspiration. You carry on appreciating films how you like. For the record, I like *Frankenstein* a lot, and other Whale films too.

Eddy Ting

weve got your permission to watch movies how we like, have we? thats big of you, in fact its monsterous. maybe youd of let us if youd kept your shit to yourself.

Lights, Gamera, Action

I love monster films, my screen name is the book I'm writing about them, and I don't want Mr Meehan to stop posting. Have you got any more quirky ideas about monsters, Mr Meehan?

Phil Meehan

Most people think *The Bride of Frankenstein* is misnamed because Elsa Lanchester plays the monster's mate and not the scientist's, but I think it works with the gay subtext where Ernest Thesiger is Colin Clive's bride and they have an unnatural daughter. Remember Thesiger seduces Clive away from his wife with whom he had a son at the end of the first film. Now they don't have one, because the film has turned time back so the narrative can deviate.

LIGHTS, GAMERA, ACTION
Why do you have to bring perverts into it? They're everywhere now, but they weren't allowed then. You said you didn't want to spoil films and now you have. You're trying to make it dirty when it never was. We watch monster films to get away from all that, so why can't you leave them alone?

PHIL MEEHAN
I don't believe I put anything in. James Whale was gay, which gives us insights into several of his films. His friend Thesiger made no secret that he was and used to sell his needlework while they were filming *Bride*. They made *The Old Dark House* with Charles Laughton, Elsa Lanchester's husband, who was gay as well. In that film Thesiger's called Femm, and he lives up to the name in both.

KARLOFFANN
So your point is what exactly? Who are you trying to smear? Don't you dare say that about Boris. He was happily married and a gentleman. I think these people that want us to believe everybody's homosexual only ever have one reason, they're it themselves and want the rest of us to join them.

PHIL MEEHAN
I'm as straight as the edge of your screen, and my lady is as well. Your sexuality shouldn't dictate how closely you look at a film. You just need to be prepared to see what's in front of you and while you're at it have a second look.

Fearful Implications

GETAGRIP

What do you know about her screen? Better not be spying on us or we'll hunt you down. Watch out we don't think you're as homophobic as you're trying not to sound. You don't know arse about her sexuality either. Or maybe you want us thinking you're a phobe so we won't know you're gay. Bit confused, are you, Phil? Make up your brain.

LIGHTS, GAMERA, ACTION

I think Mr Meehan is trying to confuse us. I watch films to see the characters, not who they really are or people like him say they are. Have you finished making things up about films, Mr Meehan? Haven't you got anything to say about *Son of Frankenstein*?

PHIL MEEHAN

It's the last one where Karloff keeps his brain.

GLENN STRANGER

Sounds like youre losing your's.

PHIL MEEHAN

I think I'd better take it elsewhere before someone steals it or my ability to think.

KARLOFFANN

Don't go till you've said what you meant about Boris's brain in *Son of Frankenstein*.

PHIL MEEHAN

After he and Ernest Thesiger split up Colin Clive must have had a son who's grown up to be Basil Rathbone. Karloff learned to speak in

Brains

Bride but now he can't, because being struck by lightning leaves you speechless in their world. Bela Lugosi lost his chance to play the monster in the first film, but now he's the monster's friend, and later they'll get closer than you'd believe friends could. After this film things get monstrously complicated.

KARLOFFANN

You still haven't told us about the brain, and what are you trying to say about Boris and Bela?

PHIL MEEHAN

In *Ghost of Frankenstein* the monster's turned into Lon Chaney Junior, but Lugosi's as much his friend as ever. He could be recognising his old friend's brain inside a new head. I'm saying they were friends, since they worked on several films besides the Frankensteins, but I expect you all know they were rivals as well. Cedric Hardwicke is yet another Frankenstein, and Lionel Atwill's his assistant in charge of brains, but Hardwicke's also the ghost of the original monster maker and tells himself to put a better brain in the monster. Lugosi wants it to be his, but the monster's after the brain of a little girl he befriended, presumably to make up for throwing someone like her in a lake in the original film. That would have had to be the first sex change operation in Hollywood. Hardwicke means to put in the brain of an assistant the monster killed, but Atwill tricks him into using Lugosi's. When the monster comes round he has Lugosi's voice, and we can hear Bela's triumph at being the creature at last. Only the operation has blinded him, as if whenever the monster comes back he has to leave a sense behind.

LIGHTS, GAMERA, ACTION

I'd say you've lost yours. Why did you need to bring a sex change into it? They'd never have had ideas like that back then. You might as well say Lionel Atwill grew a new arm because the monster pulled it off in *Son of Frankenstein*. And while you're at it why don't you say Dwight Frye came back as a villager in *Ghost of Frankenstein* because he'd had enough of being killed off for helping Frankenstein in *Frankenstein* and then in *Bride* as well.

PHIL MEEHAN
Sorry for the sex change, and thank you for the extra notions!

GETAGRIP
What are you thanking him for? He was having a joke, you brainless clown.

LIGHTS, GAMERA, ACTION
I'm not a him. Girls have brains as well.

KARLOFFANN
You bet we have, bigger than a lot of men's. They could do with having ours.

PHIL MEEHAN
To be fair, we can't tell gender from a name like LGA. I was thanking her for inspiration, because I've been thinking aloud on here, trying out ideas to give students. Thanks to everyone who indulged me.

GLENN STRANGER
Your saying your a teacher? Thats like gamera saying hes a girl.

LIGHTS, GAMERA, ACTION
I'm not just saying. What are you trying to do to their brains, Mr Meehan?

Brains

Phil Meehan
To make them look again at films they think they've finished with and have fun while they do.

Lights, Gamera, Action
Have you finished having your fun? There are still four films to go. Let's hope you've run out of twisted ideas or you haven't seen them.

Phil Meehan
I have, and they get more complicated. For a start, in *Frankenstein Meets the Wolf Man* Ilona Massey is Frankenstein, but we won't say anything about gender change. Lugosi is the monster, but now his brain has brought his body with it, which means Lon Chaney's has to find another role. He's the wolf man who was killed at the end of his own film, and now he's resurrected by the full moon. Come to think, Rathbone played Wolf von Frankenstein in *Son*, so he was a wolf man too. And thanks for reminding me about Frye and Atwill. Dwight is a villager who's grateful to get some dialogue, and Atwill is the burgomeister, having come back to life after Chaney with Lugosi's brain killed him last time.

Lights, Gamera, Action
At least you didn't bring in sex change, except you did. Have you still not finished?

All To Reel
Obsessed with sex change, aren't you, Gam? No wonder you hide your name.

Phil Meehan
House of Frankenstein brings in extra monsters. Last time Dracula

Fearful Implications

showed up on the screen he was Lon Chaney, who was either the count's son or the man himself. Now Chaney can't stop being the wolf man, and so John Carradine has to be Dracula, since presumably Lugosi's brain is still in the Frankenstein monster's head, though he's turned into Glenn Strange when he's found where he was buried under the castle at the end of the last film, along with the wolf man. Karloff has graduated from monster to scientist in charge of brains, but though he promises hunchback J. Carroll Naish that he'll find him a better body he never transfers a single brain. Lionel Atwill has got his police job back, but there's no sign of Dwight Frye, because he's definitively dead.

Lights, Gamera, Action
That's awful. You shouldn't be a teacher if you make a joke of people dying.

Phil Meehan
I'm not a teacher, you should have seen I'm a lecturer, and I rather think students can cope. Anyway, Frye died long before I should think you were born.

Lights, Gamera, Action
You don't know how old I am and you won't be finding out either.

All To Reel
Don't let the sissy shut you up, Phil. You carry on sharing your brains with us.

Phil Meehan
House of Dracula reunites the monsters and keeps some of them the same. Now that Karloff has reclaimed his brain he's gone elsewhere,

Brains

leaving Onslow Stevens to carry on the operations. Stevens means to cure the wolf man by brain surgery and give Dracula blood transfusions to turn him into a man. They're Chaney and Carradine again, and Glenn Strange shows up in a cave under the doctor's castle. Though he's still the monster, some scenes turn him into Karloff or Chaney, and you have to wonder whose brain has ended up in him. Atwill has kept his police job but he's changed his name from Arnz to Holtz. Hunchback Carroll Naish is now hunchback Martha O'Driscoll. Are these films really about the impermanence of personality? That's how they seem to fit together.

Getagrip

No they aren't and no they don't. Rather play with films than stand up for people, would you, Phil? If you're supposed to be a lecturer you're meant to look after them.

Phil Meehan

I've already told you I'm better than supposed, and who am I meant to be defending against what?

Getagrip

Too busy pumping up your brain to read what someone else said about sissies? It isn't homophobic just to say it, not caring is as well.

All To Reel

There's no fucking homophobes round here. That's just what your lot call anyone that wants to stay normal.

Phil Meehan

I didn't realise the comment about sissies was intended to be homophobic, which I'm absolutely not. I thought it was about sensitivity even if it wasn't called for.

KARLOFFANN
Don't say any more or you'll be tying your brain into a bigger knot. You've got no more ideas, so go away. Even you couldn't make anything out of Abbott and Costello.

PHIL MEEHAN
I'll have to disagree with that. This time the brain surgeon is Lenore Aubert, who plans to transfer Lou Costello's brain to Glenn Strange's head. Chaney is the wolf man and tells Abbott and Costello they're in the house of Dracula, perhaps thinking he's still in the last film. Lugosi is Dracula but forgets he is at one point and shows up in a mirror. Costello turns into the wolf man at a masked ball. Perhaps Aubert is Frankenstein, since the film is *Abbott and Costello Meet Frankenstein* and she's stored his research in her brain. Is that enough for everyone?

KARLOFFANN
You're getting really desperate, aren't you, crippling a comedy so it'll fit your brain. If you've got any students I hope they're laughing at all this.

PHIL MEEHAN
Anyone can laugh. I said it was about having fun.

LIGHTS, GAMERA, ACTION
Then stop trying to ruin ours. Like Karloffann says that's a comedy, so don't try making it something else.

Brains

PHIL MEEHAN
Let me just point out that it was filmed as *The Brain of Frankenstein*, which rather fits my thesis.

LIGHTS, GAMERA, ACTION
It's a thesis now, is it? I thought just students did those. And I think you've made that title up like a lot more you've been saying.

PHIL MEEHAN
I've made nothing up. Try searching for the title, and then you might apologise.

LIGHTS, GAMERA, ACTION
I don't need to search to know I don't believe you, and I'd swap brains with you before I'd apologise. I don't even believe in your name.

PHIL MEEHAN
That's quite a laugh, Miss Gamera, considering what you call yourself. I ought to have acted like the rest of you and made up a name.

LIGHTS, GAMERA, ACTION
Just so everyone knows, I searched for your name and it isn't listed as a lecturer anywhere. What's it meant to be? Film Me Ann or Fill Me In? I believe you're laughing at us for missing the joke.

PHIL MEEHAN
It's no joke. It's me and I'm it. I'm afraid it looks as if the joke's your name and the book you claim you're writing. You ought to realise it isn't original. It's all over the internet, where I expect you found it even if you didn't realise. The net is part of everyone's brain.

Fearful Implications

Lights, Gamera, Action
My brain's nowhere except here in my head. What are you trying to make me think?

Phil Meehan
I'm saying your name and that title is everywhere, but I think the book is only in your brain. If I'm wrong do prove it. Post a chapter or a few as evidence.

Lights, Gamera, Action
I'm not putting anything on here for anyone to steal.

Phil Meehan
Somehow I didn't think you would. You can't prove anything is real by hiding it, you know. If you won't post any chapters, how about a few of your ideas? We've seen none except the ones you didn't mean to give me.

Getagrip
Maybe that's what Phil He Mean wants us to believe. Maybe he's inside your computer like we thought he could be.

Gail Lloyd
Excuse me, could you all stop disturbing my daughter?

Phil Meehan
May we know who you're talking about and who you're saying you are?

Gail Lloyd
I'm Ann's mother, the girl who's been posting as Lights, Gamera, Action, and I want you to stop bullying her.

Brains

PHIL MEEHAN
You're the girl, are you? You're saying you're her. Do you share a brain by any chance? It doesn't seem to be functioning too well. And is Ann short for FrAnnKenstein? There's already one Ann here, and I wonder if there's only one.

GAIL LLOYD
I think it's your brain that needs some attention. Just so you know, she's vulnerable and you're doing her no good. I can't believe you're bullying her over such trivial things either.

PHIL MEEHAN
At least I don't talk about myself in the third person, and you're the one who's been inciting me, Miss Gamera. Gail, would that be I LGA mixed up? And is Lloyd short for Cellulloyd? That's a joke.

ALL TO REEL
Sounds more like Gay fucking Lloyd to me.

GAIL LLOYD
I don't play games with words and films like you, Mr Meehan or whatever your name may be. And just so you're aware, Ann isn't as strong as she likes everyone to think. She's sixteen and she's in a wheelchair.

PHIL MEEHAN
You know my name perfectly well. I don't pretend to be anyone I'm not. She isn't a hunchback as well by any chance, Miss Gamera? Did you piece her together out of your own head? Isn't one body enough for you? Would you like it to be in a film? I'd better stop before you accuse me of bullying.

Fearful Implications

GAIL LLOYD

You're a real monster, aren't you? I can see how much you enjoy it. You aren't affecting me, and you'll have to find another victim, because my daughter won't be here any more. I hope you're proud of driving her off somewhere she thought she'd find minds like hers.

PHIL MEEHAN

After brains, was she? If you want me to feel guilty you'll have to show me why. Let's see you prove who you are, Ann Lloyd.

GAIL LLOYD

I shouldn't even have posted her name, and I'm certainly not giving you any more details. People like you need to be kept at a distance.

PHIL MEEHAN

People like what? What are you saying I am? I've only been responding how I've been made to respond. I'm sending you a private message in case you really are who you say. If I show you who I am I hope you'll do the same for me.

GETAGRIP

Been quiet for a while, hasn't it? Maybe they've switched their brains off.

GLENN STRANGER

Looks like Filmy Ann and Gay Lloyd must of got together somewhere else, except more like theyre both him.

PHIL MEEHAN

I'm back and I'm nobody else, but I have to apologise. I was wrong about Ann Lloyd and wrong to harass her. She's disabled as her mother said. I'm leaving the group now, but I hope she'll give it another chance. If she does I hope you'll all treat her better than I did.

GLENN STRANGER

Your giving up pretending to be her and her ma, more like. Maybe you was trying to involve us in the arguements you made out you was haveing and it didnt work. Maybe your tired of sharing your brain round till you want to be Gammy again. Theres a good name for somebody that says theyre in a wheelchair.

PHIL MEEHAN

All right, I'll stop pretending so that nobody can mistake the truth. I was never a teacher or a lecturer. I tried to teach but couldn't cope, and then I put in for lecturing but my ideas got laughed down. At least that's giving me time to make them into a book. That's the honest truth, and I've told it about Ann Lloyd as well.

GLENN STRANGER

Writing two books now, are you, Gammy? Better do one before you start the other. Dont try telling us how to act, though. Dont bother showing up as your mammy either, Mammy Gammy. If you come saying youre Gammy youll get treated like it, and if you cant cope like you said you couldnt then piss off.

PHIL MEEHAN

For christ's sake, I'm exactly who I say. Can't you see I've given up pretending? And you know their real names now and what they are. Can't you believe in anything?

Fearful Implications

Glenn Stranger

Yeh, I believe your like youre monsters, always turning into someone else.

Phil Meehan

I'm. Ban. Ging. My. Head. A. Gainst. The. Screen. Am. I. Get. Ting. Through. To. You? What. Do. I. Have. To. Do. To. Get. Some. Sense. In. Side. Your. Head?

Glenn Stranger

Trying to play monster, are you, Gam? Watch out you dont hurt your brain. Youd hurt for real if we ever met and thats a promise.

Phil Meehan

I'd look forward to it. Somebody wouldn't be walking away from it. Just tell me where you are and we'll see who's the real monster.

Glenn Stranger

Message on it's way to you right now, Gammy.

Karloffann

Have we lost someone again? It's quieter than ever.

Getagrip

I'd say the topic's died on us.

Eddy Ting

feels as dead as all them actors.

Phil Meehan

So did Glenn.

Brains

Karloffann
That's your latest joke, is it? You're not in on it, are you, Glenn?

Phil Meehan
He won't be answering even if I didn't get his brain out. I think I touched it, though.

Karloffann
What a nasty thing to say, even as a joke. Don't let him use you for it, Glenn.

Getagrip
That's right, Glenn, don't you let him pretend. Just give us all a shout.

Eddy Ting
come on glenn, youve shut up long enough, you dont want anyone believing him.

Phil Meehan
I thought you all liked monsters. You've created one and now you don't believe in him, so he'll have to hunt you down. You won't be really gone, because he'll keep you in his brain. It's as near as you'll come to fame without being in a film. If you're reading this and you don't believe, he'll find you. Glenn would say so if they put him back together, and it's his tongue that's talking. It's saying use your brains while you can.

Getting Through

"We need to get him out of his room, Bob."

"He'll be reading his magazines if he isn't putting them in order."

"It can't be healthy for him to be stuck up there all day."

"I'm agreeing with you, Jean. Reading all that rot isn't healthy either, time machines and spaceships as if real life isn't good enough for us."

"He's got a better mind than that, and we don't want him ending up a hermit when we're gone."

"Almighty God grant us a long time yet, but he can't make friends while he's shutting himself in."

"Then we need to do something, Bob, because I don't think he will on his own."

"If we get rid of all that stuff he reads he won't have anything to stay up there for."

"Is that going a bit far, do you think? Suppose we just tell him how long he can spend in there?"

"I've had enough of never seeing him all day. It's worse than having a lodger. I'm sorting this out right now and for good. Those magazines are going out the window if that's what it takes."

Fearful Implications

As Desmond heard a door open downstairs he leapt off the bed, clutching the magazine he'd been reading. Even if he found somewhere to hide it from his father, his bedroom shelves were full of more than he could hide. A bright shard of panic had lodged in his brain, and the rest of him felt brittle as a reflection in a mirror. His father was tramping up the stairs, and the relentless sound made Desmond feel suffocated, even worse than being in a crowd affected him. He wasn't far from crumpling the magazine, because he thought he might never learn the end of the story he'd begun. He was backing into a corner, where he could crouch and hug his treasure so hard that nobody would take it from him, when he saw that the shelves and their contents had taken refuge in the dressing-table mirror.

Why did it remind him of a window? He had to go close to be sure that none of the spines of the magazines, which were arranged by title and then by date, were reversed. He could read every word and every digit with an ease that felt like passing through the glass. He didn't know whether he was stooping towards it or straightening up when it showed his father entering the room. "Finished reading, have you, son?" his father said.

Although his glasses enlarged his eyes, they showed none of the determination Desmond had tried to prepare for. "Not yet," Desmond said.

"When you do we were wondering if you'd like to go out for a walk."

Desmond thought this must be designed to lure him away from his room. "What about my magazines?"

"You can leave those till we're home, can't you? Come and get some fresh air."

Desmond could only conclude his father had experienced a change of heart on his way upstairs. He watched his father leave the room and listened while he rejoined Desmond's mother. Were they having a discussion Desmond couldn't hear? Surely his mother had to question why his father had gone back on his decision. Its retraction left Desmond's head feeling eagerly capacious, and he lay on the bed, where a quilt not quite as teenage as himself bore a map of the stars, to finish reading his tale. Once the narrator had stopped migrating to his bodies in alternate universes, Desmond went downstairs. "Ready to be sociable?" his mother said.

To test her attitude he said "I was making space for next month's magazines."

"That's right, you keep everything tidy like you always do."

Presumably his father had persuaded her in favour of Desmond's reading. There weren't many people in the park, which let Desmond's mind feel as wide as the sky. The bright stud of the sun held the blue expanse in place and lent leaves on the trees the energy to unfurl while discovering more colour, so many greens that he couldn't even think of counting them. The only problem was how tense his parents grew whenever they saw a dog. "Don't let it come near him," his mother used to call out, "he doesn't like them," and his father wouldn't merely shoo but stamp. "Dodge the dog," Desmond had taken to muttering like a charm, low enough that he could hope his parents didn't hear. He knew he embarrassed them, and their dogged attempts to hide their feelings simply made it worse. It left him anxious to qualify for university, however many years that took, and leave home.

All this came back to him on the day of the English Literature examination. As he opened the folder and read all the topics he found himself wishing he could flee back to a time when the examination had represented hope. Now he saw he'd been so bound up in the magazines the intervening years had brought him that he'd revised nothing like enough. There wasn't a single question he could even start to answer. The examination hall seemed to have grown oppressively dim, and the sky beyond the long windows was as dull as his mind. The nearest window displayed his face, and as he watched it twist with panic he recalled the mirror in his bedroom.

Had it come to his aid that day? Could his reflection help now? He'd begun to feel no more substantial than it looked. He glanced at the invigilator, who was leafing through papers on her desk. Before she could notice what he was doing and disqualify him on suspicion of cheating, he picked up the folder and turned it to the window. The print on the cover was big enough to be legible in the reflection, especially since it wasn't reversed. Before he finished taking a breath he felt his body regain its substance while a sensation like a splinter that was lodged between his eyes subsided into his head.

He wasn't sure what to expect on reopening the folder. Though none of the questions had changed, they no longer daunted him. Once he took time to ponder them he found he knew more than enough. He was completing his final answer when the invigilator announced the last five minutes of the session. "Needn't have worried," he told his parents, knowing they had.

He could have fancied they'd saved up their muffled concern for the day his father drove him and a vanload of magazines to the university they'd helped him choose. Desmond failed to see why his parents should worry, since he had a room to himself and space for every magazine. At first he was happy to learn of a society for people like him, despite his reservations about its name, Sci Fine. It met in a pub, in a small crowded noisy room further shrunken by a pall of smoke from ragged amateur cigarettes. At least there were almost no girls in the group, though Desmond supposed he would have to cope with some of those eventually, never having managed at school. The girls in the society had to be more like him if they liked science fiction. He did his best to stay in the room and make himself heard, but felt as if the heat and noise and the closeness of so much flesh had merged into a solitary intolerable medium that was gathering on him. Retreating outside, he waited under a lamp that made his shadow imitate his slightest twitch and magnified every movement of his hands. When the group emerged he accosted the secretary, a longhaired student half Desmond's width. "I think you should change your name."

The secretary's mouth shrank towards imitating an exclamation mark in collaboration with his beaky nose. "What's your problem with my name?"

"Not yours, the Sci Fine one." Was the secretary making what some people called a joke? "Just the fine bit," Desmond said. "It sounds like you want to fine people."

"Not to me." A glance at his friends let the secretary add "Not to anyone."

"Don't you like Sci File? It could be with a pee aitch like scientists use."

Without bothering to glance at the others the secretary said "We don't, no."

As he and his entourage sauntered away a girl murmured "I do."

She was as blond as Desmond had ever seen the sun, with a small pert lightly highlighted face and a figure that would have graced the cover of any of his magazines. He imagined her in a space helmet and bikini—he'd lingered over similar pictures—and decided he might like some girls in the flesh after all. Just the same, he felt provoked to ask "Why?"

"I thought it was quite witty, your joke."

He hadn't been aware of making one or even that he could. The revelation left him feeling there was more to him that he had yet to discover. Her was wondering if he should thank her when she said "Are you new?"

"No, I'm nineteen."

Fearful Implications

This time she seemed uncertain whether he was joking. "What's your name?"

"Desmond. What's yours?"

"I'll have a lager and lime."

"That's a peculiar name."

Her frown was faint enough to let her face stay pretty. "It's Dianne with two ens and an e."

"That's more like one." To demonstrate maturity, which might involve overcoming his aversion to crowds, he said "I'm going for a drink."

"Is that an invitation, Desmond?"

"It can be if you want."

Apparently she did. At least there were empty booths in the main bar. "You sit down," he said in a bid to ensure they had one to themselves. "Do you still want a lager and lime?"

"That was rather the idea."

The price of this and a pint of beer took him aback. As he carried them to the booth the barman put on a tape of the latest Beatles album, and Desmond had to fight an urge to tell the man to turn it down as he would have told his parents. He centred his tankard on a beermat while he gave Dianne the bad news. "That was three and six."

"You're saying you'd like me to pay."

"Weren't you going to?"

She appeared to take this as an accusation. Opening her bag, a scaly item reminiscent of the body of a lizard flattened by a mangle, she produced a purse that might have been its offspring, which she unclasped as well. Once Desmond pocketed the coin, having waited for Dianne to place it on the table, a Beatles song about the universe took the place of conversation. When it was over Dianne said "You like science fiction, then."

"Of course I do." Perhaps this sounded too harsh, although only because he was having to talk over the next song, which was all about I and me and mine, though not Desmond himself. "Which magazines do you like?" he said.

"*Galaxy*'s my favourite."

"That's the worst one. The name doesn't mean anything. Even the way they print it is wrong."

Dianne laughed before appearing to decide she shouldn't have. "Wrong how?"

"The letters all feel spiky in your head."

"Not in mine, and the name means plenty. You know what a galaxy is."

"That magazine's not one. You can't just stick a word on things and say that's what they are." Since it was plain she was as unable to grasp his reasoning as he ought to have expected any girl to be, Desmond said "*Amazing* is amazing, and *Astounding* is astounding, and *Authentic* is authentic..."

Her face began to lose expression before he came to the fantastic, but he carried on to the end, by which time she'd halved her drink. "Which is your favourite?" she said.

"All of them except yours."

He thought she was inclined to smile or even grin, but she did neither. "We'll agree to differ, then," she said.

"You can't just say that. You have to ask me if I do, and I don't."

Dianne reached for her handbag and stood up. "Excuse me, please," she said, though he wasn't in her path.

Several manly gulps of beer left his mouth tasting increasingly metallic, unless panic did. Had he driven her away? When the Beatles began exhorting someone to get back he knew Dianne wouldn't do so. Had she even bothered to pretend she was heading for the Ladies? She wasn't to be seen as he made for the Gents.

Fearful Implications

Though he'd touched nothing but himself, he spent more than a minute at a sink. Since the roller towel would have been recycled, he wiped his hands with toilet paper. In the extended mirror above the sinks he saw his forehead glistening with sweat, which it presumably had been while he was talking to Dianne. As he raised a hand to rub away the shameful evidence of tension he caught sight of his wristwatch in the mirror.

It wasn't reversed, unless his perceptions were, and what would that have to mean? That he was the reflection, confronted by himself beyond the glass? When he reached his other hand towards the mirror he had no idea what he was expecting to feel. He remembered feeling nothing as he straightened up. As soon as he emerged into the bar he saw Dianne in the booth. "Sorry I was such a time," she said. "It's my round."

He might have asked where she'd been, but he was nervous of breaking some kind of spell. She waved away his move to help her carry the drinks to the booth. "Have you brought any magazines with you?" she said.

He liked how she was continuing the conversation as if they hadn't disagreed. This kind of agreement he could take. "All of them except for your one," he said.

"Then we could be a team."

"We could be our own group and have the name they didn't want." Since she seemed open to the notion Desmond said "Would you like to see my magazines?"

"I'd love to, but let's not waste our drinks."

Presumably she'd sensed his impatience, which had him digging his fingertips into his thighs while she lingered over her lager. As she took the final sip he headed for his room so fast that he almost forgot to look back to confirm she was following. He switched on his light and retreated to the window, leaving her more space to admire his achievement. "You're fearfully tidy," she said.

"A tidy home means a tidy mind."

"I could learn from you. I should be tidier."

"Learn all you like." When she ventured to the shelves he said "You can borrow one if you take care of it."

"I'll treat it like one of my own."

"Does that mean taking care?"

As though forgiving an insult Dianne said "Of course."

Desmond eased his oldest issue of *Amazing* off the shelf. "You'd better start with this one."

When she returned it two days later it looked as unread as it always had, so that he wasn't sure she'd even opened it until he questioned her about the contents. He was happy to lend her the next issue, and able to concentrate on lectures now that he needn't worry about her doing any damage. She was taking science while he took modern literature, and so he could put her out of his mind except whenever they met. This was increasingly often even when she wasn't bringing back a magazine, and the first time his parents came to check how Desmond was progressing she met them as well. She was still meeting them a year later, a date Desmond celebrated as fantastic, since that was the magazine she was borrowing now. "I hope you two aren't getting up to mischief," his mother said like a line she'd rehearsed.

"Some of us believe in waiting till we're married," Dianne told her.

"More power to you and anybody like you," Desmond's father said. "His mother and I did."

The three of them seemed more embarrassed than Desmond found any need to feel. He'd discovered that he quite liked not just kissing

Fearful Implications

Dianne but poking his tongue in and running his hands over her, but beyond this lay territory he felt nervous of exploring. When his parents left for home he suspected he and Dianne were meant to overhear his father murmuring "I think she's going to be ideal for him."

"For each other," Desmond's mother said quite like a rebuke.

Not only Dianne stayed ideal throughout Desmond's university years, which felt nowhere near as long as that. It seemed appropriate that his magazine she was reading when their studentship ended was *Venture*, since they would be setting out on one. His thesis on alternate universes as fictional searches for an ideal world earned him a degree, and Dianne gained its equal in science. As they each took the stage at the graduation ceremony both of them had already been accepted for a job, and their wedding followed shortly after.

When Dianne said "I do" Desmond thought she was repeating the first words she'd addressed to him. He had the odd impression that his life contained echoes of events or even consisted of them. He was disconcerted by how many guests at the reception he didn't know—friends of his parents and Dianne's—and relieved when they dispersed. He was on the way to relaxing until his father said as a farewell "You two be good, now."

"We'll be listening for tiny feet soon," his mother said.

Apparently champagne had swept away their worries, but Desmond's only multiplied once he grasped that his mother hadn't meant there were mice in the bridal suite. Even the bedroom threatened to overwhelm him, especially the four-poster that looked crystallised with dazzling linen. The bathroom with its fat white towels and puffy toilet seat offered no refuge. He stared at the mirror until his eyes stung as though they'd been soaped, which failed to turn the image of his watch around. As he bruised his fingertips against the glass Dianne called "I'm ready, Desmond."

"Turn the light off," he shouted in case not seeing helped.

A pale glow from floodlights in the hotel car park turned the bed into a shrouded ghost of itself. The canopy squatted four-legged over the area of action. Dianne's head was sprouting over the quilt, which was blank as an unwritten page. Perhaps he should think of it as a cover on which he could imagine a picture, Dianne's body attired like a cute spacewoman, but the image dwindled into a shard of pain when he climbed into bed and discovered how naked she was. He rubbed her and poked at her mouth and wished his penis was as manageable as his tongue. The unresponsive protrusion continued to flap as he climbed aboard Dianne, and as soon as it touched her it shrivelled. He had to struggle not to close his hand over it, to protect it from the spiky nest it had encountered. At least he couldn't see his pitiable toil in the dressing-table mirror, though the edges of the glass were visible. He was staring at the nuptial cards Dianne had arranged in front of the mirror—he was striving to feel they could encourage him somehow—when he read a manufacturer's name on the back of a card.

Though it was in the mirror, it was the right way around. He almost sprawled off the bed in his haste to make sure, driven by an instinct to see himself. As he craned around the headboard for a sight of his blurred face Dianne protested "What are you doing, Desmond?"

He couldn't reach the mirror, but he felt his penis try, which proved to be enough. At once he felt as substantial as it had grown. "It's all right now," he said, gagging her with his tongue as he boarded her once more. This time his penis found a hospitable entrance in the spiky place. "Oh," Dianne started to declare, and before long so did he.

Very little time seemed to have passed—certainly less than three months—when she phoned him from the industrial laboratory, where he imagined her mixing the contents of phials in the manner of a scientist dressed like a model on a cover. "Are you sitting down?" she said.

He was preparing new books to be shelved, one of the library tasks he found most satisfying. "That's one thing I'm doing," he said.

"Soon there'll be more of us, Desmond."

He felt nervous of learning "Where?"

"Right here at the moment." Before he could urge her to be clear Dianne said "We've made a bit of the future."

This sounded as if it belonged in a magazine, though he couldn't think how. "Which bit?"

"We won't know for a little while yet. Either a boy or a girl."

His bewilderment must have been visible, since one of the library assistants was blinking at him like a query in code. "My wife's saying either a boy or a girl," Desmond said.

Her eyes widened with delight, and she informed her colleagues "Desmond's having a baby."

"I'm not. I can't. You mean my wife is." As this caught up with him he told Dianne "Well done."

"You're responsible as well, Desmond."

Although he didn't think this was an accusation, it left him feeling hemmed in. What might be expected of him? He was glad to return to the books, and later to the magazines at home, where he'd persuaded Dianne to file hers among his even though the spiky type on the spines felt invasive. Despite her condition she looked no different at first, but presumably her state led her to suggest he should learn to cook. He set about it while her shape grew so unfamiliar that he thought she could no longer appear on a magazine except as some species of alien. At least this meant that bedtime required him just to drape an arm around her increasing circumference until she fell asleep. Sometimes he found himself gazing across the bedroom at the mirror while he waited to follow her into unconsciousness. Dreaming made him feel he was in someone else's dream or was the dream itself, and he did his utmost to waken.

Perhaps his interrupted sleep was to blame for a persistent sense that he wasn't entirely awake in the daytime, not to mention in danger of dreaming. Every dinner he made for Dianne and presumably for her parasite felt like a version of an earlier meal, since he hadn't many recipes at his disposal. The sight of himself in the kitchen window only reminded him how limited he was, in some areas at any rate. Whenever his parents came to the apartment for dinner his mother helped him at his task, and she was peppering a casserole on his behalf when Dianne raised her voice in the main room, louder than Desmond liked. "I think I need to go to hospital."

As he hurried after his mother he called "Why, what's wrong?"

"I can't believe you said that," his mother said. "Sometimes I feel I don't know my son at all. Nothing's wrong, is it, Dianne? Everything is as it should be."

Desmond hardly thought so. Why couldn't babies be produced the way they were in several of his magazines—generated in a phial and developed in a laboratory like Dianne's? His father gave him a look that summarised agreement with Desmond's mother, and Desmond felt excluded, wishing he were someone else or a better model of himself. "I'll drive us," his father said.

He helped Dianne to clamber onto the back seat of the car, since aiding her hadn't immediately occurred to Desmond. Gripping Dianne's hand, his mother said "Go as fast as you dare, Bob."

On the motorway he drove faster than Desmond had ever seen him drive. Desmond felt useless and desperate to take control of events somehow. He might as well have reverted to his childhood self for all the benefit he was to anyone—all the use he'd failed to be for too much of his life. He gazed at Dianne in the mirror while his father overtook lorry after elongated lorry, but she didn't meet his eyes. If her reflection looked at him, what might that do? A lorry with a logo the length of a terrace of houses—**FUTURE SOLUTIONS**—drifted backwards past her window, and he was about to draw her attention to the words when her face contorted, grimacing violently. He sensed she was keeping in a cry so as not to distract his father, and the insight made him feel as if he'd discovered at last that there was more to him. He twisted around, reaching for her hand. "I'm here if—"

His elbow thumped his father in the face and knocked his glasses off. Perhaps lurching to retrieve them robbed his father of control, though in any case he must have been left little better than blind, or perhaps he meant to head for sanctuary on the hard shoulder. The car slewed into the path of the Future Solutions lorry, and the oncoming cab filled the side windows. In a moment the world shattered like a mirror.

Some of the high sounds were human, some were screeches of metal. Desmond hardly realised he'd squeezed his eyes tight shut until he opened them. The car was full of glass and silence and an increasing amount of bright red, well on the way to blotting out its sources. Desmond risked a glance in the mirror, though the movement sent a dull pain through his neck and downwards, and was about to look away in haste when his attention fastened on the sight beyond the contents of the back seat. He could read the maker's name on the front of the lorry, because the letters weren't reversed.

He lowered his head until he could see nothing worse in the mirror than the name. When he stretched out a hand to the glass, expanding the pain that had occupied his spine, he saw the hand was spattered red, though not from him. He almost snatched it back so as not to see it, but he had to do whatever he could do—whatever the mirror could.

Getting Through

He needed to be somewhere the last few minutes had never happened to his family or him. As he touched the glass he found he couldn't feel it, but he seemed to hear his mother speak. "We need to get him out," he thought she said.

Extending the Family

"Is this Mr Lasky?"

"No, it's Cliff."

"May I have a word with Mr Lasky?"

"Who's after him?"

"The name is Kenneth Trent. I'm looking at his house, or one of them."

"Sounds like you've got a buyer, Mr L."

Cliff's voice gives way to another. "Sid Lasky."

"Mr Lasky, Kenneth Trent. Could we talk about the property you meant to renovate?"

"Cliff tells me you're looking to buy."

"I'm afraid that isn't me. I overlook your house. I don't suppose you could be letting anybody live there while it's in that state."

"What's my house to do with you?"

"We met in the street once, don't you recall? You wanted an eye kept on it. That's why I have your number."

"So what do you think you're seeing?"

"A baby and a little boy and presumably the father, except he doesn't look nearly old enough. You'll agree nobody like that should be in there."

"I don't know anything about them, and I wonder if you realise how hard squatters are to shift."

"You'll need to, won't you? For the sake of your property if not for their sakes."

"I'll be looking into it."

"Better soon. I don't like how the father is behaving. Yes, you're being discussed."

The last remark is aimed at the youth in the room Trent is looking down on. He would have expected Lasky to grasp this, but the old man demands "With whom?"

"With you, Mr Lasky. We're talking about him."

"I'm quite aware who's who. I'll do what's required in my own time and without seeking your approval, Mr whatever your name is."

"Trent," Trent says, but he's talking to himself. The youth at the window across the back yards—the closer one spread with rugs of turf that flank a flagged path to the alley, the other cluttered with rubble—has just finished mouthing at him, so that Trent could imagine the phone has been dubbing his voice, however imperfectly synchronised. On the far side of the room scattered with takeaway cartons, the baby in a spavined crib next to a drooping patch of wallpaper starts to wail as though it has been waiting for its father to fall silent. As the youth tramps to the crib he shouts "Shut the curtains, Billy. Some old twat thinks we're his show to watch."

Dropping his phone, on which Trent assumes he has been playing a game, the boy trudges to the window. His unhealthily pale face is a shrunken version of his father's—small reddish eyes, sharp nose and cheekbones, a pallid slash of a mouth. Why does it seem familiar? Was the father a pupil at one of the schools to which Trent was supplied in the last years of his career? As Billy stares up at him the boy's lips twist into a grimace Trent imagines him giving a teacher. The boy grabs one of the curtains that lend the window a gloomy penumbra and drags it across the glass, swinging monkey-like on it as it stutters halfway. The rail can't support even his meagre weight, and crashes to the floor.

"What did you do now, you little shit?" The father darts across the room to deal his fallen son a vicious kick. "You shut up, Colum, or you'll get some too," he tells the baby in his arms as it adds to the sounds of woe, and then he glares at Trent. "Don't feel left out, you old twat. Got some for you as well."

Trent won't be the first to look away. The youth needs to understand he's being watched, but this doesn't prevent him from turning on the boy, who has dodged out of reach. "Give it a hug," the youth tells him.

Trent thinks he's entrusting the baby to his son until the boy slouches to fetch a nippled bottle, which he fills from a carton of milk on the floor. As Billy sets about warming the bottle by pressing it against his chest the father says "I'll be cleaning up the mucky little bastard."

An April wind chills Trent's fingertips as he inches the sash of the window up to help him eavesdrop for the children's sake. He hears the baby's cries beyond the frosted glass of a bathroom window while water falters down a drain. Is there any hot water in that house? The transom of the frosted window jerks open, and a hand flings a soiled plastic nappy into the yard. The father dumps the baby in the cot while he finds a nappy somewhere out of sight, and pins the infant down with one hand on its chest until he succeeds in positioning the plastic. "Give us the bottle," he shouts, having fixed the adhesive tags.

Trent is afraid the milk may fail to quell the baby, but its silence lingers when the youth deposits his burden in the cot. "Got to feed you too, have I?" he complains. "You're not getting curry. Don't want you farting when I've got to have you in the bed."

Fearful Implications

He types an order on his phone, and Trent feels as if the family he's compelled to watch has stolen his appetite. He mustn't starve himself, and he calls the Darling Dhal to deliver his dinner. When a doorbell rings he can't tell which building it's in. Perhaps it was both, because on returning to his apartment he sees dinner has arrived opposite as well. He dines out of cartons at a table near the window while the youth and his son sit gobbling on the floor, and comes back from binning the remains to find the father yelling at the boy for abandoning his meal. Trent is surrounded by shelves of books he has been meaning to find time to read at last, but now he feels unequal to any that might make demands on him. He falls back on a detective novel, only to be dogged by a fancy that Roger Ackroyd's doctor keeps uttering a word the father opposite appears unable to do without, a monotonous monosyllabic repetition that puts Trent in mind of the tuneless thumping of a stereo. Though he's reluctant to forsake his vigil, the word eventually drives him to seek his bed.

His bedroom faces the other house, and he raises the window an inch. In the night he hears the boy's cries, which set off the younger brother's and provoke shouts of virtually inarticulate rage. Trent stumbles to the window but can see nothing in the unlit room across the yards. His pulse takes even longer to subside than the uproar does, and sleep stays clear of him long after the baby's wails have been exhausted. By the time he rises red-eyed he knows he has to make a call.

It oughtn't to be up to him to contact the authorities, and he recalls the last number he called. A voice answers almost at once—speaks, at any rate. "It's your Mr Trent again."

"That's who I am and no mistake. Mr Lasky, please."

"He's not available right now."

"Then who were you just talking to? Kindly put him on at once."

"Don't worry, Cliff, I'll deal with him." In a moment Lasky says "What's your problem this time, Mr Trent?"

"I was wondering how soon you'll be looking into the situation we discussed."

"When it suits me. In my own time. I thought I'd made that plain."

Trent has stayed clear of the window so as not to be seen phoning, but ventures to it now. Just Billy is visible in the dilapidated room. Though the boy is intent on his phone, he glances up at once. "The old twat's there again," he shouts.

"That's an example of how your tenants are behaving, Mr Lasky."

"I've not the least idea what you mean. They're no tenants of mine and not a thing to do with me."

The father has come to his window, displaying the baby like a trophy if not a challenge. "They're in your rooms," Trent insists. "That's not how anyone should live, let alone children. I believe the social services would agree."

"If you're so concerned, why don't you pester them instead."

"I should have thought you might want to talk to them yourself."

Trent is distracted by a grotesque fancy that the youth is mouthing his words. The boy's lips and the baby's are moving as well, but he hears only his own voice until Lasky says "You thought wrong."

He's gone before Trent can speak again. The boy and his father are smirking as if they heard the call prove useless. The youth is still brandishing the baby, which makes Trent wary of worsening its situation, and he moves out of sight before he searches his phone for a number. The council switchboard makes him jab several keys as a requirement of rewarding him with a less artificial voice. "I want to report a family in danger," Trent says at once.

"Do you have a name and address for me?"

"I can tell you the address." Trent gives it and says "There's a boy about seven called Billy and a baby by the name of Colum, and a father too young for them."

"It sounds like the Williams family again." This isn't said to Trent, but she informs him "We believe they're known to us."

"You aren't telling me you've seen how they're living."

"How are you saying that is, Mr . . ."

"Trent. Kenneth Trent. You wouldn't keep a dog in there. I can see it all from where I am."

"When did Maggie visit them?" A hand muffles a discussion, and then the woman says "Their worker happens to be in your area. We'll see if she has time to look in."

"Do more than see," Trent retorts, but only to himself. Surely he has time to use the bathroom while he awaits the intervention. Afterwards he's dressing in the bedroom when he hears a harsh shrill cry across the yards: "Give me it now." When it's repeated with exactly the same cadence he gathers it's the first line of a piece of music, though it doesn't sound much like one to him, and doing duty as a ringtone. He hears Williams answer the phone with a respectful attitude bordering on mockery, but he can't make out any words.

He's breakfasting on coffee and a bagel from which he had to scrape a tinge of greenish mould when a doorbell shrills. He sees Williams clutch the baby to his chest and shove his son out of the room, and then they appear beyond the frosted glass. Are they hiding from the social worker? They've grown so still that Trent could imagine he's staring at an impressionistic daub of a family group. He's willing them to betray some movement when his apartment doorbell summons him, and he stumps down the corpulently carpeted stairs to the front door. A woman is retreating across the concrete car park that used to be a garden. "Can I assist you?" Trent calls.

She turns like a mime of reluctance. She's large-boned with a wide flat face suggestive of a poster for concern, and her plumpness may be designed to look maternal. "Mr Trent?"

"Guilty as charged."

"Maggie Renfrew." She bustles to the doorstep before adding "I understand you were in touch with us."

"If you're the social people I was. I hope you're planning to take a good look at the situation I reported."

"Just now the client's with his children in the park."

"Is that what he told you when you rang to warn him you were visiting?" As her face grows professionally blank Trent says "Come up and look."

"I don't want to be late for my next service user."

"It won't take a minute," Trent pleads. "Someone besides me needs to see."

He's hoping the Williams family may have emerged from concealment, but the main room opposite is deserted. "They're hiding in the bathroom," he insists, "keeping the baby quiet somehow."

He strains his stinging eyes until they bring him hints of figures that can only be the lurkers in the bathroom. The social worker has already turned to him. "I'm not sure what you're expecting me to see."

"Look at the room they're all living in." Trent jabs a finger at it, only to realise the angle of the sunlight has rendered the window as opaque as a screen awaiting a projection. "Wait till the light goes," he urges. "You'll see what he's reduced his family to."

"Approved accommodation will be found for them." She's scrutinising Trent rather than the apartment opposite. "And I've seen a young man trying to do his best for his family against very considerable odds," she says. "We can't all enjoy your advantages."

"We must be thinking of two different people. If you trust him that much, why did you go to the house when he'd told you he wasn't there?" As her face renews its blankness Trent says "And do you know what happened to the mother, assuming there's only one?"

"There was, yes. I'm very much afraid she died."

"Of what, if you don't mind my asking?"

"We don't give out that kind of information."

"Then I'm guessing an overdose."

"I can't spend any more time on this, Mr Trent. Please be advised the situation is in hand."

She's making for the door when Trent glimpses movement beyond the frosted glass. "I think they're coming out," he cries. "Watch and you may see them."

She strides to the window and almost instantly away from it. "There's nothing to see, Mr Trent," she says and gives the room a longer look. "Maybe you should keep your imagination for your books."

"This has nothing to do with my imagination."

"Then maybe it should have. Try imagining what it must be like to be Mr Williams and his family."

"I had to do enough along those lines when I was teaching."

From the stairs she offers him an afterthought. "Maybe now it's time for you to learn."

"I don't need to learn how to deal with his kind," Trent tells the slam of the front door. The sunlight has unveiled the window opposite. Williams looks poised to dump or even drop the baby in the cot, but glances warily about and lays the infant down. When he meets Trent's eyes he utters several words Trent would never have permitted in a classroom, and then appears to mouth "Give me it now." It's his phone, and the screen or the caller's name lights up his face.

He mutters at the phone and then rounds on his son. "Just going up the road. You stay with Colum," he says, miming a backhand slap that makes the boy flinch. "You can do whatever needs doing. About time you learned."

Trent thinks he sounds too much like the social worker. The boy should be learning, but at school. Trent doesn't look away or even blink while he backs across the room as if he's imitating Williams and gropes behind him for an armchair. When he grasps its fat arms he finds it too cumbersome to drag, and has to dodge around it to shove it to the window. He sidles onto it and plants his fists on the windowsill, and sees Billy staring at him.

For a while the boy lets fly words he may well have learned from his father. Trent feels as if he has been trapped into competing not to blink. He has no idea how long they remain in their stance like tomcats paralysed by a confrontation, but eventually the baby starts to wail. The boy sneers at Trent before making for the cot, where he fumbles at the trousers of his grubby grey track suit. Trent lurches to his feet, hauling the window all the way up. "Don't do that," he shouts, "you wretched creature."

Perhaps he should have kept the last phrase to himself. He would have done his best in any classroom. The boy swings around, preceded by his flailing penis, and swaggers to the window while the baby continues to wail. Having forced the sash up, he directs an unhealthily orange stream in Trent's direction and waves the emptied member at him, then yanks up his trousers and sprawls on the floor with his phone, leaving the baby to howl.

While Trent dreads how the father may react, he's at least equally afraid to see the boy deal with the infant. Should he offer help? Even if this wouldn't be met with contempt or worse, the boy would never let him in. He can only watch until his eyes smart and the images of boy and baby flicker like imperfect simulations—like the figure that throws the door open and grimaces savagely at the howls from the cot. "Told you to fix him," he shouts and deals the boy a kick that lifts him off the floor. Over the chorus of cries Williams snatches the baby out of the cot and stomps with him to the bathroom.

He reappears with a used nappy in one of the hands that are holding the child. Having deposited the infant in the cot, he flings the nappy out of the window with such force that it lands in the yard of Trent's house. Soon clouds of smoke from offstage make the purpose of his recent outing clear. "You're getting none," he tells his elder son, who responds with a pitiful sniff. Smoke gathers over the cot, and an intense smell of cannabis seems to soften and expand Trent's skull. What may it be doing to the youngsters in the room? He keeps his phone out of sight while he jabs the emergency icon and asks for the police.

"I want to report a cannabis user."

The voice representing the law sounds unimpressed. "What were they doing?"

"He is right now. I can smell how much."

"You need to be careful it doesn't affect you." With little increase in enthusiasm she says "What is the address?"

"His, you mean, obviously." Trent supplies it and adds "The name's Williams."

"Not yours."

"Of course not mine. I don't know the rest of it, but there's a small son Billy and a baby Colum."

"We'll send someone as soon as we can. Please be aware the number you called is reserved for emergencies."

"I'm looking at one. He's smoking in front of the children. If it can affect me as you suggest, it must be affecting them."

"Have you contacted social services?"

Extending the Family

"They were worse than useless. I'm hoping you won't be."

Might this antagonise her? It doesn't matter so long as the police do their job. He rings off before she can ask for his details and grips the windowsill while he watches the apartment opposite. Extravagant masses of smoke drift over supine Billy's head to settle on the cot, and Trent has begun to feel time has slowed to the pace of the smoke when he hears a doorbell. Williams darts to the window, stubbing a fat cigarette out on his tongue before swallowing the remnant, and wafts at the air. He snarls at Billy as he almost trips over him on the way to stowing a plump translucent greenish package under the baby's mattress, and then he makes at not much speed to answer a protracted outburst of the doorbell.

The baby hasn't stirred by the time Williams reappears with a pair of police a good deal closer to his age than to Trent's. He looks so resolutely deferential that Trent is sure they'll see through the pretence, but they halt in the doorway while Williams indicates the cot, then loiter as he beckons to his son. Whatever they ask the boy, it makes everyone look at Trent. "It was me all right," he declares just as the police turn their backs to him. "The cot," he shouts, "it's under there," but they leave the apartment, taking Williams with them.

If they're arresting him, what will become of the children? The boy has fallen flat again to play on his phone, and the baby isn't moving. When the door opens Trent is ready to imagine his concern for them has brought someone to look after them, but the door lets Williams in. He stalks to the window to offer Trent a gesture to go with the words he sends, and then retrieves his prize from the cot. He's rolling another cigarette for Trent to see when they both hear a doorbell. It's in Trent's house.

As Trent opens the front door the police step forward in unison. "We understand you called us," the woman says.

"Mr Williams said so, did he? Then he told the truth for once. Couldn't you smell what he was up to? Why didn't you go in?"

"Because the youngest child isn't well," her colleague says. "We made the decision to let it sleep."

Their superficial efficiency reminds Trent of head teachers of their age, quite a few of whom dismissed his experience. "That was a ruse to keep you away. Didn't you hear me saying that was where he hid his drugs?"

"We saw no evidence of drug abuse." As Trent makes to protest the policewoman says "Is there some reason you haven't asked us in?"

"None whatsoever unless you object to books."

"That would depend what kind they are."

"What kind would they have to be?"

As though she has abandoned the subject she tells him "Mr Williams says you made the allegation before he could contact us."

"Why is anyone like him going to want you?" When she confines reproof to her eyes Trent says "Contact you about what?"

"About your behaviour." It's the policeman's turn to speak. "He says you exposed yourself to his son."

"Why, the lying little—" Trent manages to regain enough control to say "I don't know which of them is lying, but the boy showed himself to me." He's sure he senses contempt, which provokes him to demand "Did Williams say he saw me? Then he's a bigger liar than I thought. He wasn't even there."

Could they mistake this for an admission? Trent can't judge as the policewoman says "We'll need your name."

"Kenneth Trent, and I don't care who knows it. Maybe I should have all of theirs."

"That isn't necessary," the policeman says, adding a cautionary look. "We may want to see you again."

Extending the Family

"I'm not the one you should be seeing," Trent says, slamming the door with such force that he's afraid he may have roused the baby and the father's rage at it. Of course he's thinking of the wrong house, though he can't recall who else lives in his. He hurries upstairs to find the entire Williams family waiting for him.

The boy is at the window with his father, who is holding up the baby like a doll. The sight leaves Trent barely able to think. Lasky should be faced with it, not him. He stubs a wincing finger on his phone as he drops into the chair. "Speaking for Sid Lasky," a voice informs him.

"I wonder if that means you're him."

"This is Mr Lasky's phone. He isn't here right now."

"You're Cliff again, are you? Just let him know I've called the social workers and the police. I imagine he'd rather they weren't seen at his house."

Silence is the answer. Williams and Billy have been mouthing every one of his words, and their lips didn't stop moving even when his did. Throughout the conversation the father pumped the baby's arms up and down, causing its mouth to take ventriloquial shapes in its sleep. Why hasn't this wakened it? His fears for it prompt Trent to make another call. "Can I speak to Maggie Renfrew urgently, please."

"She's out visiting all day."

Surely the woman isn't her, however similar she sounds. "Then can you contact her? It's about the Williams case."

"Did you phone earlier? It's Mr Trent, isn't it? Maggie has already made a visit."

"Yes, to me. She didn't bother seeing them. I'm telling you those children are terribly at risk." The family is imitating him again, another reason he's enraged. "I can tell you who owns the property," he says. "Sid Lasky's the name. Surely if you people speak to him he'll have to help."

Fearful Implications

"I don't know if that's likely."

"You've had dealings with him too, have you? I rang his office earlier but I couldn't tell you if I reached him. His secretary, if that's who I spoke to, he's something of an obstructive type."

"His secretary."

"He calls himself Cliff. I did wonder if it could have been Lasky putting on a performance."

"Mr Trent, Cliff is Mr Lasky's carer. Mr Lasky doesn't have an office any longer. He's in a home."

Is she trying to confuse Trent? Certainly the figures mouthing at the edge of his vision are. "It's being left to me, is it?" he says in a rage so intense it seems to blot out his surroundings. "Don't anybody think I'm less than equal to it. I often had to be the police and the social services even though they were never my job."

He could almost fancy the watchers are mouthing his words before he utters them, forcing him to speak. The impression aggravates his fury, and as he shoves the chair backwards he feels the carpet rip. "You did that, you wretches," he cries and marches out of the house.

An alley leads alongside the suppressed garden and the nine-foot wall of the back yard opposite. The far half is carpeted with litter, and there are holes suggestive of embrasures in the yard wall. He hears Williams urging "Come on" but has no idea whether this is aimed at him. The cracked concrete of the front garden of the other house is strewn with so many obstacles—the charred remains of a plastic bin, a child's deconstructed tricycle, oily fragments of at least one car—that they might be intended to deter intruders. He nearly trips up more than once as he limps to the front door.

Its rusty digits lie on the fractured doorstep. They've left their outlines on the scaly paint, and the house has the same number as his. None of the metal slots beside the grimy doorbells contain names. He would rather not ring any of the bells, but how else can he gain entry? Perhaps somebody other than Williams may let him in. He fumbles with his keys as if they're some kind of charm while he tries to decide which bells are least likely to belong to the apartment opposite his. How senile has he grown? Without thinking he has slipped his front-door key into the dislocated lock. Of course it won't work—but the unhinged door stumbles inwards.

Trent pads across the gloomy hall strewn with brown official envelopes and tiptoes rapidly up the splintered carpetless stairs. As he sets a cautious foot on the first-floor landing, which is barely lit by a dusty skylight, he hears Williams beyond the door ahead of him. "He's here."

He dashes across the landing to fling the door wide. "Yes, I'm—"

His challenge peters out, because the room is empty—not just utterly bare but deserted. He reels towards the bathroom, which contains nothing but fixtures, all of them perilously damaged. A greasy kitchen is bereft of utensils apart from a pan brimming with scummy water. A loose board clatters underfoot as he totters across the main room. He's on his bewildered way out when he hears a series of sprawling thuds beyond the window. The Williams family is in his room.

As the father hurls handfuls of books at the floor Billy clambers up the shelves, on one of which the baby is pulling a paperback apart. "Get out of there," Trent shouts. "Leave those alone." When nobody even glances at him he flounders out of the room.

The stairs feel capable of collapsing beneath him, and so does the world. Dodging obstacles outside the house almost throws him on his face. At his front door he's seized by a fear that his key won't work. It admits him, and he struggles up the stairs to hear what he could imagine is a belated echo. "He's here."

Fearful Implications

"You won't escape me this time," he vows, snatching out his phone. He'll take photographs of the intruders before he calls the police. He throws his door open, but the phone he's raising to capture the miscreants almost falls out of his unsteady hand. While the floor of his room is a mass of broken books, nobody is to be seen.

The bathroom and the kitchen are equally unoccupied. He picks his enraged way between the vandalised books to the window, but the apartment opposite is as empty as before. "I'll find you," he cries, only to stare at the task that surrounds him. He's stooping to retrieve a relatively undamaged volume when he catches sight of a solitary page on the floor.

It isn't from any of the books, unless it was hidden inside one. It has been torn out of a diary. Although the date printed at the top is more than sixty years old, he recognises the teenage handwriting all too well, and the aggressively adolescent style of the entry. *smoked too much weed today—remembered stuff i must have wanted to forget—had to keep an eye on little cousin Gus—needed to pee so much i nearly did on him because he was a pain—peed out of window instead and some neighbour saw, so i peed at him—see if more dope lets me forget again—*

He tries to be dismayed just by the immaturity of the handwriting. Perhaps that was caused by the drug. The thought can't fend off the shame of what he read, and he can only hope it leaves him again soon. The inside of his head feels as if it's sliding into a dark pit, and he's barely able to waver over to the chair. He slumps in it, clutching his phone while he gropes at a number on the screen. "Cliff," he pleads. "Come and take me where I have to live."

Still Hungry

"Bert."

"No, it's Bertram."

"Yeah, whichever. Pregnant woman and a girl in trackies just come out of food and they've bought nothing. Now she's sending the kid off and I'm betting that's a decoy. You check the mother."

Bertram is in women's clothing, a joke that became one more of the things Jane couldn't stand about him. Stacks of flattened jumpers flank him while he locates the customer. She's bonily thin but frontally swollen, and the idea of ascertaining how genuine her condition is dismays him. He's making his casual way between two ranks of headless dresses when someone clutches at his left hand. "Mister, can you help me find my mam?"

She's in a grubby rumpled track suit that must have started out bright green, not an outfit Bertram would have chosen if he and Jane had ever succeeded in producing a child. She looks about six but short for her age. Plumpness dulls her pale face topped with unkempt mousy curls, and he's ashamed of thinking that her small cold moist hand feels like tripe. "That's the kid," his earpiece says. "Keep hold of her."

Fearful Implications

He feels shifty for pretending to be helpful. "What does your mother look like?"

The girl's stare summarises how unreasonable adults are. "Like me, only bigger."

It's true, even of the garish track suit. The woman is dodging at speed through a crowd of empty coats, and Bertram takes a firm grip on the child's hand as he heads his quarry off. "Excuse me, madam, I think this is your daughter."

He's in time to block the mother's escape from an aisle of nightdresses. "There you are, Lucy," she complains as her pallid pudgy face struggles to find lines with which to sketch a frown. "I said not to go where I can't see you."

Bertram's earpiece intervenes. "Keep them there, Bert. Management's on the way."

He used to tell Jane the device made him feel like a robot. Sometimes he longs for the strength of one, but just now he wishes he were as emotionless. He doesn't realise how resolutely he's grasping the child's hand until the woman says "You can let her go now, mister."

There's no point in fancying he can save the child. As he releases the hand he says "Stay there for a minute, please. Somebody would like to speak to you."

"Got no time now. Luce, you run."

Though the child looks bemused by the change of direction, she darts around Bertram. When the mother makes to follow he stretches out his arms on both sides of him, entangling his fingers in the embroidery of a nightdress. "You let me look after my little one," she protests and stoops to dart past him, which dislodges an item from her bulging midriff—a sleeve that dangles over her stomach. Bertram's instincts override prudence, and he gives the sleeve a tug, dislodging not just a child's track suit with the price tag still attached but a miniature avalanche of bars of chocolate.

"You keep your hands off me," she cries, sounding far too much like Jane before she left him, and then turns conversational. "You're not going to arrest me, are you, hon? I only did it for the little one. I'm all she's got. We had to leave her dad."

Bertram isn't paid to be sympathetic. That's a manager's job if it's anyone's. He's about to detain her with a neutral comment when she says "Lucy, go on when you're told."

As Bertram glances back to see the girl hesitating by the exit, her mother shoves a rack of nightdresses aside and sprints through the gap. He makes a grab for her but misses, and as he chases her several men who have just entered the store block his way. "Let her off, feller," one says. "She's got a kid."

If Bertram follows her into the mall his occupational insurance won't accompany him. As she and her daughter vanish into the crowd he unhooks the phone from his belt and warns his colleagues in the other shops. Annie from the food department is clearing the sweets into a plastic basket, and hands him the track suit. "You could take it upstairs if you liked, Bertram."

On the top floor he finds Mrs Deacon in Babes And Bigger. Her smile of eager helpfulness subsides when she sees Bertram isn't a customer. "What are you doing with that?" she says across the counter.

"You didn't see it being stolen." When Mrs Deacon makes this and her resentment plain he says "Were you talking to a little girl at all?"

"As a matter of fact I was. She seemed quite a pleasant child."

"That's how her mother distracts people while she's stealing."

"That can hardly be the child's fault, can it, Mr Bertram? Perhaps some of us have more of a feeling for children."

"It's just Bertram, and I didn't get the chance." As he spreads the crumpled track suit on the counter he feels as if he's trying to erase the girl. "We all make mistakes," he says in a bid to placate Mrs Deacon. "I could have. The woman sent the girl to make me think she needed help."

"It's a pity you couldn't respond, then."

He did his best, and nearly says so. Even if he let his marriage down, he's better at his job. The glass lift in the middle of the store lets him look out for suspicious characters, but he has seen none by the time he reaches the ground floor. He's among the televisions, several aisles of windows on luminous landscapes, when Mr Chalfont finds him. "Bertram," the manager says, though he makes this sound quite a task. "Just keep your eyes on the job."

"I dealt with the situation as soon as control tipped me off."

Mr Chalfont's face is etched with lines like a sketch of stress completed by its features. "I'm talking about now," he says, "while you're listening to me. I just hope there won't be any comeback from your actions earlier."

"What kind of comeback?"

"You're well aware you have no business touching customers."

"She wasn't a customer, she was a thief."

"She was still entitled to the proper treatment. She could sue for being searched in public. It might go against the store, especially when a child's involved."

"But I found the stolen goods on her. We must have that on tape."

"The angle makes it look as if you could have been planting them."

"I hope you know I never would have."

"It doesn't matter what I think. You'd better hope it doesn't matter what anybody else thinks either," Mr Chalfont says and burdens Bertram with a stony look.

He runs a mistrustful finger along the top of every screen he passes

Still Hungry

on his way to the lift, which elevates him saintlike. Bertram is leaving the televisions behind when the glowing landscapes are replaced by a shaky vista of a station platform, and he halts before he quite knows why. The mother and daughter he failed to apprehend are on the underground platform with their backs to an oncoming train.

Whatever the woman is shouting, none of the televisions lets out a sound. Where is she declaring she won't go? Bertram thinks she could be saying jail, but her lips shape a different word. She takes the child's hand in both of hers, a gesture he can't help finding ominous. He wishes he could intervene, but he had his chance. She releases the small hand and lifts her daughter into her arms. Hugging her with a fierceness Bertram imagines he feels, she leaps in front of the train.

The back of his fist bruises Bertram's lips, trapping a dismayed gasp. The falling bodies seem to hover almost supine—perhaps the image from the phone that filmed them has been slowed down—before the train hits them. It carries them forward until they're dragged under the circular saw of a wheel, and Bertram looks away. How can television show such details, especially at this time of day? Presumably the broadcast is a newsflash someone neglected to edit. He doesn't glance at the screens again until they recover their landscapes, and then he makes for Desmond, who's in charge of the department. "Did you see them?" Bertram says and finds his voice has grown as shaky as the rest of him. "I had to chase them out for stealing."

Desmond gives his resolutely bearded squarish head a puzzled shake, perhaps since the items in his section are too cumbersome to steal or, given his lack of emotion, because he didn't notice the report the televisions somehow picked up. The silenced shout and the suicidal leap replay themselves in Bertram's skull until it's time to head for home. The trains are just reverting to their schedule, and staff in yellow tabards patrol the platforms. In his apartment, which he's rented since

Fearful Implications

Jane kept the house, he listens to the local radio while he dines on the remaining half of last night's pizza from Stow That Dough, but there's no news of the deaths. He was planning to watch the kind of action film Jane would have complained throughout, only now he finds it hard to concentrate. He pauses the film so as to listen to each newscast, and is ready for bed by the time he hears that a homeless woman and her daughter—Bridie and Lucy Darwin—were killed by a train. He shouldn't have expected the media to report the woman's words, and he lies awake in the dark trying to deduce them. At last he lurches out of a jerky sleep, having grasped her final word. It feels as though he has just heard her say "Not going to starve."

He's glad to see the dawn, and at first he's glad to go to work. Mr Chalfont is letting staff in like a resentful doorman, and Bertram tries not to feel ashamed to say "Did you see we won't be sued? That woman and her child I had the trouble with, they were killed by a train."

"Then I very much hope it won't be associated in any way with us."

Bertram feels more accused than ever, and retreats to the control room. As he hangs his padded coat up, the security monitors shift their viewpoints with a concerted flicker. Did he glimpse a small shape scurrying down an upward escalator? "Caught short, Bert?" Cy calls as Bertram hurries out, a question undeserving of an answer.

The glass lift shows Bertram nobody at large except staff, but what's that mark on the floor of a frozen foods aisle? It looks like a trail of earth. He has to go down on his knees to identify the substance: a scattering of chocolate. The wrappers of several bars in the racks placed by the tills to tempt children have been bitten through. "I think we've got mice," he says.

He's addressing Annie, but Mr Chalfont hurries over to mutter "Keep your voice down. Just clear this up, Ann, and Bertram, you see to tracing the problem."

Still Hungry

The intermittent trail leads to the escalators. Is there an infestation somewhere underneath? Bertram sees crumbs of chocolate on the restless metal treads, and finds traces on the next higher escalator. He thinks he can distinguish increasingly faint marks all the way up to Babes And Bigger, where he halts by a gathering of children's track suits. "Mrs Deacon, can you page Mr Chalfont? He'll want to see this."

The manager peers where Bertram indicates and then stares at him. "What am I meant to see?"

"Those are bites, aren't they? It's where the trail ends."

"I see no trail." Mr Chalfont scrutinises Bertram while saying "I'll look for the culprit myself."

Bertram can no longer make the trail out either, and although the marks on several track suits look like bites, they're larger than any rodent could have made. If they represent a manufacturing fault he's surprised they weren't noticed, but it's not his job to insist they should be. As Mr Chalfont takes the lift down, Mrs Deacon says "Try not to let him upset you, Mr Bertram."

"I'm more upset about the woman and her child I told you about. She threw them both under a train."

"How can you know that?"

"They showed it on television yesterday afternoon."

"It wasn't in our paper last night. My dad likes me to read the local news to him."

Perhaps a caprice of the network transmitted the video directly from somebody's phone to the televisions; the railway station is nearby, after all. As Bertram searches for the trail he followed, a track suit slithers off its hanger beside him. He wasn't aware of brushing against it, and when he picks it up by its gaping neck an object seems to writhe inside the left arm. Has he captured the perpetrator of the trail? He shakes the suit, but nothing emerges before the arm grows flat, and he restores the

Fearful Implications

outfit to the hanger, an action that feels like clothing childish shoulder bones. There's no sign of the trail anywhere, and he wonders how much Annie cleaned up. "Get out, whatever you are," he whispers, and the store opens its doors as if it's expelling the problem.

It's letting in the public, coming to life. Not everything is lively yet; the televisions have been switched off overnight, and the black rectangles remind Bertram of graves large enough for children. No doubt that's because of the incident they showed him, which makes the inside of his skull feel as dark as they are now. He grows tense as Desmond powers them up, and has to fend off an insistent mental image of a small face with a stained mouth or at least with the remains of one until every screen glows with a landscape.

He needs to watch the customers. Just now they feel like company as well, but why should he have the impression he's being watched? There are the security cameras, but the scrutiny seems more personal. He's on his way out of the furniture department, having guided a young couple to the cots, when a sight in one of the mirrors high up on the walls halts him. Someone far too pale is lying in a bed.

As soon as he locates the intruder he tries to laugh at his mistake. The white shape poking from beneath a quilt is an empty pillowcase. Did somebody forget to put a pillow in it? Bertram is making for the bed when he hears a rustle suggestive of rodents. His foot has caught a wad of cellophane, the wrapping from the pillowcase. As he retrieves it he glimpses movement, and could imagine the pillowcase or whatever it hides has begun not just to breathe but to hint at outlines reminiscent of a face, though one that's unappealingly incomplete. No, the pillowcase is still lying flat on a pillow. He crumples the cellophane in his fist, only to feel as if he's squeezing out some unwelcome moisture, surely only his own perspiration. He shies the wad into the bin behind the deserted counter, just as the phone at his belt vibrates.

Still Hungry

Carl is calling from the Espouse Scouse shop. "Lad in a baseball cap on his way to you. Looks like a scally to us."

From the lift Bertram sees a lanky youth stuffing a cap into a hip pocket as he dodges into the store. Bertram follows him through Count On Our Computers and Phones Alone and stays well behind him on the escalator, but when he arrives at the next floor the fellow is waiting for him. "What are you creeping after me for?"

Bertram is distracted by a reflection of the escalator he just used. It looks as if a small figure is rising at his back, not borne by the escalator but wrung from between the ascending treads. He twists around to see the escalator is unoccupied. "Expecting reinforcements?" the youth says. "What's your actual problem?"

"Only doing my job, sir."

"I'm not it. Just tell me what I've done wrong."

Bertram reassures himself he can't really be seeing ill-distinguished fragments scattered over the next highest escalator, especially since they appear to be moving. "I saw what you hid in your pocket," he blurts.

"Right, my hat. I brought it in."

The activity vanishes off or into the escalator in the mirror as Bertram demands "Why didn't you want to be seen with it on?"

"Because you people don't like anybody wearing hats in shops." The youth drags the hat out of his pocket. "Take a good look," he says. "Not yours. I bought it in Greece."

It's a canvas trilby, not a baseball cap. Bertram is preparing to apologise when the mirror shows him a man in such a cap sidling behind him to dash down the escalator. "Bastard," Bertram protests and clatters after him, too late. The shoplifter sets off an alarm as he flees into the mall, and Bertram glares at the mirrors that surround him. "Playing games, are we?" he snarls, and stares at customers who stare at him.

321

Fearful Implications

The mirrors have refrained from performing any more tricks by the time Mr Chalfont calls him into the office. "I've had a complaint about you, Bertram."

"If it was the fellow with the headgear, I was warned to look out for someone like him."

"Like won't do. You need to be one hundred per cent certain what you're seeing."

Bertram tries to shut his thought up, only to mumble "Not much chance of that round here just now."

"I strongly advise you to make sure there is." Mr Chalfont presses his lips thin as if to squeeze more words out. "And the customer says you swore at him."

"Not him, the real thief."

"Who you allowed to escape with his loot."

"I'm sorry about that. I was distracted."

"I trust you aren't blaming the gentleman you falsely confronted." When Bertram doesn't risk answering, Mr Chalfont says "If this is about the lady who committed suicide, it can't be allowed to undermine our security. I'll be having eyes kept on you, Bertram."

Bertram thinks he senses them, even once he heads for home. Someone he can't locate is eating chocolate close to him on the platform and then on the train. The smell and taste follow him to his apartment, where they put him off his dinner and invade his concentration on every film he tries to watch. They accompany him to bed despite how fiercely he brushes his teeth, and the fear that they're omens of worse keeps twitching him awake.

At the store in the morning he heads straight for food. A chocolate bar in a shredded wrapper lies on the floor by a checkout desk. Why haven't the cleaners done their job? Perhaps the culprit waited until they'd finished so as to leave the evidence to taunt Bertram. Although

Mr Chalfont let him in, Bertram thinks better of showing him. He bins the item and follows the trail he's sure has been left for him.

It leads not much better than invisibly to the escalator and vanishes in the toy department, where Bertram searches the aisles for further mischief. He's abandoning the quest when a mirror catches two objects rearing above a block of shelves behind him. They're hand puppets, and since one is larger than the other he can't help taking them for a parent and child. As he twists around they slump on the shelf, and the contents drop to the floor with two soft thuds. He stalks around the shelves, but the linoleum is bare. He fumbles the mouthpiece of his headset closer as he murmurs "Did you see that?"

"I'm seeing nobody but you, Bert, playing whatever you reckon you're playing."

"I'll catch you," Bertram vows. "I'll show them." He doesn't know how loud he spoke or who may have heard. He avoids Mr Chalfont while he ranges about the store in search of his tormentor. He has seen no further signs of a trespasser by the time the public is let in. Customers are a distraction now, and perhaps they're helping to conceal an interloper too. While he spies on anyone who seems remotely suspect, that kind of miscreant isn't his primary concern. He's sure a small invader is lurking somewhere in the maze of aisles. A glimpse of someone less than adult in Have Some Scents, a department where children surely have no business, sends him to sneak up on the intruder, only for the little girl to complain "Mummy, that man's watching me."

"Just doing what I'm paid for, madam."

"Then find somewhere more appropriate to do it," the woman says and adds an almost physically ferocious look.

Bertram turns to the mirrors, losing sight of her and her child. He rides up and down in the lift to survey the floors, even when he sees Mr

Fearful Implications

Chalfont scowling at him. The ruse shows him nothing he's determined to find, and he sets about roving the floors. As the escalator returns him to the top floor a mirror lets him see an intrusive shape in Babes And Bigger.

It has appeared at the entrance to an aisle of track suits, wavering as though its composition is unstable. It's the size of a child but a good deal less shapely. Bertram would like to take it for an improperly assembled mannequin, but its eager restlessness gives him no chance, and he tries to see as little detail as he can. On the other hand he needs to catch the malefactor while there are witnesses, and Mrs Deacon is talking to a woman at the counter.

As Bertram turns towards the aisle the figure shambles askew into it. It's heading for the women, who watch Bertram sprint into the aisle. "Got you this time," he shouts, only to snarl in disbelief. His quarry has escaped in a number of directions, apparently unseen by anyone except him, and he's grasping the shoulder of the girl who previously complained about him. "You won't trick me this time, you little bitch," he declares louder still. He should have released the girl first, especially since Mr Chalfont has come to find him.

Bertram returns to the store just once. The crowd in the mall stares at him and stays well clear. Perhaps the stale smell of chocolate repels them, unless they can see what's holding his hand. He stumbles close enough to the doors that they flinch aside. "Go in," he whispers urgently. "That's where you ought to live." He appears to be alone in watching a scrawny form, imperfectly recomposed, dart through the gap between the doors just before they meet. He's letting out a gasp of relief when it turns into a shriek, and he flails his arm so desperately it feels dislocated. He's still holding a hand.

Wherever You Look

"Aren't you going to tell everybody about Bretherton, Mr Lavater?"

Maurice is about to read a sample of his latest novel to the Friends of Cheshire Libraries when the voice from the back of the audience accosts him. "Forgive me," he says, "about what?"

"Don't say what, say whom. Simeon Bretherton."

"I'm afraid I'm still not getting you."

"The writer you put in your book you have there."

"They must have crept in when I wasn't looking. I've never heard of them."

"You put their character in."

Maurice has started to feel as bemused as most of the audience look. "Which character?"

"The one you see looking out from behind things." The speaker demonstrates to the extent of an eye, having been concealed by an extravagantly burly man in the row next to the back of the ranks of folding chairs. "And you don't know who they are," he says, "until it's too late."

"I certainly don't know anything about them. Has anybody here heard of Simeon Bretherton?" When this prompts a general shaking of heads Maurice demands "What am I meant to have written?"

"The slanted wide-brimmed hat appeared to have tilted all his features, which might still have been slipping into place. His left eyebrow was lined up with the hat, and his pale blue left eye was higher than its whitish twin. Violence or birth had skewed his long thin nose leftwards. Even his slim black moustache was less than level, canted perhaps by the permanent sneer his pallid lips presented to the world."

All this is uttered in a neutral tone presumably designed to signify quotation. Maurice finds the sentences disconcertingly familiar, which provokes him to retort "Where's that from?"

"Your thirteenth chapter."

Maurice turns the pages of *Bell's Told* so fiercely he almost tears several. It's the scene where Victorian psychic investigator Solomon Bell views portraits of his haunted client's ancestors. Perhaps the subject of the painting is behind the spectral trouble, since he summoned spirits while he was alive, but Maurice never brings him onstage in the novel. Just the same, he's disconcerted not to have recognised the paragraph. "Fair enough, it's here," he has to admit. "It's mine."

"It's Simeon Bretherton, Mr Lavater, and is your hero's name a little tribute too?"

"I'd hardly have done that for somebody I've never heard of. What do you mean, it's him?"

"It's from his story, word for word."

Is the speaker about to claim that he wrote it—perhaps that conspirators blocked its publication? "Which story?" Maurice is less than eager to learn.

"The only one of his they ever published."

"And where can we find it?"

"Wherever you look." Presumably this refers to whichever method Maurice may use to search, since the speaker says "It went out of print before you were born."

"Do you have it with you?"

"I've just brought myself."

"I think we'll have to call any similarity a coincidence, however much of one it is." Maurice is angered to think this could sound more like an admission than skepticism. "Would anybody like to hear a less contentious section?" he hopes aloud.

As he finds the passage he planned to read he's aware that a member of the audience has stood up. A glance shows him a figure in black vanishing around a library bookcase. It's his accuser, who is carrying some item, not a book. "Is that all he came for?" Maurice mutters, not entirely to himself.

He reads the scene where Bell plays bridge with his client and her family and sees faces of her ancestors peering from behind cards as they're laid on the baize. Just now it feels unnecessarily and of course coincidentally like a reference to the tale his interrogator cited. More than one library user eavesdrops on his performance, unless it's the same person who leans around a bookcase and is gone whenever Maurice glances up. He's presenting copies of his novels to the library when the secretary of the Friends brings him an apologetic look. "I've no idea who that person at the back was," she says. "He certainly wasn't with us."

"Maybe just someone else who cares about books."

"So long as we don't get too immersed in them like him."

As Maurice drives home he can't outrun the notion that whatever he told his audience, the passage the intruder quoted seems familiar, not just from Maurice's own work. He hasn't identified it by the time he reaches New Ferry, the Wirral district he has taken to calling No

Fearful Implications

Ferry, not least because he lives so far from the river where there used to be one. Eventually he succeeds in manoeuvring into a space between cars parked half on the pavement in the cul-de-sac shaped like a noose at the end of the rope of a side road, an image he's repeated in so many interviews it feels as though it has tightened on his brain. As he makes for his pebbledashed house, which is no smaller than the other dinky dwellings, front rooms flicker with the light from screens, and he wonders how many of his neighbours ever read a book.

He falls asleep still struggling to disinter the memory he's sure is buried in his brain. In the morning he makes himself ignore the impression while he tries to work on his next novel. Soon he's reduced to gazing at the distant scrap of river that glints between the houses opposite, beneath a feeble sun brought low by October. At least he can swear as loud and as furiously as he likes, since he no longer has the girlfriend who might have been his partner if she hadn't objected to the language his frustration with a first draft always provokes and her rebukes exacerbated. His parents wouldn't approve, and no doubt theirs would have even less. The thought of them reminds him how early he began reading, and then he recalls the first adult book he ever read.

Was he even as old as seven? He and his parents were spending half his summer holidays with his father's parents, whose house Maurice had thought was no more ancient than them, though of course it would have been. In its musty library, where he was allowed to browse unsupervised, he'd found a book of ghostly fiction with a skull embossed on the faded blackish spine. He remembers tales about a sheet that came to life on a bed, and someone who was given a guest room they'd had nightmares about before they'd ever seen it, and two friends who vowed that whoever died first would appear to the other. He can name them and their authors, but might he have forgotten reading a contribution by what was the writer called, Simeon Bretherton?

If he ever knew the title of the book, he doesn't now. An online search for Simeon Bretherton brings just one reference to anybody of that name, the sexton of St Aloysius Parish Church, a position the man held over a century ago. The church is in New Ferry, and the online map places it about a mile away. A glance in that direction shows Maurice the admonitory fingertip of a church spire above a roof across the road.

The information only leaves him feeling more dissatisfied. Even if the sexton wrote the ghostly tale, what help is that? Maurice needs to dismiss all the coincidences so as to work, but they've settled in his mind. Could rereading the passage he's meant to have copied give him back some control? He's searching for it, having entered the description of the hat in the onscreen box, when he realises how confused he is. He's looking for the paragraph in the book he's working on.

Of course it can't be in there, and he brings up the file of *Bell's Told*. He pores over the paragraph until the sentences begin to disintegrate into phrases and then into separate words in his skull. He has to reread the paragraph yet again to put its sense together, a process unsettlingly suggestive of reconstructing a presence. Perhaps he did indeed encounter something similar that lodged unnoticed in his head—and then he starts to feel he came upon some form of it more recently than childhood. A disquieting possibility feels unlikely as a dream, one he wouldn't want to have. Since disbelief fails to shift it, he opens more files onscreen to search for phrases that are lying low in his mind. Soon he makes a sound that can't find a word for his feelings, and before long he releases another. Each of his books contains an image he finds altogether too familiar.

In *Bell, Book and Candle* a sinister punter at a racetrack wears a hat skewed in line with his features, unless it's the other way around. In *Clear as a Bell* the coquettish wearer of an equally wide-brimmed item keeps one eyebrow raised in alignment with it while she describes an apparently spectral encounter. In *Bell Towers* the driver of a hansom cab who takes Bell unbidden into a maze of fogbound London streets looks down at him through the trap with one eye higher than its paler twin. By now Maurice feels as though an unnoticed tenant of his head has been making surreptitious bids for freedom. He very much wants to regard his depiction of the fake medium in *Give Them a Bell* as coincidental—surely many characters in fiction have a dislocated nose—except that Bell can't decide whether birth or violence is responsible for the deformity. Maurice is desperate to find no likeness in *Sound as a Bell*, but then he remembers the pimp who organises vigilantes to protect women of the street from Jack the Ripper—the pimp whose slim black moustache is canted in parallel with his permanent sneer.

Maurice is distracted by a sight across the road. Sunlight between his house and its neighbour lends a streetlamp a reduced shadow like the silhouette of a thin man sporting a hat, a sketch waiting for details to be added. He closes all the files apart from the novel in progress, only to find he can't write another word. His efforts feel like struggling not to repeat any more of the tale his childhood reading buried in his mind, but how will he know if he fails? He has to read the tale.

A new search for Simeon Bretherton only revives the sketchy facts about the sexton. Adding "story" brings no extra information, and "ghost story" is unproductive too. Maurice tries patching the entire paragraph from *Bell's Told* into the search box, just as uselessly. He needs to consult someone who might help. In moments he has a list of second-hand booksellers, and he phones the topmost at once. "Boon of Books," a woman says as though she's naming herself.

"I'm hoping you can help me find a book by an author."

"They're mostly by them, aren't they?" When Maurice fails to find much of a sound to make in response she says "Are you looking for romance?"

"Not presently, thank you." Has he somehow contacted quite the wrong kind of service? "Just a book," he says. "I thought that was what you deal in."

"Plenty of romance in those." Rather too much in a counsellor's tone she says "Tell me what you need."

"A book with a story by Simeon Bretherton."

"That doesn't sound like one of ours. We don't do books with stories in."

"Then what do they contain?"

"Love." As Maurice tries not to feel personally addressed by the word, she says "Just one story each."

Maurice does his best to laugh at himself. "Romance novels, you mean."

"That's what Boon's all about. What did you think we were?"

"More than that," Maurice says and feels unreasonable at once.

The shadow on the pavement has grown human in its stature, if less so in its shape, by the time a man answers his next call. "Just For Your Shelf."

"I'm trying to track down a book I once read."

"If it's any good we've got it or we'll get it." He sounds not far from tired of saying so, but adds "What's the name?"

"Mine? Maurice Lavater."

"Not yours. The one you think I ought to know."

"I think perhaps you might know mine. I'm a writer."

"Really." With no increase of enthusiasm the bookseller says "Published?"

Fearful Implications

"Six novels and a seventh on the way."

"Maurice Lavater." As if he's solved that problem the bookseller says "May I ask your field?"

"My publishers call them supernatural thrillers." In case this sounds defensive Maurice says "So do I."

"That explains my lack of recognition. We wouldn't have you in the shop." Before Maurice can react the bookseller says "Must I assume the book you're seeking is your kind?"

"I believe you could say so."

"I wouldn't, no." More dismissively still the bookseller says "You should consult a specialist."

When he grasps that this is all the help the man intends to offer, Maurice can't resist asking "Do you sell many books?"

"Enough." Although this sounds like a bid to end the conversation, the man says "And yourself?"

"Plenty."

"No doubt you're bound to."

Maurice is in no danger of mistaking this for praise. He terminates the call and searches furiously for names related to his field. Terrific Tomes appears to be, and he calls the number. The supine shadow has vanished. The houses are blocking the sunlight, of course; the silhouette hasn't dodged behind the streetlamp. Just the same, he's squinting at the outline of the metal post to confirm nothing else is there when a woman says "Tomes."

"Terrific, would that be?"

"That's our first name. What can we do for you today?"

"I wonder if you could find me a story by Simeon Bretherton."

"In the wings of the world."

Does this mean she can't? "If that's where you have to look," Maurice tries to hope.

"No," the bookseller says with a delicate giggle. "That's what his only story's called."

"Has it been reprinted, do you know?"

"It was only ever in *Tales of the Ghostly and the Grim*."

As the title goes some way towards rousing a memory Maurice says "Have you any idea where I should look for that?"

"I can see it now across the shop."

"I'll buy it," Maurice says almost before he finds the breath to speak. "How soon can you get it to me?"

"As soon as you've paid. You're looking at fifty-five including postage." When Maurice undertakes to pay at once she says "Let me fetch your book."

As he takes out his credit card he hears sounds suggestive of a distant struggle. The returning footsteps are slower than the ones that went away, and the bookseller says "You'd think it didn't want you reading it."

More nervously than he welcomes Maurice says "How do you mean?"

"My colleague must have wedged too many books in. You'd have thought someone was keeping hold of it on the shelf. Just tell me where I'm sending it." When Maurice gives his name she cries "Not the Bell man."

"I'm glad someone's heard of me."

"We're often asked for your books. Drop in and sign some whenever you're in our part of the country." Having copied his address with a chatter of plastic keys, she says "So there are two of you there."

"Two of whom?"

"You and Bretherton. He was the sexton at one of your local churches." Perhaps she thinks the silence means Maurice needs to be placated, since she says "You're the one people know."

Fearful Implications

"We know about him."

"I'm afraid we're a dying breed." The phone emits a rustling sound, and the bookseller adds "Well, here he is."

"Who?" Maurice feels further driven to ask "How?"

"My colleague let a draught in, as if it isn't cold enough. Don't pull that face or it'll stay lopsided, Dan." To Lavater she says "It turned up your man."

"His story, you mean."

"I'm looking at his words right now." A thud leaves Maurice unaccountably anxious until she speaks again. "He'll be with you tomorrow."

The thud was her shutting the book, of course. May its imminence let him write? His mind is strewn with fragments of Bretherton's description, and he can't think past them. In the hope of dislodging the obstacles or of coaxing his mind to relax he wanders out of the house. He's about to go for a stroll when he decides to see if anything significant is to be found at the church.

On the far side of the road that divides the district, every second street denies entry to traffic. By the time he finds St Aloysius his mind feels as tangled as the route. As he drives around the outside of the churchyard, pale figures glide from behind others of their species. They're memorials lent movement by the car, but why do some of their discoloured outlines flicker as though uncertain of their shapes? He could think his eyes are growing unreliable, or his mind—and then he sees the unsteady glare comes from lamps on the roofs of several police vehicles drawn up outside the church.

He's coasting past them and trying to make out the dim interior beyond the porch when he's overwhelmed by an aroma of cannabis so powerful it sets his head swimming. His foot falters on the accelerator, and the car stumbles to a halt. A policeman using a mobile phone stares at him, which makes Maurice stall the engine afresh once he has wrenched a shriek from the starter motor. His mime of comical incompetence brings the officer over to him. More like a warning than an invitation the policeman says "Can I help you, sir?"

"I'm a writer." Since this earns no response, Maurice adds "I was wanting to research the history."

"Too late for that now." Not much less ominously the policeman says "Should we know your name?"

"Maurice Lavater," Maurice says and fumbles out his driving licence.

"Weren't you in the paper recently?" When Maurice confirms this, though he's unsure how accusing the question sounds, the policeman says "This would have been right up your street."

"I don't deal much with drugs. Just opium because I'm writing Victorian."

The policeman gives him a searching look. "How the neighbours found out what was going on would be. The watchman for the gang, he started screaming in the night. That's why someone called us."

"Too much cannabis, do you think?"

"Too much." As Maurice starts to feel admonished the policeman tells him "The watchman said he thought someone kept looking in the windows. Said when he tried to chase them their face came off the inside of the glass."

"There'll be faces in the stained glass, I suppose."

"He said it wasn't one of those, and it kept following him round in the dark. Some of us might say it serves him right." When Maurice finds the notion too disquieting to endorse, the policeman says "What kind of research were you looking to do?"

"Whatever documents there are. Perhaps the parish magazine."

"They'll be well gone somewhere if they're anywhere. The place has been shut down for years, and the priest's house."

Fearful Implications

Maurice manages to drive away without betraying any further clumsiness. Could breathing in the smell from the cannabis factory have affected him? In that case it should have acted on the policeman as well, and wasn't the man's peaked cap a shade askew? He's out of sight by now, and Maurice sees no way of sneaking back. Instead he drives home so carefully he feels as if he's striving not to wobble his attenuated head.

When at last he finishes inching the car into the only available space near his house, the retired teacher who lives opposite hurries up to him. Her urgency disconcerts him until he realises she's being propelled by a hound large enough to feature in an Edwardian tale. She only just succeeds in tugging it to a temporary halt that lets her greet Maurice. "Written any books this week?" she says, cocking an eyebrow that's presumably meant to be humorous.

"Ah ha." While this is designed more to acknowledge than to celebrate the joke, does it resemble agreement too much? "Ha ha," Maurice adds without mirth.

When the hound hauls her onwards he makes for his desk, but can't think past the day's events. What's so significant about them? Perhaps the policeman helped him after all, and the church records have indeed been preserved somewhere. Maurice calls the central library in Birkenhead and learns that the archive has a set of the St Aloysius parish magazine. If he requests it now he can view it tomorrow.

First he'll need to wait for the package from Terrific Tomes. He makes himself a pasta dinner before spending time with the television. Vintage films generally help him relax, but all those he tries to watch contain at least one man with a moustache. When this persists in troubling him he retreats to bed. Thoughts that feel like fragments of a tale someone has already told keep him awake, not least because he has an impression that they apply to him. He can't judge how while he's unable to define them. At last he sleeps, only to dream that somebody is pounding on the inside of a lid. The sound pursues him into daylight, and he realises it's at the front door. He stumbles to the window in time to see a uniformed figure heading for a van. "Hello?" Maurice shouts, louder once he has raised the plastic sash.

"On your step."

The man might almost be fleeing the item he brought. He turns no more than momentarily to respond, so that Maurice can't be sure one side of his face is higher than the other. Perhaps it was distorted by a grimace. Maurice hurries downstairs to find a parcel not so much delivered as abandoned, its padded envelope partially unstuffed by a bid to force it through the letterbox. He shakes its greyish innards into the kitchen bin and unpicks the staples with an aching fingernail. The book wrapped in a plastic sheet like a cluster of translucent eggs is indeed *Tales of the Ghostly and the Grim*.

Maurice sprawls in a front-room chair to read Simeon Bretherton's story, which concerns a sexton who rings the church bell most enthusiastically whenever there's a funeral. His gusto appears to offend or else to rouse one of the deceased, who sets about returning piecemeal. Local villagers the sexton hasn't previously met prove to have features reminiscent of the dead man—one feature each. In preparation for Sunday mass the sexton is struggling to remove hymnals so firmly wedged into a shelf that it feels as if someone is gripping them when they yield all at once, and he almost ends up supine. Did he glimpse a shape behind the books? The shelf is empty, but beside it a mirror reveals the face looming at his back. He swings around to see he's alone in the sacristy, or at least that part of it. The lopsided sneering face is behind the glass, and sidles forth as a long thin greyish arm reaches for his head. When the priest finds the sexton's body, it bears the dead man's face.

Fearful Implications

Maurice shuts the book and lets it fall beside his chair. Now that he has finished the story, he hopes it has finished with him—hopes it stays trapped in the book. It strikes him as an incoherent piece that could only have impressed him as a child. Surely reading in context the paragraph he hadn't known he quoted will have freed him to write—but when he tries to work on his novel, his mind feels as obstructed as ever. He could fancy Bretherton's description isn't satisfied with its revival, a nonsensical notion he can't dislodge. He still has to visit the library archive, and even if he finds nothing worth the journey, perhaps leaving his desk for a while will shift the hindrance out of his mind.

In twenty minutes he's at the library, where the front entrance huddles under a massive two-storey porch between twin wings full of windows. The stone is grey as twilight beneath the sunless sky. Nobody looks at Maurice until he rests his elbows on the counter in the midst of a multitude of shelves. When a librarian approaches he says "Maurice Lavater."

"Oh yes."

This sounds nowhere close to recognition. Her colleague's glance across a table piled with new books suggests he knows the name, but Maurice finds this less than heartening, since one of the man's eyes appears to be paler than the other. "You have some parish publications for me," Maurice tells the woman.

"If I could just see your card."

Of course she isn't doubting his identity, and he hands over his library card. "Where would you like to start?" she says.

The online paragraph about the sexton gave the date of his death. "I think nineteen hundred may be what I'm after."

She hands Maurice a hefty foolscap box, which he takes to a seat, though not at once. He's wary of sharing a table with a morose man whose nose is spectacularly dislocated, and a fellow sneering so hard at a newspaper that his lips drag his moustache awry seems worth avoiding too. Instead Maurice finds an empty table by a window overlooking a lawn and a wide low shrub, its leaves reduced to blackness by the unforthcoming sky. When he opens the box, the topmost magazine lifts its flimsy cover as though it has been waiting for him.

The cover shows the church as it was more than a century ago. It doesn't mention Simeon Bretherton, but he's lying in wait on page five. The obituary praises his commitment to the church and celebrates how vigorously he used to ring the bell, though the writer stops short of specifying any occasion. Maurice finds he needs to read all this as a distraction from the photograph that accompanies the testimonial. Despite its age, it preserves every detail: the rakish wide-brimmed hat, the eyebrow raised in sympathy with the unaligned and mismatched eye, the sideways nose, the moustache lined up with the sneer.

Surely the sexton wouldn't have chosen this expression for a photograph, and Maurice can only conclude he was permanently deformed by the look. Did he write his appearance into his story in a bid to set it apart from him? Maurice hasn't realised he's clenching his face until he feels it relax. He very much hopes the insight he has gained will let him return to his own tale. He lifts his head as though his mind has raised it and his consciousness, and meets the eyes of the face outside the window.

He could imagine he's still looking at the photograph in the magazine, or at any rate he's desperate to think so. When he wavers to his feet and ventures closer, the face advances too. Was it wearing a hat to begin with? It is now. No, that's the blackened shrub, which he misperceived because his right eye isn't functioning too well. He rubs the eye, an activity the watcher imitates with a finger on a pallid eyeball.

Fearful Implications

Perhaps Maurice is grimacing even though he thought he'd managed to relax, and the watcher is copying him. Maurice leans forward and sees the patch of grass where the tilted shrub stands—sees the grass through the face. Now his viewpoint no longer lets the shrub pose as a hat, but he ducks forward again and again in a wild attempt to rid himself of the appearance on the glass. Before anyone can reach him he has smashed the window with his face, and the opposite as well. He's no further use to me, but now I'm in your book.

AFTERWORD
THE OLD GROWS NEW

SOME THINGS ARE BEYOND me now. On a recent walk along the Wirral Way nature trail Jenny and I made a detour not far from the site of Arthur Pendemon's house to revisit a favourite place, a cave to which we used to scramble with our children. I took time to realise how I can no longer risk the climb, or shin up the popular rock at Thurstaston (a name I misspelled throughout the first edition of *Thieving Fear*, having misperceived it ever since I first encountered it). As we sat on a bench below the cave to contemplate the past, a couple who might have represented our younger selves made the ascent with ease and clambered past the cave to the sandstone ridge. It won't last, I found myself thinking, but perhaps in memory it does. Perhaps we do.

Old age brings tricks, which tend to be played on the oldster. One of mine is falling off chairs, a trait that might act as research for my Three Stooges monograph, though I really don't need to live the work so literally. I recently bought *Jack Reacher* on disc and was suitably engrossed, only for Jenny to tell me once we'd watched it that we already had, and indeed there was the previous copy on the shelf. If my mind is offering the chance to experience films as if for the first time, I wish it had chosen *Psycho* instead, daunting though the implications may be (indeed, fearful). At least I can still write, even if I've taken to intermittently omitting or repeating words and even phrases in the first draft. I hope I'm remote from that terminal state that caused Kingsley Amis to write "seagulls" over and over, perhaps a note to himself or a complaint about a distraction. So long as what I present to the reader is acceptable, there's some point to me yet. You must decide. Let us see what I recall about the tales herein.

While "Speaking Still" and *The Lonely Lands*, not to mention the Brichester Mythos trilogy, suggest a preoccupation with the afterlife, this isn't a recent development: look at *The Influence*, for instance, and *Needing Ghosts*. Perhaps "Speaking Still" brings it up to date with the suggestion that the internet has changed it, possibly offering a conduit of communication or even a version of life after death. How electronic are we, after all, or have we become? Maybe my old friend Pete Crowther and I will eventually help each other solve allied mysteries, having made the promise that was kept in an Algernon Blackwood tale.

The narrative of "First a Bird" came upon me pretty well readymade as Jenny and I had recourse to a bench beside a path at Freshfield, the National Trust nature reserve up the coast from Liverpool. The reserve has provided the setting for various tales ("The Faces at Pine Dunes", "The Voice of the Beach", "The Moons"). As a windblown bush some distance from the bench turned the silvery underside of its leaves to us it began to coo, or a bird within it did. Within minutes I'd filled a page of one of the notebooks I carry, and the tale was well-nigh shaped.

When does a sight grow so familiar we no longer ponder how it has been achieved? In a sense human statues are the least spectacular species of street performer, but just consider how much discipline their

Afterword: The Old Grows New

stasis calls for. Suppose one of them were to represent an actual statue that has been removed and evoke the nature of its subject? One central theme of our field is the past that refuses to be denied or laid to rest. Some or all of this must have given rise to "The Stillness". Once I had amassed enough instances of the titular state I wrote the tale.

"The Fourth Call" was written at the behest of my old friend Steve Jones, for an anthology that aimed to find terror in the twelve days of Christmas. Alas, the book was stillborn. With typical determination, Steve found my story a new home in an anthology of folk horror. I suppose I could be said to have invented a new bit of folklore, or at least some of my characters did. Let us hope it remains fictitious.

The idea behind "The Dreamed" was the business with the passports, but as you may have seen, the development grew stranger. Mine often do. Arriving at a foreign hotel after a protracted trip—hours at the airport, more of those on the plane, some extra on the transfer once your luggage has lumbered out of hiding—can be a fraught experience, and some of ours helped set off this story. I think it also draws in a general way on holiday panics we've had: Jenny's bag snatched in Barcelona, the collapse of Thomas Cook halfway through a stay in Lesvos the firm had booked for us, a New England blizzard that threatened to ground our connection to the flight home. As well as all this, an October holiday in a Halkidiki resort on the Greek mainland provided incidents I used: the place felt much as I've described, dismantled fairground rides and shut-down tavernas included.

I came up with "Someone to Blame" for an anthology reviving classic monsters. Does it require knowledge of the original James tale? If any of my readers have yet to encounter that, I envy them the experience of meeting it for the first time, but also hope my story worked in its own independent way. I'm inclined to feel enjoyment of

Fearful Implications

a work of fiction oughtn't to depend on awareness of an external context. While knowing your Homer helps you appreciate Joyce's *Ulysses*, I don't think that's mandatory, any more than spotting the Arthurian allusions is essential to having a good time with David Lodge's *Small World*. If I bury a reference in my own stuff, I try to ensure the passage still works narratively for the reader who isn't privy to the secret—for instance, *Thieving Fear* contains a background detail I imagine most readers will find insignificant except as an element of the scene, but it has earned a few knowledgeable chortles.

"How He Helped" was conceived for an anthology on the theme of future human evolution. The amiably persistent editor, Darren Speegle, was kind enough to give me so much time I couldn't very well refuse. Maintaining his benevolence, he declared my contribution audacious. I trust the reader takes the protagonist's thoughts in the same way Horridge's in *The Face That Must Die* should be read. Still, sometimes bad intentions can have a positive result.

"The Bill" returns to a recurring theme of mine: vagaries of perception. You could say this starts with how the reader interprets the title, which I meant to accrue significance as the tale progressed. Given the theme, the protagonist's profession virtually chose itself. Once I'd settled on it I set out to incorporate all the everyday elements of the job. Developing such a narrative structure, as I often do, increasingly reminds me of working out a set of variations in music, not that I've ever done so myself.

"Girls Dream" was commissioned for an anthology of tributes to a director and his film: perhaps you can guess which and whose. "A Name for Every Home" began life as a story quite unlike itself, as others of mine have. My initial notion involved a suburb where the house names grew increasingly occult and ominous. Once the protagonist proved to be a postman, the story found a different route. The original

Afterword: The Old Grows New

tale has yet to be told, and perhaps it will be. "The Fun of the Fair" waited decades to be written, after all.

What can I say of "The Run of the Town"? The story roots the motif of the malevolent statue in contemporary events, although I started from the notion of the calls that only seem to be addressed to dogs, then found an element that would render this idea meaningful. I hadn't realised until now that it's the second statue to exert the power of an ousted past in this book.

"Fully Boarded" is the second Greek story it contains. My favourite Hellenic lodging is the Deep Blue Sea in Georgioupolis on Crete. The resort is splendid too, but marred by one accommodation complex, which offers or perhaps insists on full board. I'll refrain from naming it, but numerous reviews on TripAdvisor make it unmistakable despite a rash of five-star writeups, so be warned. Forlorn boarders bidding to liberate themselves from the shackles of their wristbands frequently flee to the local tavernas, where the staff are in no doubt where they've escaped from. On our first visit to Georgioupolis we stayed in a self-catering apartment in the complex, before we discovered the Deep Blue Sea. By now it should be clear where "Fully Boarded" came from. It's one of my stories that hardly need an uncanny element, but I hope this adds an extra dimension.

Some years ago the genial Dan Coxon invited writers to contribute to an anthology of weird fiction with a distinctly British flavour, not least in the settings. I was happy to provide, but disconcerted (no fault of his) to find my stuff cited in the invitation email as an example of the kind of work he favoured. I hope "The Devil in the Details" fitted the bill, though it feels odd to have to live up to oneself. Like its author, the tale does feel quite British.

An essay could be written about the relationship between humour and horror, which is why I wrote one ("The Grin Beneath the Flesh", collected in *Ramsey Campbell, Certainly*). In person, quite a bunch of horror writers are comedians: Robert Bloch, Pete Atkins, Dennis Etchison (even if you mightn't think so from his fiction, though he regarded some of it as comic)... I've often said that if I didn't write horror I might give stand-up comedy a go, which doesn't mean I'd be any good at it, of course. Meanwhile I created such a comedian, derived from memories of childhood radio shows, in "Some Kind of a Laugh". The onstage death of Tommy Cooper, to prolonged laughter and applause, was on my mind while I wrote.

"Play With Me" was written for a young folks' anthology of tales of terror, but apparently fell short of requirements. Here it is, for what it's worth. Years ago Jenny and I walked to Hilbre Island, a nature reserve off the West Kirby point of the Wirral peninsula. Decades earlier we'd proposed to take Robert Aickman there, but he warned us that the tides came in faster than a horse can gallop. During our successful visit I overheard a lady lying on the grass tell her child to stay by her shadow. How could I have failed to find a tale in this?

It's Christmas yet again, at least in my fiction. "But Once a Year" was written for an anthology of wintry stories, a book that sank from sight, alas, with the hibernal sun. I tried it out on a leading horror magazine, only to learn eleven months later that the editor had swiftly decided against it but forgotten I'd submitted it. At last it found a home in *ParSec*, edited by the splendid Ian Whates for PS Publishing, who had commissioned it in the first place. Such are the adventures publishing can bring. Is there any aspect of the festive season I haven't turned about to reveal its darker side? That sounds like a challenge...

Does "Brains" need any contextualisation? Not, I should say, if you know your internet. While I wouldn't be without its encyclopaedic qualities, too often it resembles the kind of state where any departure

Afterword: The Old Grows New

from a prevailing belief attracts a mob determined to shame the offender and re-educate them. At times it's reminiscent of a schoolyard. "I won't be your friend if you don't stop being their friend." "You have to join our gang or we won't let you play anywhere." "Miss, never mind what we're doing, look what they're doing over there." "I won't like you if you like that book." For the record, Phil Meehan's accounts of the Frankenstein films are based on the facts, however personally interpreted.

Although "Getting Through" isn't directly autobiographical, in my teens I wasn't too unlike Desmond. When I started work in the civil service at the age of sixteen I'd had very little contact with girls, and I can only be grateful that the symptoms of my inexperience weren't more apparent, to whatever extent I hid them. I speedily became obsessed with a colleague—let's call her J to spare any embarrassment, even sixty years later—and assuaged my undefined desire by inserting her name in a tale. Soon she was supplanted in my obsessions by G, and I asked August Derleth to substitute the name, which (more patiently than I deserved, I'd say) he did. Later I contrived an excuse to include her among the dedicatees of a book. I rather think both girls were already engaged, but in the world bounded by my head such details either went unnoticed or couldn't be allowed to matter.

"Extending the Family" was my response to a request for a tale on the theme of abjection. It's meant to address a tendency I confess to indulging too often myself: rejecting somebody's behaviour as unpardonably alien even though I'd behaved likewise in my youth. I don't mean to suggest I acted like the youthful father in my tale, but I certainly had my irresponsible moments. Incidentally, I gather opening a tale with untagged dialogue is frowned upon by some for breaking a rule writers are required to follow. It's worked for better writers than I am, and in any case it works for me.

Fearful Implications

"Still Hungry" was conceived for an anthology on the theme of haunted buildings, specifically any except houses. A department store suggested itself, and a security guard as protagonist, after which the development seemed inevitable (and rather parallels the moral issues raised in "The Bill" or at any rate reconsiders them; indeed, the stimulating editor Eric J. Guignard prompted both stories). Just one word identifies the town where the store is located.

"Wherever You Look" takes as its theme a method I learned from M. R. James: letting the uncanny skulk behind the prose and gradually grow more unmistakable. Also lurking in the tale is a fear of inadvertent plagiarism. I hope I head off any tendency to pinch. Long ago I had a splendid idea involving binoculars, but I fear it owed its splendour to Fritz Leiber, who'd already developed it in *Our Lady of Darkness*. If I catch myself using a borrowed idea or at any rate one already used elsewhere, I try at least to find a variation. Once, too late, I realised on proofreading a reissue of a novel that I'd recently reused an image of my own, having thought I'd come up with it for the first time, from decades earlier. I can only hope the present book contains no recycling. That would be my tip.

Ramsey Campbell
Wallasey, Merseyside
26 November 2022